$100

A
MURIEL SPARK
TRIO

Books by Muriel Spark

A
Muriel Spark
Trio

THE COMFORTERS

THE BALLAD OF PECKHAM RYE

MEMENTO MORI

J. B. Lippincott Company
Philadelphia & New York

1962

A MURIEL SPARK TRIO

The Comforters Copyright 1957 by Muriel Spark

The Ballad of Peckham Rye Copyright © 1960 by Muriel Spark

Memento Mori Copyright © 1959 by Muriel Spark

PRINTED IN THE UNITED STATES OF AMERICA

Library of Congress Catalog Card Number 62–14653

Contents

The
Comforters

To
ALAN AND EDWINA BARNSLEY
with love

Part One

1

On the first day of his holiday Laurence Manders woke to hear his grandmother's voice below.

"I'll have a large wholemeal. I've got my grandson stopping for a week, who's on the B.B.C. That's my daughter's boy, Lady Manders. He won't eat white bread, one of his fads."

Laurence shouted from the window, "Grandmother, I adore white bread and I have no fads."

She puckered and beamed up at him.

"Shouting from the window," she said to the baker.

"You woke me up," Laurence said.

"My grandson," she told the baker. "A large wholemeal, and don't forget to call on Wednesday."

Laurence looked at himself in the glass. "I must get up," he said, getting back into bed. He gave himself seven minutes.

He followed his grandmother's movements from the sounds which came clearly through the worn cottage floorboards. At seventy-eight Louisa Jepp did everything very slowly but with extreme attention, as some do when they know they are slightly drunk. Laurence heard a clink and a pause, a tinkle and a pause, breakfast being laid. Her footsteps clicked like a clock that is running down as she moved between the scullery and the little hot kitchen; she refused to shuffle.

When he was half dressed Laurence opened a tiny

drawer on the top of the tall old-fashioned chest. It contained some of his grandmother's things, for she had given him her room. He counted three hairpins, eight mothballs; he found a small piece of black velvet embroidered with jet beads now loose on their thread. He reckoned the bit of stuff would be about $2\frac{1}{2}$ inches by $1\frac{1}{2}$. In another drawer he found a comb with some of his grandmother's hair on it and noted that the object was none too neat. He got some pleasure from having met with these facts, three hairpins, eight mothballs, a comb none too neat, the property of his grandmother, here in her home in Sussex, now in the present tense. That is what Laurence was like.

"It is unhealthy," his mother had lately told him. "It's the only unhealthy thing about your mind, the way you notice absurd details, it's absurd of you."

"That's what I'm like," Laurence said.

As usual, she knew this meant deadlock, but carried on,

"Well, it's unnatural. Because sometimes you see things that you shouldn't."

"Such as?"

She did not say, but she knew he had been in her room prying into her messy make-up drawer, patting the little bottles like a cat and naming them. She could never persuade him that this was wrong. After all, it was a violation of privacy.

Very often Laurence said, "It would be wrong for you but it isn't for me."

And always Helena Manders, his mother, would reply "I don't see that," or "I don't agree," although really she did in a way.

In his childhood he had terrorised the household with his sheer literal truths.

"Uncle Ernest uses ladies' skin food, he rubs it on his elbows every night to keep them soft" . . . "Eileen has got her pain" . . . "Georgina Hogg has three hairs on her chin when she doesn't pull them out. Georgina has had a letter from her cousin which I read."

These were memorable utterances. Other items which he aired in the same breath, such as, "There's been a cobweb on the third landing for two weeks, four days and fifteen hours, not including the time for the making"— these were received with delight or indifference according to mood, and forgotten.

His mother told him repeatedly, "I've told you repeatedly, you are not to enter the maids' rooms. After all, they are entitled to their privacy."

As he grew older he learned to conceal the sensational portions of his knowledge, imparting only what was necessary to promote his reputation for being remarkably observant. In those days his father was capable of saying, on the strength of a school report,

"I always knew Laurence would outgrow that morbid phase."

"Let's hope he has," Helena Manders had said. Parents change. In those days, Laurence was aware that she half-suspected him of practising some vague sexual perversion which she could not name, would not envisage, and which in any case he did not practise. Then, it was almost to put her at ease, to assure her that he was the same Laurence as of old, that he said, during the holidays of his last term,

"Eileen is going to have a baby."

"She's a good Catholic girl," Helena protested; she was herself a Catholic since her marriage. None the less, on challenging Eileen in the kitchen, the case turned out to be so. Eileen, moreover, defiantly refused to name the man. Laurence was able to provide this information.

"I've always kept up with Eileen's correspondence," he explained. "It enlivens the school holidays."

15

"You've been in that poor girl's room, reading her letters behind her back, the poor thing!"

"Shall I tell you what her boy-friend wrote?" Laurence said tyrannously.

"I'm shocked as you know," she said, accepting that this made no impression. "How you, a good Catholic—but apart from that, it's illegal, I believe, to read letters addressed to others," she said, defeated.

Merely to give her the last word he pointed out, "Well, you've got them married, my dear. A good Catholic marriage. That's the happy result of my shocking perusal of Eileen's letters."

"The end doesn't justify the means."

Pat it came out just as he had expected. An answer for everything. All the same, incidents like this helped to deaden the blow when she realised that Laurence was abandoning, and finally had abandoned religion.

Louisa Jepp sat at the table writing out her football pools as she waited for Laurence.

"Come down!" she said to the ceiling, "and leave off your snooping, dear."

As soon as he appeared she told him, "If Manchester City had won last week I should have got thirty thousand."

Louisa folded her football coupon and placed it under the clock. She gave all her attention to Laurence and his breakfast.

She was half gipsy, the dark one and the youngest of a large red-haired family, which at the time of her birth owed its prosperity to the father's success as a corn dealer. The success was owing to good fortune in the first place, his having broken jail while waiting to come before the Bench, never afterwards returning to his gipsy tribe. It was a hundred and thirty years after this event that Louisa was sitting down to breakfast with Laurence.

Louisa's hair remains black, though there is not much of it. She is short, and seen from the side especially, her form resembles a neat double potato just turned up from the soil with its small round head, its body from which hang the roots, her two thin legs below her full brown skirt and corpulence. Her face, from the front, is square, receding in planes like a prism. The main lines on her face are deep, they must have been in gradual evidence since she was thirty, they seem carved to the bone. But the little wrinkles are superficial, brushing the surface of her skin, coming and going like innumerable stars when she puckers a smile or unfolds a look of surprise. Her eyes are deep-set and black. Her hands and feet very small. She wears rimless spectacles. She is still alive, not much changed from that day when Laurence came down to breakfast. She was wearing a brown dress, a brown woollen jacket with gilt buttons, and a pair of diamond earrings embedded in her ears.

When Laurence had sized her up, as he always did with everyone, he dipped his fork into a jar and drew out something long, white and pickled.

"What can this be?"

"Chid'lings," she said. "They are beautiful."

He was accustomed to Louisa's food: whelks, periwinkles, milts and roes, chitterlings and sweetbreads, giblets, brains and the tripes of ruminating animals. Louisa prepared them at long ease, by many processes of affusion, diffusion and immersion, requiring many pans of brine, many purifications and simmerings, much sousing and sweetening by slow degrees. She seldom bought an ordinary cut or joint, and held that people who went through life ignoring the inward vitals of shells and beasts didn't

17

know what was good for them.

"If you won thirty thousand in the pool, what would you do?" Laurence said.

"Buy a boat," she replied.

"I would paddle you up and down the river," Laurence said. "A houseboat would be nice. Do you remember that fortnight on the houseboat, my first year at prep school?"

"I mean a boat for crossing the sea. Yes, it was lovely on the houseboat."

"A yacht? Oh, how grand."

"Well, a good-sized boat," said Louisa, "that's what I'd buy. Suitable for crossing the Channel."

"A motor cruiser," Laurence suggested.

"That's about it," she said.

"Oh, how grand."

She did not reply, for he had gone too far with his "Oh, how grand."

"We could do the Mediterranean," he said.

"Oh, how grand," she said.

"Wouldn't it be more fun to buy a house?" Laurence had just remembered his mother's plea, "If you get an opportunity do try to persuade her to take a little money from us and live comfortably in her own house."

She answered, "No. But if I won a smaller sum I'd buy this cottage. I'm sure Mr. Webster would sell."

"Oh, I'd love to think of you having the cottage for your very own. Smugglers Retreat is such a dear little house." Even as he spoke Laurence knew that phrases like "your very own" and "dear little house" betrayed what he was leading up to, they were not his grandmother's style.

"I know what you're leading up to," said Louisa. "Help yourself to the cigarettes."

"I have my own. Why won't you let father buy the cottage for you? He can afford it."

"I manage very nicely," said Louisa. "Smoke one of these—they come from Bulgaria."

"Oh, how grand!" But he added, "How extremely smart and where did you get them from?"

"Bulgaria. I think through Tangiers."

Laurence examined the cigarette. His grandmother, a perpetual surprise. She rented the cottage, lived as an old-age pensioner.

Her daughter Helena said frequently, "God knows how she manages. But she always seems to have plenty of everything."

Helena would tell her friends, "My mother won't accept a penny. Most independent; the Protestant virtues, you know. God knows how she manages. Of course, she's half gipsy, she has the instinct for contriving ways and means."

"Really! Then you have gipsy blood, Helena? Really, and you so fair, how romantic. One would never have thought——"

"Oh, it comes out in me sometimes," Helena would say.

It was during the past four years, since the death of her husband, penniless, that Louisa had revealed, by small tokens and bit by bit, an aptitude for acquiring alien impenetrable luxuries.

Manders' Figs in Syrup, with its seventy-year-old trade mark—an oriental female yearning her draped form towards, and apparently worshipping a fig tree—was the only commodity that Louisa was willing to accept from her daughter's direction. Louisa distributed the brown sealed jars of this confection among her acquaintance; it kept them in mind of the living reality underlying their verbal tradition, "Mrs. Jepp's daughter was a great beauty, she married into Manders' Figs in Syrup."

"Tell your father," said Louisa, "that I have not written

to thank him because he is too busy to read letters. He will like the Bulgarian cigarettes. They smell very high. Did he like *my* figs?"

"Oh yes, he was much amused."

"So your mother told me when she wrote last. Did he *like* them?"

"Loved them, I'm sure. But we were awfully tickled."

Louisa, in her passion for pickling and preserving, keeps up with the newest methods. Some foods go into jars, others into tins sealed by her domestic canning machine. When Louisa's own figs in syrup, two cans of them with neatly pencilled labels, had arrived for Sir Edwin Manders, Helena had felt uneasy at first.

"Is she having a lark with us, Edwin?"

"Of course she is."

Helena was not sure what sort of a lark. She wrote to Louisa that they were all very amused.

"Did they enjoy the figs?" Louisa pressed Laurence.

"Yes, they were lovely."

"They are as good as Manders', dear, but don't tell your father I said so."

"Better than Manders'," Laurence said.

"Did you taste some, then?"

"Not actually. But I know they were most enjoyable, Mother said" (which Helena had not said).

"Well, that's what I sent them for. To be enjoyed. You shall have some later. I don't know what they are talking about—'much amused.' Tell your father that I'm giving him the cigarettes for enjoyment, tell him that, my dear."

Laurence was smoking his Bulgarian. "Most heady," he said. "But Mother takes a fit when you send expensive presents. She knows you have to deny yourself and——"

He was about to say "pinch and scrape," using his mother's lamenting words; but this would have roused the old lady. Besides, the phrase was obviously inaccurate; his grandmother was surrounded by her sufficiency, always behind which hovered a suspicion of restrained luxury. Even her curious dishes seemed chosen from an expansive economy of spirit rather than any consideration of their cost in money.

"Helena is a sweet girl, but she does deceive herself. I'm not in need of anything, as she could very well see, if she took the trouble. There is no need for Helena to grieve on my account."

Laurence was away all day, with his long legs in his small swift car, gone to look round and about the familiar countryside and coastline, gone to meet friends of his own stamp and education, whom he sometimes brought back to show off to them his funny delicious grandmother. Louisa Jepp did many things during that day. She fed the pigeons and rested. Rather earnestly, she brought from its place a loaf of white bread, cut the crust off one end, examined the loaf, cut another slice, and looked again. After the third slice she began at the other end, cutting the crust, peering at the loaf until, at the fourth slice, she smiled at what she saw, and patting the slices into place again put back the loaf in the tin marked "bread."

At nine o'clock Laurence returned. The sitting-room which looked out on the village was very oblong in shape. Here he found his grandmother with visitors, three men. They had been playing rummy, but now they were taking Louisa's refreshments, seated along each side of the room. One was in an invalid chair; this was a young man, not more than twenty-four.

"Mr. Hogarth, my grandson; my grandson, Mr. Webster; and this is *young* Mr. Hogarth. My grandson is on the B.B.C., my daughter's son, Lady Manders. You've heard him give the commentaries on the football and the races, Laurence Manders."

"Heard you last Saturday." This was Mr. Webster, the oldest guest, almost as old as Louisa.

"Saw you this morning," Laurence said.

Mr. Webster looked surprised.

"With the baker's van," Laurence added.

Louisa said, "Laurence is very observant, he has to be for his job."

Laurence, who was aglow from several drinks, spoke the obliging banality, "I never forget a face," and turning to the elder Hogarth he said, "For instance, I'm sure I've seen your face somewhere before." But here, Laurence began to lose certainty. "At least—you resemble someone I know but I don't know who."

The elder Hogarth looked hopelessly at Louisa, while his son, the boy in the invalid chair, said, "He looks like me. Have you seen me before?"

Laurence looked at him.

"No," he said, "I haven't. Nobody at all like you."

Then, in case he should have said the wrong thing, considering the young man was a cripple, Laurence rattled on,

"I may take up detective work one of these days. It would be quite my sort of thing."

"Oh no, you could never be a detective, Laurence," Louisa said, very seriously.

"Now, why not?"

"You have to be cunning to be a detective. The C.I.D. are terribly sly and private detectives will stoop to anything. You aren't a bit sly, dear."

"I notice extraordinary things," Laurence boasted casually, lolling his brown head along the back of the sofa.

"Things which people think are concealed. Awful to be like that, isn't it?"

Laurence had the feeling that they didn't like him, they suspected him. He got nervous, and couldn't seem to say anything right. They more and more seemed not to like him as he went on and on compulsively about the wonderful sleuth he would make. And all the time he was talking he actually was taking them in, sleuth-like.

Their presence in his grandmother's house was strange and surprising, and for that reason alone did not really surprise him. Louisa is pouring out tea. She calls the young Hogarth "Andrew." His father is "Mervyn" to her. Webster is "Mr. Webster."

Mr. Webster with his white hair, white moustache and dark nautical jacket is not easy to identify with his early-morning appearance—the tradesman in a sandy-brown overall who calls with the bread: Laurence felt pleased with himself for recognising Mr. Webster, who wore brown suede shoes, size ten by Laurence's discernment, whose age might be going on seventy-five, and who, by his voice, is a Sussex man.

Mervyn Hogarth was thin and small. He had a washed-out sandy colouring. Louisa had prepared for him a thin slice of brown bread and butter.

"Mervyn has to eat often, in small snacks, for his gastric trouble," Louisa explained. By his speech, the elder Hogarth is a knowing metropolitan product. God knows what he is doing at Louisa's, why he is on sufficiently familiar visiting terms for first names and gastric confidences. But Laurence was not a wonderer. He observed that the elder Hogarth wore unpressed flannels and an old ginger tweed jacket with the air of one who can afford to go careless. The son Andrew, with full red lips, was square and large-faced with glasses. He was paralysed in the legs.

As Louisa asked Laurence, "Did you have a nice outing, dear?" Andrew winked at him.

Laurence resented this, an injustice to his grandmother. He felt averse to entering a patronising conspiracy with Andrew against the old lady; he was on holiday for a special reason connected with a love affair, he wanted a change from the complications of belonging to a sophisticated social group. The grandmother refreshed him, she was not to be winked about. And so Laurence smiled at Andrew, as if to say, "I acknowledge your wink. I cannot make it out at all. I take it you mean something pleasant."

Andrew started looking round the room; he seemed to have missed something that should be there. At last he fixed on the box of Bulgarian cigarettes on Louisa's sideboard; reaching out he opened the box and helped himself to one. Mr. Webster tried to exchange a glance with Louisa disapproving of her guest's manners, but she would not be drawn in to it. She rose and passed the open box to Laurence.

Andrew told him, "They are Bulgarian."

"Yes, I know. Rather odd, aren't they?"

"They grow on one," Andrew remarked.

"Bulgarian!" his father exclaimed. "I must try one!"

Louisa silently passed the cigarettes. She inclined her head demurely towards Laurence, acknowledging an unavoidable truth: the fact that three stubbed-out fat Bulgarian ends already lay in the ash-tray beside Mervyn Hogarth's chair.

Louisa sat passively witnessing Hogarth's performance as he affected to savour a hitherto untried brand of cigarette.

"My dear Louisa, how exotic! I don't think I could cope with many of these. So strong and so . . . what shall I say?"

24

"Pungent," said Louisa patiently, as one who has heard the same word said before by the same man in the same place.

"*Pungent,*" Mervyn repeated, as if she had hit on the one only precise word.

He continued, "A flavour of—the Balkans, a tang as of—of——"

Louisa obliged him again, "Goats' milk."

"That's it! Goats' milk."

Louisa's black shiny buttons of eyes turned openly on Laurence. He was watching the man's face; he glanced towards the ash-tray with its evidence of the pose, then looked at Mervyn again. Louisa began to giggle inaudibly as if she were gently shaking a bottle of cough-mixture within herself. Mr. Webster caught her movement with the corner of his eye. From where he was seated, and his neck being stiff, he had to swivel round from the waist to get a better view of Louisa. At this sign, her face puckered slightly, but presently she composed herself like a school-girl.

Laurence said to Andrew, "Do you live round here?"

Father and son replied simultaneously. Mervyn said, "Oh, no"; Andrew said, "Oh, yes."

Louisa's mirth got the better of her, and though her lips were shut tight she whinnied through her nose like a pony. Mr. Webster clicked his cup into his saucer as if the walls had spoken.

The Hogarths immediately attempted to rectify their blunder. Both started together again—Mervyn: "Well, we live in London mostly——" Andrew: "I mean, we're here most of the time——" The father decided to let Andrew take over.

"And we sometimes go abroad," he concluded limply.

Laurence looked at his watch, and said hastily to Andrew, "Coming for a drink? There's about fifteen minutes to closing." Then he saw his blunder. For the moment the boy had looked quite normal, not a cripple at all.

"Not tonight thanks. Another time, if you're staying," Andrew said, unsurprised.

"Laurence is stopping till the end of the week," said Louisa.

Laurence hurried out. They could hear his footsteps crossing the quiet road and down the village street towards the Rose and Crown.

Mr. Webster spoke. "Charming boy."

Louisa said, "Yes, and so clever."

"Interesting lad," Mervyn said.

"I was wondering . . ." said Andrew.

"What, dear?" Louisa asked him.

"Hadn't we better clear off till next week?"

Mr. Webster twisted round to face the old lady. "Mrs. Jepp," he said, "I did not think you would permit your grandson meeting us. I understood he was to be out this evening. I trust he will not be upset in any way."

"My!" said Louisa graciously. "He won't be upset, Mr. Webster. Young people are very democratic these days."

That was not what had been meant. Mervyn spoke next.

"I think he will ask questions. It's only natural, Louisa, after all, what do you expect?" He lit one of the Bulgarian cigarettes.

"Whatever questions should he ask?"

"He is bound to wonder . . ." said Andrew.

"He's bound to ask who we are, what we're doing here," said Mervyn.

Mr. Webster looked sadly at Mervyn, pained by some crudity in the other's words.

"My!" said Louisa. "Laurence will certainly ask all about you. Would you care for another game, gentlemen?"

26

Mervyn looked at the clock.

Andrew said, "He'll be back after the pub closes, won't he?"

Mr. Webster smiled paternally at Louisa. "The matter is not urgent," he said, "we can leave our business till the end of the week, if you know of an evening when your grandson will be out."

"It can be discussed in front of Laurence," she said. "Laurence is a dear boy."

"Of course," said Mervyn.

"That's just what we mean," said Andrew. "The dear boy shouldn't be made to wonder——"

Louisa looked a little impatient. Something was defeating her. "I did hope," she said, "that we could avoid making any difference between Laurence and ourselves. I assure you, with discretion we could say all we want to say in Laurence's presence. He has not got a suspicious nature."

"Ah, discretion," Mr. Webster said, "my dear Mrs. Jepp, discretion is always desirable."

Louisa beamed warmly at him, as at one who had come nearest to understanding her.

Mervyn spoke. "I understand you, Louisa. You can't bear to participate in separated worlds. You have the instinct for unity, for co-ordinating the inconsistent elements of experience; you have the passion for picking up the idle phenomena of life and piecing them together. That is your ideal, it used to be mine. Reality, however, refuses to accommodate the idealist. It is difficult at your age to grasp a fact which you have never had occasion to recognise, but——"

"I don't know what you mean," Louisa said, "not at any age I wouldn't know."

"Of course."

"You are too far away," she said, but then she perked up. "Now Mervyn, if you feel I'm too old-fashioned in my ways I will quite understand. You may always withdraw from our arrangements."

Mervyn, who had stood up, sat down again. Andrew gave an unsmiling laugh which caused Louisa to look at him with surprise.

Andrew responded: "He spoke about doing detective work. He seems to be quite smart in the head."

"Laurence is doing nicely on the wireless. He would never make a detective, nothing so low."

"He would make a good informer," Andrew said, and from the privilege of his invalid chair looked squarely at her.

"My, you need not continue with us, Andrew dear, if anything troubles you. In which case, of course, *we* shouldn't continue, should we?" She looked at Mervyn and Mr. Webster, but they did not answer. They rose then, to leave. As he took her hand Mr. Webster said, "You see, Mrs. Jepp, your dear grandson *is* exceedingly observant. That was the only reason I had for questioning the wisdom."

Louisa laughed. "Oh, he never misses anything. I've never met anyone like him for getting the details. But, you know, the dear boy can't put two and two together."

"You mean," said Mervyn, "that he lacks the faculty of reflection?"

"I mean," said Laurence's grandmother, "that he could be more intelligent in some ways than he is. But he's clever enough to get on in the world, and he has a sweet nature, that's what matters."

"And if he asks any questions . . ." said Andrew.

"Oh, he *will* ask questions," Louisa answered him.

There was no doing anything with her.

"Oh, Mrs. Jepp, you will be discreet won't you? I'm sure you will," said Mr. Webster.

"My grandson can't put two and two together—not so's to make four." She looked rather amused so as to make them rather uncomfortable.

"He's leaving on Friday?" Mervyn asked.

"Yes, I'm afraid so."

"Friday evening then?" said Mervyn.

"Yes," she answered with melancholy.

"See you Friday," said Andrew.

"Thank you, Mrs. Jepp, for a most pleasant evening," said Mr. Webster.

Because Laurence had started writing a letter, resting the paper on a book on his knee, Louisa was clearing part of the table for him, saying, "Come, love, sit up at the table, it's more comfortable."

"No, I always write like this."

Louisa spread a white cloth over the corner reserved for Laurence.

"Always put a white cloth under your papers when you write a letter. It's good for your eyes because it reflects back the light. Come, dear, sit up at the table."

Laurence shifted to the table and continued writing. After a few minutes he said, "The white cloth does make a difference. Much pleasanter."

Louisa, lying full-length on the sofa by the little back window where she rested till tea-time in the afternoons, replied dozily, "When I told Mervyn Hogarth of that little trick, he started working out in his head whether it could be effective or not, all about light-rays and optics. 'Try it, Mervyn,' I said, 'just try it, then you'll know for certain that I'm right.' "

"Of course," Laurence reflected absently, "it may be due

29

to something psychological."

"Oh, it's something psychological all right," said Louisa surprisingly and imponderably. Then she closed her eyes.

She opened them again a few seconds later to say, "If it's your mother you're writing to give her my love."

"I'm writing to Caroline, actually."

"Then give her my love and say I hope she feels better than she was at Easter. How has she been lately?"

"Miserable. She's gone away to some religious place in the north for a rest."

"She won't get much of a rest in a religious place."

"That's what I thought. But this is one of Mother's ideas. She gets together with her priests and builds these buildings. Then they dedicate them to a saint. Then mother sends her friends to stay in them."

"But Caroline isn't a Catholic."

"She's just become one."

"I *thought* she was looking thin. How does that affect you, dear?"

"Well, of course Caroline's left me, in a way. At least, she's gone to live somewhere else."

"Well!" said the old woman, "that's a nice thing!"

"We might get married some day."

"Ah, and if not?" She looked at him with a reserved wonder as she added, "Does Caroline know what she's doing? The one certain way for a woman to hold a man is to leave him for religion. I've known it happen. The man might get another girl, but he never can be happy with anyone else after a girl has left him for religious reasons. *She* secures him for good."

"Is that really true?" Laurence said. "How very jolly. I must tell Caroline."

"Oh well, my love, it's all for the best. I hope you can marry her, soon. They wouldn't make you become a Cath-

olic, you only have to promise to bring up the children Catholics. And after all, children these days make up their own minds when they grow up. And there's nothing wrong in being a Catholic if you want to be one."

"It's a bit complicated," Laurence said. "Poor Caroline isn't well."

"Poor Caroline. That's religion for you. Give her my love and tell her to come down here. I'll feed her up. I daresay everything will come out all right."

"Grandmother has just dozed off again," Laurence wrote, "after looking up to enquire after you. The news of your conversion caused a serious expression, on her face. Made her look like one of Rembrandt's old women, but she rapidly regained her Louisa face. She wants you here, to give you things to eat.

"I hated seeing your train out at Euston and mooned off afterwards with thoughts of following you on the evening train. Met the Baron in Piccadilly Underground and walking back with him to the bookshop fell under his influence and decided against. He argued, 'The presence of a non-believer in a Catholic establishment upsets them if the unbeliever is not interested in acquiring their faith. Those places always advertise their welcome to the faithless. However, if you go merely looking for Caroline, it will upset them, you will not be welcome. Moreover, they will have it in for Caroline, for being manifestly more desirable to you that their faith.' On the whole, I decided it would be cloddish to barge in, just as well as it has turned out.

"I couldn't face the flat so went over to Hampstead. Father was in, Mother out. He let fall something that rather worries me. Apparently there's a woman by name of Hogg at the outfit you are staying at. She's a sort of manageress. Mother got her the job. God knows why. We all loathe her. That's why we've always gone out of our way for her really. She's that Georgina Hogg I think I've mentioned, the one who used to be a kind of nursery-governess before we went to school. She got married but her husband left her. Poor bastard, no wonder. We used to feel sorry for him. She suffers from chronic righteousness, exerts a sort of moral blackmail. Mother has a conscience about her—about hating her so much I mean, is terrified of her but won't admit it. Father calls her Manders' Mortification. Of course she's harmless really if you don't let her get under your skin. I think I could handle the woman, at least I used to. But best to avoid her, darling. I hope you won't come across her. I confronted Mother with her damned silliness in sending you to a place where Georgina is, at a time when you're feeling limp. She looked a bit guilty but said, 'Oh, Caroline will put Georgina in her place.' I do hope you will. If she upsets you, leave immediately and come down here to be plumped up. Such things are happening down here!

"Arrived on Sunday night. My little grandmother is a mighty woman, as I always knew. I've discovered such things! She runs a *gang*. I'm completely in the dark as to what sort of gang, but I should probably think they are communist spies. Three men. A father and son. The son's a cripple, poor chap. The father has a decided air of one *manqué*. The third gangster is rather a love, like a retired merchant sailor, fairly old. He's sweet on Grandmother. He owns the local bakery and delivers the bread himself.

"I don't know how far Grandmother is implicated in their activities, but she's certainly the boss. She's handsomely well-off. I think she only draws her pension to avoid suspicion. Do you know where she keeps her capital? In the *bread*. She sticks diamonds in the bread. Without a word of exaggeration, I came across a loaf weirdly cut at both ends, and in one end diamonds, real ones. I wondered what the hell they were at first, and picked out one of the stones ever so carefully. Diamonds look so different when they aren't set in jewellery. When I saw what it was, I put the stone back in its place. Grandmother has no idea that I'm on to this, of course. Isn't she a wonder? I wonder what her racket is. I don't think seriously of course that they are spies, but criminals of some sort. The thing is, Grandmother isn't being used, she's running the show. The main thing is, Mother mustn't find out, so be most careful, my love, what you say.

"I intend to find everything out, even if it means taking an extra week and mucking up Christmas. I've started compiling a dossier.

"Any ideas on the subject, let me know. Personally, I think Grandmother is having the time of her life, but it might be serious for her if the men are caught. I can't begin to guess what they'd be caught at. They may be jewel thieves, but that doesn't fit in with the sweet naval old fellow's character. Anything fits G'mother's.

"Grandmother openly refers to them as 'my gang,' airy as a Soho slender. Says they come to play cards. I met them here the other night, since when I've been snooping. I wish you would come for a few days and help me 'put two & two together' as G'mother says. I hope you don't get the jitters at St. Philumena's. Take it from me, you have to pick and choose amongst Catholic society in England, the wrong sort can drive you nuts. Mother knows she's done the wrong thing in sending you there. It's her passion for founding 'Centres' and peopling them, gets the better of her. Father swears she'll start a schism.

"I expect a letter from you tomorrow. Longing to hear that you have got Mrs. Hogg under control. It would be rather fun in a way if you had a set-to with her. I'd like to be there if you did. *There*, but concealed."

33

Louisa opened her eyes and said, "Put the kettle on, dear."

Laurence laid down his pen. He asked her, "Who d'you think is in charge of that religious place Caroline's gone to?"

"Who, dear?"

"Mrs. Hogg."

"In charge! I thought it was a convent."

"No, only a Centre. Georgina is a housekeeper or something."

"Does your mother know that?"

"Yes, she gave her the job."

"I think something is happening to Helena's mind," said Louisa.

"Mrs. Hogg! Just think of her, Grandmother, worming in on Caroline."

"Mrs. Hogg," said Louisa, as if she'd never heard the like. "Mrs. Hogg. Well, Caroline will fix her."

Laurence went into the scullery to fill the kettle, and shouted from there,

"You haven't seen her lately?"

His grandmother was silent. But as he returned and placed the kettle on the black coal stove, Louisa told him,

"I haven't seen her for years. A few months ago your mother wrote to suggest that Georgina Hogg should come and live here as a companion for me."

Laurence chuckled.

"You said no bloody fear, I suppose."

"I said that I would not wish to have that poisonous woman in my house for a five-second visit. It fairly puts you against Catholics, a person like that."

Laurence took up his pen again.

"I detest that woman," said Louisa.

"Grandmother is awake now," Laurence wrote. "She

34

has been delivering herself of her views on Ma Hogg. 'Poisonous' she says. It makes me rather sorry for the old Hogg being so dislikeable. Truly, she has to be savoured to be believed."

"Tell Caroline," Louisa broke in, "to be careful of Mrs. Hogg. Say she's dangerous."

"I've told her," Laurence said.

He finished his letter, and read it over.

After tea he added to it, "P.S. I forgot to mention Grandmother's cheque book. According to the stubs she donates the exact sum of her pension each week to the Prisoners' Aid Society."

He sealed the letter, then went to post it.

2

A STORM, FIERCE ENOUGH TO HOLD UP THE shipping at the mouth of the Mersey, ranged far enough inland to keep Caroline Rose indoors, where she paced the pale green corridors. Not for exercise but in order to think. A thinking-place of green corridors. The Pilgrim Centre of St. Philumena.

"Taking exercise." This was Mrs. Hogg tacking on to her, infuriating. Taking exercise. Not a question, a statement.

"Good afternoon," said Caroline.

"And feeling lonely," said Mrs. Hogg with her sort of smile. Feeling lonely, taking exercise. Caroline made no answer. The small perfect idea which had been crystallising in her mind went all to mist. All right, I am at your disposal. Eat me, bloodywell take the lot. I am feeling lonely. Rome has spoken.

"Another time," said Mrs. Hogg, "you don't want to make a private Retreat. You want to come in the summer with one of the big pilgrimages for one of the big Feasts."

"Do I?" Caroline said.

"Yes," said Mrs. Hogg. "That's what you want to do. Please call me Georgina by the way. I'll call you Caroline. Sometimes we have as many as a hundred and thirty pilgrims to stay. And of course thousands for the day pilgrimages. Sir Edwin and Lady Manders and Father Ingrid had no idea what they started when they started St. Philu-

36

mena's. You must meet the Manders."

"I know them," said Caroline.

"Oh, you do. Are you one of their converts? They are always making converts."

"Converts to what?" said Caroline in the imperative need to be difficult. Caroline vented in her mind her private formula: *You are damned. I condemn you to eternal flames. You are* caput, *as good as finished, you have had it, my dear.* More expressive, and therefore more satisfying than merely "Go to hell", and only a little less functional than a small boy's "Bang-bang, you're dead!"

"Converts to the Faith, of course," Mrs. Hogg was saying.

During her three days' stay at St. Philumena's she had already observed Mrs. Hogg. On her first evening Caroline overheard her:

"You have to take what's put before you here. Sometimes we have as many as a hundred and thirty pilgrims. Suppose a hundred and thirty people all wanted tea without milk——"

Her victim, a young lawyer who was recovering from dipsomania, had replied, "But I only say don't *trouble* to put milk in mine."

"It isn't what you say, it's what you get."

They sat later at a polished oak refectory table silently eating a suet-laden supper which represented the monastic idea at St. Philumena's. Their mouths worked silently, rhythmically, chew-pause-chew-pause-swallow-pause-chew. A Sister from the convent next door was reading aloud the "holy work" prescribed for mealtimes. Caroline recognised the Epistle of St. John, and listened, fixing her eyes on the white blouse of Mrs. Hogg opposite. Soon her mind was on Mrs. Hogg, and the recent dispute about the tea.

She began to take in the woman's details: an angular face, cropped white hair, no eyelashes, rimless glasses, a small fat nose of which the tip was twitching as she ate, very thin neck, a colossal bosom. Caroline realised that she had been staring at Mrs. Hogg's breasts for some time, and was aware at the same moment that the woman's nipples were showing dark and prominent through her cotton blouse. The woman was apparently wearing nothing underneath. Caroline looked swiftly away, sickened at the sight, for she was prim; her sins of the flesh had been fastidious always.

That was the first evening.

And this was the third day. At the end of the long corridor they turned. Caroline looked at her watch. Mrs. Hogg did not go away.

"The Manders converted you. They are always converting somebody."

"No. Not in my case, they didn't."

"The Manders are *very* nice people," said Mrs. Hogg defensively.

"Charming people."

"*Very* good people," Mrs. Hogg insisted.

"I agree," said Caroline.

"You couldn't possibly disagree. What made you a Catholic then?"

"Many reasons," Caroline said, "which are not too easy to define: and so I prefer not to discuss them."

"Mm . . . I know your type," Mrs. Hogg said, "I got your type the first evening you came. There's a lot of the Protestant about you still. You'll have to get rid of it. You're the sort that doesn't mix. Catholics are very good mixers. Why won't you talk about your conversion? Conversion's a wonderful thing. It's not *Catholic* not to talk about it."

The woman was a funny old thing in her way. Caroline suddenly felt light-hearted. She giggled and looked again at her watch.

"I must be going."

"Benediction isn't till three o'clock."

"Oh, but I've come here for rest and quiet."

"But you're not in Retreat."

"Oh yes, you know, I *am* in retreat." Then Caroline remembered that the popular meaning of "retreat" in religious circles was an organised affair, not a private retiring from customary activities, so as to possess one's soul in peace. She added, "I mean, I've retreated from London, and now I'm here for rest and quiet."

"You were speaking plenty to that young lawyer this morning."

In her private neurotic amusement Caroline decided to yield. Ten more minutes of Mrs. Hogg. The rain pelted with sudden fury against the windows while she turned to the woman with a patronising patience.

"Tell me about yourself, Mrs. Hogg."

Mrs. Hogg had recently been appointed Catering Warden. "If it wasn't for the Faith I couldn't hold down the job. On my feet from six till two, then on again at three and then two hours' break till supper and then there's the breakfast to think about. And I've got a great number of Crosses. That young lawyer you've got in with, the other night he said, 'I don't take milk in my tea'—did you hear him? Sometimes we have as many as a hundred and thirty. Suppose a hundred and thirty people wanted tea without milk——"

"Well, that would be fairly easy," said Caroline.

"Suppose they each wanted something different."

"All at the same time?" said Caroline.

Seeing Mrs. Hogg's expression at this moment, Caroline

thought, "Now it has struck her that I'm an enemy of the Faith."

But Mrs. Hogg righted herself; her mechanism was regulated for a chat.

"I'll tell you how I came here—it was a miracle. Our Lady sent me."

But Caroline's mood had changed again. Her sophisticated forbearance departed and constriction took its place; a pinching irritated sense of being with something abominable, not to be tolerated. She had a sudden intense desire to clean her teeth.

"Oh tell me about the miracle," Caroline said. Her tone was slightly menacing. "Tell me all the details." These scatty women with their miracles. Caroline thought, "I hate all women and of all women Mrs. Hogg. My nerves are starting up again. The next few eternal minutes are important. I must mind what I say. Keep aloof. Watch my manners at all costs."

"Well," Mrs. Hogg was saying, "I was of two minds whether to take a post in Bristol with a lady who was having her baby at home—I'm a registered midwife, you know, although most of my experience has been as a governess. One time I was housekeeper to a priest for two years. That was in Birmingham. He was sent to Canada in 1935, and when we said goodbye he said, 'Well, Mrs. Hogg——' "

"What about the miracle?" said Caroline, and to cover up her testiness overdid it and added, "I can't hear enough about miracles."

And, privately she consoled herself with the words, "Little dear"—for that was how she spoke to herself on occasion, "you will receive letters tomorrow morning from the civilised world."

"Well, you know," Mrs. Hogg was saying, "to *me* it was a miracle. I was debating whether to take the job in

Bristol or a permanent place in the north with a deaf lady. A letter arrived, it was a Tuesday morning, to say that the lady in Bristol had gone to hospital because of some complications, and was having her baby there. The husband sent me a week's money. Then in the afternoon another letter arrived from the other place. No, I'm wrong, it was the next morning. The deaf lady had died. So there I was without a job. So I said to Our Lady, 'What am I going to do now?' and Our Lady said, 'Go back to St. Philumena's and think it over.' I'd already stayed at St. Philumena's on one of the big Retreats——"

"Did you actually hear a voice?" Caroline enquired.

"A voice?"

"I mean, when you say, 'Our Lady said,' do you mean she spoke audibly to you?"

"Oh no. But that's how Our Lady always speaks to me. I ask a question and she answers."

"How do you hear her answer, then?"

"The words come to me—but of course you won't know much about that. You have to be experienced in the spiritual life."

"How do you know the words come from the Blessed Virgin?" Caroline persisted relentlessly. Mrs. Hogg moved her upper lip into an indecent smile. Caroline thought: "She desires the ecstasy of murdering me in some prolonged ritualistic orgy; she sees I am thin, angular, sharp, enquiring; she sees I am grisly about the truth; she sees I am well-dressed and good-looking. Perhaps she senses my weakness, my loathing of human flesh where the bulk outweighs the intelligence."

Mrs. Hogg continued: "I know it was Our Lady's message because of what happened. I came to St. Philumena's, and saw Lady Manders who was here just at that time. When I told her the position she said, 'Now, there *is* a job for you here, if you like to try it. We want to get rid of the Catering Warden, she isn't strong enough for the job. It's hard work, but Our Lady would help you.' So I came for a month's trial. That was in the autumn, and I'm loving it, every minute of it."

"That was the miracle," Caroline said.

"Oh, it *was* a miracle. My arriving here just when Lady Manders wanted to make a change in the staff. I only came, really, to think things over. But I can tell you, I don't have much chance to sit on my behind and think. It's hard work. And I always put duty first, before everything. And I don't mind the work; Our Lady helps me. When the kitchen girls grumble about the work, I always tell them, 'Our Lady will do it for you.' And she does."

"In that case, there's no need for them to do it," Caroline said.

"Now listen to me, Caroline," said Mrs. Hogg. "You want to speak to a priest. You haven't really got the hang of the Catholic Faith. You want to speak to Father Ingrid."

"You are wrong," Caroline said. "I've heard him speaking once from the pulpit. Once was enough. I must go now."

The bell was ringing for Benediction. "That's not the way to the chapel," Mrs. Hogg called after her as Caroline walked swiftly along the green-walled corridors.

Caroline did not reply. She went to her room and began to pack her things, neatly and calmly. St. Philumena's was a dead loss, Caroline told herself; "For one who demands much of life, there is always a certain amount of experience to be discarded as soon as one discovers its fruitlessness."

She excelled at packing a suitcase. She told herself "I'm good at packing a suitcase," forming these words in her mind to keep other words, other thoughts, from crowding in. The three days of St. Philumena's were bleating to high heaven for formulation, but she kept them at bay as she muttered, "Shoes there. Books here. The comb-bag in that corner. Blouses flat on the bed. Fold the arms. Like that. Then fold again. This way, that way. Hot-water bottle. Nothing rattling. Crucifix wedged in cotton wool. Catholic Truth Society pamphlet to read in the train. I am doing what I am doing."

In this way, she subjugated St. Philumena's for half-an-hour. She had devised the technique in the British Museum reading room almost a year ago, at a time when her brain was like a Guy Fawkes night, ideas cracking off in all directions, dark idiot-figures jumping round a fiery junk-heap in the centre.

In the train Caroline swung her case on to the rack and sat down. The case jutted out at an angle. Caroline got up and pushed it straight. She had the carriage to herself. After a while she rose again and moved the case to the middle of the rack, measuring by the mirror beneath until there was an equal space on either side. Then she sat down in her corner-seat facing it. She sat perfectly still while her thoughts became blind. Every now and then a cynical lucidity would overtake part of her mind, forcing her to comment on the fury of the other half. That was painful. She observed, "The mocker is taking over."

"Very funny, very funny," said Caroline out loud. A woman just then passing in the corridor observed her talking to herself. Caroline thought, "Good God, now my trouble is growing noticeable."

The shock of having been observed brought some relief. As her mental pain subsided, Caroline began to reflect. "Am I justified? I bloody well am." Carefully and intently she began to recollect what St. Philumena's had been like.

On her second evening when she had joined the other residents in the recreation room, "I must remember they are called 'pilgrims,'" she thought. She had already made the blunder of referring to them as "residents."

Anyway, there were eight of them besides Caroline. She brought them one by one to mind as she sat, still as a telegraph-post, in the train which carried her to London.

That evening she had looked very seldom at her fellow guests, but now revoking, she peered into their eyes, stared up and down at their clothes, scrutinised the very skin on their faces.

She recalled them, first singly, and then in a half-circle round the fireplace; she could even see herself.

And as the train chugged south, her memory dwelling continuously on the fireside group, while at the same time she repeated mentally the formula of the rosary, touched the beads imperceptibly in her pocket, which she did for its outward effect on her person, the automatic act of the rosary prevented her from fidgeting in her agitation, it stopped her talking aloud to herself, made her unnoticeable. For the group round St. Philumena's fire inflamed her; after all, she was a most jumpy woman at the best of times.

Two nights ago that group were exchanging anecdotes about the treatment of Catholics in England by non-Catholics. It was their favourite theme.

"What do you think, they won't employ Catholics on the passenger transport where my mother lives."

"Not one Catholic child got a scholarship. . . ."

"Forty per cent were Catholics, but not one . . ."

It was well-known, said a large florid lady from the West of Ireland, that the University of Cambridge would not take Catholics.

"Oh no, that's not true," Caroline said at once.

"And they do their best for to set the Catholics asunder," the lady from the West of Ireland went on.

"Not noticeably," Caroline said.

The young lawyer agreed with her, but his testimony was suspect. The lady from Ireland whispered aloud to her neighbour,

"He's curing from alcohol, poor lad."

The lawyer added, "Of course, there's always a prejudice in certain quarters," which put him right with the company.

"My brother in the public library, when they found he was a Catholic . . ."

As the atrocities mounted up, the lady from the West of Ireland continued to ply Caroline, "What d'ye make of that? . . . Isn't it awful? What d'ye think of it?"

At last, rising to leave, "I think it very quaint," Caroline answered.

Throughout, Mrs. Hogg had been volubly present. She too had offered some relishes, had known what persecution was, and her eyes were frequently directed towards Caroline the suspect.

Recalling these proceedings, Caroline recalled too a similar fireside pattern, her family on the Jewish side with their friends, so long ago left behind her. She saw them again, nursing themselves in a half-circle as they indulged in their debauch of unreal suffering; "Prejudice!" ". . . an outright insult!" Caroline thought, "Catholics and Jews; the Chosen, infatuated with a tragic image of themselves. They are tragic only because they are so comical." But the thought of those fireside martyrs, Jews and Catholics, revolted Caroline with their funniness. She thought she might pull the emergency cord, halt the train, create a blinding distraction; and even while planning this action she reflected that she would not positively perform it.

But in her own rapacity for suffering, Caroline seized and held the images of the world she had left years ago and the world she had newly entered. She tugged and pulled the rosary in her pocket, while her thoughts, fine as teeth, went into action again and again with the fireside congregations of mock martyrs, their incongruity beside the real ones . . . it was an insult.

It was in the dining-car that Caroline got round once more to Mrs. Hogg. Mrs. Hogg stuck in her mind like a lump of food on the chest which will move neither up nor down. Suddenly Caroline realised that she was bolting her lunch, and simultaneously the memory of mealtimes at St. Philumena's returned, with the sight of Mrs. Hogg chewing in rhythm with the reading from the Scriptures delivered in the Sister's refined modulations: "Beloved, let us love one another, love springs from God. . . . If a man boasts of loving God, while he hates his own brother, he is a liar . . . the man who loves God must be one who loves his brother."

Caroline thought, "The demands of the Christian religion are exorbitant, they are outrageous. Christians who don't realise that from the start are not faithful. They are dishonest; their teachers are talking in their sleep. 'Love one another . . . brethren, beloved . . . your brother, neighbours, love, love, love'—do they know what they are saying?"

She had stopped eating, was conscious of two things, a splitting headache and Mrs. Hogg. These bemused patterers on the theme of love, had they faced Mrs. Hogg in person? Returning to her carriage Caroline passed a married couple who had been staying at St. Philumena's, on their way to the dining-car. They had been among the

46

fireside company. She remembered that they were to have left today.

"Oh, it's you, Miss Rose! I didn't think you were leaving so soon."

People were pressing to pass, which gave Caroline a chance to escape. "I was called away," she said, moving off.

The couple had been received into the Church two months ago, so they had told the company round the fire.

Their new-found faith was expressed in a rowdy contempt for the Church of England, in which the woman's father was a clergyman. "Father was furious when we went over to Rome. Of course he's Anglo-Catholic; they have holy water and the saints; everything bar the Faith; too killing." She was a large-boned and muscled woman in her mid-thirties. She had set in her final development, at the stage of athletic senior prefect. She had some hair on her face. Her lower lip had a minor pugilistic twist. Of the two, she made the more noise, but her husband, with his smooth thin face, high pink colouring, who looked as if he never needed to shave, was a good support for his wife as they sat round the fire at St. Philumena's. He said, "The wonderful thing about being a Catholic is that it makes life so easy. Everything easy for salvation and you can have a happy life. All the little things that the Protestants hate, like the statues and the medals, they all help us to have a happy life." He finished there, as if he had filled up the required page of his school exercise book, and need state no more; he lay back in his chair, wiped his glasses, crossed his legs.

At this point the West of Ireland took over, warning them, "Converts have a lot to learn. You can always tell a convert from a cradle Catholic. There's something different."

47

The dipsomaniac lawyer, with his shiny blue suit, said, "I like converts," and smiled weakly at Caroline. His smile faded away before Mrs. Hogg's different smile.

At Crewe, Caroline got the compartment to herself again. She began to reflect that Mrs. Hogg could easily become an obsession, the demon of that carnal hypocrisy which struck her mind whenever she came across a gathering of Catholics or Jews engaged in their morbid communal pleasures. She began to think of her life in London, her work, Laurence to whom she must send a wire; he would be amused by her account of St. Philumena's. She began to giggle, felt drowsy, and, settling into her corner, fell asleep.

3

WHEN LAURENCE RETURNED TO THE COTTAGE
after posting his letter to Caroline his grandmother handed
him a telegram.

He read it. "It's from Caroline. She's back in London."

"Yes, funny, I had a feeling it was from Caroline."
Louisa very often revealed a mild form of the gipsy's
psychic faculties. "Fancy, what a pity you've posted that
letter to Liverpool."

As Laurence set off to the post office again to telephone
Caroline, he said, "Shall I ask her to come down here?"

"Yes, certainly," Louisa said with that inclination of
her head which was a modified form of the regal gesture.
When he was small she used to tell Laurence "Don't just
answer 'Yes'; say 'Yes, certainly,' that's how Queen Mary
always answers."

"How do you know that, Grandmother?"

"A person told me."

"Are you sure the person was telling the truth?"

"Oh yes, certainly."

"Tell Caroline," Louisa called after him, "that I have
some blackberries in my tins," meaning by this to tell
Laurence of her genuine desire for Caroline's visit.

"All right, I will."

"And ask the post office to give you back the letter.
There's no reason to send it all the way to Liverpool."

"Oh, they won't fish it out without a fuss," Laurence told

her. "They never give you back a letter, once it's posted. Not without a fuss."

"Oh, what a pity!"

"It doesn't matter," Laurence said. "I'll be seeing Caroline. I wonder why she left so soon?"

"Yes, I wonder why."

Caroline's number was engaged when he rang. The sky had cleared and the autumn sun, low in the sky, touched the countryside. He decided to go to Ladle Sands, a half-hour's walk, from where he could try Caroline's number again, and by which time the pubs would be open. He was impatient to talk to Caroline. His desire to get her interested and involved in the mystery surrounding his grandmother was almost a fulfilment of a more compelling desire to assert the continuing pattern of their intimacy.

Laurence had no success with Caroline's phone that night. He pursued the exchange with mounting insistence on the urgency of getting through; they continued to reply in benumbed and fatalistic tones that the phone was out of order, it had been reported.

A queer buzzing sound brought Caroline to the telephone just before midnight. "Your receiver has been off. We've been trying to get a call through from Sussex." They were extremely irate.

"It hasn't been off," said Caroline.

"It must have been misplaced. Please replace your receiver."

"And the call? Are you putting it through?"

"No. The caller has gone now."

Caroline thought, "Well, he will ring in the morning." She lay on her divan staring out at the night sky beyond her balcony, too tired to draw the curtains. She was warmed by the knowledge that Laurence was near to hand, wanting to speak to her. She could rely on him to take her side, should there be any difficulty with Helena over her rapid departure from St. Philumena's. On the whole she did not think there would be any difficulty with Helena.

Just then she heard the sound of a typewriter. It seemed to come through the wall on her left. It stopped, and was immediately followed by a voice remarking her own thoughts. It said: *On the whole she did not think there would be any difficulty with Helena.*

There seemed, then, to have been more than one voice: it was a recitative, a chanting in unison. It was something like a concurrent series of echoes. Caroline jumped up and over to the door. There was no one on the landing or on the staircase outside. She returned to her sitting-room and shut the door. Everything was quiet. The wall, from which direction the sounds had come, divided her sitting-room from the first-floor landing of a house converted into flats. Caroline's flat occupied the whole of this floor. She had felt sure the sounds had come from the direction of the landing. Now she searched the tiny flat. The opposite wall separated the bed-sitting-room from the bathroom and kitchen. Everything was quiet there. She went out on to the balcony from where she could see the whole length of Queen's Gate. Two servicemen clattered up the street and turned into Cromwell Road. The neighbouring balconies were dark and empty. Caroline returned to the room, closed the windows and drew the curtains.

She had taken the flat four weeks ago. The house held six flats, most of which were occupied by married couples or young men who went out to their offices every day. Caroline knew the other tenants only by sight, greeting them in passing on the staircase. There were occasional noises at night, when someone had a party, but usually the house was quiet. Caroline tried to recall the tenants in the flat above hers. She was not certain; they all passed her landing on their way upstairs and she herself had never gone beyond the first floor.

A typewriter and a chorus of voices: "What on earth are they up to at this time of night?" Caroline wondered. But what worried her were the words they had used, coinciding so exactly with her own thoughts.

Then it began again. Tap-tappity-tap; the typewriter. And again, the voices: Caroline ran out on to the landing, for it seemed quite certain the sound came from that direction. No one was there. The chanting reached her as she returned to her room, with these words exactly:

"What on earth are they up to at this time of night?" Caroline wondered. But what worried her were the words they had used, coinciding so exactly with her own thoughts.

And then the typewriter again: tap-tap-tap. She was rooted. "My God!" she cried aloud. "Am I going mad?"

As soon as she had said it, and with the sound of her own voice, her mind was filled with an imperative need to retain her sanity. It was the phrase "Caroline wondered" which arrested her. Immediately then, shaken as she was, Caroline began to consider the possibilities, whether the sounds she had heard were real or illusory. While the thought terrified her that she was being haunted by people—spirits or things—beings who had read her thoughts, perhaps who could read her very heart, she could not hope for the horrible alternative. She feared it more; she feared that those sounds, so real that they seemed to have come from the other side of the wall, were hallucinations sent forth from her own mind. Caroline sat for the next half-hour dazed and frightened, wondering what to do. She dreaded a repetition of the experience, yet prayed for some sign that her mind was not unhinged. The question began to appear as one on which she could herself decide; it was like being faced with a choice between sanity and madness.

She had already concluded that the noise could not have come from anyone in the house. The fact that her feelings and reflections were being recorded seemed to point to some invisible source, the issue being, was it objectively real or was it imaginary? If the sounds came from some real, invisible typewriter and voices, Caroline felt she was in danger, might go mad, but the experience was not itself a sign of madness. She was now utterly convinced that what she had heard was not the product of her own imagination. "I am not mad. I'm not mad. See; I can reflect on the situation. I am being haunted, I am not haunting myself." Meantime, she was trembling, frightened out of her wits, although her fear was not altogether blind.

Tap-click-tap. The voices again: *Meantime, she was trembling, frightened out of her wits, although her fear was not altogether blind.*

"Christ!" she said. "Who *is* it there?" Although she had decided quite reasonably that no one in the house could be responsible for those sounds, none the less when she actually heard the voices again, so clear, just behind the wall, she sprang up and began to search every corner of the flat, even under the divan, which was too low to conceal a human body; even in the little cupboard where the gas meter was fixed. The activity took the edge off her panic, and although she knew she would not find her tormentors in this way, she put all her energy into the search, moving furniture, opening and shutting doors. She suspected everything, however improbable; even that the sound might be contained in some quite small object —a box with a machine inside, operated from a distance. She acted upon these suspicions, examining everything closely in case she should find something strange.

There was suddenly a knocking from the ceiling. Caroline propelled herself out of the flat and switched on the landing lights.

"Who's there?" she called up the stairs. "Who is it?" Her voice was strained high with fear.

There was a movement above her, round the bend of the stair. A shuffle, and the opening of a door on the second landing. A woman's voice whispered fiercely, "Keep quiet!"

Looking straight above her, Caroline saw the top half of a woman leaning over the banister, long wisps of grey hair falling over her face and her loose white garment showing between the banisters. Caroline screamed, was too late to stop herself when she recognised the woman as the occupant of the flat above.

"Are you drunk?" the angry tenant breathed at her. "What do you mean by waking the house at this time of night? It's twenty-two minutes past one, and you've been banging about moving furniture and slamming doors for the last hour. I haven't slept a wink. I've got to go out to business in the morning."

Another door opened on the second floor, and a man's voice said, "Anything the matter? I heard a girl scream." The woman scuttled back into her room, being undressed, and finished her complaint with her head only showing outside her door.

"It was that young woman downstairs. She's been making a disturbance for the past hour. Did you hear her?"

"I certainly heard a scream," the man's voice said.

Caroline ran up a few steps so as to see the speakers from the bend in the staircase. "I got a terrible fright when I saw you," she explained to the woman. "Was that you knocking?"

"Indeed it was," said the woman. "I'll complain about this in the morning."

"Were *you* using a typewriter?" Caroline began to enquire. She was helpless and shaky. "I heard a typewriter, and voices."

"You're mad!" said the woman, as she withdrew and shut the door. The young man had also retreated.

Caroline returned to her rooms, and, rapidly and stealthily, began to pack a small suitcase. She wondered where she would spend the rest of the night. A lonely hotel room was unthinkable, it would have to be a friend's house. She moved about, jerkily snatching at the necessary articles as if she expected some invisible hand, concealed in each object, to close over hers before she had got possession of it. She was anxious to make as little sound as possible, but in her nervousness bumped into the furniture and knocked over a glass dish. To protect herself from the noises of her movements, she contracted a muscle somewhere behind her nose and throat, which produced the effect in her ears as of a rustling breeze—it dulled the sound of her footsteps, making the whole operation sound quieter than it was.

Caroline pressed down the lid of her small case. She had decided where to go for the night. The Baron; he was awake, or at least available, at all hours. She opened the case again, remembering that she had packed her money; she would need it for the taxi to the Baron's flat in Hampstead. She was absorbed by the pressing need to get out of her flat at the earliest possible moment, and as she searched among her clothes she did not even notice, with her customary habit of self-observation, that she had thrown her night-things together anyhow. The difference between this frenzied packing operation and the deliberate care she had taken, in spite of her rage, to fold and fit her possessions into place at St. Philumena's less than a day ago failed to register.

Tap-tick-tap. Tap. She did not even notice Click-tappity *with her customary habit of self-observation, that she had thrown her night-things together anyhow. The difference between this frenzied packing operation and the deliberate care she had taken, in spite of her rage, to fold and fit her possessions into place at St. Philumena's less than a day ago failed to register. Tap.*

Coat—hat—handbag—suitcase; Caroline grabbed them and hustled out of the door, slamming it to. She rattled downstairs and out of the front door, which she slammed behind her. At the top of Queen's Gate, turning in from Old Brompton Road, she got a taxi and secured herself inside it with a slam of the door.

"It is quite a common thing," Willi Stock said. "Your brain is overworked." This was the Baron speaking. He stood by the electric fire with its flicking imitation coals, sipping Curaçao.

Caroline sipped hers, curled up on the sofa, and crying. Absorbing the warmth of the fire and of the liquor, she felt a warmth of gratitude towards the Baron. For the last hour he had been explaining her mental condition. She was consoled, not by the explanations, but by the fact of his recognisable face, by the familiar limitations of his mind, and by the reality of his warm flat and his bottle of Curaçao.

For the first time in her life, she felt that Willi Stock was an old friend. Regarding him in this category, she was able to secure her conscience in his company. For the Baron belonged to one of the half-worlds of Caroline's past, of which she had gradually taken leave; it was a society which she had half-forgotten, and of which she had come wholly to disapprove. It was over a year since she had last seen the Baron. But Laurence had kept up with him, had mentioned him from time to time, which confirmed Caroline in her feeling that she was in the company of an old friend. She greatly needed the protection of an old friend till daylight.

He said, "Eleanor is away on tour just now."

Caroline said, "I know, Laurence had a postcard."

Eleanor Hogarth was the Baron's mistress.

"Did he?" said the Baron. "When was that?"

"Oh, last week sometime. He merely mentioned it."

They called him the Baron because he called himself Baron Stock. Caroline was not aware from what aristocracy he derived his title: nor had anyone enquired; she was sure it was not self-imposed as some suggested. He came originally from the Belgian Congo, had travelled in the Near East, loitered in Europe, and finally settled in England, a naturalized British subject. That was fifteen years ago, and he was now nearing fifty. Caroline had always felt that the Baron had native African blood, without being able to locate its traces in any one feature. She had been in Africa, and had a sense of these things. It was a matter of casual curiosity to her; but she had noticed, some years ago, when Africa's racial problems were being discussed in company with the Baron, he had denounced the blacks with ferocious bitterness, out of all proportion to the occasion. This confirmed Caroline's judgment; there was, too, an expression of pathos which at times appeared on the Baron's face, which she had seen in others of concealed mixed colour; and there was something about the whites of his eyes; what it was she did not know. And altogether, having observed these things, she did not much care.

The Baron had set up a bookshop in Charing Cross Road, one of those which keep themselves exclusively intellectual. "Intellect-u-al," the Baron pronounced it. He would say, "Of course there are no intellect-u-als in England."

It had been the delight of Caroline and Laurence to recall the day when they looked in on the Baron at Charing Cross Road, to find him being accosted by a tiny woman with the request:

"D'you have any railway books for children?"

The Baron reared high and thin on the central expanse of grey carpet and regarded her silently for half a second.

"Railway books for children," she repeated. "Books with pictures of trains and railways."

The Baron said: "Railway books for children, Madam? I do not think so, Madam." His arm languidly indicated the shelves. "We have Histor-ay, Biograph-ay, Theolog-ay, Theosoph-ay, Psycholog-ay, Religio-n, Poetr-ay, but railway books for children. . . . Try Foyles across the road, Madam."

He raised his shoulders and eyebrows as he turned to Laurence and Caroline. "My father," he said, "knew a man in the Belgian Diplomatic Service who was the author of a railway book for children. It was very popular and sold quickly. A copy was sent to a family in Yugoslavia. Of course, the book contained a code message. The author was revising the book for the second edition when he was arrested. That story is my total experience of railway books for children. Have you read this work on Kafka?—it has just come in, my darlings, my Laurence and my Caroline."

In this way, Baron Stock was an old friend.

Caroline lay in the dark warm room on a made-up sofa bed. The Baron had left her just after four had struck. She had stopped crying. In case she should want them, the Baron had left a bottle of aspirins on a chair by the sofa. Caroline reached out for the bottle, unscrewed the cap and extracted the twist of cotton wool which she had hoped to find. She stuffed a piece in each ear. Now she was alone, it seemed to her that she had been playing a false role with the Baron. It was the inevitable consequence of her arrival at his flat, in a panic, at a late hour; "Willi! Let me in, I've been hearing voices!"

After that, she was forced to accept his protection, his friendliness; was glad of it. And when he had settled her by the fire:

"Caroline, *my* dear, how slender and febrile you've become! What kind of voices? How extremely interesting. Was it a religi-ous experience?"

She had begun to weep, to apologise.

"Caroline, *my* dear, as you know, I never go to bed. Seriously, I never go to bed unless it's the last possible alternative. I am delighted beyond words—Caroline, my dear, I am so honoured—your distress, my dear—if you can realise how I feel."

And so she had to play the part. Now, alone in the dark, she thought, "I should have faced it out at the flat. I shouldn't have run away."

The Baron, of course, was convinced she was suffering from a delusion.

"It happens to many many people, my dear. It is quite nothing to worry about. If the experience should recur you will have a course of analysis or take some pills and the voices will go away. But I doubt that the phenomenon will recur. You have been under a considerable strain from what I hear of your severed relations with Laurence."

"We haven't parted, really, you know."

"But you now have separate establishments?"

"Yes, I've got rooms in Kensington. Laurence is keeping on the flat for the time being. He's away in the country. I must get in touch with him tomorrow, first thing." She gave the deliberate impression of not wanting to talk any more.

"In Sussex? With Mrs. Jepp?"—a genuine curiosity in his voice.

"Yes."

"I met her one day about three years ago. Laurence introduced me. A fine old lady. Wonderful for her age. Quite excellent. Do you see much of her?"

"I saw her last Easter," Caroline said, "she was grand."

"Yes, she is grand. She doesn't visit London, of course?"

"No," Caroline said. "That must have been her last trip when you met her. She hasn't been to London since."

"She doesn't care for the Hampstead ménage?"

"Well, she's an independent soul," said Caroline absently.

She had only half taken in the Baron's chatter, although he continued to speak of Louisa.

"I must get in touch with Laurence first thing," Caroline repeated. "Mrs. Jepp isn't on the 'phone. I'll send a wire. Oh, Willi!—those voices, it was Hell!"

Now, lying awake in the dark, Caroline recalled the conversation, regretting that she had shown such a supine dependence on the Baron. More and more she thought, "I should have stayed at home and faced whatever was to be faced." She knew she had tough resources. And as she tormented herself, now, into confronting her weakness, painfully she recollected the past hour; some of the talk which she had let slip so drowsily through her mind came back to her. It had struck her in passing that the Baron had seemed extraordinarily interested in Laurence's grandmother. He was the last person one would expect to have remembered—and by name—an undistinguished old lady to whom he had been introduced casually three years ago. Mrs. Jepp was not immediately impressive to strangers, was not at all the type to impress the Baron.

Through the darkness, from beside the fireplace, Caroline heard a sound. *Tap*. The typewriter. She sat up as the voices followed:

The Baron had seemed extraordinarily interested in Laurence's grandmother. He was the last person one would expect to have remembered—and by name—an undistinguished old lady to whom he had been introduced casually three years ago. Mrs. Jepp was not immediately impressive to strangers.

Caroline yelled, "Willi! Oh, my God, the voices. . . . Willi!"

Through the wall she heard him stir.

"Did you call, Caroline?"

Eventually he shuffled in and switched on the light.

Caroline pulled the bulky borrowed dressing-gown over her shoulders, her eyes blue and hard with fright. She had grasped the rosary which she had tucked under the cushion at her head. Her fingers clung shakily to the beads as a child clings to its abracadabra toy.

"*My* dear Caroline, what a charming picture you make! Don't move for a second, don't move: I am trying to recall —some moment, some scene in the past or a forgotten canvas.—One of my sister's friends perhaps—or my nurse. Caroline, my dear, there is no more exquisite sight than that of a woman taken unawares with a rosary."

Caroline slung the beads on the post of the chair. The thought flashed upon her, "He is indecent." She looked up at him sharply and caught him off his guard; his mouth and eyes drooped deadly tired, and he was resisting a yawn. She thought, "After all, he is kind; it was only a pose."

"Tell me about the voices," he said. "I heard nothing, myself. From what direction did they come?"

"Over there, beside the fireplace," she answered.

61

"Would you like some tea? I think there is tea."

"Oh, coffee. Could I have some coffee? I don't think I'm likely to sleep."

"We shall both have some coffee. Stay where you are."

Caroline thought, "He means that he isn't likely to sleep, either." She said, "I'm awfully sorry about this, Willi. It sounds so foolish, but it really is appalling. And you must be dead tired."

"Coffee and aspirins. *My* Caroline, you are not to apologise, I am delighted——"

But he could hardly conceal his sleepiness. As he returned bearing their coffee, with a bottle of brandy on a tray, he said, as one who keeps the conversation flowing, notwithstanding a tiger in the garden, "You must tell me all about the voices." He saw her removing the cotton-wool plugs from her ears, but pretended not to notice. "I have always believed that disembodied beings inhabit this room," he went on, "and now I'm sure. Seriously, I'm sure—indissuasively convinced, Caroline, that you are in touch with something. I do so wish I had been able to give you some phenobarbitone, an excellent sedative; or something to make you sleep. But of course I shall sit up with you, it's nearly five already . . ."

He said no more about hallucinations, by which Caroline understood that he now really believed that she was crazy. She sipped her coffee submissively and jerkily, weeping all the time. She told him to leave her.

"Of course not. I want to hear about the voices. It's most intriguing, really."

She felt better for the effort to describe what had happened, although the fact gnawed at her that the Baron was finding the episode a strain and a nuisance. But ruthlessly, in her own interest, she talked on and on. And as she talked she realised that the Baron was making the best of it, had resigned himself, was attending to her, but as one who regards another's words, not as symbols but as symptoms.

He got out of her that the clicking of the typewriter always preceded the voices, and sometimes accompanied their speech. How many voices there were, she could not say. Male or female? Both, she told him. It was impossible to disconnect the separate voices, because they came in complete concert; only by the varying timbres could the chorus be distinguished from one voice. "In fact," she went on, wound-up and talking rapidly, "it sounds like one person speaking in several tones at once."

"And always using the past tense?"

"Yes. Mocking voices."

"And you say this chorus comments on your thoughts and actions?"

"Not always," said Caroline, "that's the strange thing. It says 'Caroline was thinking or doing this or that'—then sometimes it adds a remark of its own."

"Give me an example, dear. I'm so stupid—I can never grasp——"

"Well," said Caroline, unwhelming herself of a sudden access of confidence in the Baron's disinterestedness, "take tonight. I was dropping off, and thinking over my conversation with you—

"—as one does—" she added,

"—and it drifted to my mind how you had remembered meeting Laurence's grandmother; I thought it strange you should do so. Next thing, I heard the typewriter and the voices. They repeated my thought, something like, 'It came to her that the Baron'—you know we always call you the Baron, '—that the Baron had been extraordinarily interested in Laurence's grandmother.' That's what the voices said. And then they added something to the effect that

63

the Baron was the last person who would remember, and remember by name, an old woman like Mrs. Jepp merely from a passing introduction three years ago. You see, Willi, the words are immaterial——"

"You're mad," said the Baron abruptly.

Caroline felt relieved at these words, although, and in a way because, they confirmed her distress. It was a relief to hear the Baron speak his true mind, it gave her exactly what she had anticipated, what seemed to her a normal person's reaction to her story. Fearing this, she had been purposely vague when, earlier in the evening, she had explained her distress: "A typewriter followed by voices. They speak in the past tense. They mock me."

Now that she had been more explicit, and had been told she was mad, she felt a perverse satisfaction at the same time as a suffocating sense that she might never communicate the reality of what she had heard.

The Baron hastily recovered. "I use 'mad' of course in the colloquial sense. In the way that we're *all mad,* you know. A little crazy, you know. Amongst ourselves, I mean —the intelligentsia are all a little mad and, my dear Caroline, that's what makes us so nice. The sane are not worth noticing."

"Oh, quite," said Caroline. "I know what you mean." But she was wondering, now, why he had spoken so viciously: "You're mad!"—like a dog snapping at a fly. She felt she had been tactless. She wished she had chosen to cite a different example of the voices.

"Someone is haunting me, that's what it is," Caroline said, hoping to discard responsibility for offending the Baron.

He seemed to have forgotten his role as the intrigued questioner; his air of disinterested curiosity was suspended while he told Caroline exactly why and how Mrs.

64

Jepp had impressed him. "You see, she is a charac-ter. So small and yet her strength—her aged yet vivid face. So dark, so small. I could never forget that face."

With surprise, Caroline thought, "He is defending himself."

"And she looked so debonair, my dear, in a deep blue velvet hat. Her brown wrinkles. Quite a picture."

"Three years ago, was it, Willi?"

"Almost three years—I remember it well. Laurence brought her into the shop, and she said, 'What a lot of books!' "

He gave an affectionate chuckle, but Caroline did not join him. She was thinking of Louisa Jepp's last visit to London, three years ago. Certainly, she did not possess her blue hat at that time, Caroline was acquainted with all Louisa's hats. They were purchased at long intervals, on rare occasions. And only last Easter, Caroline had accompanied the old lady to Hayward's Heath where they had spent the afternoon, eventually deciding on that blue velvet hat which had so pleased Louisa that she had worn it on every occasion since.

"A blue hat?" said Caroline.

"My dear, believe it or not, a blue. I recall it distinctly. Blue velvet, curling close to her head, with a fluffy black feather at the side. I shall never forget that hat nor the face beneath it."

That was the hat all right.

In the face of the Baron's apparent lie—to what purpose?—and the obvious fact that her account of the voices had somehow provoked it, Caroline began to gather her own strength. The glimmering of a puzzle distinct from her own problem was a merciful antidote to her bewilderment. She kept her peace and sipped her coffee, knowing that she was delivered at least from this second mockery, the Baron posing as a credulous sympathiser, his maddening chatter about psychic phenomena, while in reality he waited for the morning, when he could hand her over to Laurence or someone responsible. The Baron might think her mentally unhinged, but by a mercy she had made it clear, though quite unintentionally, that her condition was dangerous for him. In fact, she had forced him to take her seriously, to the extent that he made excuses for himself and lied.

She considered this, but when she looked at him, saw him still courteous in his extreme tiredness, her tears returned.

"Oh, Willi! How can I ever thank you? You are so kind."

"So kind," she repeated, she herself like a tired infant whose tongue cannot extricate, itself from a single phrase, "So kind, so kind——" And so, in her gratitude, she gave away what advantage she had gained and became once more a distracted woman seeking the protection of an old friend.

The Baron, as if he too would make a concession, and anxious to place her in a less pathetic light, asked,

"What are you writing these days?"

"Oh, the same book. But I haven't done much lately."

"The work on the twentieth-century novel?"

"That's right. *Form in the Modern Novel.*"

"How's it going so far?"

"Not bad. I'm having difficulty with the chapter on realism."

Suddenly she felt furious with the voices for having upset her arrangements. She had planned to start work that week; to put all her personal troubles out of her mind. And now, this ghastly humiliating experience.

She broke down again. "It ought not to have happened

to me! This sort of thing shouldn't happen to an intelligent woman!"

"It is precisely to the intelligent that these things happen," said the Baron. Both he and Caroline were drinking brandy neat.

After a while the Baron made more coffee, and then, thank God, it was dawn.

The Baron had put up a protest, but eventually he had let her leave his flat. By daylight she had revived, with that unaccountable energy to which nervous people have access, not only in spite of a sleepless and harrowing night, but almost because of it. The Baron had put up a protest but he had let her go after she had promised to keep in touch with him during the day. She wanted to be out of his flat. She wanted to return to Kensington. And to contact Laurence; he would return to London. She would have to face the housekeeper at her flat; she was sure the other tenants must have complained of the last night's turmoil. "The housekeeper is a brute, Willi," Caroline had said, as she collected her things.

"Give her ten shill-ings," said the Baron.

"It's a man."

"Give him two pounds."

"Perhaps a pound," said Caroline. "Well, Willi, I do thank you."

"Two pounds would be on the safe side," pursued the Baron.

"I'll make it thirty shillings," said Caroline, seriously.

The Baron began to giggle quietly. Then Caroline, thinking it over, was taken with laughter too.

"I like to haggle."

"All women do."

On the way to Hampstead Underground, she sent

Laurence a wire. "Come immediately something mysterious going on."

"The voices may never come back," she thought. In a way she hoped they would. Laurence might easily be the means of tracking them down by some sheer innocent remark. That was the sort of thing he could do. She did not think the voices would speak to her if she was with anyone else. But Laurence would investigate. She had almost a sense of adventure in her unnatural exhilaration. It was a sharp sunny day. In the train, she put a pound note and a ten-shilling note in a separate place in her handbag, and smiled; that was for the housekeeper. On the whole, she hoped the voices would return, would give her a chance to establish their existence, and to trace their source.

It was nearly nine-thirty when she reached Queen's Gate. A convenient time. The tenants had left for their offices, and the housekeeper had not yet emerged. She closed the door quietly and crept upstairs.

Laurence kept the door of the telephone box open to let in the sun and air of the autumn morning.

"Still no reply?"

"Sorry, no reply."

"Sure you've got the right——?"

But the operator had switched off. He was sure she hadn't got the right number—at least—maybe—— Caroline must have gone somewhere else for the night. Perhaps she had gone to Mass.

He rang his parents' home. There had been no word from Miss Rose. His mother was at Mass. His father had just left. He sent Caroline a wire from the village post office, and went for an exasperated walk, which turned cheerful as he anticipated Caroline's coming to stay at his grandmother's. He had arranged to prolong his holiday for another week. When he reached the cottage half an hour later, he found a wire from Caroline.

"There's been a mix-up at the post office," he told Louisa.

"What, dear?"

"I sent Caroline a wire, and apparently Caroline has sent one to me. But they must have got the messages mixed up somehow. This is the message I sent to Caroline. The very words."

"What, dear? Read it out, I don't understand."

"I'll go and speak to the post office," Laurence said swiftly, leaving at once. He was anxious to avoid the appearance of concealing the wire from his grandmother, after admitting that it contained his own message. He read it again. "Come immediately something mysterious going on." It ended, "love Caroline."

At the post office, where a number of Louisa's neighbours were buying tea and other things, Laurence caused a slight stir. His outgoing message was compared with the one he had just received. He distinctly overheard the postmaster, in their little back office, say to his daughter, "They've both used the exact same words. It's a code, or something fishy they've arranged beforehand."

He came out and said to Laurence, "The two telegrams are identical, sir."

"Well, that's funny." Laurence repeated the words, "something mysterious going on."

"Yes, it seems so," said the man.

Laurence cleared off before the question could become more confused and public. He went into the phone box and asked for Caroline's number. It was ringing through. Immediately she answered.

"Caroline?"

69

"Laurence, is that you? Oh, I've just come home and found a wire. Did you send a wire?"

"Yes, did you?"

"Yes, how was it supposed to read? I'm so frightened."

The little parlour in the Benedictine Priory smelt strongly of polish; the four chairs, the table, the floors, the window-frame gleamed in repose of the polish, as if these wooden things themselves had done some hard industry that day before dawn. Outside, the late October evening sun lit up the front garden strip, and Caroline while she waited in the parlour could hear the familiar incidence of birds and footsteps from the suburban street. She knew this parlour well, with its polish; she had come here weekly for three months to receive her instruction for the Church. She watched a fly alight on the table for a moment; it seemed to Caroline to be in a highly dangerous predica-ment, as if it might break through the glossy surface on which it skated. But it made off quite easily. Caroline jogged round nervily as the door opened. Then she rose as the priest came in, her friend, ageing Father Jerome. She had known him for so many years that she could not remember their first meeting. They had been in touch and out of touch for long periods. And when, after she had decided to enter the Church, and she went weekly to his Priory, her friends had said,

"Why do you go so far out of London for instruction? Why don't you go to Farm Street?" Caroline replied,

"Well, I know this priest."

And if they were Catholics, her friends would say,

"Oh, it doesn't matter about the particular priest. The nearest priest is always the best one."

And Caroline replied, "Well, I know this priest."

She wondered, now, if she did know him. He was, as usual, smiling with his russet face, limping with his bad

70

leg, carrying a faded folder from which emerged an untidy sheaf of crumpled papers. "I got two days off last week to copy parts of Lydgate's *Life of Our Lady* at the British Museum. I've got it here. Do you know it? I'll read you a bit presently. Glorious. What are you writing? You look tired, are you sleeping well? Are you eating proper food? What did you have for breakfast?"

"I haven't slept properly for a week," said Caroline. Then she told him about the voices.

"This started after you got back from St. Philumena's?"

"Yes. That's a week ago today. And it's been going on ever since. It happens when I'm alone during the day. Laurence came up from the country. He's moved into my flat. I can't bear to be alone at nights."

"Sleeping there?"

"In the other room," said Caroline. "That's all right, isn't it?"

"For the time being," said the priest absently.

He rose abruptly and went out. The thoughts shot through Caroline's brain, "Perhaps he's gone to fetch another priest; he thinks I'm dangerous. Has he gone to fetch a doctor? He thinks I should be certified, taken away." And she knew those thoughts were foolish, for Father Jerome had a habit of leaving rooms abruptly when he remembered something which had to be done elsewhere. He would be back presently.

He returned very soon and sat down without comment. He was followed almost immediately by a lay brother, bearing a tray with a glass of milk and a plate of biscuits which he placed before her. This brought back to her the familiarity of the monk and the parlour; only last winter in the early dark evenings after they had finished the catechism, Father Jerome would fetch Caroline the big editions of the Christian Fathers from the monastery library, for she had loved to rummage through them. Then, when he had left her in the warm parlour turning the pages and writing out her notes, he had used to send the lay brother to her with a glass of milk and biscuits.

Now, while she sipped the milk, Father Jerome read aloud a part of *The Life or Our Lady*. He had already started putting it into modern English, and consulted her on one or two points. Caroline felt her old sense of ease with the priest; he never treated her as someone far different from what she was. He treated her not only as a child; not only as an intellectual; not only as a nervy woman; not only as weird; he seemed to assume simply that she was as she was. When he asked, she told him more clearly about the voices.

"I think," she said, "that they are really different tones of one voice. I think they belong to one person."

She also said, "I think I am possessed."

"No," he said, "you are not possessed. You may be obsessed, but I doubt it."

Caroline said, "Do you think this is a delusion?"

"How should I know?"

"Do you think I'm mad?"

"No. But you're ill."

"That's true. D'you think I'm a neurotic?"

"Of course. That goes without saying."

Caroline laughed too. There was a time when she could call herself a neurotic without a sense of premonition; a time when it was merely the badge of her tribe.

"If I'm not mad," she said, "I soon will be, if this goes on much longer."

"Neurotics never go mad," he said.

"But this is intolerable."

"Doesn't it depend on how you take it?"

"Father," she said, almost as if speaking to herself to clarify her mind, "if only I knew where the voices came from. I think it is one person. It uses a typewriter. It uses

72

the past tense. It's exactly as if someone were watching me closely, able to read my thoughts; it's as if the person were waiting to pounce on some insignificant thought or action, in order to make it signify in a strange distorted way. And how does it know about Laurence and my friends? And then there was a strange coincidence the other day. Laurence and I sent each other a wire with exactly the same words, at the same time. It was horrifying. Like predestination."

"These things can happen," said Father Jerome. "Coincidence or some kind of telepathy."

"But the typewriter and the voices—it is as if a writer on another plane of existence was writing a story about us." As soon as she had said these words, Caroline knew that she had hit on the truth. After that she said no more to him on the subject.

As she was leaving he asked her how she had liked St. Philumena's.

"Awful," she said, "I only stayed three days."

"Well," he said, "I didn't think it was your sort of place. You should have gone to a Benedictine convent. They are more your sort."

"But it was you recommended St. Philumena's! Don't you remember, that afternoon at Lady Manders', you were both so keen on my going there?"

"Oh sorry. Yes, I suppose we were. What didn't you like?"

"The people."

He chuckled. "Yes, the people. It's a matter of how you take them."

"I believe it is," said Caroline as though she had just thought of something.

"Well, God bless you. Get some sleep and keep in touch."

She found Laurence in when she returned to the flat in

73

Queen's Gate. He was fiddling about with a black box-like object which at first she took to be a large typewriter.

"What's that?" she said, when she saw it closer.

"Listen," said Laurence.

He pressed a key. There was a whirring sound and the box began to talk with a male voice pitched on a peculiarly forced husky note. It said, "Caroline darling, I have a suggestion to make." Then it went on to say something funny but unprintable.

Caroline subsided with laughter and relief on to the divan.

Laurence did something to the instrument and the words rumbled forth again.

"I knew your voice right away," Caroline said.

"I bet you didn't. I disguised it admirably. Listen again."

"No!" said Caroline. "Someone might overhear it. Dirty beast you are."

He replayed the record and they both laughed helplessly.

"What have you brought that thing here for?" Caroline said. "It might have given me a dreadful fright."

"To record your spook-voices. Now see. I'm placing this disc in here. If you hear them again, you press that. Then it records any voice within hearing distance."

He had placed it against the wall where the voices came from.

"Afterwards," he explained, "we can take out the disc and play it back."

"Maybe those voices won't record," Caroline said.

"They will if they're in the air. Any sound causes an occurrence. If the sound has objective existence it will be recorded."

"This sound might have another sort of existence and still be real."

"Well, let's first exhaust the possibilities of the natural order——"

"But we don't know all the possibilities of the natural order."

"If the sound doesn't record, we can take it for granted that it either doesn't exist, or it exists in some supernatural order," he explained.

She insisted, "It does exist. I think it's a natural sound. I don't think that machine will record it."

"Don't you want to try it?" He seemed disappointed almost.

"Of course. It's a lovely idea."

"And better," he said, "than any ideas you've had so far."

"I've got a good one now," Caroline said. "I'm sure it's the right one. It came to me while I was talking to Father Jerome."

"Let's have it," he said.

"Not yet. I want to assemble the evidence."

Caroline was happy. Laurence looked at himself in the mirror, smiled, and told himself, "She says I'm a dirty beast."

The flat was untidy. Caroline loved to see her own arrangement of things upset by Laurence. It was a double habitation now. They had told the housekeeper that they had got married. He was only half satisfied with the story, but he would put the other half on the bill, Laurence predicted. She was used to being called "Mrs. Manders": it was easy, as if they had never parted, except for the knowledge that this was an emergency set-up. Another week, at the most, and then something would have to be done. She regretted having disclosed her plight to the Baron. He had been pressing Laurence to get Caroline into a nursing home. She did not mind this suggestion, so much as the implication. "A nursing home." He meant a refined looney-bin. Laurence opposed it; he wanted to take her back with him to his grandmother. The Baron had carried the story to Helena, who offered to pay Caroline's expenses at a private nursing home for Catholics. Helena did not mean a looney-bin, however.

"I wouldn't mind a few weeks' rest in a nursing home," Caroline had told Laurence. "I don't think they could do away with the voices, but they might deafen me to them for a while. It would be a rest."

Laurence had been altogether against this.

And he had a mystery of his own to solve. "I wrote and told you all about it. I'd just posted the letter to St. Philumena's when I got your first wire to say you'd returned to London. I daresay it will be forwarded."

"Do tell me." Caroline had half expected to hear of a "mystery" similar to her own.

"Well, the thing is, Grandmother is mixed up with some highly suspect parties. At first I thought she was running a gang, but now, all things considered, I think she may be their stooge."

"No," said Caroline. "Quite definitely, your grandmother isn't anyone's stooge."

"Now, d'you think that, honestly?—That's what I feel myself really. You must come and see for yourself."

"I'll think about it," Caroline had said.

Four times during the past week, while Laurence had been out, she had heard the typewriter and the voices.

Then she had told Laurence. "I'll see Father Jerome. If he advises a nursing home, it's a nursing home. If he says go to your grandmother's, I'll come. I could always go into a nursing home later on."

But she had forgotten to put these alternatives to Father

Jerome. And now, she did not feel it mattered.

"I'll come to Sussex," she said.

"Really, will you? Is that what the holy pa advised?"

"No. I forgot to mention it. He advised food and sleep."

Laurence knew Caroline's nervous responses to food and sleep at the best of times. But she didn't laugh with him. Instead, she said, "I feel better. I think the worst of my trouble is over; I begin to see daylight."

He was used to Caroline's rapid recoveries, but only from physical illness. In past years, he had known her prostrated by the chest complications to which she was subject: bronchitis, pleurisy, pneumonia. Once or twice she had lain for several days, running a temperature, burning with fever. Then, overnight or in the course of an hour in the afternoon, or waking in the late morning after a kindling night, there would come a swift alteration, a lightning revival of her sick body; Caroline would say, "I am better. I feel quite well." She would sit up and talk. Her temperature would drop to normal. It was almost as though she were under a decision, as if her body, at such times, were only awaiting her word, and she herself submissively waiting for some secret go-ahead within her, permitting her at last to say, "I am better. I feel well." After such rapid reversals Caroline would feel depressed, would crave that attention due to an invalid which she had not cared about in her real danger. Frequently in the days that followed, she would say, "I'm not better yet. I'm still weak." But there was never any conviction in this. It became a joke eventually, for Laurence to say for months after her illnesses, "You're still an invalid. You're not better yet," and Caroline, too, would tell him, "You make breakfast today, dear. I'm still an invalid. I'm feeling *very unwell.*"

Laurence thought of these things when he heard Caroline, on her return from the Priory, tell him, "I feel better. . . . I begin to see daylight." He recognised this signal; he himself had nursed her through her illnesses over the past six years. Those were mostly times of poverty before his parents had accepted his irregular life with Caroline; before he got his job on the B.B.C.; before Caroline had got her literary reputation.

Caroline knew what he was thinking. He had not expected her to recover so abruptly from this sort of illness. He had seen it coming on for the past six months.

And now he was thinking—"So she is better. She sees daylight. Is it just like that? Can she be right? No more melancholia. No more panic at the prospect of meeting strangers. No worry, no voices? Only the formal convalescence, the 'invalid' period, and then the old Caroline again. Can it be so?"

Caroline saw on his face an expression which she remembered having seen before. It was a look of stumped surprise, the look of one who faces an altogether and irrational new experience; a look partly fearful, partly indignant, partly curious, but predominantly joyful. The other occasion on which she had seen this expression on Laurence's face was during an argument, when she told him of her decision to enter the Church, with the consequence that they must part. They were both distressed; they hardly knew what they were saying. In reply to some remark of Laurence she had rapped out, nastily, "I love God better than you!" It was then she saw on his face that mixture of surprise and dismay, somehow revealing in its midst an unconscious alien delight, which she witnessed now once more when she told him, "The worst is over. I see daylight."

"But remember I'm still an invalid," she added. He laughed quite a lot. She was sorry to have to disappoint him. She knew he would be expecting her "recovery" to be something different from what it was going to be, and that he was wondering, "How does she know she won't hear those voices again?"

He said, "Do you really feel that everything's going to be all right now, darling?"

"Yes," she said. "I'm perfectly O.K. Only a bit tired, but now, you see, I know what the voices are. It's a creepy experience but I can cope with it. I'm sure I've discovered the true cause. I have a plan. I'll tell you something about it by and by."

She lay on the divan and closed her eyes.

"I'm worried about you," he said.

"You mean, the voices. You mean I can't be well if I go on hearing them."

He thought for a moment. "Let's see if this machine records anything."

"All right," said Caroline. "But supposing it doesn't, what difference does that make?"

"Well, in that case, I think you should try to understand the experience in a symbolic light."

"But the voices are voices. Of course they are symbols. But they are also voices. There's the typewriter too—that's a symbol, but it *is* a real typewriter. I hear it."

"My Caroline," he said, "I hope you will hear it no more."

"I don't," Caroline said.

"Don't you? Now, why?"

"Because now I know what they are. I'm on the alert now," Caroline said. "You see, I really am quite better. Only tired." She raised her voice a little, and said, "And if anyone's listening, let them take note."

Well, well!

"I bet they feel scared," said Laurence quite merrily.

79

She slipped off her skirt, and slid between the sheets of the divan.

He thought, "And yet, she does look better. Almost well again, only tired."

She was dozing off when he left her; he had to run over to Hampstead to see his mother; she had telephoned to him rather urgently. He promised Caroline to be back in time to take her out to dinner. Before he went he reminded her of the tape-recorder.

"Don't forget to press that lever if anything should happen," he said. "Sure you'll be all right?"

"Perfectly O.K.," said Caroline drowsily. "I could sleep for a fortnight."

"Good. Sleep well. And if you want anything, you know, just ring my mother. I'll be over there myself in about twenty minutes."

Caroline was very quickly asleep. And even as she slept, she felt herself appreciating her sleep; told herself, this was the best sleep she had had for six months. She told herself to sleep on, for she would wake up presently, and then she would mean business.

At this point in the narrative, it might be as well to state that the characters in this novel are all fictitious, and do not refer to any living persons whatsoever.

Tap-tappity-tap. At this point in the narrative . . . Caroline sprang up and pressed the lever on the dictaphone. Then she snatched the notebook and pencil which she had placed ready, and took down in shorthand the paragraph above; she did not start to tremble until after the chanting chorus had ended. She lay trembling in the darkening room, and considered the new form of her suffering, now that she was well again and committed to health.

4

THERE WERE CHRYSANTHEMUMS AND ASTERS IN the bowls, chrysanthemums and asters almost discernible on the faded loose upholstery in the drawing-room. They needed to be replaced, but Helena Manders had never replaced them, in order that the Knighthood, which had occurred when the covers were already past their best, should make no difference. The Manders put up with many discomforts so that the Knighthood should make no difference. The fire was lit because of Laurence coming. No fires till November, as a rule.

"Are you in a hurry?" Helena said, because now Laurence had arrived and was looking at his watch. He did this because he knew that when his mother wanted to see him about any particular business, she would usually forget the business until he was ready to go, causing him to stay for dinner or to stay the night; or she would forget the business until after he had gone, in which case she would ring him again and he would have to go again.

Laurence did not mind visiting his parents at Hampstead, he even enjoyed going there to stay for meals, or for days and weeks; only this had to be in his own time, when the time was ripe, when the time came round for him to say to himself, "I would like to go over to Hampstead." When he was summoned there, he couldn't be bothered greatly.

And so he looked at his watch. He said, "I've only got

an hour. I'm dining with Caroline. I would have brought her, only she's resting."

"How is Caroline?"

"She says she's better. I think she is, really."

"Do you? And the hallucinations, have they disappeared? Poor girl, she wouldn't tell me much."

"I don't know," said Laurence. "I don't know if she's better. She says she feels better."

"Not going into a nursing home? That would be best."

"No. I'm taking her down to Grandmother's tomorrow, in fact."

"I am worried, Laurence."

She looked worried. Her face had no confidence. There was a ladder in her stocking. She had said she wanted to see him urgently, and within the first five minutes she was coming to the point. There were other signs that she was very worried.

"I asked you to come, Laurence, because I'm so worried."

He sat on the arm of her chair, he put his arm round her shoulder, and said,

"Is it to do with Caroline and me?"

"No," she said.

Laurence got up and poured himself a drink. His mother had not offered him a drink. She was worried.

"Georgina Hogg came to see me yesterday."

"Oh! What did she want?"

"I don't know. She told me an extraordinary story. I'm so worried."

"About Caroline? I told you Caroline had left St. Philumena's on Georgina Hogg's account. Can you blame her?"

"No, of course not."

"You shouldn't have sent Caroline to that place. You know what Georgina's like."

"Well, Father Jerome agreed——"

82

"But he doesn't know Georgina Hogg. You should never have given her that job. What took you to do that? She's such a frightful advertisement for the Church."

"I just thought," said Helena. "One tries to be charitable. I thought. She said a miracle seemed to have brought her back to me. I thought, 'Perhaps she has changed.' One never knows, in our Faith. Anything can happen to anyone."

"Well, Georgina hasn't changed apparently. Still the same psychological thug as she always was. I think honestly she's to blame for Caroline's relapse. She must have touched a raw nerve."

Helena said, "Pour me a drink, Laurence."

"What will you have?"

"Same as you."

Laurence gave her a drink as strong as his own, which she didn't object to on this occasion.

"What's on your mind, darling? What does Georgina want now?"

"I don't know. She came to tell me something."

"Felt it was her duty, as usual? What did she say about Caroline?"

"That's right, that's what she said, about it being her duty. She didn't say much about Caroline but she told me an extraordinary story about my mother going in for some terribly illegal business. She suggested that Mother was a receiver of stolen property."

"My dear, what made her say that?"

Helena was apologetic. She didn't quite know how to tell Laurence what her protected servant had done.

"I don't quite know how to tell you, Laurence. I thought Georgina had changed. And of course she's got a justification, an excuse. Caroline didn't leave her address. She says a letter came for Caroline the day after she left.

Georgina took upon herself to open it, just to see the address of the writer, she said, meaning to return it. Then she found the letter came from you. She read it, as she felt that was her duty to me. You see, Laurence, she has an excuse for everything."

"But that's illegal. No one has any right to open a letter addressed to someone else. Only the Post Office can do that, when the person it's addressed to can't be traced. And even then, officially they only look at the signature and the address on the letter. No one *at all* has a right to read the substance of a letter addressed to someone else," Laurence said. He was fairly raging.

"I told her that, Laurence. I'm worried, dear."

"What did she mean, she felt it was her duty to you to read my letter to Caroline?"

"I don't know. Perhaps she thought there was something between you of which I wasn't aware. I put her right on that score."

"Did you tell her it's a serious crime to do what she's done?" Laurence was on his third whisky.

"Hush, dear," said his mother, forgetting his size, "I don't know if we're in a position to talk about crime to Georgina Hogg. You must tell me all you know about Grandmother. You should have told me right away."

"Did the Hogg show you my letter, or did she only tell you what I wrote?"

"She offered to let me read it. I refused."

"Good," said Laurence. "That keeps our own standards up."

His mother smiled a little and looked at him. But she returned to her anxiety. "Georgina was very high-minded about what you wrote about *her*, whatever it was."

"She didn't offer to return my letter to me, I suppose? It's my property."

84

"No, she refused," said Helena.

"And what's her excuse for *that?*"

"Feels it's her duty. She says that these things are too often hushed up."

"Blackmail?" Laurence said.

"She didn't ask for anything," said Helena. Then, as if these exchanges were so many tedious preliminaries, she said, as one getting down to business, "Laurence, that was true wasn't it—what you wrote to Caroline about Grandmother?"

"Yes. But I don't think Grandmother's a criminal. I didn't say that. Possibly she's being used by a gang of criminals." He did not sound very convinced of this.

Helena said, "I've been blind. I've been simply inattentive these past four years since my father's death. I should have made it my business to look after my mother. I should have forced her to accept——"

"Where's Georgina now? Has she gone back?"

"No. She has given notice. I don't know where she's staying. I was too stunned to ask."

"What is she going to do about the letter?"

"She said she would keep it, that's all."

"What is she going to do about Grandmother?"

"She wouldn't say. Oh Laurence, I'm so worried about your grandmother. Tell me all about it. Tell me everything."

"I don't know everything."

"This about diamonds in the bread. I can't believe it, and yet Georgina was so serious. I like to know where I am. Tell me what you discovered."

"All right," Laurence said. He knew that his mother had a peculiar faith that no evil could touch her. It made her adaptable to new ideas. Laurence had seen her coming round to one after another acceptance where his own vagaries were concerned. Especially now, when she sat worried in her shabby drawing-room, wearing her well-worn blue with the quite expensive pearls, a ladder in her stocking, Laurence thought, "She could get through a jungle without so much as a scratch."

When he had finished talking she said, "When will you leave for Ladylees?"

"Tomorrow, as early as possible. By train; my car's going in for repair. I'll hire one at Hayward's Heath for the few days."

"Don't take Caroline."

"Why not?"

"She isn't strong enough, surely, to be mixed up in this?"

"I should say it would do her good."

"She will be in your way, surely, if you intend making enquiries."

"Not Caroline. She's too cute."

"Tell Caroline to keep in touch with me, then. Ask her to phone every day and let me know what's happening. I can depend on Caroline."

"Whisky makes you snooty," he said. "You can depend on me too."

"Wheedle the truth out of your grandmother," she pleaded.

As he started to leave, she said shyly in case there should be any offence, "Try to find out how much it will cost us to get her out of the hands of these crooks."

Laurence said, "We don't know who's in whose hands, really. Better not mention it to Father just yet; it may turn out to be something quite innocent, a game of Grand-mother's——"

"I won't trouble your father just yet," she assured him abruptly. "He does so admire my mother." Then she added, "To think that our old trusted servant should do a thing like this."

He thought that a bit of hypocrisy—that "old trusted servant" phrase.

"You think I'm a hypocrite, don't you?" his mother said.

"Of course not," he replied, "why should I?"

"Everything O.K.?"

Caroline woke at the sound of Laurence's voice. She was very sleepy still; this protracted waking up was also a sign that she was getting better. Muzzily, she was not sure if Laurence had said "Everything O.K.?" or if this was something as yet unspoken, which it was her place to ask. So she said, all muzzed, sitting up, "Everything O.K.?"

Laurence laughed.

She rose sleepily and went into the bathroom to wash and change, leaving the door open to talk through.

"Any incidents?" said Laurence.

She was awake now. "Yes," she told him. "Lord Tom Noddy on the air."

"Who?"

"Madame Butterfly."

"And did you remember the tape-machine?"

"Um. I pressed the button. But I don't know if it's recorded anything."

She sounded diffident. Laurence said:

"Shall I try?" He was afraid the experiment might upset her, might turn the luck of Caroline's health.

"Yes, do."

He arranged the recording device, and pressed a lever. It gave a tiny whirr, then came the boom of Laurence's voice. "Caroline darling . . ." followed by the funny, unprintable suggestion.

Caroline came out of the bathroom to listen, towel in

hand. They were both eager for the next bit. It was a woman's voice. Laurence looked up sharply as it spoke: "That's a damned lie. You're getting scared, I think. Why are you suddenly taking cover under that protestation?"

That was all. "Good Christ!" said Laurence.

Caroline explained, rather embarrassed. "That was my voice, answering back. It seems, my dear, that these visiting voices don't record. I didn't really think they would take."

"What did they say to you? Why did you reply like that? What made you say 'It's a lie'?"

She read him the shorthand notes she had taken.

"So you see," she said with a hurt laugh, "the characters are all fictitious."

Laurence fiddled absently with the machine. When she stopped talking, he told her to hurry and get dressed. He kissed her as if she were a child.

As she made up her face she told him excitably, "I have the answer. I know how to handle that voice."

She expected him to ask, "Tell me how." But he didn't; he looked at her, still reckoning her in his regard as if she were a lovable child.

Then he said, "Mother's worried. I'm afraid there's going to be a big shemozzle about Grandmother."

It seemed to Laurence, then, that it was unsatisfactory for Caroline to be a child. He felt the need of her co-ordinating mind to piece together the mysterious facts of his grandmother's life. He felt helpless.

"You'll help me with my grandmother, won't you?" he said.

"Why?" she said gaily. "What are you going to do to your grandmother?" She looked mock-sinister. She was getting better. Laurence looked from her face to the short-hand notebook on the table, from the evidence of her normality to the evidence of her delusion. Perhaps, he thought, a person could go through life with one little crank and remain perfectly normal in every other respect. Perhaps it was only in regard to the imaginary aural impressions that Caroline was a child.

He said, "Mrs. Hogg read the letter I sent to you at St. Philumena's."

"You mean, she opened my letter and read it?"

"Yes, it's appalling. In fact, it's criminal."

Caroline smiled a little at this. Laurence remembered the same sort of smile fleeting on his mother's face that afternoon in spite of her worry. He realised what it was the two women had smiled the same smile about.

"I admit that I've read other people's letters myself. I quite see that. But this is a different case. It's frightful, actually."

Having established, with her smile, the fact that she considered him not altogether adult, Caroline said, "On the level, is it serious?" And she began to question him as an equal.

They switched off the fires and lights, still talking, and left the flat.

At about half-past eleven, since they had decided to make a night of it, they went to dance at a place called the Pylon in Dover Street. There was hardly any light, and Caroline thought, Thank God for that.

For, after dinner at a restaurant in Knightsbridge, they had been to Soho. First, to a pub where some B.B.C. people were unexpectedly forgathered who called Laurence "Larry"; and this was a washout so far as Laurence was concerned. His mind was on his grandmother, and the spoiling of his disinterestedness, his peace, by Mrs. Hogg. He was on leave, moreover, and did not reckon to meet with his colleagues in those weeks. Next they had gone to a literary pub, where it rapidly became clear that the Baron had spread the story of Caroline and her hysterical night at his flat.

At the first pub, after they had left, a friend of Laurence had said, "That's Larry's form of perversion—beautiful neurotic women. They have to be neurotic."

It was understood that every close association between two people was a perversion. Caroline sensed the idea they had left behind them when they left this pub. Laurence, of course, knew it, but he didn't mind; he accepted that, for instance, "perversion" was his friends' code-word for anyone's personal taste in love. While Caroline and Laurence were on their way to the second pub, this friend of Laurence's was saying, "All Larry's girls have been neurotics." This was true, as it happened.

Later, in the taxi, Caroline said to Laurence, "Am I noticeably neurotic, do you think?"

Her eyes were huge and deep, unsettled, but she had the power of judgment in other features of her face.

He said, "Yes, in a satisfactory way." And he said presently, "All my girls have been neurotics."

Caroline knew this but was glad to hear it again from Laurence; his words made articulate her feeling of what was being said in the pub they had left. She knew most of Laurence's previous neurotic girls; she herself was the enduring one.

Presently again, and Laurence said,

"There are more interesting particulars about neurotic women. You never know what you mayn't find on their persons and in their general carry-on."

In the second pub, where a fair fat poet said to Caroline, "Tell me *all* about your visions, my dear"; and another poet, a woman with a cape and a huge mouth, said, "Is there much Satanism going on within the Catholic Church these days?"; and another sort of writer, a man of over fifty,

asked Caroline who was her psychoanalyst, and told her
who was his—at this pub Caroline collected, one way and
another, that the Baron had been mentioning this and that
about her, to the ageless boys and girls who dropped in on
him at his bookshop in Charing Cross Road.

The fat poet went steadily on about Caroline's "visions";
he said they would be good for her publicity. Caroline and
Laurence had been on short drinks, and both were rather
lit up.

"Wonderful publicity," they both agreed.

And the over-fifty, in his brown coat of fur-fabric, persisted,

"I could tell you of a psychiatrist who——"

"We know one," Laurence said, "who analyses crazy
pavements."

Caroline told the girl in the cape, did she know that
Eleanor Hogarth had deserted the Baron?

"No!"

"Yes. He put me up for the night at his flat last week.
All her things were gone. Not even a photograph. He only
mentioned her once. He said she was away on tour, which
was true; he said nothing about the break. Then Laurence
found out definitely—he finds out everything, of course."

"Gone off with someone else?"

"Don't know, really. But she's left him, not he her; I
know that."

"Poor Willi."

"Oh, one can't blame her," said Caroline, satisfied that
the story would now spread.

The girl in the cape said, "Have you tried to convert the
Baron?"

"Me? No."

"R.C.s usually try to convert everyone, however hopeless. I thought that was a sort of obligation."

For good measure, Caroline quoted of the Baron what

she heard said of someone else: "He exhausted his capacity for conversion when he became an Englishman."

Indeed, the Baron was rather scrupulous about his English observances and confident that he had the English idea, so that his contempt for the English, their intellect, their manners, arose from a vexation that they did not conform better to the idea. To this effect, Caroline exchanged her views on the Baron with the girl in the cape.

"But you know," said the girl, "there's another side to Willi Stock. He's an orgiast on the quiet."

"A what?"

"Goes in for the Black Mass. He's a Satanist. Probably that's why Eleanor left him. She's so awfully bourgeois."

Caroline suddenly felt oppressed by the pub and the people. That word "bourgeois" had a dispiriting effect on her evening—it was part of the dreary imprecise language of this half-world she had left behind her more than two years since.

Laurence was talking to the blond fat poet who was inviting him to a party at someone else's house next week, describing the sort of people who would be present; and as Caroline got up, Laurence caught her eye just as this man was saying, "You can't afford to miss it."

Laurence piloted her out to the taxi, for she had been wobbly even when they arrived. But the momentary revulsion had sobered her.

They went to a coffee house, then on to the West End, to the Pylon, where, Caroline thought, thank God the lights are dim and the people not too distinguishable. The West End was another half-world of Caroline's past.

Eleanor Hogarth had a close look at the couple moving in the sleepy gloom before her. They had a square foot of floor-space, which they utilised with sweet skill, within its

92

scope manœuvring together like creatures out of natural history. This fascinated Eleanor; she was for a few moments incredulous at the sight of Caroline and Laurence in these surroundings, since she had never seen them before in a night-club, nor dancing.

Eleanor waved from her table; it was too far away from them to call, decently. Eventually Caroline saw. "Oh, see, there's Eleanor."

And there she was, with her business partner, white-haired young-faced Ernest Manders. This was Laurence's uncle, his father's younger brother who had gone into ballet instead of Manders' Figs in Syrup.

When Laurence was quite little he had informed his mother,

"Uncle Ernest is a queer."

"So he is, pet," she answered happily, and repeated the child's words to several people before she learned from her husband the difference between being a queer and just being queer. After this, it became a family duty to pray for Uncle Ernest; it was understood that no occasion for prayers should pass without a mention of this uncle. And with some success apparently, because in his fortieth year, when his relations with men were becoming increasingly violent, he gave them up for comfort's sake; not that he ever took to women as a substitute. Laurence had remarked to Caroline one day,

"I've gradually had to overcome an early disrespect for my Uncle Ernest."

"Because he was a homosexual?"

"No. Because we were always praying specially for him."

He was a religious man and likeable. Caroline got on well with him. She said he was her sort of Catholic, critical but conforming. Ernest always agreed with Caroline that the True Church was awful, though unfortunately, one couldn't deny, true.

She could not much bear Eleanor these days, though it was through Eleanor that she had first met Laurence. At one time these women were friends, exceedingly of a kind; that was at Cambridge, when, in their boxy rooms, they had leaned on the ignoble wooden fittings which were stained with rings from cocoa-mugs, and talked of this and that; mostly about the insolence of their fellow students and the insolence of their elders, for both girls had potential talents unrecognised. They were united in discontentment with the place as a place; its public-tiled washrooms, its bed-sitting-rooms, and other apartments so insolently designed. Eleanor left after a couple of terms to go into ballet. She might easily have gone to an art school, for she also had the art-school gift. It was Eleanor who had removed from one of the ground-floor corridors, and from its place on a wall, the portrait of a former Principal, keeping it for a whole night, in the course of which, by means of innumerable small touchings, she had made a subtle and important alteration in the portrait, which remains undetected to this day.

The thing about Eleanor, Caroline held, was that her real talent was for mimicry, and so she could have taken up any trade with ease, because all she had to do was to mimic the best that had already been done in any particular line, and that gave the impression of the expert.

Caroline was abroad during Eleanor's marriage; she did not know much about it, only that she had left her husband after the war, and under her married name had started a dancing school with a male partner, Ernest Manders. A few months later, Caroline and Laurence had set up together, by which time Eleanor's relationship with the Baron was becoming established. What irritated Caroline now about her old friend was the fact that she had seemed not to change essentially in the years since their Cambridge days, and was apparently quite happy with herself as she was. Now Laurence was another like that. But Caroline could like in Laurence many characteristics which in others she could not tolerate. And she was aware of the irrationality and prejudice of all these feelings, without being able to stop feeling them.

But she said, so that her contempt for Eleanor should be concealed,

"Look at the band-leader. Who does he look like?" She mentioned a Cambridge don, with his rimless glasses and the sideways mouth. Eleanor laughed and laughed. She had been drinking more than Caroline that evening. "So he does." Then she told Caroline a story from which it emerged that this don was dead.

"I didn't know that," said Caroline, being shocked then that Eleanor had laughed at her joke. When she saw Caroline involuntarily putting her face serious, Eleanor affirmed, "But the band boy is the image of the man, just the same."

Then Eleanor started picking out other members of the band, likening them to men they had agreed in despising during their friendship days. And she got Caroline to laugh, putting their meeting on a basis of workable humour, considering they were supposed to be enjoying themselves: and this was only possible by reference to the one kindly association between the two women, their college friendship. Caroline got over her annoyance at being caught out putting on a grave religious face when Eleanor had laughed at a dead man. And while she entered into Eleanor's amusement, she felt almost dumb about her suspicion that Eleanor was humouring her on account of her neurosis. She was right; this was exactly Eleanor's idea as she sat with her dark-brown head leaning over towards Caroline's much darker brown.

Two bottles of gin appeared out of the gloom. Laurence, on his third drink from the first bottle, said,

"I've never felt more sober in my life. Some occasions, it just won't 'take,' you simply can't get drunk."

Eleanor looked sorry for him, as if she knew he had worry on his mind from Caroline. This annoyed Caroline, because she knew he was worrying about his grandmother most of all.

While she danced with Ernest, who was weird to dance with, flexible, almost not there at all, so that she felt like a missile directed from a far distance, she saw Laurence examining Eleanor's cigarette case in his nosey way, and thought, "He keeps trying to detect whatever it is he's looking for in life." She admired his ability to start somewhere repeatedly; his courage; even if it was only in a cigarette case.

Soon, Laurence and Eleanor were dancing, then she saw that they sat down, and that Eleanor was talking in a confiding way; Eleanor was making small circular movements with her glass, stopping only to sigh reflectively into it before she drank, as often happens towards the end of a drinking night, when a woman confides in a man about another man.

Round the walls of the Pylon, so far as the walls could be discerned, were large gilt picture frames. Inside each, where the picture should be, was a square of black velvet, this being the Pylon's sort of effectiveness. As she smoothed her slight feet with Ernest, so limp, over their portion of dancing-floor, Caroline caught her view of Eleanor's head, described against one of the black squares of velvet in the background, just like a framed portrait, indistinct, in need of some touching-up.

5

"I SAID, 'WILLI, THIS CAN'T GO ON, IT SIMPLY cannot go on.'" Eleanor was getting maudlin. She was not a neurotic particularly, but that was not why Laurence didn't much care for her. It was only that he rather liked the Baron, and Eleanor, though her infidelities were her own affair, had never kept very quiet about them, except to the Baron himself who never suspected them.

Laurence, gazing intently at her small gold cigarette case as if it were the book of life itself, nodded his acknowledgement of her confidences.

"If he had been unfaithful," she went on, "I could have understood, I could have forgiven. But this obscenity—and apparently it's been going on for years—I never suspected. Of course I always knew he was interested in diabolism and that sort of thing, but I thought it was only theory. He had all the books, and I thought like a collector you know. But apparently it's been going on for years, the Black Masses, and they do frightful things, ask Caroline, she'll know all about the Black Mass. I feel it's a sort of personal insult to me personally, as if I'd found him out dabbling with a whore. And I said, 'Willi, you've got to choose, it's either me or these foul practices—you can't have both.' Because I tell you, Laurence, it was an insult to my intelligence apart from everything else. He said he was amused by my attitude. Amused. I'm not melodramatic, and further*more*, I'm not religious, but I do know that the Black

Mass has a profoundly evil influence truly, Laurence. In fact, I wouldn't be surprised if he hasn't done something to Caroline."

"How d'you mean, dear?"

"Well, I don't know if it's true, but I heard that she spent a night with Willi recently——"

"Yes, he was sweet to her really. She was ill at the time. But I think that was the climax, somehow. I think she's getting better now."

"But I heard that she started hearing things after that night. I heard that and you can't help hearing things when people tell you, however unlikely."

Laurence did not quite get the hang of this sentence, and while he was working it out Eleanor persisted,

"Hasn't Caroline been hearing things?"

"About you, dear?"

"No, voices. Spirits. Hearing——"

"Come and dance," said Laurence.

This was their second attempt. She was even less steady than before, and it took him all his time to keep her upright. He said, "Too many people, what d'you think?"

"Yes," she said, "let's sit down and drink."

Ernest and Caroline were already returned. Eleanor said immediately, "Caroline, what do you think of the Black Mass?"

Caroline's mood had become gay and physical; she was still jiggering about with her hands in time to the music. "No idea," she answered, "but ask the Baron. He's the expert, so I'm told." Then she remembered that Eleanor had left the Baron, so she said, "Laurence, stop peering at Eleanor's cigarette case, like an old Jew looking for the carat mark."

Laurence said, "I'm trying to read the motto."

On the front of the case was a tiny raised crest. Caroline

poked her head in beside Laurence's with exaggerated curiosity. "A wolf's head," said Laurence. "What's the motto? I can't read it."

"Fidelis et—I can't remember, for the moment," Eleanor said. "I did know. It's the Hogarth crest. Only a Victorian rake-up, I imagine. My ex-husband gave me that case for a wedding present. He had a passion for putting his family crest on everything. Spoons, hairbrushes, you never saw the like. Caroline, seriously, don't you think the evil influence that's over us all is due to these Black Masses? I've found out about Willi. I suppose you've known all the time, but I didn't dream. And it takes place at Notting Hill Gate, as you probably know."

Laurence had given her a weak drink, but now, sipping it, she noticed this, and said to Ernest reproachfully, "I'm drinking lemonade, virtually. Don't be so mean with that gin, Ernest."

Caroline was fascinated by Eleanor's performance. Indeed, it was only an act; the fascination of Eleanor was her entire submersion in whatever role she had to play. There did not seem to be any question of Eleanor's choosing her part, it was forced on her, she was enslaved by it. Just now, she appeared to be under the control of liquor; but she was also and more completely under the control of her stagey act: that of a scatty female who'd been drinking; wholeheartedly, her personality was involved, so that it was impossible to distinguish between Eleanor and the personality which possessed her during those hours; as well try to distinguish between the sea and the water in it.

Caroline was fascinated and appalled. In former days, Eleanor's mimicry was recognisable. She would change her personality like dresses according to occasion, and it had been fun to watch, and an acknowledged joke of Eleanor's. But she had lost her small portion of detachment; now, to watch her was like watching doom. As a child Caroline, pulling a face, had been warned, "If you keep doing that it will stick one day." She felt, looking at Eleanor, that this was actually happening to the woman. Her assumed personalities were beginning to cling; soon one of them would stick, grotesque and ineradicable.

"She's got the Black Mass on the brain," Ernest was sighing.

"So would you if you'd been living with a diabolist," said Eleanor, contorting her face according to her role of the moment. And she drawled, placing a hand on Caroline's hand, looking intensely into her eyes,

"Caroline, my poor Caroline. You're haunted by spirits, aren't you? And you know who's behind it, don't you?"

The performance was becoming more and more corny. Caroline tried to revert to their earlier farce about the band and their Cambridge friends.

"But she's haunted," said Eleanor, still gazing at Caroline.

Caroline had never felt less haunted. She was almost shocked to find how she seemed to derive composure from the evidence of her friend's dissolution.

"I've never felt less haunted," Caroline said.

"*I'm* haunted," said Ernest, "by the fact that we're nearly bankrupt, and Eleanor has abandoned our only form of security."

"Willi can't withdraw financially. But he'll ruin us all another way. I know it. I feel it. He's working a tremendous power against us," Eleanor drivelled.

"What was your husband's name?" Laurence asked her.

"You *are* haunted, my dear girl," Eleanor insisted, still gazing upon Caroline's face.

"Hogarth." It was Ernest who supplied the name, smiling like a conjurer who has produced the rabbit.

"Mervyn," said Eleanor belatedly.

"I believe I've met him. Does he live at Ladle Sands in Sussex by any chance?"

"Yes," said Eleanor. "Don't remind me *please*. He ought to be in prison. I've had a tragic life, Laurence. Ernest, haven't I had a tragic life?"

"Desperately," said Ernest.

"And the tragedy of that poor cripple boy," said Eleanor. "Caroline, I've never told you about my marriage. What a mess. He had a son by a former marriage, quite helpless. What could I do? These tragedies occur everywhere through influences of evil spirits, that I do believe. You've given me sheer *lemonade*, Ernest, don't be mean with the gin."

"You're getting tight," said Ernest.

"Can you blame me? Caroline, do you realise the sheer potency of the Black Mass? It's going on all the time."

"I shouldn't worry," said Caroline. "It's only an infantile orgy. It can't do much harm."

"Have you ever been to a Black Mass?"

"No. It takes me all my time to keep up with the white Mass on Sundays."

"What's the white Mass? Ernest, tell me what's the white Mass?"

"She means the Mass, dear. The ordinary Catholic Mass," Ernest said.

"Oh, but this is different. The Black Mass has tremendous power. It can actually make objects move. Nobody touches them. They move. I've read heaps about it. There are naked girls, and they say everything backward. And obscenity. Ernest, you don't take me seriously, but you just *go* to a Black Mass, and see. I challenge you. *I* wouldn't dare go. I'd die."

Caroline and Laurence spoke simultaneously, "Catholics can't go to Black Masses."

"Not allowed," Ernest explained.

"They treat you like kids," said Eleanor, "don't they, Laurence?" she said, for she knew he had lapsed from religion.

"That's right," he said agreeably.

"Why is the Black Mass forbidden, if there isn't some tremendous evil in it?" she persisted, her hand on Caroline's.

"I don't say there isn't great evil in it," Caroline replied, "I only say it's a lot of tomfoolery."

"I wouldn't dismiss it so lightly as that," Ernest argued.

"It depends on how you regard evil," Caroline said. "I mean, as compared with the power of goodness. The effectuality of the Black Mass, for instance, must be trivial so long as we have the real Mass."

"I wouldn't dismiss the power of evil lightly," Ernest insisted. "It does exist, obviously."

"I thought," said Eleanor, "that Catholics all believed the same thing. But I can see you don't."

"Caroline is being mystical," Ernest said.

"Caroline is a mystic," said Eleanor. "I've always said so. She's a mystic, isn't she, Laurence?"

"Every time," said Laurence, very pleasantly.

"And the trouble with these mystics, they theorise on the basis of other people's sufferings, and in the end they belittle suffering. Caroline, if you'd suffered as much as I've suffered, you wouldn't be talking like something out of this world."

"I won't compete with you on the question of suffering," Caroline spoke acidly, for, after all, she rather fancied herself as a sufferer.

"Poor girl, you are haunted by the evil ones," Eleanor said,. which was maddening just at that moment.

"I shouldn't have much to do with Willi," Eleanor continued. "Take my advice and keep clear."

"Poor Willi!" Caroline said with a happy laugh, though meaning malice.

"The Baron is charming, bless him," said Laurence, in an absent way, for he was conferring with Ernest over paying their bill.

"Willi makes his money out of the Black Mass," Eleanor stated. "That's where he gets it from, I'm sure."

"Oh, surely it can't be a business matter?" Laurence put in again.

"They do quite a trade in consecrated wafers," said Eleanor.

"In *what?*" Caroline said, seriously disturbed for the first time since the subject was mentioned.

Laurence said, "I doubt if they make a point of the wafers being consecrated."

"I believe they do," Ernest said. "I'm afraid that seems to be the whole point of the Black Mass."

"It's a very rare thing these days," Caroline said. "Satanism fizzled out in the 'twenties."

"Oh, did it?" Eleanor said, getting ready to argue the point.

Laurence interrupted with, "Why did you say your ex-husband should be in prison?"

"Mind y'r own business, lovey." Eleanor screwed up her face into an inebriate smile.

"Is there a relation of his, do you know, called Georgina Hogg?"

"I can see," said Caroline, "we've reached the stage where each one discourses upon his private obsession, regardless——"

"I just wondered," Laurence explained, "because that crest on Eleanor's cigarette case is the same as the one on some of Georgina's possessions."

Eleanor did not reply. She had a look of drunken incoherence which may have covered any emotion.

"Possibly derived from the same name, originally," Caroline suggested. " 'Hogg' and 'Hogarth.' "

When they went to get their coats Caroline had to take Eleanor's arm to keep her steady, although she felt a slight electricity singing in her own limbs. In the cloakroom Eleanor revived a little, and putting on her lipstick shifted over her attitude to the woman-to-woman basis. "Men are clods.

"And keep away, Caroline, do, from the Baron.

"And Laurence said something about a woman called Hogg? I couldn't quite catch—I'm so sleepy, so tight." In evidence, she yawned with her mouth all over her face.

Caroline replied with exaggerated precision, annoyed at having to repeat what Eleanor already knew.

"Yes. She was a nursemaid or governess with the Manders years ago. Laurence thought there might be some connection between her and your husband because the crest on your cigarette case is the same as the crest on Mrs. Hogg's possessions, apparently."

"A nursemaid with a family crest?"

"Apparently. It's quite possible," said Caroline.

"There may be some original connection between the names 'Hogg' and 'Hogarth,' " Eleanor said, as if she had not heard Caroline's remark to this effect, and had just thought of it herself.

"Quite," said Caroline, and noticed that this abrupt finality did not have a satisfying effect on Eleanor.

As they waited for their coats Eleanor asked,

"Where are you living now?"

"In Queen's Gate, quite near our old flat."

"And Laurence?"

"Laurence is still in the old flat."

"Officially, that is?" said Eleanor.

"What d'you mean?"

"Well, dear Carrie, I heard that Laurence couldn't tear himself away from you, and was stopping over at your new place."

"Oh, that's only a temporary arrangement. I haven't been well."

"A temporary arrangement! You Roman Catholics can get away with anything. You just nip into the confessional in between temporary arrangements, so to speak."

"We sleep in separate rooms, as it happens." Then Caroline was furious with herself for making this defence where none was due. Laurence wouldn't like it, either. "I rate friendship infinitely higher than erotic love," she added, trying to improve matters, but making them worse.

They found Laurence and Ernest outside with a taxi.

"Let's walk a little way and get some air," Caroline said to Laurence.

"Oh, then we'll walk with you. That would be nice," said Eleanor.

But Ernest, with his tact, got her into the cab. Before they said goodnight, Eleanor, slurred and mouthy, declared, "Now Laurence, take care of Caroline. She's just been telling me that you both sleep in separate rooms. It's a good story if you stick to it. And it must be a frightful strain either way. No wonder Caroline's haunted."

They left London next day by car, though Laurence's M.G. was overdue for repair, instead of going by train. This was owing to their getting up late and frittering the day in talk, first about poor Eleanor, as they agreed she was, then about themselves.

Caroline had not slept much that night. To start with it was after four o'clock by the time she parted from Laurence who was sleeping on a camp-bed in the kitchen.

She lay awake for about half an hour and then she was visited by the voices, preceded by the typewriter. This was the first time it had happened while Laurence was in the flat.

As soon as she heard the familiar tapping she called softly to Laurence; he was quite near, only a few yards away through the open door.

"Are you awake?"

He was instantly awake. "Yes?"

"Don't come. Only listen. Here's that noise again. Keep quiet."

It had already started its chanting. She switched on the light and grabbed her notebook and pencil. She missed the first bit, but she got:

". . . *next day by car, though Laurence's M.G. was due for repair, instead of going by train. This was owing to their getting up late and frittering the day in talk, first about poor Eleanor, as they agreed she was, then about themselves. Click. Click.*"

"Did you hear that?" Caroline then called out to Laurence.

"No, my dear, I didn't hear a thing."

He had got out of bed and now came in, looking anxious. "Are you all right?"

She was sitting up, gazing at her shorthand notes.

"I can't make this out," she said. "I can't make it out at all."

She read it to him.

"You're thinking ahead. Don't worry about tomorrow. We can sleep late and catch an afternoon train."

"I didn't imagine these words. They were told me," she stated, but unprotesting factually.

"Shall I come in beside you?"

"Make some tea first."

He did this, while Caroline continued gazing at the notebook.

When he brought their tea, he said, "I'll come in beside you."

It was a three-quarter divan and so there was just room. Caroline considered the situation as she drank her tea, then she said,

"I'll be all right by myself, really I will."

"It's cold in the kitchen," said Laurence.

He began to snuggle down.

"I'll put a pillow down the middle," Caroline said.

"Wouldn't a bread-knife and a prayer book do instead?"

"Clear off," said Caroline.

"All I want is a beautiful night's sleep."

"Same here," she said.

Eventually they brought in the camp-bed from the kitchen and settled down alongside. He reflected how strangely near impracticable sexual relations would be between them, now that Caroline thought them sinful. She was thinking the same thing.

It was past eleven when they woke next morning.

It was while they cooked their omelettes for lunch that she told Laurence, as if it were an undeniable fact, of her theory about the author making a book out of their lives.

Laurence knew that people with obsessions could usually find evidence to fit their craziest convictions. From the time he had learned about the voices, he had been debating within himself what this might mean to his relationship with Caroline. He had hoped that the failure of the tape-machine to record the sounds would prove her delusion to her. And when this failed to impress her he wondered whether it would be possible for him to humour her fantasy indefinitely, so that she could be the same Caroline except for this one difference in their notions of reality; or whether reality would force them apart, and the time arrive when he needs must break with, "Caroline, you are wrong, mistaken, mad. There are no voices; there is no typewriter; it is all a delusion. You must get mental treatment."

It was on his tongue to tell her so when, standing in her dressing-gown cooking the eggs and bacon, she told him, "I've discovered the truth of the matter"; the truth of the matter being, it transpired, this fabulous idea of themselves and their friends being used as characters in a novel.

"How do you know it's a novel?"

" 'The characters in this novel are all fictitious,' " she quoted with a truly mad sort of laugh.

"In fact," she continued, "I've begun to study the experience objectively. That's a sign, isn't it, that I'm well again?"

He thought not. He went so far to suggest, "Your work on the novel form—isn't it possible that your mind——"

"It's convenient that I know something of the novel form," Caroline said.

"Yes," he said.

He argued a little, questioned her. Was the author disembodied?—She didn't know. If so, how could he use a typewriter? How could she overhear him? How could one author chant in chorus?—That she didn't know, that she didn't know. Was the author human or a spirit, and if so——

"How can I answer these questions? I've only begun to ask them myself. The author obviously exists in a different dimension from ours. That will make the investigation difficult."

He realised, then, that he was arguing madness upon madness, was up against a private revelation. He almost wished he were still a believer, so that he could the more forcefully use some Catholic polemic against her privacy.

"From the Catholic point of view, I should have thought there were spiritual dangers in holding this conviction."

"There are spiritual dangers in everything. From the Catholic point of view the chief danger about a conviction is the temptation to deny it."

"But you ought to subject it to reason."

"I'm doing so," Caroline said. "I have started investigations," and she was becoming delighted with this talk.

He said then, "Don't you think the idea of an invisible person tuning into your life might possibly upset your faith?"

"Of course," she said. "That's why he ought to be subjected to reason!"

"Well," he said wearily, "I've never heard of a Catholic being allowed to traffic with the unknown like this."

"The author is doing all the trafficking," she explained. "But I'm going to make it difficult for him, you'll see."

"The whole thing is far too gnostic," he said.

That did amuse her. "That does amuse me," she said; "you expressing yourself so orthodox."

"It makes damn all difference to me if you're a heretic, darling, because you're sweet. But sooner or later you'll come bump against authority. Did you tell Father Jerome about this idea?"

"I mentioned the possibility. I had only just realised it."

"Didn't he object?"

"No, why should he? It isn't a sin to be a little cracked in the head." She added, "I know that I am slightly insane."

"No," he said gently, "you are quite sane, Caroline."

"From your point of view," she insisted, "I am out of my senses. It would be a human indignity to deny it."

He thought, "How cunning of her to get round it that

way," and he remembered that with madness comes cunning.

"You have a mild nervous disorder," he said.

"I have what you ought to call a delusion. In any normal opinion that's a fact."

"Caroline, don't distress yourself, dear."

"The normal opinion is bound to distress me because it's a fact like the fact of the author and the facts of the Faith. They are all painful to me in different ways."

"What can I do?" he said, as he had said many times in the past days. "What can I do to help you?"

"Will you be able to make an occasional concession to the logic of my madness?" she asked him. "Because that will be necessary between us. Otherwise, we shall be really separated." She was terrified of being entirely separated from Laurence.

"Haven't I always tried to enter your world?"

"Yes, but this is a very remote world I'm in now."

"Not really," he said. "You're as good as normal in every other way."

He wondered if she was hurt by this. He wondered he had not courage enough to make her see a mental doctor.

She said, "We shall have to keep this secret. I don't want the reputation of being crackers more than necessary. The Baron has broadcast enough already."

It was a pact. But less than a couple of hours later he saw how irksome it could be.

They had already frittered the best part of the day, and it was past four when Laurence, after telephoning the station about the trains, said,

"We'd better go by car. It's O.K. for the one trip, and I can get it seen to at Hayward's Heath quite quickly. Then we can have the use of it, much more convenient."

"Oh, you can hire a car at Hayward's Heath," Caroline said quickly. "I want to go by train. We must go by train."

"Don't be awkward. Get dressed, and I'll get the car out. Trains are hateful if you have the alternative of a car."

"Awkward is just what I'm going to be," Caroline said. She started hunting for her notebook.

"I've just jerked up to the fact," she said, "that our day is doing what the voices said it would. Now, we chatted about Eleanor. Then about ourselves. All right. We've frittered the day. The narrative says we went by car; all right, we must go by train. You do see that, don't you, Laurence? It's a matter of asserting free will."

He quite saw. He thought, "Why the hell should we be enslaved by her secret fantasy?"

"I don't see," he said, "why we should be inconvenienced by it one way or another. Let's act naturally."

But he saw that Caroline had it very much on the brain that her phantom should be outwitted in this one particular.

"Very well," he said. He felt his honesty under threat of strangling. He desired their relationship to continue with the least possible change, but ever since her conversion it had been altering. Laurence could not feel that they were further apart than before, but he felt, now, that Caroline was on shifting ground, liable to be swept beyond his reach at any moment. He was not sure if he was agile enough to keep contact with her, nor that the effort would be worth it beyond a point at which Caroline might become unrecognisable.

These misgivings nearly choked him while he said to Caroline,

"All right, we'll go by train."

But when, at this, she turned gay, he thought predominantly, "She will help me with Grandmother in spite of her illness. The holiday will be good for Caroline. We still need each other." Also he thought, "I love the girl." And his excitement at the thought of unravelling his grandmother's mysteries somehow made Caroline more lovable.

She was dressed and had packed for them both, to make up to Laurence for his concession. It was half-past five. Laurence was telephoning a wire to his grandmother, to expect them about eight o'clock.

"She probably prepared lunch," he said, as he put down the receiver.

"Laurence, that's too bad of us."

"But she'll be so happy when we arrive, she won't say a word. Are you ready?"

Standing by her desk when he had finished phoning, Laurence had torn a few outdated pages off the calendar.

"That brings you up to date," he said.

She remarked ruefully, "I tear off the weeks automatically, when I'm sitting at the desk. It's a reproach when the calendar gets behind the times. Really, I must get down to my book soon."

They were ready to leave. Laurence lifted the suitcases. But she was still staring at the calendar.

"What's today?" she asked. "It isn't November the first, is it?"

"That's right. November already. Do make haste."

"All Saints' Day," she continued, "you know what that means?"

Like most people who are brought up in the Catholic faith, Laurence was quick in recollecting such things. "A Holiday of Obligation," he said.

"And I haven't been to Mass!"

"Oh, it can't be helped. Don't worry. It isn't considered a mortal sin if you genuinely forgot."

"But I'm obliged to attend a Mass if there's an opportunity, since I have remembered. There's probably a late Mass at the Oratory. Probably at six-thirty. I'll have to go to that. You do see that, don't you Laurence?"

"Yes, I quite see that." So he did; he found it easy to see the obligations of the Catholic religion; it was part of his environment. He found it much easier to cope with Caroline's new-found Catholicism than her new-found psychicism. He also found it easy to say,

"We can't let Grandmother down again. Wouldn't that be a valid excuse for missing Mass?"

And he quite expected her reply,

"You go ahead by car, and I'll come by a later train."

And therefore, happy at regaining his liberty on the question of taking his car, he said with ease,

"It would be more fun if we both went by car after your Mass. We could make it by eight o'clock."

She felt relieved on the whole. Her great desire to travel by train was dispersed by the obvious necessities of going to Mass, and of not messing Laurence around any further.

Presently he said, "Sure you won't mind," for he understood the question was safely settled for her, and he did not wish to play the tyrant. So he had the luxury of asking her several times, "Quite sure, dear, it's all right? You don't mind coming by car?"

"After all," she told him, "it isn't a moral defeat. The Mass is a proper obligation. But to acquiesce in the requirements of someone's novel would have been ignoble."

He gave academic consideration to this statement and observed, "The acquiescence is accidental, in which sense the nobility must oblige."

She thought, "The hell of it, he understands that much. Why isn't he a Catholic, then?" She smiled at him over her drink, for their immediate haste was over and Laurence

had fished out the bottle which she had packed in his suitcase, very carefully in its proper corner.

Brompton Oratory oppressed her when it was full of
people, such a big monster of a place. As usual, when she
entered, the line from the Book of Job came to her mind,
"Behold now Behemoth which I made with thee."

Before the Mass started, this being the Feast of All Saints,
there was a great amount of devotion going on before the
fat stone statues. The things worth looking at were the
votive candles, crowds of these twinklers round every altar;
Caroline added her own candle to the nearest cluster. It
occurred to her that the Oratory was the sort of place
which might become endeared in memory, after a long
absence. She could not immediately cope with this huge
full-blown environment, for it antagonised the diligence
with which Caroline coped with things, bit by bit.

Having been much in Laurence's company for the fortnight past, and now alone in this company of faces, in the
midst of the terrifying collective, she remembered more
acutely than ever her isolation by ordeal. She was now
fully conscious that she was under observation intermittently by an intruder. And presently her thoughts were
away, dwelling on the new strangeness of her life, and although her eyes and ears had been following the Mass
throughout, it was not until the Offertory verse that she
collected her wits; *Justorum animae* . . . from sheer intelligence, the climax of the Mass approaching, she had to
let her brood of sufferings go by for the time being.

"You're always bad-tempered after Mass," Laurence observed as they cruised through the built-up areas.

"I know," she said. "It's one of the proofs of the Faith so
far as I'm concerned. It's evidence of the truth of the Mass,
don't you see? The flesh despairs."

"Pure subjectivism," he said. "You're something of a Quietist, I think. And quite Manichaean. A Catharist." He had been schooled in the detection of heresies.

"Anything else?"

"Scribe and Pharisee," he said, "alternately according to mood."

"The decor of Brompton Oratory makes me ill," she told him, as another excuse. For when he had met her after the Mass she had turned most sour.

"You don't refer to the 'decor' of a church," he said—"at least, I think not."

"What is it then?"

"I'm not sure of the correct term. I've never heard it called a 'decor.' "

"Very useful, your having been brought up a Catholic," said Caroline. "Converts can always rely on your kind for instruction in the non-essentials."

Eventually, they had clear road. Caroline pulled their spare duffle from the back seat and arranged it over her head and shoulders, so that she was secluded inside this tent, concealed from Laurence; then he guessed she was trying to suppress her irritable mood. In fact, it was getting on her nerves more and more that the eyes of an onlooker were illicitly upon them. Her determination to behave naturally in face of that situation made her more self-conscious.

Laurence was thinking about his grandmother, and as he did so, he speeded up.

Two days had passed since Mrs. Hogg had paid her bleak visit to Helena. Strangely, when Caroline had heard of this, she had seemed incredulous: and now, when he reverted to the subject:

"No. Helena must be mistaken. I can't conceive Mrs. Hogg as a blackmailer."

"But you've seen what she's like."

"I don't think that particular vice is quite in her line. Opening your letter—that I do visualise. I got the impression that she's a type who acts instinctively: she'd do any evil under the guise of good. But she wouldn't engage in deliberate malice. She's too superstitious. In fact, Mrs. Hogg is simply a Catholic atrocity, like the tin medals and bleeding hearts. I don't see her as a cold-blooded blackmailer. Helena must have imagined those insinuated threats." And so Caroline rattled on, overtaken by an impulse to talk, to repeat and repeat any assertion as an alternative to absolute silence. For in such a silence Caroline kept her deepest madness, a fear void of evidence, a suspicion altogether to be distrusted. It stuck within her like something which would go neither up nor down, the shapeless notion that Mrs. Hogg was somehow in league with her invisible persecutor. She would not speak of this nor give it verbal form in her mind.

Laurence could not see her face, it was behind the duffle coat. He felt exasperated by Caroline's seeming to take Mrs. Hogg's part, if only that little bit.

"We've known her for twenty-odd years. We know her better than you do, dear. She's vicious."

She snapped back at him. And so, in his need for their relations to return to a nice normal, he said peaceably,

"Yes, I suppose old Georgina means well. But she's done a lot of harm one way and another, and this time she's gone too far. We can't have Grandmother tormented at her time of life, no matter what mischief the old lady's up to. We can't, can we?" So Laurence tried to calm her testiness and engage her sympathy.

Caroline did soften down. But she surprised him when she declared vehemently, "I don't know that Mrs. Hogg wants to torment your grandmother. I don't really think your grandmother is involved in any suspicious activity. I think you're imagining it all, on the strength of a few odd coincidences."

It was strange. Normally, Laurence's concession, his "Yes, I suppose old Georgina means well" should have evoked something quite agreeable from Caroline.

So he tried again. "There's something else to be considered. That clue I got from Eleanor's cigarette case. I'm sure the crest is the same as Georgina's. There is some connection between Georgina and this Hogarth couple, I'm convinced of it."

She did not reply.

"Strange, wasn't it, my discerning that crest, quite by chance?"

"By chance." Caroline repeated the words on a strained pitch.

"I mean," said Laurence obligingly, but misunderstanding her, "that God led me to it, God bless him. Well, it's a small world. We just bump into Eleanor and——"

"Laurence," said Caroline, "I don't think I'm going to be much help to you at Ladylees. I've had enough holiday-making. I'll stay for a couple of days but I want to get back to London and do some work, actually. Sorry to change my mind but——"

"Go to hell," Laurence said. "Kindly go to hell."

After that they stopped at a pub. When they resumed their journey Caroline began patiently to state her case. They had lost half an hour, and Laurence drove swiftly into Sussex.

"From my point of view it's clear that you are getting these ideas into your head through the influence of a novelist who is contriving some phoney plot. I can see clearly that your mind is working under the pressure of someone else's necessity, and under the suggestive power of some irresponsible writer you are allowing yourself to become an amateur sleuth in a cheap mystery piece."

"How do you know the plot is phoney?" he said, which was rather sweet of him.

"I haven't been studying novels for three years without knowing some of the technical tricks. In this case it seems to me there's an attempt being made to organise our lives into a convenient slick plot. Is it likely that your grandmother is a gangster?"

Just ahead of them two girls in a shining black open racer skimmed the wet road. Automatically Laurence put on speed, listening intently to Caroline at the same time, for it was difficult to grasp her mind at this fantastic level.

"That's a Sunbeam Alpine," he remarked.

"Are you listening to what I'm saying, dear?"

"I am, truly," he said.

"Your grandmother being a gangster, it's taking things too far. She's an implausible character, don't you see?"

"She's the most plausible person I know. She'd take in anyone. That's the difficulty."

"I mean, as a character, don't you see? She's unlikely. So is Mrs. Hogg. Is it likely that the pious old cow is a blackmailer?"

"I think it likely that she's done *you* a lot of harm. She must have got properly on your nerves. She's an evil influence. You haven't been the same since you met her."

Above the throb and tapping of the engine and the rain, he heard her, "You don't know what you're talking about!"

"No," he said.

"Do you really think, Laurence, that the coincidence of the crest on Eleanor's cigarette case with the one on Mrs. Hogg's hairbrushes is plausible?"

"Well," he said, "I didn't invent the coincidence. There it was."

"Quite," she said.

They were losing on the Sunbeam Alpine. Laurence put on speed, so that the noise of the engine made conversation impossible. But when he had regained his ground, doing an easy fifty over the bright wet road, she asked him,

"Do you want to understand my point of view, Laurence?"

"Yes, darling, I do. Try to be reasonable."

"It's a question of what you choose," she said. "If you hadn't been on the look-out for some connection between the Hogarths and poor Mrs. Hogg you wouldn't have lit on the crest. And you wouldn't have been looking for it if you hadn't been influenced in that direction. I nearly fell for the trick myself, that night I stayed with the Baron. He happened to let fall a remark; it seemed to point to the suspicion that he'd been seeing your grandmother secretively during the past year, and quite often. But personally, I reject the suspicion—I refuse to have my thoughts and actions controlled by some unknown, possibly sinister being. I intend to subject him to reason. I happen to be a Christian. I happen——"

"You think the Baron's been seeing Grandmother?" Laurence pressed her. "How did you come to think that? It's very important, dear, do tell me."

The Sunbeam Alpine was still ahead of them. The girl at the wheel said something to her companion, who looked round. They obviously expected a race. Laurence accelerated.

"No," Caroline said. "That's just the point. I won't be involved in this fictional plot if I can help it. In fact, I'd like to spoil it. If I had my way I'd hold up the action of the novel. It's a duty."

"Do tell me what the Baron said about my grandmother," Laurence said. "That would be the reasonable thing, my dear."

"No, it would involve me. I intend to stand aside and see if the novel has any real form apart from this artificial plot. I happen to be a Christian."

She said a good deal more against the plot. Laurence thought in his misery, "She really is mad, after all. There's no help for it, Caroline is mad." And he thought of the possibility of the long months and perhaps years ahead in which he might have to endure the sight of Caroline, his love, a mental chaos, perhaps in an asylum for months, years.

She said a great deal more about the artificial plot. Once she broke off to warn him.

"Laurence, don't try to chase those girls. They've got a supercharger."

But he took no notice, and she continued to assure him of her resolution not to be involved in any man's story.

It was all very well for Caroline to hold out for what she wanted and what she didn't want in the way of a plot. All very well for her to resolve upon holding up the action. Easy enough for her to criticise. Laurence speeded up and touched seventy before they skidded and crashed. The Sunbeam Alpine slowed down and turned back. Laurence was still conscious, though the pain in his chest was fierce, when he saw the girls get out of their shiny racer and come towards his, where he lay entangled in his wreckage.

He saw Caroline too, her face covered with blood beside him, one of her legs bent back beneath her body most unnaturally, a sight not to be endured after he had noted her one faint moan and one twist.

Part Two

6

A WOMAN CAME IN THREE DAYS A WEEK TO DO
housework for Louisa Jepp. It was on one of those days
that Mrs. Hogg called at the cottage.

Mrs. Jepp, keeping her on the doorstep, said,

"I cannot ask you to come inside, Mrs. Hogg. My woman
is all over the floors. Is it anything in particular?"

"Perhaps this afternoon," Mrs. Hogg said, and she was
looking over Louisa's shoulder into the interior, right
through to the green back garden.

"No. This afternoon I'm going to see my grandson in
hospital. Master Laurence has had an accident. Is it anything in particular, Mrs. Hogg?"

"I would like to enquire for Laurence."

"That's kind of you. Master Laurence is progressing *and*
Miss Caroline, though she's more serious. I shall say you
enquired." Louisa did not for the world suggest that Mrs.
Hogg might have anything further to say.

"I have a message for Laurence. That's why I came
personally."

"All the way from the North of England," stated Louisa.

Mrs. Hogg said, "I'm here for the day. From London."

"Come round to the back and we shall sit in the garden."

It was a day of mild November light and sun. Louisa
led the way among her pigeons across the small green patch
to the bench in front of her loganberry bush.

Mrs. Hogg sat down beside her, fished into her carrier
bag and pulled out an old yellow fox cape which she ar-

123

ranged and patted on her shoulders.

"This time of year," she said.

Louisa thought, "My charwoman is turned out more ladylike, and yet this woman is of good family." She said, "Is it anything special, your message for Master Laurence?" And while there was time she added on second thoughts, "He is quite able to read although not sitting up yet, if you would care to write a note."

"Oh no," said Mrs. Hogg.

Louisa thought, "I thought not."

"No, I shouldn't trouble him with a letter, poor Laurence, letters can cause trouble," Mrs. Hogg said. She seemed glad of the rest after the up-hill walk from the station. Observably, she gathered strength while Louisa sat beside her expressly making no reply.

"I learn," said Mrs. Hogg, "that you call me a poisonous woman."

"One is always learning," Louisa said, while her black eyes made a rapid small movement in her thinking head. Mrs. Hogg saw only the small hands folded on the brown lap.

"Do you not think it is time for you," said Mrs. Hogg, "to take a reckoning of your sins and prepare for your death?"

"You spoke like that to my husband," said Louisa. "His death was a misery to him through your interference."

"I nursed Mr. Jepp day and night——"

"No," said Louisa, "only night. And then only until I discovered your talk."

"He should have seen a priest, as I said."

"Mrs. Hogg, what is your message for Master Laurence?"

"Only that he is not to worry. I shall take no legal action against *him*. He will understand what I mean. And, Mrs.

Jepp," she continued, "you are lonely here living by your-self."

"I am lonely by no means. I shall give no such foolish message to Master Laurence. If you have any grievance against him, I suggest you write to Sir Edwin. My grandson is not to be troubled at present."

"There's the matter of slander. In my position my character in the world is very important."

"You have got hold of Master Laurence's letter to Miss Caroline," Louisa said in a voice she sometimes used when she had played a successful hand at rummy through guess-work.

"You really must remember your age," said Mrs. Hogg. "No good carrying on as if you were in your prime."

"I will not have you to stay with me," Louisa said.

"You need a companion."

"I am not feeble. I trust I shall never be so feeble as to choose you for a companion."

"Why do you keep diamonds in the bread?"

Louisa hardly moved nor paused at all. Indeed it entered her mind: how like Laurence to have found the hiding place!

"I will not deny, that is my habit."

"You are full of sin."

"Crime," said Louisa. "I would hardly say 'full'. . . ."

Mrs. Hogg rose then, her lashless eyes screwed on Louisa's brown hands on her brown lap. Was the woman really senile, then?

"Wait. Sit down," Louisa said, "I should like to tell you all about the crime." She looked up, her black old eyes open to Mrs. Hogg. The appealing glance was quite convincing.

Thus encouraged, "You must see a priest," said Mrs.

Hogg. None the less, she sat down to hear Louisa's confession.

"I am in smuggling," said Louisa. "I shan't go into the whys and hows because of my memory, but I have a gang of my own, my dear Georgina, what do you think of that?" Louisa peered at Mrs. Hogg from the corner of her eye and pursed her lips as if she were kissing the breeze. Mrs. Hogg stared. Was she drunk perhaps? But at seventy-eight, after all——

"A *gang?*" said Mrs. Hogg at last.

"A gang. We are four. I am the leader. The other three are gentlemen. They smuggle diamonds from abroad."

"In loaves of bread?"

"I won't go into the ways and whats. Then I dispose of the diamonds through my contact in London."

Mrs. Hogg said, "Your daughter doesn't know this. *If* it's true."

"You have been to see Lady Manders, of course? You have told her what was in that letter you stole?"

"Lady Manders is very worried about you."

"Ah yes. I will put that right. Well, let me tell you the names of the parties involved in my smuggling arrangements. If you know everything I'm sure you won't want to worry my daughter any more."

"You can trust me," said Mrs. Hogg.

"I'm sure. There is a Mr. Webster, he is a local baker. A real fine person, he doesn't go abroad himself. I had better not say what part he plays in my smuggling arrangements. Then there's a father and son—such a sad affair, the boy's a cripple but it does him so much good the trips abroad, the father too. Their name is Hogarth. Mervyn is the father and Andrew is the son. That is my gang."

But Mrs. Hogg looked in a bad way just then. The dreadful fluffy fur slipped awry on her shoulder. Violently she said, "Mervyn and Andrew!"

"That is correct. Hogarth they call themselves."

"You are evil," said Mrs. Hogg.

"You won't be needing that letter," said Louisa, "but you may keep it just the same."

Mrs. Hogg gathered her fur cape around her huge breasts, and speaking without a movement of her upper lip in a way that fascinated Louisa by its oddity, she said, "You're an evil woman. A criminal evil old, a wicked old," and talking like that, she made off. Louisa climbed to her attic, from where she could see the railway station set in a dip of the land, and, through her father's old spyglass, Mrs. Hogg eventually appeared like a shady yellow wasp on the platform.

When Louisa came downstairs, she said to her charwoman, "That visitor I had just now."

"Yes, Mrs. Jepp?"

"She wanted to come and look after me as I'm getting so old."

"Coo."

Louisa opened a drawer in the kitchen dresser, took out a folded white cloth, placed it carefully at the window end of the table. She brought out her air-mail writing paper and her fountain pen and wrote a note of six lines. Next she folded the letter and laid it on the dresser while she replaced the white cloth in the drawer. She put away her fountain pen, then the writing paper, took up the note and went out into her garden. There she sat in the November mildness, uttering repeatedly and softly "Coo. Coo-oo!" Soon a pigeon flashed out from its high loft and descended to the seat beside her. She folded the thin paper into a tiny pellet, fixed it into the band on the silver bird's leg, stroked its bill with her brown fingers and let it go. Off it flew, in the direction of Ladle Sands.

It is possible for a man matured in religion by half a century of punctilious observance, having advanced himself in devotion the slow exquisite way, trustfully ascending his winding stair, and, to make assurance doubly sure, supplementing his meditations by deep-breathing exercises twice daily, to go into a flat spin when faced with some trouble which does not come within a familiar category. Should this occur, it causes dismay in others. To anyone accustomed to respect the wisdom and control of a contemplative creature, the evidence of his failure to cope with a normal emergency is distressing. Only the spiritual extremists rejoice—the Devil on account of his crude triumph, and the very holy souls because they discern in such behaviour a testimony to the truth that human nature is apt to fail in spite of regular prayer and deep breathing.

But fortunately that situation rarely happens. The common instinct knows how to gauge the limits of a man's sanctity, and anyone who has earned a reputation for piety by prayer, deep breathing and one or two acceptable good works has gained this much for his trouble, that few people bring him any extraordinary problem.

That is why hardly anyone asked Sir Edwin Manders for a peculiar favour or said weird things to him.

He had coped, it was true, with the shock of the car accident; Laurence and Caroline were seen into safe hands. He floated over Helena's anxiety on the strength of his stout character. He might have managed to do something suave and comforting about Helena's other worry—her mother's suspected criminal activities. He might have turned this upset of his social tranquillity to some personal and spiritual advantage, but then he might not. Helena instinctively did not try him with this problem. She did not know what Louisa was up to, but she understood that the difficulty was not one which the Manders' cheque book could solve. Helena would not have liked to see her husband in a state of bewilderment. He went to Mass every morning, confession once a week, entertained Cardinals. He would sit, contemplating deeply, for a full hour in a silence so still you could hear a moth breathe. And Helena thought, "No, simply no" when she tried to envisage the same Edwin grappling also with the knowledge that his mother-in-law ran a gang, kept diamonds in the bread—stolen diamonds possibly. Helena took her troubles to his brother Ernest who sailed through life wherever the fairest wind should waft him, and for whom she had always prayed so hard.

"I feel I ought not to worry Edwin about this. He has a certain sanctity. You understand, don't you, Ernest?"

"Yes, of course, dear Helena, but I'm the last person, as you know, to cope with Louisa's great gangsters. If I could invite them to lunch at my club——"

"I'm sure you could if they are my mother's associates," Helena said.

A week later, Helena went to the flat at Queen's Gate where Caroline had lodged. It was the job of packing up the girl's possessions. Caroline's fracture would keep her in hospital for another month at least. The housekeeper, a thin ill-looking man, who, on Helena's delicate enquiries, proved not to be ill but merely a retired lightweight boxer, let her in. Nice man, she thought, telling herself that she had a way with people: Laurence and Caroline had said he was frightful.

Helena was expecting Ernest to join her. She sat for a moment on Caroline's divan; then, it was so restful, she decided to put her feet up and recline among the piled-up cushions until he should arrive. The room had been tidied up, but it was clear that Laurence and Caroline had made a sort of home of the place. The realisation did not really shock Helena, it quickly startled her, it was soon over. Years ago she had come to a reckoning with the business between Laurence and Caroline and when they had parted, even while she piously rejoiced, she had felt romantically sad, wished they could be married without their incomprehensible delay. But still it was a little startling to see the evidence of what she already knew, that Laurence had been sharing the flat with Caroline, innocently but without the externals of innocence. The housekeeper had asked her, "How are Mr. and Mrs. Manders? What a shame, so newly married." Helena had kept herself collected, revealed nothing. That sort of remark—and this place with Laurence's tie over the back of the chair—caused the little startles, soon over.

"I was resting. I'm so tired running backwards and forwards to the country," she told Ernest when he was shown up by that nice little man.

For the first few days after the accident, till Caroline was out of her long bruised sleep, Helena had stayed intermittently at a local hotel and at Ladylees with her mother. She had been watchful, had said nothing to upset the old lady. Once in the night she had turned it over in her mind to have it out with Louisa—Mother, I'm driven mad with anxiety over this accident, I can't be doing with worry on your account as well. Laurence told me . . . his idea . . . your gang . . . diamonds in the bread . . . tell me, is it true or not? What's your game . . . what's your source of income . . . ?

But supposing there was nothing in it. Seventy-eight, the old woman. Helena considered and considered between her sleeps. Suppose she has a stroke! She had refrained often from speaking her mind to Louisa in case she caused the old lady a stroke, it was an old fear of Helena's.

So she said nothing to upset her, had been more than ever alert when, on returning to the cottage one evening after her hospital visiting, Louisa told her, "Your Mrs. Hogg has been here."

Then Helena could not conceal her anxiety.

"But I sent her away," said Louisa, "and I don't think I shall see her again."

"Oh, Mother, what did she want?"

"To be my companion, dear. I am able to get about very nicely."

"Nothing worrying you, Mother? Oh, I wish you would let us help you!"

"My!" said Louisa. "I vow, you are all a great comfort to me, and once the children are recovered we shall all be straight with the world."

"Well," said Helena, "I brought you a present from Hayward's Heath, I was so happy to see Laurence looking better."

It was a tin-opening gadget. The old woman got out the tomato basket in which she kept a few handy tools. Helena held the machine against the scullery door while her mother screwed it in place, the old fingers manipulating the screwdriver slowly but without a tremor.

"It's a great life if you don't weaken," Louisa remarked as she twisted the screws in their places.

"That will be handy for you," said Helena, "won't it?"

"Yes, certainly," Louisa said. "Let's try it now." They opened a tin of gooseberries. "It was just what I wanted to open my cans," said Louisa. "You must have guessed. You have a touch of our gipsy insight in you, dear. The only thing, you don't cultivate it."

"Now that's an exaggeration, really, Mother. Buying you a can-opener doesn't prove anything specially psychic, now does it?"

"Not when you put it that way," said Louisa.

Helena had already taken advantage of one of her mother's outings to search the bread bin. There were no diamonds anywhere evident, neither in the bread nor in the rice and sugar tins, nor nestling among the tea nor anywhere on the shelves of the little pantry. There Louisa also kept the sealed bottles and cans of food, neatly labelled, which she canned and bottled herself from season to season.

"Georgina wasn't horrid to you, or anything?" This was Helena's last try.

"She is not a pleasant woman by nature. I can't think why you ever took up with her. I would never have had her in my house."

"She's had a hard life. We felt sorry for her. I don't think she can do any harm. At least . . . well, I think not, do you?"

"Everyone can do harm, and do whether they mean it or not. But Mrs. Hogg is not a decent woman."

Everything stood so quiet, Helena wondered if perhaps Laurence had been mistaken, his foolish letter useless in Mrs. Hogg's hands.

And that was what she told Ernest when he was shown up to Caroline's flat. She had allowed this hope to grow on her during the weeks following the accident when, sometimes alone, sometimes with her husband, she had motored back and forth between London and the country hospital. Laurence was a case of broken ribs, he could be moved home very soon. Caroline had come round, her head still bandaged, her leg now caged in its plaster and slung up on its scaffold. She had started to make a fuss about the pain, which was a good sign. Everything could have been worse.

"I doubt very much that there was anything in that suspicion of Laurence's. It caused me a lot of worry and the accident on top of it. Everything could have been worse but I'm worn out."

"Do you know," said Ernest, "my dear, so am I."

Those revelatory tones and gestures!—she watched Ernest as he picked up Caroline's blue brocade dressing-gown with the intention of folding it, helping Helena to pack, but there—before he knew what he was doing he had posed himself before the long mirror, draping the blue stuff over one hip. "Sumptuous material!"

Helena surprised herself by the mildness of her distaste. "The room is full of Caroline," she remarked. "I feel that I am seeing things through Caroline's eyes, d'you know?"

"So do I," said he, "now you come to mention it."

Helena knelt by the large suitcase she had brought. Her fair skin was drawn under its frail make-up.

"We could make a pot of tea, Ernest. The meter may need a shilling."

He put on the kettle while she considered his predicament in life. Caroline had always been able to accept his category. It was easier, Helena thought, to accept his effeminacy now that he had given up his vice and had returned to the Church, but even before that Caroline had declared, on one occasion of discussing Ernest, "I should think God would say, 'Don't dare despise My beloved freak, My homosexual.' "

Helena had replied, "Of course. But if it goes against one's very breathing to respect the man——? Oh, love is very difficult."

"I have my own prejudices," Caroline had said, "so I understand yours. Ernest doesn't happen to be one of mine, that's all."

Helena, adrift in these recollections, caught herself staring at Ernest. She lifted the phone, spoke in reply to the housekeeper's "Yes, what number?"—"May we have a little

133

milk, please? We've just made some tea and we have no milk."

Whatever he said caused Helena to exclaim when she had put down the receiver.

"Rather beastly abrupt that man! I thought him so nice before."

She apologized for the trouble when the man brought the milk, to which he made no reply at all.

"The man's a brute, Ernest," she said. "He knows the sad circumstances of our being here."

But she settled down with Ernest now, observing the peculiar turn of his wrist—he showed a lot of wrist—as he poured out their tea. Caroline with her sense of mythology would see in him a beautiful hermaphrodite, she thought, and came near to realizing this vision of Ernest herself.

"I managed to see Laurence yesterday," Ernest said, "remarkably well, isn't he, considering?"

"Thank God," Helena said.

"He gave me this"—a red pocket notebook—"and told me what he knew about your mother's friends."

"D'you know, Ernest, I don't think there's anything to fear. I kept my eyes open those few days I spent at the cottage, but I noticed nothing suspicious. Laurence must have been mistaken, I can't help thinking. And apparently Mrs. Hogg has come to the same conclusion; she actually descended on my mother while I was out. Mother was very calm about it—simply sent her away. I've no doubt—though Mother didn't say so—that Mrs. Hogg came about Laurence's letter."

"That's exactly what I should have thought. Exactly that." Ernest was now folding Caroline's blue dressing-gown, very meticulously. "But," he said, "I happen to know vaguely one of the men in Mrs. Jepp's gang."

"Oh, who's that?"

"Mervyn Hogarth. Eleanor used to be married to him. Now, *he's* most odd. Laurence thinks Mrs. Hogg may be related to him."

Helena said it was unlikely. "I've never heard her mention the name Hogarth." She took the notebook from him and turned its pages. The meagre dossier Laurence had prepared had a merciless look of reality. It revived Helena's fears. She was happiest when life could be reduced to metaphor, but life on its lofty literal peaks oppressed her. She peered at the stringent notes in Laurence's hand.

"What do you think of this, Ernest? Is my mother involved or not?"

"Why don't you ask her?"

"Oh, she would never say."

Ernest said, "Laurence thinks we should investigate. I promised him we would, in fact."

Helena read aloud one of the unbearable pages of the notebook:

Mervyn Hogarth: The Green House, Ladle Sands. Lives with crippled son (see Andrew Hogarth). No servants. Ex-library workshop. Bench tools. Mending (?) broken plaster statuettes. St. Anthony. S. Francis. Immac. Concept. —others unrecognisable. No record in S.H. Ex Eleanor.

"I can't make this out," she said, "broken plaster and the saints—are they Catholics, the Hogarths?"

"I think not," Ernest said.

"What does 'S.H.' stand for?"

"Somerset House. There's apparently no record of them there. They may have been born abroad. I shall ask Eleanor, she'll know."

"Laurence has explained all these notes to you?"

"More or less. Please don't upset yourself, Helena."

135

"Oh, I did hope there was nothing more to be feared. Explain all this to me, please."

She kept turning the pages, hoping for some small absurdity to prove the whole notion absurd that her aged mother should be involved in organised crime. She had a strong impulse to tear up the book.

"There wasn't time to go through the whole of it with Laurence. He wants me to go and stay nearby for a couple of weeks, so that I can investigate under his supervision and consult him on my daily visits."

"No," Helena said, "that won't do. We can't weary Laurence in his state. I want him moved to London at the first opportunity."

Ernest agreed. "It would be very inconvenient for me to leave London at this time of the year. But Laurence was keen. Perhaps there's some other way——"

Helena looked at Ernest reclining now on Caroline's divan in such a hollowed-out sort of way. Shifting sand, we must not build our houses on it. But Helena was not sure whether he didn't possess some stable qualities in spite of the way the family regarded him. She realised her inexperience of Ernest: Caroline had a more lucid idea of him.

"Of course," Helena said, "it would cheer Laurence up tremendously, someone visiting him every day. Now that they're out of danger I can only manage twice a week. Caroline too, you would visit Caroline too?"

"I'm not sure that I can get away."

"Ernest, I will pay your expenses of *course*." She was almost glad of his resistance, it proved him to be ever so slightly substantial.

"If you would," he said, "it would be a help. But I shall have to talk to Eleanor. This time of year is difficult, and we aren't doing so well just now."

"Please," she said, "don't confide in Eleanor."

"Oh, I shouldn't mention any family business."

They talked back and forth until it became needful to Helena that Ernest should go to reside at Hayward's Heath for two weeks.

"We must get to the bottom of this intrigue without upsetting my mother," she declared. "Laurence understands that perfectly. I'm sure his recovery depends on our doing something active. We must be *doing*. I know you are discreet, Ernest. I don't want Mother to have a stroke, Ernest. And we must pray."

"I'll try to see Hogarth," he promised. "Maybe I can get him to meet me in London."

He was pouring out their second cups, with that wrist, of which there was a lot showing, poised in a woman's fashion which nibbled at Helena's trust in him.

"I have no misgivings," she declared, "I have implicit trust in you, Ernest."

"Dear me," said Ernest. She thought how Caroline with her aptitude for "placing" people in their correct historical setting had once placed Ernest in the French Court of the seventeenth century. "He's born out of his time," Caroline had explained, "that's part of his value in the present age." Laurence had said placidly, and not long ago, "Ernest never buys a tie, he has them made. Five-eighths of an inch wider than anyone else's."

Parents learn a lot from their children about coping with life. It is possible for parents to be corrupted or improved by their children. Through Laurence, and also of later years through Caroline, Helena's mental organisation had been recast. She was, at least, prepared for the idea that Ernest was not only to be tolerated in a spirit of what she understood as Christian charity, but valued for himself, his differences from the normal. Helena actually admired

137

him a little for what she called his reform. But when he gave up his relations with men she had half expected an external change in Ernest; was disappointed and puzzled that his appearance and attitudes remained so infrangibly effeminate, and she understood that these mannerisms were not offensive to people like Laurence and Caroline. Helena possessed some French china, figurines of the seventeenth century which she valued, but the cherishing of Ernest while he was in her presence came hard enough to present her with an instinctive antagonism; something to overcome.

Ernest had folded while she packed nearly everything. What couldn't be packed was ready to be carried to the car. "Let's have a cigarette, we've worked hard."

"I suppose," she said, "that machine belongs to Caroline. We had better have the man up to make sure we haven't left anything of ours, or taken away what's theirs."

Ernest, curling himself on a low footstool, lifted the cover off the machine. "It's a tape-recorder. Caroline probably used it for her work."

"I have implicit trust in you, Ernest. I've come to you before anyone. I don't want to inconvenience you of course, and if it's a question of expense——"

"Thank you, Helena. But I can't promise—I'll try of course—this time of year we have our bookings, our classes. Maybe Hogarth will agree to come to London."

"I'm so grateful to you, Ernest."

He fiddled with the tape machine, pressed the lever. It gave a faint whirr and the voice came with an exaggerated soppy yak: "Caroline, darling. . . ."

Within a few seconds Helena had recognised Laurence's voice; a slight pause and it was followed by Caroline's. The first speech was shocking and the second was nonsense.

Ernest said, "Hee, silly little dears."

Helena lifted her coat, let Ernest help her on with it.

"Will you send for the man, Ernest? Give him a pound and ask if everything's all right. I'll take some of the loose things down to the car. No, ten shillings will do."

She felt almost alone in the world, wearily unfit for the task of understanding Laurence and Caroline. These new shocks and new insights, this perpetual obligation on her part to accept what it went against her to accept. . . . She wanted a warm soft bath in her own home; she was tired and worried and she didn't know what.

Just as she was leaving, Ernest phoning for the house-keeper said,

"Look, there's something. A notebook, that's Caroline's I'm sure."

A red pocket notebook was lying on the lower ledge of the telephone table. He picked it up and handed it to Helena.

"What a good thing you saw it. I'd quite forgotten. Caroline was asking specially for this. A notebook with shorthand notes, she asked for it." Helena flicked it open to make sure. Most of it was in shorthand, but on one of the pages was a list in longhand. She caught the words: *Possible identity.*

"This must be connected with Laurence's investigations," Helena said.

She turned again to that page while she sat in the car waiting for Ernest with the bags, but she could make nothing of it. Under *Possible identity* were listed

> Satan
> a woman
> hermaphrodite
> a Holy Soul in Purgatory

"I don't know what," said Helena, as she put it away carefully among Caroline's things. "I really don't know what."

7

Just after two in the mild bluish afternoon a tall straight old man entered the bookshop. He found Baron Stock alone and waiting for him.

"Ah, Mr. Webster, how punctual you are, how very good of you to make the journey. Come right through to the inside, come to the inside."

Baron Stock's large personal acquaintance—though he had few intimate friends—when they dropped in on the Baron in his Charing Cross Road bookshop were invariably greeted with this request, "Come to the inside." Customers, travellers and the trade were not allowed further than the large front show-place; the Baron was highly cagey about "the inside," those shabby, comfortable and quite harmless back premises where books and files piled and tumbled over everything except the three old armchairs and the square of worn red carpet, in the centre of which stood a foreign-looking and noisy paraffin stove. Those admitted to the inside, before they sat down and if they knew the Baron's habits, would wait while he placed a sheet of newspaper on the seat of each chair. "It is exceedingly dusty, my dears, I never permit the cleaners to touch the inside." When the afternoons began to draw in, the Baron would light a paraffin lamp on his desk: the electricity had long since failed here in these back premises, "and really," said the Baron, "I can't have electricians coming through to the inside with their mess." Occasionally one of his friends would say, "It looks a simple job, I think I could fix your lights, Willi." "How very obliging of you." "Not at all, I'll do it next week." But no one ever came next week to connect up the electricity.

"And how," said the Baron when he had settled Mr. Webster on a fresh piece of newspaper, "is Mrs. Jepp?"

Mr. Webster sat erect and stiff, turning his body from the waist to answer the Baron.

"She is well I am pleased to say, but worried about her grandson I am sorry to say."

"Yes, a nasty accident. I've known Laurence for years of course. A bad driver. But he's coming home next week, I hear."

"Yes, he had a handsome escape. The poor young lady's leg is fractured, but she too might be worse, they tell us."

"Poor Caroline, I've known her for years. Her forehead was cut quite open, I hear."

"Slight abrasions, I understand, nothing serious."

"Such a relief. I hear everything in this shop but my informants always exaggerate. They are poets on the whole or professional liars of some sort, and so one has to make allowances. I'm glad to know that Caroline's head has no permanent cavity. I've known her for years. I am going to visit her next week."

"If you will pardon my mentioning, Baron, if you intend to be in our part of the country, I think at the moment you should not make occasion to call on Mrs. Jepp. The Hogarths have had to cancel their trip to the Continent and they frequently call at the cottage."

"What was the trouble? Why didn't they go?"

"Mrs. Jepp had the feeling that the Manders were about to investigate her concerns. She thinks there should be no further trips till the spring. The Hogarths were ready to leave, but she stopped them at the last minute. She is not at all worried."

"It sounds fairly worrying to me. The Hogarths do not suspect that I am involved in your arrangements?"

"I don't think you need fear that. Mrs. Jepp and I are very careful about mentioning names. You are simply Mrs. Jepp's 'London connection.' They have never shown further curiosity."

"And the Manders? I suppose Laurence has put them up to something, he is so observant, it's terrifying. I am never happy when he goes to that cottage."

"Mrs. Jepp is very fond of him."

"Why, of course. *I* am very fond of Laurence, I've known the Manders for years. But Laurence is most inquisitive. Do you think the Manders are likely to suspect my part in the affair?"

"If anything, their interest would reside in myself and the Hogarths. I do not think you need worry, Baron."

"I will tell you why I'm anxious. There is no risk of exposure either from the Hogarths or from the Manders. In the one case they themselves are involved. In the other case the old lady is involved and the Manders would of course wish to hush up anything they found out. But it happens that I am interested in Mervyn Hogarth in another connection. I have arranged to be introduced to him, and I do not wish to confuse the two concerns."

Mr. Webster thought, "Ah, to do with the woman, Hogarth's former wife," but he was wrong.

"Hogarth is up in London today," he informed the Baron, "I saw him on the train, but I thought best to remain unseen."

"Sure he didn't see you? No chance of his having followed you here out of curiosity?"

"No, in fact I kept *him* in sight until he disappeared into a club in Piccadilly. Ho, ho, Baron."

He handed the Baron a small neat package. "I had better not forget to give you this," he said, still chuckling in an old man's way.

The Baron opened it carefully, taking out a tin marked in Louisa Jepp's clear hand, "Soft herring roes."

"Mrs. Jepp was particularly anxious that you should eat the actual herring roes," Mr. Webster said. "She bade me say that they are very nourishing and no contamination can possibly arise from the other contents of the tin."

"I shall," said the Baron, "I shall."

He slid the tin into his brief case, then opening a double-locked drawer took out a bundle of white notes. These he counted. He took another bunch and did likewise, then a third; from a fourth lot he extracted a number of notes which he added to the three bundles. He replaced the remainder of the notes in his drawer and relocked it before handing the bundles to Mr. Webster. Then he wrote three cheques and handed them over.

"They are dated at three-weekly intervals. Please check the amount," he said, "and then I will give you this good strong envelope to put them in."

"Much the safest way," said Mr. Webster as he always did, referring, not to the envelope but to the method of payment. "Much the safest in case of enquiries," he added as always.

When this business was done, and the notes packed into their envelope and locked away in Mr. Webster's bag, the Baron said,

"Now, a cigar, Mr. Webster, and a sip of Curaçao."

"Very well, thank you. But I mustn't delay long because of the time of year."

The shop door tinkled. "Tinkle," said the Baron, and rising, he peered through a chink in the partition that separated the grey-carpeted front shop from the warm and shabby inside. "A barbarian wanting a book," the Baron remarked as he went forth to serve his customer.

Returning within a few seconds, he said,

"Do you know anything of diabolism?"

"I've seen witchcraft practised, many times in the olden days; that was before your time, Baron; mostly in South American ports."

"You are a sail-or," said the Baron. "I have always thought you were a sail-or."

"I was a merchant seaman. I have seen witchcraft, Baron. In those countries it can be fearful, I can tell you."

"I am interested in diabolism. In a detached way, I assure you."

"Ho, I am sure, Baron. It isn't a thing for a temperate climate."

"That is why," said the Baron, "I am interested in Mervyn Hogarth. You would call him a mild and temperate man?"

"Well, Baron, he doesn't say much though he talks a lot. Myself I don't care for him. But Mrs. Jepp tolerates, she tolerates. She is thinking perhaps of the poor son. This *trading* of ours, it gives him something in life. Poor lad, poor lad."

"Would it surprise you, Mr. Webster, to know that Mervyn Hogarth is the foremost diabolist in these islands?"

"I should never have thought of the man as being foremost in anything."

"How does he strike you, tell me?"

"Between ourselves, Baron, he strikes me, between ourselves, as a cynic, as they say, and a misanthropist. A tedious fellow."

"Devoted to his son, though?"

"I don't know, I do not. He behaves well to the lad. Mrs.

Jepp believes, and this is between ourselves, Baron, that he only sticks to the boy in order to spite his former wife. At least that was her impression when she first met them."

"This diamond trading was Mrs. Jepp's idea, wasn't it?"

"Oh yes. Oh, and she enjoys it, Mrs. Jepp would be the last to deny it."

"They don't need money, the Hogarths?"

"No. Hogarth himself is comfortable. The unfortunate young man does so enjoy evading the customs, Baron."

The Baron put a finger to his lips with a smile. Mr. Webster lowered his voice as he thanked his host for the replenishment of his glass.

"Evading the customs has made a great difference to young Andrew Hogarth. It has given him confidence," Mr. Webster said in low tones.

"When Mrs. Jepp first suggested this arrangement to me—for it was she, you know, who approached me with the scheme, she came straight in to the shop here a few days after I had met her with Laurence and stated her proposition most admirably; I could see her quality. Well, when she put it to me she added that if I should agree to come in with her, I must undertake not to enquire into the *methods* used by the more active agents. When I had thought over her suggestion and had satisfied myself that the plan was genuinely and well conceived—allowing for the usual risk which I do not find unpleasurable—I agreed exactly to Mrs. Jepp's terms. I mention this, because frankly I would not be within my rights if I asked you by what means the Hogarths convey their valuables. Up to the past few months I have not been greatly interested in that side of the transactions, but now I am greatly inter*ested* because of my interest in the actions of Mervyn Hogarth."

"I do not know their method," said Mr. Webster, and

the Baron could not tell if he were speaking the truth or not, so unaltered were his sharp blue eyes.

"Hogarth is a diabolist. I am intensely inter*ested* in Hogarth for the reason that I am *inter*ested in the psychology of diabolism. You do not know the madness of scholarly curiosity, Mr. Webster. To be interested and at the same time disinterested. . . ."

"I can well understand it, Baron. But I should not have thought the elder Mr. Hogarth indulged in any exotic practices. He seems to me a disillusioned man, far from an enthusiast."

"That is the interesting factor," said the Baron excitedly. "From all I have discovered of the man's personality, he is drenched in disillusionment, an intelligent man, a bored man; an unsuccessful man with women, indifferent to friendships. Yet, he is a fanatical diabolist. You will keep my confidence, Mr. Webster."

"Baron, of course. And now I must be going."

"A fanatic," said the Baron as he escorted Mr. Webster from the inside to the outside. "A pity the Hogarths did not go abroad. I would have called on Mrs. Jepp. She may have been persuaded to tell me more of Mervyn Hogarth. However, I shall be meeting him myself very soon, I believe."

"Good day to you, Baron."

"My regards to Mrs. Jepp." And he added, "Be assured, Mr. Webster, the risk is neglig-ible."

"Oh, Hogarth is not dangerous."

"I do not mean Hogarth. I mean our happy trade. We are amateurs. There is a specially protective providence for amateurs. How easily the powerful and organised professionals come to grief! They fall like Lucifer——"

"Quite so, Baron."

"But we innocents are difficult to trip up."

"I shouldn't call us *innocents*. Ho!" said Mr. Webster stepping forth.

"That's the point. . . ." But by this time the old man had gone out of hearing.

"I don't pretend to understand women," Mervyn Hogarth stated over the brandy. He looked at his host as if he were not sure he had said the right thing, for there was a touch of the woman, a musing effect in the baby-faced, white-haired man.

"The lamb was not right or else the sauce, I fear," Ernest Manders mused. After all, he had not gone to Sussex. He had contrived a better plan.

"I take it you are speaking in good faith?" Mervyn Hogarth was saying.

"The lamb——?"

"No, no, the subject we were discussing, I take it——"

"Do let's take it that way, Mr. Hogarth."

"Manders, I meant no offence. I wanted to make my mind clear—only that. It seems to me a definitely odd suggestion to come from Eleanor, she knows my position, definitely."

"It was only, you see, that we're temporarily in a tight place. Baron Stock has withdrawn his support. Naturally Eleanor thought of you. It was a kind of compliment."

"Oh, definitely."

"And if you can't, you can't, that is quite understood," said Ernest.

"Have you approached your brother?"

"Yes. My brother Edwin is a mystic. He is not interested in dancing and will only invest in that which interests him. But he gave us fifty pounds. Eleanor bought a dress."

147

"I can imagine Eleanor would."

"I am myself very detached from money," Ernest remarked, "that is why I need so much of it. One simply doesn't notice the stuff; it slithers away."

He sat back in his chair as if he had the whole afternoon. His guest had discovered that the business proposition for which he had been summoned was an unprofitable one.

"A quarter to three," said Mervyn Hogarth. "My word, the time does fly. I have one or two things to do this afternoon. People to see. Bore."

"There *was* something else," Ernest said, "but if you're rushed, perhaps another time."

"Perhaps another time"—but Mervyn Hogarth did a little exercise in his head which took no time at all, but which, had it been laboured out, would have gone like this:

Fares 13*s.* but had to come to London anyway; dreariness of food but it was free; disappointment at subject of discussion (Ernest had invited him to discuss "matters of interest to you") but satisfaction about Eleanor's break with Stock and consequent money difficulties; annoyance at being touched for money but satisfaction in refusing; waste of time but now Manders wants to say something further, which might possibly redeem the meeting or on the other hand confirm it as a dead loss.

The process passed through his mind like a snap of the fingers and so, when Ernest said, "There *was* something else, but if you're rushed——"

"Something else?" Hogarth replied.

"Perhaps another time," Ernest said.

"Oh, I'm not rushed for the next half-hour. Do carry on."

"Well," said Ernest, "it may interest you or it may not.

I feel, you know, I've brought you up to London on a disappointing inducement—I did think honestly it would please you to be substantially connected with the dancing school—and Eleanor was sure you would—I hope you don't feel it impertinent on our part."

"He is like a woman," Mervyn thought. "It's just like lunching with a woman." And he assured Ernest that he hadn't minded a bit: "only too sorry I can't spare a penny. What was the other question you wanted to mention?"

"Yes, well, that may be of interest and it may not. It's just as you feel. The lamb was most peculiar, I must apologise. It's the worst club lunch I do ever remember. I would send a complaint, only I did fire watching with the chef, who is most really nice and almost never has an off day like this."

"A very good lunch," said Mervyn sadly.

"*Sweet* of you to say so," said Ernest.

"This further question——?"

"Truly you've time? I should so like to say a few words, something which you might be interested in. You know my brother Edwin?"

"I haven't met Sir Edwin Manders."

"He is very rich. You know Helena?"

"His wife, that is? I know *of* her."

"She's rather sweet. You've met her mother?"

"As a matter of fact I do know Mrs. Jepp."

"Mrs. Jepp," said Ernest.

"Fine old lady. Lives quite near my place," said Mervyn.

"Yes, I know that," said Ernest. "You visit regularly, I hear."

"I hear," said Mervyn, "that her grandson had an accident."

"Only a broken rib. He's recovering rapidly."

"Ah, these young people. I met the grandson."

"I know," said Ernest.

It was creeping on three o'clock and their glasses had been twice filled. Ernest thought he was doing rather well. Mervyn was hoping against time, but really there was no excuse for prolonging the afternoon. Ernest had made it clear, in the soft mannerly style of pertinacity, that the Manders family had started to smell out the affairs of Louisa Jepp. Mervyn would have liked to hit Ernest for his womanly ways, and he said,

"I must say, Manders, I can't reveal any of Mrs. Jepp's confidences."

"Certainly not. Are you going abroad soon?"

"I take it this farce of asking me to lunch in order to ask me for a loan was really intended to create an opportunity to ask——"

"Oh dear, I can't possibly," said Ernest, "cope. I am so— am so sorry about the lunch. 'Farce' is the word exactly. I do wish I had made you take duck. Most distressing, I did so think you'd be interested in Eleanor's academy, it is top-ranking absolutely if she only had the capital. How dire for you, how frightful my dear man, for me."

"Your questions about Mrs. Jepp, I can't possibly answer them," said Mervyn, looking at his watch but unpurposed, settling into his chair, so that Ernest in his heart shook hands with himself: "He is waiting for more questions, more clues towards how much I'm in the know." He said to his guest, "I mustn't keep you, then. It's been charming."

Mervyn rose. He said, "Look here," and stopped.

"Yes?"

"Nothing, nothing." But as he stood on the top doorstep taking his leave from Ernest he said, "Tell Eleanor I shall think over her proposition. Perhaps after all I shall think it over and scrape up a little to help her out. But it's very grim these days, you realize, and I have my poor boy. He's a heavy expense."

"Don't think of it," said Ernest. "Please don't dream."

"Tell Eleanor I shall do what I can."

For about four minutes after his guest's departure Ernest was truly puzzled by these last-minute remarks. Then he sat back in a cushiony chocolate-coloured chair and smiled all over his youthful face, which made his forehead rise in lines right up to his very white hair.

He was in Kensington within half an hour, and at the studio. He saw Eleanor in one of the dressing cubicles off the large upper dancing floor, and pirouetted beautifully to attract her attention.

She sleeked her velvet jeans over her hips, pulled the belt tight as she did always when she wanted to pull her brains together.

"How did you get on? Anything doing?"

"I think so," he said.

"He'll put up the money?"

"I think so," he said.

"Ernest, what charm you must have with men. I would have sworn you wouldn't get an old bit of macaroni out of Mervyn, especially seeing I'm to benefit by it. He's so mean as a rule. What did he say? How did you do it?"

"Blackmail," Ernest said.

"How did you do it, dear?"

"I told you. It isn't certain yet, of course. And yet—I'm pretty sure you'll get the money, my dear."

"How did you manage it?"

"Blackmail by mistake."

"What can you mean? Tell me all."

"I gave him lunch. I explained your difficulties. Asked

for a loan. He said no. Then I asked him some other questions about something else, which he took to be a form of blackmail. Then, as he was leaving, he succumbed."

"What questions—the ones he thought were a blackmailing effort?—What were they?"

"Sorry, can't say, my dear. Something rather private."

"Concerning me?" said Eleanor.

"No, nothing at all to do with you, honestly."

"Nothing honestly to do with me?"

"Honestly."

Then she was satisfied. Ernest left her intent on her calculations, anticipating the subsidy from Mervyn Hogarth. She sat cross-legged on a curly white rug with pen and paper, adding and multiplying, as if the worries of the past had never been, as if not even yesterday had been a day of talking and thinking about bankruptcy. Before he left she said to Ernest, "Don't forget to draw on expenses for the lunch."

"Helena?"

"Hold the line a minute."

"Helena?"

"Who's that? Oh, it's you, Ernest."

"I saw Hogarth."

"Already? Where?"

"At my club. For lunch. Frightful serious little man with a Harris tweed jacket."

"Ernest, you are a marvel. You will let me pay for it of course."

"I thought you might like to know how things went. Such a glum little fellow."

"Tell me all. I'm on edge to know."

"Laurence is right. There is certainly something going on between your mother and Hogarth."

152

"*What's* going on?"

"He wouldn't say, of course. But it's something important enough to make him most unhappy, most eager to appease us. A bleak little bodikin actually. We had such unfortunate food, lamb like tree-bark, no exaggeration. He thinks we know more than we do. That's one up for us, I feel."

"Certainly it is. Can you come right over, Ernest? You could take a taxi."

"It would cost ten bob."

"Where are you speaking from?"

"South Kensington underground."

"Oh well, come by tube if you like. But take a taxi *if* you like."

"I'll be with you presently."

While Ernest was telephoning to Helena that afternoon Mervyn Hogarth climbed the steps of a drab neglected house at Chiswick. He pressed the bell. He could hear no sound, so pressed again, keeping his finger on it for a long time. Presumably out of order. Just as he was peering through the letter-box to see if anything was doing inside, the door opened so that Mervyn nearly stumbled over the threshold into the body of the blue-suited shady-looking man with no collar, who opened it.

"Is Mrs. Hogg living here at present?" Mervyn said.

He was acquainted with the place, Georgina's habitual residence when in London. He had been to the place before and he did not like it.

On that day Caroline Rose in hospital heard the click of a typewriter, she heard those voices,

He was acquainted with the place, Georgina's habitual residence when in London. He had been to the place before and he did not like it.

153

It is not easy to dispense with Caroline Rose. At this point in the tale she is confined in a hospital bed, and no experience of hers ought to be allowed to intrude. Unfortunately she slept restlessly. She never did sleep well. And during the hours of night, rather than ring for the nurse and a sedative, she preferred to savour her private wakefulness, a luxury heightened by the profound sleeping of seven other women in the public ward. When her leg was not too distracting, Caroline among the sleepers turned her mind to the art of the novel, wondering and cogitating, those long hours, and exerting an undue, unreckoned, influence on the narrative from which she is supposed to be absent for a time.

Tap-tick-click. Caroline among the sleepers turned her mind to the art of the novel, wondering and cogitating, those long hours, and exerting an undue, unreckoned, influence on the narrative from which she is supposed to be absent for a time.

Mrs. Hogg's tremendous bosom was a great embarrassment to her—not so much in the way of vanity, now that she was getting on in life—but in the circumstance that she didn't know what to do with it.

When, at the age of thirty-five she had gone to nursery-govern the Manders' boys, Edwin Manders remarked to his wife,

"Don't you think, rather buxom to have about the house?"

"Don't be disagreeable, please, Edwin. She has a fine character."

Laurence and Giles (the elder son, killed in the war) were overjoyed at Georgina's abounding bosom. Giles was the one who produced the more poetic figures to describe it; he declared that under her blouse she kept pairs of vegetable marrows, of infant whales, St. Paul's Cathedrals, goldfish bowls. Laurence's interest in Georgina's bulging frontage was more documentary. He acquired knowledge of her large stock of bust-bodices, long widths of bright pink or yellow-white materials, some hard as canvas, some more yielding in texture, from some of which dangled loops of criss-cross straps, some with eyelets for intricate tight-lacing, some with much-tried hooks and eyes. He knew exactly which one of these garments Georgina was wearing at any given time; one of them gave her four breasts, another gave her the life-jacket look which Laurence had seen in his dangerous sea-faring picture books. He knew the day when she wore her made-to-measure brassière provided at a costly expense by his mother. That was about the time Georgina was leaving to get married. The new garment was a disappointment to the children, they felt it made her look normal, only, of course, far more so. And they knew their mother was uneasy about these new shapely protrusions which did so seem to proceed heraldically far in advance of Georgina herself; the old bust-bodices were ungainly, but was this new contraption decent?

"I will lift up mine eyes to the hills," little Giles chanted for the entertainment of the lower domestics.

The boys did not share their mother's view of Georgina's character. They were delighted when she was to leave to marry her cousin.

"What's wrong with her cousin, then?"

"Be quiet, Laurence, Miss Hogg will hear you."

They had found her to be a sneak, a subtle tyrant. Prep school, next year, was wonderfully straightforward in comparison.

Her pale red-gold hair, round pale-blue eyes, her piglet "flesh-coloured" face: Georgina Hogg had certain attractions at the time of her marriage. Throughout the "tragic" years which followed (for when misfortune occurs to slightly absurd or mean-minded people it is indeed tragic for them—it falls with a thud which they don't expect, it does not excite the pity and fear of the onlooker, it excites revulsion more likely; so that the piece of bad luck which happened to Georgina Hogg was not truly tragic, only pathetic)—throughout those years since her marriage, Mrs. Hogg had sought in vain for an effectual garment to harness her tremendous and increasing bosom. She spent more money than she could afford in the effort; it was like damming up the sea. By that time of her life when she met Caroline Rose at St. Philumena's she had taken to wearing nothing regardless beneath her billowing blouses. "As God made me," she may have thought in justification, and in her new-found release.

. . . *"As God made me," she may have thought in justification, and in her new-found release.*

"Bad taste," Caroline commented. "Revolting taste." She had, in fact, "picked up" a good deal of the preceding passage, all about Mrs. Hogg and the breasts.

"Bad taste"—typical comment of Caroline Rose. Wasn't it she in the first place who had noticed with revulsion the transparent blouse of Mrs. Hogg, that time at St. Philumena's? It was Caroline herself who introduced into the story the question of Mrs. Hogg's bosom.

Tap-tap. It was Caroline herself who introduced into the story the question of Mrs. Hogg's bosom.

Caroline Rose sighed as she lay in hospital contemplating her memory of Mrs. Hogg. "Not a real-life character," she commented at last, "only a gargoyle."

Mervyn Hogarth, when he was admitted to Georgina's lodgings by the lazy dog-racing son of her landlady, was directed to Georgina's room. As he mounted the stairs towards it, he heard the swift scamper of mice, as if that part of the house were uninhabited. He knocked and jerked open the door. He saw her presently, her unfortunate smile, her colossal bust arranged more peculiarly than he had ever seen it before—and he had seen it in many extraordinary shapes—all lopsided, one side heaving up and the other one rolling down, for, possibly in the flurry of confronting him, the right shoulder strap of her bodice had snapped.

He took in her appearance without being fully aware of it, so anxious was he to speak his mind, give her warning, and be at peace.

Mrs. Hogg said, collecting herself though lopsided,

"You're late, Mervyn."

He sidled into an easy chair while she made to light the gas-ring under the kettle.

"No tea for me," he said. "Tell me," he said, "why you have started interfering. You've been to see Mrs. Jepp. What's your game?"

"I know what yours is," she said. "Smuggling." She sat down in her chair by the window so that the side where her bust-bodice had burst was concealed from him.

"Mrs. Jepp told you that."

"Yes, and it's true. She can afford to be truthful."

"Andrew is involved," he said.

"Ah yes, it's all in keeping, you have ruined Andrew already. It's only to be expected that you're making a criminal of him."

"Why exactly did you go to Mrs. Jepp?"

"I know I can do her some good if I have the chance. She's a wicked old woman. But I didn't know she had got thick with you and Andrew. When she told me 'Mervyn and Andrew Hogarth' I was stabbed, stabbed to the heart." And taking her handkerchief she stabbed each eye.

Mervyn Hogarth, looking at her, thought, "I never pity myself. A weaker mind would be shattered by the perversity of my life. There would be plenty of pity if I were a man who indulged in self-pity."

Georgina was speaking. "Bigamy and now diamond smuggling. Diamond smuggling"—she repeated this crowning iniquity with dramatic contempt, upturning her profile. She looked very like Mervyn in profile.

He determined to frighten her, though he had intended only to warn.

Georgina Hogg had no need to worry about her odd appearance that afternoon, for Mervyn, though he looked straight at her, could not see her accurately. She had stirred in him, as she always did, a brew of old troubles, until he could not see Georgina for her turbulent mythical dimensions, she being the consummation of a lifetime's error, she in whom he could drown and drown if he did not frighten her.

There was no need for him to fear that the woman profiled in the window would ever denounce him openly for his bigamous marriage with Eleanor.

In their childhood he had watched his cousin Georgina's way with the other cousins—Georgina at ten, arriving at the farm for the summer holidays with her bloodless face, reddish hair, lashless eyes, her greediness, would tell the cousins,

"I can know the thoughts in your head."

"You don't know what I'm thinking just now, Georgina."

"Yes I do."

"What then?"

"I shan't say. But I know because I go to school at a convent."

There was always something in her mouth: grass— she would eat grass if there was nothing else to eat.

"Georgina, greedy guts."

"Why did you swing the cat by its tail, poor creature, then?"

She discovered and exploited their transgressions, never told on them. She ruined their games.

"I'm to be queen of the Turks."

"Ya Georgina lump of a girl, queen of the fairies!"

Even Mervyn, though a silent child, would mimic, "I'm to be queen of the turkeys!"

"You stole two pennies," and in making this retort Georgina looked as pleased as if she were eating a thick sandwich. Mervyn, the accused, was overpowered by the words, he thought perhaps they were true and eventually, as the day wore on, believed them.

He had married her in his thirty-second year instead of carving her image in stone. It was not his first mistake and her presence, half-turned to the window, dabbing each eye with her furious handkerchief, stabbed him with an unwanted knowledge of himself.

"I have it in me to be a sculptor if I find the right medium . . . the right environment . . . the right climate . . . terrific vision of the female form if I could find the right model . . . the right influences," and by the time he was forty it became,

"I had it in me . . . if only I had found the right teachers."

By that time he had married Georgina instead of hacking out her image in stone. A *mistake*. She turned out not at all his style, her morals were as flat-chested as her form was sensuous; she conversed in acid drops while her breasts swelled with her pregnancy. He left her at the end of four months. Georgina refused to divorce him: that was the mistake of marrying a Catholic. Wouldn't let him see the son; a mistake to marry a first cousin, the child was crippled from birth, and Georgina moved him from hospitals to convents, wherever her various jobs took her. In her few letters to Mervyn, she leered at him out of her martyrdom. He sent her money, but never a message in reply.

At intervals throughout the next twenty years Georgina would put in appearances at the Manders' house in Hampstead, there to chew over her troubles. Helena hardly ever refused to see her, although she could hardly abide Georgina's presence. As the years passed, Helena would endure these sessions with her distasteful former servant, she would express banal sympathies, press small gifts into Georgina's hand and, when the woman had gone, "offer up" the dreary interview for the Holy Souls in Purgatory. Sometimes Helena would find her a job, recommending her to individuals and institutes with an indiscriminate but desperate sense of guilt.

"I am sure you are better off without Mr. Hogg," Helena would say often when Georgina bemoaned her husband's desertion.

"It is God's will, Georgina," Helena would say when Georgina lamented her son's deformity.

Georgina would reply, "Yes, and better he should be a cripple than a heathen like Master Laurence."

That was the sort of thing Helena put up with, partly out of weakness and partly strength.

One day after a long absence Georgina had arrived as of old with her rampant wounded rectitude. On this occasion she kicked the Manders' cat just as Helena entered the room. Helena pretended not to notice but sat down as usual to hear the story.

"Lady Manders," said Georgina, dabbing her eyes, "my son has gone."

Helena thought at first he must be dead.

"Gone?" she said.

"Gone to live with his father," Mrs. Hogg said. "Imagine the deception. That vile man has been seeing my boy in the hostel, behind my back. It's been going on for months, a great evil, Lady Manders. The father has money you know, and my poor boy, a good Catholic——"

"The father has taken him away?"

"Yes. Andrew has gone to live with him."

"But surely Mr. Hogg has no right. You can demand him back. What were the authorities thinking of? I shall look into this, Georgina."

"Andrew is of age. He went of his own free will. I wrote to him, begged him to explain or to see me. He won't, he just won't."

"Were you not informed by the authorities before Andrew was removed?" Helena asked.

"No. It was very sudden. All in an afternoon. They say they had no power to prevent it, and I was in Bristol at the time in that temporary post. It's a shocking thing, a tragedy."

Later Helena said to her husband,

"Poor Mrs. Hogg. She had reason to be distressed about it. I wish I could like the woman, but there's something so unwholesome about her."

"Isn't there!" he said. "The children never cared for her, remember."

"I wonder if her son disliked her."

"Shouldn't be surprised."

"Perhaps he's better off with Mr. Hogg."

"Shouldn't be surprised."

There was only one disastrous event which Georgina Hogg omitted to tell the Manders. That was the affair of Mervyn's bigamous marriage under the assumed name "Hogarth."

Mrs. Hogg shifted from the window to turn up the gas fire.

She said to Mervyn,

"Making a criminal out of Andrew."

"He likes the game."

"Bigamy," she said, "and now smuggling. You may get a surprise one day. I'm not going to sit by and watch you ruining Andrew."

But he knew she would never dissipate, in open scandal, the precious secret she held against him. He counted always and accurately on the moral blackmailer in Georgina, he had known in his childhood her predatory habits with other people's seamy secrets. Most of all she cherished those offences which were punishable by law, and for this reason she would jealously keep her prey from the attention of the law. Knowledge of a crime was safe with her, it was the criminal himself she was after, his peace of mind if she could get it. And so Mervyn had exploited her nature without fear of her disclosing to anyone his bigamy (another "mistake" of his), far less his smuggling activities. It was now three years since Mrs. Hogg had made her prize discovery of the bigamy. She had simply received an anonymous letter. It informed her that her husband, under the name of Hogarth, had undergone a form of marriage in a registry office with the woman who had since shared his home. Georgina thought this very probable—too probable for her even to confide in Helena who might have made investigations, caused a public fuss.

Instead, Georgina made her own investigations. The letter, to start with: on close examination, obviously written by Andrew. She rejoiced at this token of disloyalty as much as the contents agitated her with a form of triumph.

They were true. Georgina turned up at Ladle Sands, Sussex, where the couple were established, and made a scene with Eleanor.

"You have been living with my husband for some years."

"Quite right," said Andrew who was present.

"I must ask you to leave," Eleanor had kept repeating, very uncertain of her ground.

It was as banal as that.

Eleanor left Mervyn Hogg, now Hogarth, shortly after this revelation of his duplicity. She re-enacted the incident many times to the Baron. She made the most of it but her acting ability was inferior to her power of dramatic invention; what Eleanor added to the scene merely detracted from the sharp unambiguous quality of the original which lingered now only in the memories of Andrew and Georgina, exultant both, distinct though their satisfactions, and separated though they were. All the same, the Baron was impressed by Eleanor's repeated assertion, "Mrs. Hogg is a *witch!*"

Georgina wielded the bigamy in terrified triumph. Her terror lest Eleanor should take public action against the bigamist was partly mitigated by the fact that Eleanor had a reputation to keep free of scandal.

"But my name would suffer more than hers. I've always been respectable whereas she's a dancer," Georgina declared on one of her unwelcome visits to Ladle Sands. On the strength of the bigamy she had made free of Mervyn's house.

"Moreover," she declared, "the affair must be kept quiet for Andrew's sake."

"I'm not fussy," Andrew said.

"Imagine if my friends the Manders got to hear," Georgina said as she propped a post-card picture of the Little Flower on the mantelpiece.

For a year she made these visits frequently, until at length Mervyn threatened to give himself up to the police. "Six to twelve months in jail would be worth it for a little peace," he declared.

"Good idea," said Andrew.

"You are possessed by the Devil," his mother told him as she departed for the last time with a contemptuous glance at some broken plaster statuettes lying on a table. "Mervyn has taken up modelling, no doubt!"

Mervyn continued to tell himself, as he sat in that room in Chiswick late in the afternoon, that if he were a man given to indulge in self-pity he would have plenty of scope. It was one mistake after another. It came to mind that on one occasion, during his matrimonial years with Eleanor, he had slipped while crossing her very polished dancing floor. Polished floors were a mistake, he had broken an eye-tooth, and in consequence, so he maintained, he had lost his sense of smell. Other calamities, other mistakes came flooding back.

It was not any disclosure of his crimes that he feared from Georgina, he was frightened of the damage she could do to body and soul by her fanatical moral intrusiveness, so near to an utterly primitive mania.

Georgina was speaking. "Repent and be converted, Mervyn."

He shuddered, all hunched in the chair as he was, penetrated by the chill of danger. Georgina's lust for converts to the Faith was terrifying, for by the Faith she meant herself. He felt himself shrink to a sizeable item of prey, hovering on the shores of her monstrous mouth to be masticated to a pulp and to slither unrecognisably down that abominable gully, that throat he could almost see as she smiled her smile of all-forgetting. "Repent, Mervyn. Be converted." And in case he should be converted perhaps chemically into an intimate cell of her great nothingness he stood up quickly and shed a snigger.

"Change your evil life," said she. "Get out of the clutches of Mrs. Jepp."

"You don't know what evil is," he said defencively, "nor the difference between right and wrong . . . confuse God with the Inland Revenue and God knows what." And he recalled at that moment several instances of Georgina's muddled morals, and he thought again of his mistakes in life, his lost art and skill, his marriages, the slippery day when he broke the eye-tooth and another occasion not long ago when he had missed his travellers' cheques after spending half an hour in Boulogne with an acquaintance of his youth whom he had happened to meet. Added to this, he had a stomach ulcer, due to all these mistakes. He thought of Ernest Manders, the hush money. He sat down again and set about to defy Georgina.

"I'll tell you what has happened thanks to your interference in my affairs. The Manders are on our trail."

"The Manders? They dare not act. When I saw Lady Manders about my suspicions she was very very frightened about her mother."

"You told Lady Manders? You've been busy. No wonder the affair is almost common property."

"She was more frightened than grieved, I'm sorry to say," Georgina said. "She dare not act because of the mother being involved."

"The old woman takes a very minor part in our scheme. Do you suppose we put ourselves in the hands of that senile hag?"

"She isn't senile, that one."

"Mrs. Jepp has very little to do with us. Almost nothing. The Manders are after us; they intend to make a big fuss. You see their line?—Preying on a defenceless old lady. That was the line Ernest Manders took when I met him today."

"Ernest Manders," Georgina said, "you've been seeing that pervert."

"Yes, he's blackmailing us. Thanks to your interference. But I won't be intimidated. A few years in prison wouldn't worry me after all I've been through. Andrew will get off, I daresay, on account of his condition. A special probationary home for him, I reckon. He wouldn't care a damn. Our real name would come out of course and you would be called as witness. Andrew doesn't care. Only the other day he said, 'I don't care a damn.' "

"You've ruined Andrew," she declared, as she always did.

He replied: "I was just about to take Andrew on a pilgrimage to the shrine at Einsiedeln, but we've had to cancel it thanks to your interference."

"*You* go on a pilgrimage!" she said. "I don't believe you would go on a holy pilgrimage, I don't believe that."

Sir Edwin Manders had been in retreat for two weeks.

"Edwin has been in retreat for two weeks," said Helena. Ernest, dining with her, noticed that she had said this three times since his arrival, speaking almost to herself. "I suppose," he thought, "she must love him," and he was struck by the strangeness of this love, whatever its nature might be; not that his brother was unlovable in the great magnanimous sense, but it was difficult to imagine wifely

166

affection stretching out towards Edwin of these late years, for he had grown remote to the world though always amiable, always amiable, with a uniform amiability.

For himself, trying to approach his brother was an unendurable embarrassment. Ernest had decided that his last attempt was to remain the last.

"A temporary difficulty, Edwin. We had expensive alterations carried out at the studio. Unfortunately Eleanor has no head for business. She was under the impression that Baron Stock's financial interests in the school were secure from any personal—I mean to say any personal—you see, whereas in fact the Baron's commitments were *quite* limited, a mere form of patronage. Do you think yourself it would be a worth-*while* venture, for yourself, to satisfy your desire to promote what Eleanor and I are trying to do?" and so on.

Edwin had said, all amiable, "To be honest now, Ernest, I have no real attraction to investing in dancing schools. But look, I'll write you a cheque. You are not to think of repayment. I am sure that is the best way to solve your problem."

He handed Ernest the slip he had signed and folded neatly and properly. He was obviously at ease in his gesture; nothing *in* the transaction to cause reasonable resentment but Ernest was in horrible discomfort, he was unnerved, no one could know why.

Ernest began to effuse. "I can't begin to thank you, Edwin, I can't say how pleased Eleanor . . ." What he had meant to say was: "We don't want a gift—this is a business proposition," but the very sight of his smiling brother blotted out the words.

"Why, don't think of it,"—Edwin looked surprised, as if he had written the cheque a long-forgotten twenty years ago.

Ernest fumbled the gift into his pocket and in his nervousness exaggerated his effeminate movements. Blandly the brother spoke of the ballet, of the famous dancers he had seen; this for goodwill; Ernest knew that his brother had withdrawn for many years since into a life of interior philosophy, as one might say. The arts had ceased to nourish Edwin. It was sweet of him to talk of ballet, but it put Ernest out dreadfully, and altogether he had to go home to bed. Next day he remembered the cheque, looked at it, took it to Eleanor.

"Fifty pounds! How mean! Your brother is rich enough to *invest!*" Ernest was vexed at her tone.

"Do modify your exclamation marks," he said. "He doesn't want to invest in the school, don't you see? He tried so hard to be nice. Fifty pounds is a generous gift."

Eleanor bought a dress, black grosgrain with a charming backward swish which so suited her lubricious poise that Ernest felt better. With the money left over from the dress Eleanor paid down a deposit for an amber bracelet.

"Wouldn't your brother be dismayed if he knew how his sacred money was being spent?"

"No, he would not be angry at all," Ernest said, "not even surprised."

For the fourth time Helena murmured,

"Edwin has been in retreat for two weeks."

"When he returns," Ernest said, "you must tell him the whole story, much the best way."

"First we shall settle the business. I never tell Edwin my troubles until they are over."

"I feel there is nothing more to worry about. Hogarth was really scared, poor bilious little bloke he was. I pulled a gorgeous bluff."

"If he was scared there must be something in our suspicions. Laurence was right."

"Does it matter if we never know exactly what your mother's been doing, so long as we put an effective stop to it?"

"I should like to know a little more," said Helena. "But Mother is very deep, Ernest. So deep, and yet in her way so innocent. I must say I feel it a shortcoming on my part that I can't accept her innocence without wondering how it *works*. I mean, those diamonds in the bread, and where she gets her income from. It's a great defect in me, Ernest, but I'm bound to wonder, it's natural."

"Perfectly natural, dear," said Ernest, "and I shouldn't reproach myself."

"Oh *you* have nothing to reproach yourself about, Ernest dear."

Ernest had meant to imply, "I shouldn't reproach myself *if I were you*," but he did not correct her impression. A light rain had started to pat the windows.

"Let's employ a firm of private detectives and be done with it," he suggested.

"Oh no, they might find out something," she said quite seriously.

Ernest, who hated getting wet, departed soon after dinner in case the shower should turn into a steady drencher.

He had been gone nearly half an hour and it was nine-thirty, Helena thinking of saying her rosary, and of bed with a hot-water bottle since it was chilly, when the door-bell rang. Presently the middle-aged housekeeper put her head round the drawing-room door.

"Who is it, Eileen?"

"Mrs. Hogg. I've sat her in the hall. She wants to see you. She said she saw the drawing-room light." This Eileen knew Mrs. Hogg; she was the one whose marriage was long ago precipitated by Laurence, his reading of her love letters. Though she had only recently returned to the Manders' service after much lively knocking about the world, she retained sufficient memory of her kitchen-girl days and especially of Mrs. Hogg to resent that woman's appearances at the house, her drawing-room conferences with Lady Manders.

"I was just going to bed, Eileen. I thought an early night——"

"I'll tell her," said Eileen, disappearing.

"No, send her up," Helena called out.

Eileen put her head round the door again with the expression of one who demands a final clear decision.

"Send her up," Helena said, "but tell her I was just going to bed."

An absurd idea came into Helena's mind while she heard the tread of footsteps ascending the stairs. She thought, "How exhilarating it is to be myself," and the whole advantage of her personality flashed into her thoughts as if they were someone else's—her good manners and property, her good health, her niceness and her modest sense and charity; and she felt an excitement to encounter Mrs. Hogg. She felt her strength; a fine disregard, freedom to take sides with her mother absolutely if necessary.

It was hardly necessary. Mrs. Hogg was docile. She began by apologising for her previous visit about Laurence's letter. "My nerves were upset. I'd been overdoing things at St. Philumena's. Some days as many as a hundred and thirty pilgrims——"

"Of course, Georgina," Helena said.

Georgina went on to explain that she'd been thinking things over. Clearly, she had misread that letter from Master Laurence. It was all a joke, she could see that now.

"You never should have read it in the first place. It wasn't addressed to you."

"I did it for the best," said Mrs. Hogg dabbing her eyes. And she handed the letter to Helena.

"What's this?" Helena said.

"Laurence's letter. You can see for yourself how I was misled."

Helena tore it in two and tossed it on the fire.

"I hope you will do nothing more about it," Georgina said.

"About what? The letter is burned. What more should I do about it?"

"I mean, about your mother. Poor old lady, I'm sure she's a holy soul," Georgina said, adding, as she watched Helena's face, "at heart."

The interview continued for half an hour before Helena realised how desperately anxious the woman was to put a stop to all investigations. It was barely a month since Mrs. Hogg had descended upon her mother at the cottage. Helena was puzzled by this change of attitude and yet her suspicions were allayed by the sight of Mrs. Hogg dabbing her tearful eyes.

"I'm glad you have come to your senses, Georgina."

"I meant everything for the best, Lady Manders."

"I understand you called to see my mother. Why was that?"

Georgina was startled. Helena was made aware of one of her suspicions being confirmed: something more than she knew had passed between her mother and Mrs. Hogg.

"I thought she might want a companion," Mrs. Hogg said feebly. "You yourself suggested it not long ago."

Helena felt her courage surge up. "You mean to say that you offered your services to Mrs. Jepp at a time when you believed her to be a criminal?"

"A Catholic can do a lot of good amongst wicked people."

"My mother is not a wicked person, Georgina."

"Yes, I quite see that."

A knock at the door, and "Your bottle is in your bed, Lady Manders."

"Thank you, Eileen."

Mrs. Hogg rose. She said, "I can take it, then, that the matter is closed."

"What on earth are you worrying about? Of course there is no more to be done," said Helena.

"Thank God! Now I shall feel easy in my mind."

"Where are you placed now? Have you got a job?" Helena said as if by habit.

"No, Lady Manders."

"Have you anything in mind?"

"No. It's a worry."

"Come and see me tomorrow at five."

Before she went to bed Helena rang Ernest.

"Are you up, Ernest?"

"No, in bed."

"Oh, I've woken you up, I'm sorry."

"No, I was awake."

"Just to say, Ernest, that Mrs. Hogg came here after you left. For some reason she's highly anxious to stop all enquiries. She apologised for her suspicions."

"Well, that's all to the good, isn't it?"

"Yes, I know. But don't you see this sudden change is rather odd, just at this time?"

"Are you sure she has nothing to do with Hogarth?" Ernest said in a more wakeful voice.

"Well, I've never heard her mention the name. Is he a Catholic?"

"Shouldn't think so."

"Then definitely she wouldn't be *friendly* with the man in any way. She's got a religious kink."

"You don't think she means to attempt blackmail? These blackmailers beetle round in a curious way, you know."

"No. She actually brought me Laurence's letter. I burned it in front of her. I carried the thing off well, Ernest."

"Of course. Well, we've nothing more to worry about from Mrs. Hogg's direction."

She was grateful for that "we." "Perhaps we haven't. I told her to come and see me tomorrow about a job. I want to keep my eye on her."

"Good idea."

"But personally," said Helena, "I am beginning to think that Georgina is not all there."

At that hour Mr. Webster lay in his bed above the bakery turning over in his mind the satisfaction of the day. In spite of his tiredness on his return from London he had gone straight to Mrs. Jepp, had repeated with meticulous fidelity his conversation with the Baron and together they had reckoned up the payment and their profits as they always did.

"I am glad I sent herring roes," Louisa said. "I nearly sent fruit but the herring roes will be a change for Baron Stock. Herrings make brains."

"What a day it's been!" said Mr. Webster, smiling round at the walls before he took his leave.

For Baron Stock it had also been "a day." He hated the business of money-making, but one had to do it. The bookshop, if it had not been a luxurious adjunct to his personality, would have been a liability.

After sweet old Webster had gone, the Baron closed his bookshop for the day and, taking with him Louisa Jepp's tin of herring roes, went home. There he opened the can, and tipping the contents into a dish, surveyed the moist pale layers of embryo fish. He took a knife and lifting them one by one he daintily withdrew from between each layer a small screw of white wax paper; and when he had extracted all of these he placed the paper pellets on a saucer. These he opened when he was seated comfortably before his fire. The diamonds were enchanting, they winked their ice-hard dynamics at him as he moved over to the window to see them better.

"Blue as blue," he said, an hour later when he sat in the back premises of a high room in Hatton Garden.

The jeweller said nothing in reply. He had one eye screwed up and the other peering through his glass at the gems, each little beauty in turn. The Baron thought afterwards, as he always did, "I must make a new contact. This man swindles me." But then he remembered how terse and unexcitable the jeweller was, so different from those gem-dealers who, meeting with each other on the pavements at Hatton Garden, could not contain for two seconds their business verve, nor refrain from displaying there and then their tiny precious wares, produced out of waistcoat pockets and wrapped in tissue paper. It was inconceivable that the Baron's silent dealer should ever be seen on the street; possibly he never went home, possibly had no home, but sat in vigilance and fasting from dawn to dawn, making laconic bargains with such people who arrived to sell diamonds.

Later that evening the Baron sipped Curaçao in his flat and decided that doing business was exhausting. Once every three months, this trip to Hatton Garden and the half-hearted haggle with the jeweller, exhausted him. He reclined as in a hammock of his thoughts, shifting gently back and forth over the past day, and before he went to bed he began to write a letter to Louisa.

"The herring roes, my dear Mrs. Jepp, have provided

174

the most exquisite light supper for me after a most *exhausting* (but satisfying) day. I put them on toast under the grill—delicious! I admire your preservative process. The contents of your tin were more delicate than oysters, rarer than . . ." But his mind drifted to other delicacies, mysterious Mervyn Hogarth, the inter-esting black arts.

What a day it had been, also, for Mervyn Hogarth, who had returned to Ladle Sands to find Andrew in one of his ugly moods. When he was in such moods Andrew would literally spit on everyone. Andrew had been left in charge of a village woman whom he had spat at so much she had gone home long before the arranged time, leaving the young cripple alone as darkness fell. When Mervyn at last got to bed he tried to read himself to sleep, but the "mistakes" of the day started tingling; he lay in darkness fretting about the cunning of Ernest Manders, the tasteless lunch, the blackmail; and he murmured piteously to himself "What a day, what a day," far past midnight.

And what a day for Mrs. Hogg, that gargoyle, climbing to her mousy room at Chiswick where, as she opened the door, two mice scuttled one after the other swiftly down their hole beside the gas meter.

However, as soon as Mrs. Hogg stepped into her room she disappeared, she simply disappeared. She had no private life whatsoever. God knows where she went in her privacy.

8

IT IS VERY MUCH TO BE DOUBTED IF MERVYN Hogarth had ever in his life given more than a passing thought to any black art or occult science. Certainly he was innocent of prolonged interest in, let alone any practice of, diabolism, witchcraft, demonism or such cults. Nevertheless Baron Stock believed otherwise.

It was not till the New Year that the Baron was able to assemble his evidence. He confided often in Caroline, for since her return to London they met as frequently, almost, as in earlier days. She lived now in a flat in Hampstead, quite near the Baron, with only a slight twinge in her leg before rainy weather to remind her of the fracture, and in reminding her, to bring the surprise of having had a serious accident.

"It is strange," said the Baron, "how Eleanor left me, her reasons. Did you ever hear?"

Caroline said, "I know she had suspicions of your participating in Black Masses and what not."

"I'm not surprised," the Baron said. "A woman of Eleanor's limited intellig-ence is incapable of distinguishing between interest in an activity and participation in it. I am interested, for instance, in relig-ion, poetr-ay, psycholog-ay, theosoph-ay, the occult and of course demonolog-ay and diabolism, but I participate in none of them, practise none."

"And your chief interest is diabolism," Caroline observed.

"Oh yes, utterly my chief. As I tried to explain to Eleanor at the time, I regard these studies of mine as an adult pursuit; but to actually take part in the absurd rituals would be childish."

"Quite," said Caroline.

"I have, of course, attended a few Black Masses and the ceremonies of other cults, but purely as an observer."

Caroline said, "Um."

It was a gusty day, and from the windows of Caroline's top-floor flat, only the sky was visible with its little hurrying clouds. It was a day when being indoors was meaningful, wasting an afternoon in superior confidences with a friend before the two-barred electric heater.

"Eleanor would not be reasoned with," the Baron went on. "And for some reason the idea of living with a man whose spare-time occupation was black magic appalled her. Now the curious thing is, I've since discovered that her former husband Mervyn Hogarth is a *raging* diabolist, my dear Caroline. That is obviously why she deserted him."

"Never mind, Willi. You're as well apart from Eleanor, and she from you."

"I've got over it. And you," he said, "are as well without Laurence."

"Our case is different," she said snappily. "There's love saved up between Laurence and me, but no love lost between you and Eleanor."

"No love lost," he said, "but still it hurts when I think of her."

"Of course," she said nicely.

"But not enough, my Caroline," said he, "to induce me to give up these investigations. People are unaccountable. One finds barbarity and superstition amongst the most unlikely. The subject, the people, excite me in-tensely. At present my attention is almost entirely on this Mervyn Hogarth. He is, I assure you, Caroline, the foremost diabolist in the kingdom. I go so far as to employ agents. I have him watched."

"Oh, come!" Caroline said.

"Truly," said the Baron. "I have him watched. I get reports. I have compiled a dossier. I spend a fortune. The psychology of this man is my main occupation."

"Dear me. You must miss Eleanor more than I thought."

"What d'you mean?"

"Obviously your obsession with Eleanor's former lover is a kind of obsession with Eleanor. You are looking in him for something concealed in her, don't you see! Obviously you are following the man because you can't follow Eleanor, she has eluded you, don't you see? Obviously——"

"Physician, heal thyself," said the Baron with what he thought was aptness.

"Oh, I may be wrong," said Caroline mildly. The indoor afternoon idea went limp and she was reminded of her imprudence when, in hospital, she had begun to confide her state of mind to the Baron on the occasion of his visits. She knew he would not keep her confidences any more than she his.

But unable to leave well alone she said, "Why really does it trouble you even if Hogarth is a diabolist? I could understand your fanaticism if you had any religion to defend. Perhaps unawares you are very religious."

"I have no religion," he said. "And I don't disapprove of diabolism. For my part, it is not a moral interest; simply an intellectual passion."

She teased him, but did not watch her words. "You remind me of an African witch-doctor on the trail of a witch. Perhaps you picked up the spirit of the thing in the Congo

—weren't you born there?" Then she saw her mistake, and the strange tinge in the whites of his eyes that had made her wonder at times if the Baron had native blood. He was extremely irritated by her remark.

"At least," articulated he, "I pursue an intelligible objective. Diabolism exists; the fact can be proved by the card index of any comprehensive library. Diabolism is practised: I can prove it to you if you care to accompany me to Notting Hill Gate on certain nights—unless, of course, you are too bound by the superstitious rules of your Church. Mervyn Hogarth exists. He practises diabolism; that fact is available to anyone who cares to insti-gate private enquiries into his conduct. You on the other hand," he said, "assert a number of unascertainable facts. That chorus of voices," he said, "who but yourself has heard them? Your theories—your speculations about the source of the noises? I think, Caroline *my* dear, that you yourself are more like a witch-doctor than I am."

This upset Caroline, whereupon she busied herself with tea-cups, quick movements, tiny clatters of spoons and saucers. As she did this she protested nebulously.

"The evidence will be in the book itself."

Now Caroline, one day when the Baron had visited her in hospital, had told him,

"Those voices, Willi—since I've been in hospital I have heard them. But one thing I'm convinced of"—and she indicated her leg which had swollen slightly within the plaster case so that it hurt quite a lot—"this physical pain convinces me that I'm not wholly a fictional character. I have independent life."

"Dear me," said the Baron, "were you ever in doubt of it?"

So she told him, confidentially, of her theory. He was

intrigued. She warmed to the sense of conspiracy induced by the soft tones of their conversation, for it was an eight-bed ward.

"Am I also a charact-er in this mysterious book, Caroline?" he asked.

"Yes you are, Willi."

"Is everyone a character?—Those people for instance?" He indicated the seven other beds with their occupants and visiting relatives and fuss.

"I don't know," Caroline said. "I only know what the voices have hinted, small crazy fragments of a novel. There may be characters I'm unaware of."

The Baron came to see her every week-end. On each occasion they discussed Caroline's theory. And although, profoundly, she knew he was not to be trusted with a confidence, she would tell herself as he arrived and after he had gone, "After all, he is an old friend."

One day she informed him, "The Typing Ghost has not recorded any lively details about this hospital ward. The reason is that the author doesn't know how to describe a hospital ward. This interlude in my life is not part of the book in consequence." It was by making exasperating remarks like this that Caroline Rose continued to interfere with the book.

The other patients bored and irritated her. She longed to be able to suffer her physical discomforts in peace. When she experienced pain, what made it intolerable was the abrasive presence of the seven other women in the beds, their chatter and complaints, and the crowing and clucking of the administering nurses.

"The irritant that comes between us and our suffering is the hardest thing of all to suffer. If only we could have our sufferings clean," Caroline said to the Baron.

A visiting priest on one occasion advised her to "offer

up" her sufferings for the relief of some holy soul in Purgatory.

"I do so," Caroline declared, "with the result that my pain is intensified, not at all alleviated. However, I continue to do so."

"Come, come," said the priest, youthful, blue-eyed behind his glasses, fresh from his seminary.

"That is a fact, as far as my experience goes," said Caroline.

He looked a trifle scared, and never stopped for long at Caroline's bedside after that.

On those Saturday afternoons the Baron had seemed to bring to Caroline her more proper environment, and for the six weeks of her confinement in the country hospital she insulated herself by the phrase "he is an old friend" against the certainty that the Baron would, without the slightest sense of betrayal, repeat and embellish her sayings and speculations for the benefit of his Charing Cross Road acquaintance. Much was the psycho-analysing of Caroline that went on in those weeks at the back of the Baron's bookshop, while she lay criticising the book in the eight-bed ward. Which was an orthopaedic ward, rather untidy as hospital wards go, owing to the plaster casts which were lying here and there, the cages humping over the beds and the trolley at the window end on which was kept the plaster-of-paris equipment, also a huge pair of plaster-cutting scissors like gardening shears, all of which were covered lumpily with a white sheet; and into which ward there came, at certain times, physiotherapists to exercise, exhort and manipulate their patients.

The Baron, it is true, while he discussed "the book" with her, had no thought for the Monday next when he should say to this one and that,

"Caroline is embroiled in a psychic allegory which she

is trying to piece together while she lies with her leg in that dreary, dreary ward. I told you of her experience with the voices and the typewriter. Now she has developed the idea that these voices represent the thoughts of a disembodied novelist, if you follow, who is writing a book on his typewrite-r. Caroline is apparently a character in this book and so, my dears, am I."

"Charming notion. She doesn't believe it literally though?"

"Quite literally. In all other respects her reason is unimpaired."

"Caroline, of all people!"

"Oh it's absol-utely the sort of thing that happens to the logical mind. I am so fond of Caroline. I think it all very harmless. At first I thought she was on the verge of a serious disorder. But since the accident she has settled down with the fantasy, and I see no reason why she shouldn't cultivate it if it makes her happy. We are all a little mad in one or other particular."

"Aren't we just, Willi!"

Laurence was out of hospital some weeks before Caroline.

"I can't think what possesses you," he said, when at last he was able to see her, "to confide in the Baron. You asked me to keep your wild ideas a secret and naturally I've been denying all the rumours. It's embarrassing for me."

"What rumours?"

"They vary. Roughly, it goes that you've dropped Catholicism and taken up a new religion."

"What new religion?"

"Science Fiction."

She laughed, then winced, for the least tremble hurt her leg.

"Sorry," said Laurence who had promised not to make her laugh.

"I never expected the Baron to keep his peace on any subject," she said. "I rather like talking to him, it amuses me. I've been lonely here, sick as well."

She could see that Laurence was more niggled by the Baron's attentiveness than by her actual conversations with him.

To return to that afternoon in the New Year when Caroline unwittingly hurt the Baron by comparing him to an African witch-doctor.

After tea, which she made in two pots: green for the Baron and plain Ceylon for herself, the Baron attempted to compensate for his anger. He told her a story in strictest confidence which, however, she repeated to Laurence before the day was out.

"Once, on Eleanor's behalf—shortly after her divorce from her daemonical Hogarth, and in connection with a financial settlement, I went to call on him at his house in Ladle Sands. I had not informed him previously of my intention to call, believing that if I did so he would refuse to see me. I hoped to catch him by chance.—Many were such services, I assure you, Caroline, that I performed for Eleanor. Well, I called at the house. It is fairly large with some elegance of frontage, Queen Anne; set well back from the road and concealed by a semi-circle of plane trees within a high hedge that had not been trimmed for months. The garden was greatly neglected. The house was empty. Peering through the letter-box I could see a number of circular letters lying on the hall table. From this I assumed that the Hogarths had been absent for some weeks, having arranged for their personal letters to be forwarded. I went round to the back of the house. I was curious. At that time, you must understand, I was greatly in love with Eleanor, and the house where she had lived with Hogarth inter-ested me in the sense that it gave me a physical con-

183

tact with a period of Eleanor's past which I knew only from what she had chosen to tell me.

"The back premises were even more untidy than the front. The kitchen garden gone to seed and stalk, and an important thing that I am going to tell you is this. At the door of an outhouse lay a pile of junk. Empty boxes, rusty broken gardening tools, old shoes. And amongst these a large number of broken plaster statuettes—religious objects of the more common kind that are sold by the thousand in the repositories attached to the Christian shrines. These were hacked about in a curious way. The heads were severed from many of them, and in some cases the whole statue had been reduced to fragments. There were far too many of these plaster pieces to be accounted for by accidental breakage. Even at that time—I knew nothing of Hogarth's occult activities then—I assumed that there had been a wholesale orgy of deliberate iconoclasm. In cases where the body was intact, only the head or limbs being severed, I noticed how cleanly the cleavage occurred, as if cut by an instrument, certainly not smashed by a fall, not that.

"Then I must tell you, Caroline, what happened while I was engaged in examining these extraordinary bits of clay. The back premises were skirted by a strip of woodland. This was about thirty yards from the outhouse where I was standing. The sound of a dog growling caused me to turn and observe this direction, and soon I saw the dog emerge from the wood towards me. It was a black spaniel, very well cared for. I picked up a stick in case it should attack me. It approached with its horrid growling. However, it did not make straight for me. As soon as it got within five yards it started to walk round me in a circle. *It encircled me three times,* Caroline. Then it bounded towards the heap of broken statues and sat, simply sat, in front of the heap as though defying me to touch them.

"Of course I went away, walking casually in case the dog should leap. But what I am trying to tell you, Caroline, is that the black dog was Mervyn Hogarth."

"What did you say?" said Caroline.

"I did not realise at the time," said the Baron, stirring his green tea, "I merely thought it an uncommonly be-haved dog. Of course I am speaking to you confidentially, it is not the sort of thing one can tell one's acquaintances, however intimate. But I feel you have an understanding of such things, especially as you yourself are supernormal, clairaudient and——"

"What was that you said," Caroline said, "just now, about the dog?"

"The dog was Mervyn Hogarth. Magically transformed, of course. It is not unknown——"

"You're mad, Willi," said Caroline amiably.

"Indeed," said the Baron, "I am not."

"Oh, I don't mean *mad,* you know," Caroline said. "Just a little crazy, just a little crazy. I think of course it's a lovely tale, it has the makings of a shaggy dog."

"I wouldn't have expected you to be incredu-lous, of all people."

"Well, Willi, I ask you!"

He was serious. "What," he said, "do you make of the broken saints?"

"Maybe they had a house-full and then got fed up with them and chucked them out. Maybe they break up the statues for pleasure. After all, most of those plaster saints are atrocious artistically, one can well understand the urge."

"For pleasure," the Baron repeated. "And how do you account for the dog?"

"Dogs are. One doesn't have to account for dogs. It must

have been the Hogarths' dog——"

"It wasn't the Hogarths' dog. I enquired. They possess no dog."

"It must have been a neighbour's dog. Or a stray, looking for something to eat."

"What do you say to its having encircled me *three times?*"

"My dear Willi, I'm speechless."

"True," said the Baron, "you have no answer to *that*. Not that I have formed my opinion that Hogarth is a black magician solely from the experience which I have just described to you. I haven't told you yet about the carrier-pigeons, and many subsequent phenomena. Are you free to dine with me tonight? If you are I can tell you the whole story, and then, my Caroline, you will no longer say Willi's mad."

"We're all a little mad, Willi. That's what makes us so nice, dear. No, I'm not free tonight, I'm sorry to say. It would have been pleasant really. . . ."

He planted a friendly kiss on her cheek when he said goodbye. As soon as Caroline heard him descending in the shaky lift she went into her bathroom and taking out a bottle of Dettol poured rather a lot into a beaker of warm water. She saturated a piece of cotton wool with this strong solution; she dabbed that area on her face where the Baron had deposited his kiss.

"The Baron is crackers."

It gave Laurence pleasure to hear Caroline say these words, for he had been lately put out by the renewed friendship between Caroline and the Baron.

"The Baron," she declared, "is clean gone. He came to tea this afternoon. He related the most bats tale I've ever heard."

So she told Laurence the Baron's story. At first it amused him. Then suddenly his mild mirth changed to a real delight. "Good for the Baron!" he said. "He's actually stumbled on a clue, a very important one, I feel."

"Clue to what?" she said.

"My grandmother."

"What has the black dog to do with your grandmother?"

"The clue is in the broken statues. Why didn't I think of it before?"

"Your grandmother wouldn't break anything whatsoever. What's the matter with you, dear man?"

"No, but Hogarth would."

"You're as bad as the Baron," she said, "with your obsession about Hogarth."

Since their motor accident Laurence had been reticent with Caroline. She saw that, because he was partly afraid, he could not keep away from her, but it was not at all to her taste to nourish the new kind of power by which she attracted him. Laurence's fear depressed her. For that reason she stopped altogether discussing with him the private mystique of her life. Only when she was taken off-guard in conversation did she reveal her mind to Laurence, as when he innocently enquired,

"How is your book going?" meaning her work on the structure of the modern novel.

"I think it is nearing the end," she answered.

He was surprised, for only a few days since she had announced that the work was slow in progress.

Another thing had surprised him.

They had planned a holiday together abroad, to take place in the last two weeks in March.

At first Caroline had objected that this was too early in the year. Laurence, however, was fixed on this date, he had already applied for leave before consulting Caroline. She thought it rather high behaviour, too, when he announced that they would go to Lausanne.

"Lausanne in March! No fear."

"Do trust me," he said. "Have I been your good friend?"

"Yes, yes, but Lausanne in March."

"Then believe that I have my reasons. Do, please."

She suspected that his choice of time and place was connected with his intense curiosity about his grandmother's doings. Ernest and Helena had come to believe that the danger was over. Any illicit enterprise the old woman had been engaged in was squashed by Ernest's interference and bluff. They hardly cared to think there had been any cause for anxiety. But Laurence, who had made several week-end trips to the cottage during the past winter, seemed convinced that his grandmother's adventures were still in hearty progress. Arriving unexpectedly one recent week-day evening Laurence had found her little "gang" assembled as before, the cards in play as before, Louisa unconcerned as always. From her own lips he learned that the Hogarths had twice been abroad since January.

For his failure to pull off a dramatic swift solution of his grandmother's mystery Laurence blamed the car accident. He bitterly blamed the accident. At the same time he felt stimulated by his discovery that Ernest and Helena had between them succeeded only in putting the gang on its guard. It still remained for him to search out the old woman's craftiness. That was what he mostly desired, and not content merely to put an end to her activities, Laurence wanted to know them.

Throughout the winter his brief trips to the cottage tantalised him. He snooped round Ladylees and Ladle Sands with blank results; he had a mounting certainty that the gang was lying low. Ernest had bungled the quest.

Most of all Laurence felt up against his grandmother's frankness. She was never secretive in her talk or manner, but decidedly she refrained from disclosing her secret. All he had gained was the information that the Hogarths planned a trip to Lausanne in the last two weeks of March.

"The Hogarths go abroad a great deal, Grandmother."

"They do like travelling, my, don't they!"

He got no more out of Louisa. He applied for a fortnight's leave to start on the 15th of March.

Helena had been so far emancipated by her son that she saw nothing offensive in suggesting to him,

"Why not take Caroline with you? She needs a holiday and, poor girl, she can't afford one. I'll pay her expenses."

It was then Laurence was faced with Caroline's objection, "Lausanne in March! Why Lausanne? It will be so bleak."

But when he said, "Haven't I been your good friend? Do please agree with me this once," she agreed.

That was in the middle of February. Two weeks later she disagreed.

"I've been to the Priory to see Father Jerome," she began.

"Jolly good!" said Laurence. She had observed lately with some amusement that Laurence displayed himself keen to promote all her contacts with religion, the more as he himself continued to profess his merry scepticism. One recent Sunday when she had decided to miss church because of a sore throat, he had shown much concern, in the suggestion of a warm scarf, the providing of a gargle and transport to and from the church in his new car, to see that she did not evade the obligation. "Jolly good!" said Laurence, when he heard that she had visited the old monk whom he had known since his boyhood.

"He says," Caroline announced, "that I ought not to

189

go to Lausanne with you."

"But he knows me! Surely he knows we can be trusted together, that it's simply a companionable holiday. My goodness, it's done continually by the deadliest proper couples. My goodness, I always thought he was a reasonable broad-minded priest."

"He said that in view of our past relationship, we ought not to appear in circumstances which might give rise to scandal."

"But there's no question of sin. Even I know that. I was indoctrinated in the Catholic racket, don't forget."

"No question of sin, but he said it would disedify," Caroline said.

"We needn't tell anyone we're going together. And we're hardly likely to be seen by anyone at all in Lausanne in March."

"A furtive trip would be worse than an open one. More disedifying still. I can't go. Awfully sorry."

Her withdrawal upset Laurence more than she expected. He had not told her that, as she had guessed, his determination to visit Lausanne in March was in some way connected with his passion to play the sleuth on his grandmother. She had not reckoned with his need for her participation, and the more he argued with her the more she conceived herself well out of the affair. It reminded her too much of the pattern of events preceding the car-smash.

Laurence did not press her very far. He accepted her decision with that strange fear he now had of approaching close enough to Caroline to precipitate a row. It was on this occasion that, suppressing his disappointedness, he asked her amicably,

"How is your book going?" and she, her mind brooding elsewhere, answered, "I think it is nearing the end."

"Really? You were saying only the other day that you still had a lot to write."

Swiftly she realised her mistake, and so did Laurence. He looked rather helpless, as if enmeshed. She hated to think of herself as a spiritual tyrant, she longed to free him from those complex familiars of her thoughts which were to him so foreign.

"Naturally, I look forward to the end of the book," she said, "in a manner of speaking to get some peace."

"I meant," said Laurence with a burst of irritation, "of course, the book that you are writing, not the 'book' in which you think you are participating."

"I know," she said meekly, "that is what you meant." And to lift the heavy feeling between them she gave him her pretty civilised smile and said, "Do you remember that passage in Proust where he discusses the ambiguous use of the word 'book', and he says——?"

"To hell with Proust," said Laurence.

"Look," she said, "I don't enquire into your fantastic affairs. Leave mine alone. And look," she said, "we have nothing to say to each other this evening. I'm going home. I'll walk."

They were dining in a small restaurant only a few minutes' walk from Caroline's flat, and so her "I'll walk," falling short of its intended direness, tickled Laurence.

"I find it difficult to keep up with you these days." And to pacify her he added, "Why do you say that the 'book' is nearing the end?"

She was reluctant to answer, but his manner obliged her.

"Because of incidents which have been happening within our orbit of consciousness, and their sequence. Especially this news about your grandmother's friend."

"Which friend?" said Laurence.

"Haven't you heard about it? Helena rang me this morning, very excited, and from what I can gather it's most remarkable——"

"Which friend?"

"One of those concerning whom you entertain your daft suspicions. Andrew Hogarth. Apparently he was paralysed, and his father took him off to some little shrine of Our Lady in the French Alps. Well, he was brought back yesterday and he's actually started to move his paralysed limb. Helena says it's a miracle. I don't know about that but it seems the sort of incident which winds up a plot and brings a book to a close. I shan't be sorry."

"But they haven't been abroad since January. They hadn't planned to leave until the middle of March, at least so I understood. I have reason to believe the Hogarths are diamond smugglers, don't you understand?"

"Ask your mother," Caroline said. "She knows all about it. She's brimming full of it."

"I don't see," said Laurence, "much point, now, in going to Lausanne in March."

"Absolutely perfect. . . . A pass back there—a foul tackle and the whistle . . . the sun has come out, everything looks *absolutely perfect* with the red coats of the band . . . that feeling of—of tenseness . . . and now again for the second half . . . the first dramatic . . . absolutely perfect . . . it's a *corner,* a goal to Manchester City . . . a beautiful, absolutely . . . ."

Louisa Jepp sat beside the wireless cuddled in the entranced caress of Laurence's voice.

Much later in the day, after he had braked up loudly outside the cottage in his new car, and had settled into a chair by the stove with a newly-opened bottle of beer, he said,

"Is it true about young Hogarth?"

"He is receiving physiotherapeutic treatment," she said, with correctness, for she used and pronounced her words, however unlikely, accurately, or not at all.

"And he has actually started to use his legs?"

"Yes. He totters a little. It's too soon to say 'he walks.' "

"He was absolutely paralysed before."

"My, yes. The trips abroad did him good. I always knew they would."

"I suppose," said Laurence, "that the Hogarths have cancelled their holiday in Lausanne?"

"Oh yes. There's no need for them to go wandering in March. It's very chilly. Much better at home. Andrew is getting his treatment."

"I suppose," said Laurence, "they will be off again in the early summer?"

"Not abroad," said the old lady. "Somerset or Cornwall I should say, if the boy's fit enough."

"I suppose that means," said Laurence, "that your game is up, Grandmother?"

"Why, dear," she said, "I was thinking, as I listened to you on the wireless today, how much I wished for your sake, dear, that you could have caught us red-handed. It must be a disappointment, love. But never mind, we all have our frustrations and you were lovely on the wireless, you were *absolutely perfect.*"

"I had every clue, Grandmother. I only needed the time. If I hadn't had the smash I'd have got you last autumn, Grandmother."

"There, never mind."

"But you're in danger. An acquaintance of ours is on your trail. I heard by chance through Caroline. His name's Willi Stock, a phoney Baron——"

"No, he is quite authentic a Baron."

"You know Baron Stock, then?"

"I have met the Baron," she said.

"Well, do you know," he said, "Caroline told me last November, just before the smash, that the Baron had been seeing you last year. He described a hat you wore. Caroline recognised it, and inferred——"

"That was very stupid of the Baron, but typical, though he is nice——"

"But I didn't," said Laurence, "place much faith in what Caroline said. I thought she was sort of dreaming."

"Why, you can't be clever at everything."

"It was a good clue," said Laurence. "I ought to have followed it up. I might have got you right away. Have you any fears of the Baron?—Because if so——"

"No, no. He's my London party. Or was."

"The *Baron* has been in with you! I thought there were only the four of you."

"There are only four of us. Baron Stock was only our London agent."

"You've packed up the game, then?"

"Now, which game?" she said, puckering a smile as if to encourage him to recite a lesson.

"Smuggling diamonds through the customs," he said, "concealed in plaster figures."

"And rosary beads at times," said Louisa. Her whole body seemed to perk with delight, and to further signify her sense of occasion she passed Laurence a glass and a bottle of stout to open for her. She watched him pour the brown liquid and she watched the high self-controlled froth as one who watches a scene to be preserved in memory.

"You took a risk, Grandmother."

"There was very small risk," she said. "What there was, the Hogarths took, as I see it."

194

She drew up to the stove and sipped warmly.

"I had many a smile," she said, "considering how they came through with the merchandise."

"Several times a year," said Laurence, "at a guess."

"It has varied," she said, "over four years and eight months. Some trips were better than others. It depended so much on our continental parties. It was difficult for that end to get the right moulds for the statues. The beads were easier. But Andrew preferred the statues."

"I should have thought the customs would have got suspicious with all that coming and going. Very risky," Laurence said.

"Everything's risky," she said. "Many a laugh I had to myself when Mervyn told me about the customs men passing remarks. *Mervyn* didn't laugh, he didn't like that part of it. You see they went as pilgrims looking for a cure, Andrew in his invalid chair, you can picture him, hugging his statues with a long churchy face. So as to deceive the customs, don't you see. Each time they went to some shrine of the Virgin Mary and our contact would meet them in the town, who was a gentlemanly party I believe. But I made Mervyn and Andrew visit the shrines properly, in case they were watched. You can't be too careful with the continental police, they are very deceitful and low."

"Are the Hogarths Catholics?"

"Oh, no. Not religious at all. That was the pose, you see. Many an entertainment I had, love."

"Mother has heard about Andrew Hogarth's recovery," Laurence said.

"Yes, I wrote and told her. I thought it would be of interest to her that the young man, being a neighbour of mine, had got a cure at a Roman Catholic shrine. She likes those stories."

"Do you think it was a miracle, then?"

195

"Oh yes," she said, "I do believe in lucky places if your luck is in. Indeed Andrew was unlucky before. He got a cold in the bladder at Lourdes two years back, but Myans has brought him luck, where there's a *black* Madonna, I believe. And indeed I once knew a gentleman very up in history and fond of the olden days who had a stammer which he lost in the Tower of London."

"That sounds psychological," said Laurence.

"Oh, it's all what I call luck," Louisa said.

"You don't think Andrew's case is clearly a miracle, then?"

"Oh, quite clear a miracle, as I see him now. He can move his legs from the knees, sitting in his chair. He couldn't do that before."

"What do the doctors say?"

"They say he has to have physiotherapy. He's improving already."

"How do they explain it?"

"They say it's a marvel but they don't make mention of miracles. They brought a great crowd of students to look at Andrew up at the hospital. Andrew put an end to it, though, by swearing and spitting. He has such a temper."

"Good for him!" Laurence said. "I suppose he's thrilled to be able to move his legs?"

"I think so. But he has a temper," she said, and passing a box of cigarettes, "Have a Bulgarian."

Laurence smiled, comparing this account of Andrew with the picture in his mother's imagination of the young man miraculously cured. In Helena's eyes, the event entirely justified the Hogarths' shady activities. It justified her mother. She was content to remain vague about Louisa's late intrigues, and convinced that Ernest, through his strong hand with Mervyn Hogarth last year in the course of a luncheon, had been successful in ending the troubles, whatever they were.

When she told Laurence of Andrew's cure at the Alpine shrine, he remarked,

"They're still at the game, then."

"Nonsense," Helena replied. "At the very worst, the Hogarths might have been winding up their business, whatever it was. I expect they will both become Catholics. The young man will, surely."

"Helena wants to make a Church thing of it," Louisa told Laurence. "But she won't be able to. I'm sorry for her sake, but the Hogarths aren't interested at all in churches."

"Like me," said Laurence.

"No, not at all. They aren't interested in quite a different way from you."

The old woman had sipped from her glass only at long intervals. Even so, Laurence was fascinated to notice how little she had drunk, while giving the companionable appearance of keeping pace with him.

"I suppose," he said, "you made a packet between you."

"Yes. I meant to retire this year in any case."

Helena had developed a firm new theory about her mother's motives. "I am sure she involved herself in all that unpleasantness, whatever it was, simply to help the young man. My mother is extremely secretive. She is quite capable of *planning* to send him to the holy shrines, using the financial reward as a bribery."

Laurence reported this to his grandmother. She wrinkled her nose and sipped from her glass. "Of course I knew the trips would be good for Andrew. Psychologically. It gave him a job to do and a change now and then. The business side was good for me too. Psychologically. I shall miss it, dear, it was sport. Helena is sentimental, my!"

"What was Mr. Webster's role, Grandmother?"

"Oh, the good fellow baked the bread, and he sometimes

went to London for me."

"Now tell me where the bread comes in," said Laurence.

"You found diamonds in the bread, and you wrote to tell Caroline of it. That caused a lot of trouble."— Laurence, feeling sleepy from his day's work, the warmth and the beer, was not quite sure whether he heard or imagined these words.

"What did you say, Grandmother?"

The glass was at her lips. "Nothing, dear," she said when she had sipped.

"Tell me about the bread. Who transferred the diamonds to the bread? You know I saw them once."

"Mr. Webster," she said. "Because I desired to have my merchandise quickly, as soon as the Hogarths brought it in. For the sake of the London end. Sometimes, at first, there was a little delay owing to Andrew being poorly after the journey and leading Mervyn a dance. So we arranged that Mervyn should break up his saints and rosaries and extract the stones as soon as he returned from the trips, which was always in the morning. Mervyn would telephone Mr. Webster, because they use telephones, I stick to my pigeons. And then Mr. Webster called at the Hogarths' to deliver the bread."

"Ostensibly," said Laurence.

Louisa closed her eyes. "He called to deliver the bread as it might seem. You can't be too careful. And he took the money for it."

"Along with the diamonds."

"Yes, you are clever, dear. Mr. Webster has been invaluable. He would bring the merchandise to me on the following morning in my bread. I didn't think it would be nice to let him slip the little goods into my hand as if there were some mystery or anything shady going on."

"Wonderfully ingenious," Laurence said.

"It was sport," said Louisa.

"But totally unnecessary, the bread part of it," Laurence said.

"No, that was necessary. I never liked to have the diamonds carried loose."

"I can guess why," Laurence put in suddenly. "The police."

"Of course," she said. "I don't trust the police. Our local constable is a nice fellow, but the police all stick together if it comes to the bit, the world over."

Laurence laughed. Louisa's dislike of the police was a family joke. "It's the gipsy in her," Helena would explain.

"I should have thought," Laurence said, "that if you got the goods safely into the country, there would be no need for elaborate precautions."

"You never can tell. It was sport," Louisa said.

After a while Laurence said, "I believe Mrs. Hogg gave you some trouble."

"None at all," she said, "nor will she."

"You think she's likely to turn up again? Has she any evidence against you, Grandmother?"

"I don't know about that. But she won't trouble me, that I know. She might try, but I shan't be troubled." She added, "There are things about Mrs. Hogg which you don't know."

At a later time when Laurence learned of the relationship between Mrs. Hogg and the Hogarths, he recalled this remark of his grandmother's, and thought that was what she must have meant.

"And at a side altar, I do assure you, Caroline," said the Baron, "robed in full liturgical vestments, was Mervyn

199

Hogg alias Hogarth serving cocktails." Thus he ended his description of the Black Mass he had recently attended at Notting Hill Gate.

"It sounds puerile," Caroline said, lapsing unawares into that Catholic habit of belittling what was secretly feared.

"You as a Catholic," he said, "must think it evil. I myself do not judge good and evil. I judge by interesting or otherwise."

"It sounds otherwise to me," said Caroline.

"In fact you are right. This was a poor effort from the sinister point of view. For a really effective Black Mass you need a renegade priest. They are rare in these days, when the Faith is so thin. But Hogg is the one who inter*ests* me. He assumes the name of Hogg on the dark side of his life and Hogarth by daylight so to speak. I am preparing a monograph on the psychology of diabolism and black magic.

"And my informants tell me that Hogarth has recently un-bewitched his son, a man in his early twenties who since infancy has suffered from paralysis in the lower part of his body due to a spell. This proves that Hogarth's magical powers are not exclusively bent towards evil, it proves——"

"Tell me," said Caroline, "have you ever spoken to Mervyn Hogarth?"

"Not in his natural flesh. But I shall shortly. A private meeting is to be arranged. Unofficially, I believe, he has been into the bookshop, transformed into a woman."

"I'm sure, Willi," said Caroline, "that you are suffering from the emotional effects of Eleanor's leaving you. I am sure, Willi, that you should see a psychiatrist."

"If what you say were true," he said, "it would be horribly tactless of you to say it. As it is I make allowances for your own disorder."

"Is the world a lunatic asylum then? Are we all courteous maniacs discreetly making allowances for everyone else's derangement?"

"Largely," said the Baron.

"I resist the proposition," Caroline said.

"That is an intolerant attitude."

"It's the only alternative to demonstrating the proposition," Caroline said.

"I don't know," said the Baron, "really why I continue to open my mind to you."

At various times the Baron had described to Caroline the stages by which he had reached the conclusion that Mervyn Hogarth was a diabolist and magician. The first hint had come to him from Eleanor: "She told me he had previously been through a form of marriage with a witch. Eleanor had seen the witch, a repulsive woman. In fact, it was when she began to frequent the house in Ladle Sands that Eleanor left Hogarth."

"I shouldn't take much account of what Eleanor says. She dramatises a lot," said Caroline, and barely refrained from adding the information that Eleanor, in her college days, had been wont to send love-letters to herself. Caroline only refrained because she was not too sure if this were true.

"My subsequent experience has borne out her allegations. My subsequent investigations have proved that Hogarth is the foremost diabolist in the kingdom. One must speak as one experiences and as one finds. You, Caroline, are no exception. Your peculiar experiences are less explicable than mine: I have the evidence. The broken plaster images: a well-known diabolic practice: the black dog. If you would only enter*tain* the subject a little more you would see that I am right."

So he attempted to extort sympathy from Caroline. He

appeared to her more and more in the nature of a demanding creditor. "The result," she told herself, "of going to him with my troubles last autumn. He acted the old friend and now he wants me to do the same, which is impossible."

And she told him, "You are asking me to entertain impossible beliefs: what you claim may be true or not; I have doubts, I can't give assent to them. For my own experiences, however, I don't demand anyone's belief. You may call them delusions for all I care. I have merely registered my findings."

Caroline had been reflecting recently on the case of Laurence and his fantastic belief that his grandmother had for years been the leader of a gang of diamond smugglers. She had considered, also, the case of the Baron and his fantastic belief in the magical powers of Mervyn Hogarth. The Baron was beginning to show a sickly resemblance to Eleanor. She thought of Eleanor with her habit of giving spontaneous utterance to stray and irresponsible accusations. Caroline found the true facts everywhere beclouded. She was aware that the book in which she was involved was still in progress. Now, when she speculated on the story, she did so privately, noting the facts as they accumulated. By now, she possessed a large number of notes, transcribed from the voices, and these she studied carefully. Her sense of being written into the novel was painful. Of her constant influence on its course she remained unaware and now she was impatient for the story to come to an end, knowing that the narrative could never become coherent to her until she was at last outside it, and at the same time consummately inside it.

Eventually she told the Baron that she simply wasn't interested in black magic. She forbade the subject.

"It gets on my nerves, Willi. I have no sympathy with your occult interests. Talk about something else in future."

"You are lost," he said sadly, "to the world of ideas. You had the makings of an inter-esting mind, I do assure you, Caroline. Ah, well!"

One morning Caroline had an unexpected caller. She had opened the door of her flat unguardedly, expecting the parcel post. For a second Caroline got the impression that nobody was there, but then immediately she saw the woman standing heavily in the doorway and recognised the indecent smile of Mrs. Hogg just as she had last seen it at St. Philumena's.

"May I have a word with you, Miss Rose?" Already the woman was in the small square hall, taking up most of it.

"I'm busy," Caroline said. "I work in the mornings. Is it anything urgent?"

Mrs. Hogg glared with her little eyes. "It's important," she said.

"Will you come inside, then?"

She seated herself in Caroline's own chair and cast her eyes on the notebook in which Caroline had been writing. It was lying on a side table. Caroline leant forward and snapped the book shut.

"There is a Baron Stock," said Mrs. Hogg. "He was in your flat till after one o'clock this morning. He was in your flat till after two on Wednesday morning. You were in his flat till after midnight twice the week before last. If you think you are going to catch Laurence Manders with this carry-on——"

"You are insolent," Caroline said. "You'll have to leave."

"Till after two on Wednesday morning. Baron Stock is more attractive than Laurence Manders, I don't doubt, but I think it low behaviour and so would everyone——"

"Take yourself off," said Caroline.

She left, pathetic and lumpy as a public response. Caroline seized the phone angrily and rang Helena.

"Would you mind calling off your Mrs. Hogg. She's just been round here making wild insinuations about my private life, citing Willi Stock. She must have been watching my flat for weeks. Haven't you any control over the woman? I do think, Helena, you are far too soft with that woman. She's a beast. If there's any more trouble I shall simply call the police, tell her that."

"Dear me. I haven't seen Mrs. Hogg for months. I *am* sorry, Caroline. Won't you come round to lunch? I recommended Mrs. Hogg for a job in a place at Streatham last autumn. I haven't heard from her since. We've got a new sort of risotto, quite simple, and heaps to spare. Edwin won't be in to lunch. Have you seen Laurence lately?"

"You ought not to recommend Mrs. Hogg for jobs. She's quite vile."

"Oh, one tries to be charitable. I shall speak severely. Did she upset you seriously, Caroline?"

"No, she did not. I mean, she did, yes. But it's not what she says, it's what she is."

"She's not all there," said Helena.

Presently, Caroline sprayed the room with a preparation for eliminating germs and insects.

9

"WONDERFUL TO HAVE A WHOLE DAY UN-
planned," Caroline said. "It's like a blank sheet of paper to
be filled in according to inspiration." It was summer, on a
day which Laurence described as absolutely perfect for a
riverside picnic. They chose their spot and got the luncheon boxes out of the car. It was Laurence's day off. Helena
too had decided to have a day off.

"I've been working so hard on the committees, and
Edwin is in retreat—I should love a day in the country,"
she admitted when Laurence invited her to join them.
"But I hate intruding. You and Caroline enjoy yourselves
together, do."

But she yielded easily when Caroline too insisted on her
coming.

"All right. But you two go ahead. I'll join you before
lunch, if you tell me where to find you."

They described the area where they intended to park,
on the banks of the Medway where it borders Kent and
Sussex.

There they were at midday sunning themselves lus-
ciously and keeping an intermittent look-out for Helena's
car.

She arrived at half-past twelve, and they could see as
she bumped down the track towards them that she had
brought two people with her, a man beside her in the
front and a woman with a black hat at the back.

The couple turned out to be the Baron and Mrs. Hogg.

Helena, uncertain of their welcome, and unusually nervous, began immediately,

"Such fun. Willi phoned me just after you'd left and d'you know what, he's been meaning to come down here the first opportunity. He wants to look at an Abbey in these parts, don't you, Willi? So I made him come. And I've brought poor Mrs. Hogg, I made her come. It was a lovely ride, wasn't it? Poor Georgina's had neuralgia. She called round to the house by chance just after you'd left, so I made her come. A day in the country will do you a world of good, Georgina. We shan't interfere with your plans, Laurence. We've brought extra lunch and you can go off by yourselves if you like while we sit in the sun."

Helena looked a trifle shaky. While they prepared lunch she made the opportunity of a private word with Caroline,

"I hope you don't mind dreadfully, dear, about my bringing Georgina. She turned up so desolate, and there was I so obviously preparing the picnic basket. I asked her on impulse and of course she jumped to it—I was rather sorry afterwards, remembering how much you dislike her. Do try to ignore her and if she says anything funny to you just shake her off. I know how you feel about Georgina for I can't bear the sight of her at times, but one tries to be charitable."

"Don't you think," Caroline said, "that you misconstrue charity?"

"Well, charity," said Helena, "begins at home. And Georgina *has* been part of our household."

"Mrs. Hogg is not home," Caroline said.

"Oh dear, I wish I hadn't asked her to come. It was foolish of me, I've spoiled your day."

"The day isn't over yet," said Caroline cordially, for

the weather was glorious really.

"But still I wish I hadn't brought her, for another reason. Something happened on the way here, Caroline. It was disturbing." Caroline saw she was distressed.

"Come over here and help me to take out the bottles," Caroline said, "and tell me what happened."

"I gave Georgina a tablet for her neuralgia before we set off," Helena said, "and sat her comfortably at the back of the car. Before we were out of London I said over my shoulder, 'Are you all right, Georgina?' She replied that she was feeling sleepy. I went on chatting to Willi and thought no more of Georgina at the back. I assumed she had fallen asleep for I could hear her breathing rather heavily."

"She snores," Caroline said. "I remember at St. Philumena's I could hear her snoring six doors away."

"Well, yes, she was snoring," Helena said. "And I thought the sleep would do her good. After a while she stopped snoring. I said to Willi, 'She's dead asleep.' Then Willi's cigarette lighter gave out and he asked for some matches. I thought there were some at the back of the car, but I didn't want to wake Georgina. So I pulled up. And when I turned to reach for the matches, I couldn't see Georgina."

"Why, what had happened?"

"She simply wasn't there," Helena declared. "I said to Willi, 'Heavens, where's Georgina?' and Willi said, 'My God! she's gone!' Well, just as he said this, we saw Georgina again. She suddenly appeared before our eyes at the back of the car, sitting in the same position and blinking, as if she'd just then woken up. It was as if there'd been a blackout at the films. I would have thought I'd been dreaming the incident, but Willi apparently had the same experience.

He said, 'Where have you been, Mrs. Hogg? You vanished, didn't you?' She looked really surprised, she said, 'I've been asleep, sir.' "

"It may have been some telepathic illusion shared by you and Willi," Caroline said. "I shouldn't worry."

"Maybe it was. I haven't had an opportunity to discuss this privately with Willi. It was a most strange affair; truly I wish I hadn't brought Georgina. Sometimes I feel I can handle her, but at other times she seems to get the better of me."

"Maybe when she goes to sleep she disappears as a matter of course," Caroline said with a dry laugh so that Helena would not take her too seriously.

"What a gruesome idea. Well, I swear that she did apparently vanish. All I saw when I first looked round was the empty seat."

"Maybe she has no private life whatsoever," Caroline said, and she giggled to take the grim edge off her words.

"Oh, she has no private life, poor soul," Helena agreed, meaning that the woman had no friends.

Mrs. Hogg ate heartily at lunch. Caroline sat as far away from her as possible to avoid the sight of her large mouth chewing, and the memory of that sight when, at St. Philumena's, she had first observed Mrs. Hogg sitting opposite to her at the refectory table, chew—pause—chew—pause. Mrs. Hogg spoke little, but she was very much present.

After lunch, Caroline was stacking an empty food box in the boot of Helena's car some distance from the rest of the party, when the Baron approached her.

"Summer suits you, my Caroline," he said. "Your sun dress is charming. Green suits you, and you are plumper. I thought you a delightful picture at lunch, so secluded within your proud personality as you always seem to be and with such a watchful air."

Caroline appreciated flattery, the more so when it was plainly excessive and well laid on, for then she felt that the flatterer had really taken pains to please. So she smiled languidly and waited for the rest, not at all surprised that these remarks were a prelude to one of those "confidences" which the Baron so greatly longed to make. For, since she had forbidden the subject of black magic, the Baron had been manifestly unhappy. She realised that he had chosen her as a repository for his secret enthusiasm because of that very edginess and snap with which she responded. If, like his other friends, she could have been merely sociable about his esoteric interests, making a gay palaver of them —"Do describe the formula, Willi, for changing oneself into a fly. One could watch all one's friends. . . . Suppose one got stuck in a pot of jam"—if only she could have played buoyant and easy with the Baron, he never would have plagued her with his "confidences."

Having lubricated the way with his opening speech he proceeded instantly,

"I must tell you, Caroline, such a strange thing happened in the car as we came down. This woman, Mrs. Hogg——"

Caroline tried to be pleasant. "Helena has already told me of the incident. Obviously, Willi, you've been infecting Helena with your fancies. Obviously——"

"I do assure you, Caroline, I have never discussed any occult subject with Helena. I am very careful in whom I confide these matters. There is no other way of accounting for the strange phenomenon in the car but to accept the fact that this woman Hogg is a witch."

"Not necessarily," Caroline said, "even if she did disappear. I think she's too ignorant to be a witch." And she added, "Not that I believe in witches particularly."

"And I have made a curious discovery," the Baron continued relentlessly. "Don't you see—this woman Hogg is, I am certain, the witch to whom Mervyn Hogarth was married. The facts meet together—he *has* been known to use the name Hogg, as I told you. My informants say he always used it in his younger days. This Georgina Hogg is his witch-wife."

"Nonsense. She's an old servant of the Manders'. I believe she married a cousin. She has a crippled son somewhere."

"Has she?—Then it is certain she is the one, the witch, the wife! It is her son who was cured a few months ago by Hogarth's magic. It must be the same young man!"

"Awfully far-fetched," Caroline said. "And, Willi, all this bores me." In fact it agitated her, as he could see. "That Hogarth crest," she was thinking, "on Eleanor's cigarette case. Laurence identified it, the same as Mrs. Hogg's. . . ." She decided to speak of this to Laurence later on.

Just then Helena shouted,

"Caroline, will you fetch my book—I threw it in at the back of the boot with my little head cushion. Will you fetch that too?"

"Hell!" Caroline breathed.

It meant unloading the entire contents of the boot. The Baron helped Caroline to ease them out of the tiny space, while he talked as fast as he could, as if to get in as much as possible of his precious confidences in the next few moments.

"It is the same young man," he said, "and you will see that I am right."

"You must be wrong," said Caroline, out of breath with the effort of shifting the boxes, old petrol cans and other clutter. She was reminding herself that only the other day Helena had said, "Fancy, I told Mrs. Hogg about that wonderful miracle that happened to the Hogarth boy. I thought it might give her some hope for her own son who's a cripple. But do you know, she wouldn't believe it was a miracle—she said if it had been a real miracle the young man would have become a Catholic. Unfortunately this Hogarth boy has gone off with some woman—a rich theosophist, I understand. Perhaps I shouldn't have told Georgina that bit."

"You must be wrong," Caroline told the Baron. "Helena knows Georgina Hogg's affairs. Ask Helena, she'll confirm that Mrs. Hogg has nothing to do with Hogarth." Again, she wondered about that crest.

"Helena does *not* know," said the Baron. "And another thing, Caroline. So exciting, Caroline. I am going to see Mervyn Hogarth this afternoon. I have been informed that he is staying at an Abbey a few miles from this spot. Now why should he be staying at a religious house? He must be posing as a Catholic retreatant. I daresay that these are the means he uses for stealing the consecrated elements for use in the Black Mass. After all, he must get them from somewhere——"

Caroline caught his sleeve and nodded towards the hedge-row a few yards from where the car was parked. He looked in that direction. The black hat had just bobbed out of sight.

"Mrs. Hogg has been listening," Caroline said in a loud voice.

"Did you call me, Miss Rose?"

Mrs. Hogg came out of hiding as if she had never been in it.

"Lovely round here," she said with her smile. "Did you call? I thought you called 'Mrs. Hogg.'"

Caroline walked away quickly, followed by the Baron, while Mrs. Hogg made off along the towpath.

Caroline handed Helena the book. "It had slipped down at the very back," she said, "I had to move everything. I feel as exhausted as if I'd done a hard day's work."

"Oh, you shouldn't have—I thought Willi was doing all the heaving. Willi, why didn't you do all the heaving?"

"I did so, my Helena," said the Baron.

"Mrs. Hogg was bent behind the hedge listening to our conversation," Caroline said.

"I take an oriental view of manual labour myself," said Laurence. He was stretched in the dappling shade of a tree.

"She has nothing in her life," Helena said, "that's her trouble. She always has been a nosey type. Simply because she hasn't any life of her own. I'm sorry I brought her. I dread taking her back."

Laurence gurgled. "I think that's sweet." Helena had not told him of their creepy experience with Georgina that morning.

"I've sent her off for a walk," said Helena, looking round. "I wonder if she'll be all right." Georgina was nowhere in sight.

"Georgina is nowhere in sight," she said anxiously.

"You've sent her off; well, she's gone off," Laurence said. "Stop jittering. Relax. Read your book. There's too much talking."

"Which way did she go?" Helena said.

"Downstream, by the towpath," said Caroline.

"Silence," said Laurence. "Let nothing disturb thee," he chanted, "nothing affright thee, all things are passing. . . ."

"God never changeth," Helena continued, surprised that he had remembered the words.

The Baron was examining a map. "I should be back just after four," he said. "Will that do?"

"Perfectly," said Laurence. "Kindly depart."

"The Abbey is on the other side of the river," said the Baron, "but there's a bridge two miles down. I shall be back just after four."

He set off with his jacket trailing over his arm. Lazily, they watched him until he was out of sight round a bend.

"I wonder why he wants to see the Abbey," said Helena, "it isn't an exceptional place, nothing architecturally speaking."

"He's looking for a man he believes is staying at the Abbey. A man called Mervyn Hogarth," Caroline said deliberately.

Helena looked startled. "Mervyn Hogarth! Does Willi know him then?"

"By hearsay," Caroline said.

"That's the father of the young man who was cured," Helena said. "Has Mr. Hogarth become a Catholic, I wonder?"

"The Baron thinks," Caroline said, "that he is a magician. The Baron believes that Mervyn Hogarth is the leader of a Black Mass circle and that he's staying at the Abbey under the guise of a retreatant, but really on purpose to steal the consecrated Host."

"Oh how frightful, oh how frightful!"

"The Baron has a kink," Laurence put in.

"Exactly," said Caroline.

"It does sound a far-fetched story," Helena said. "There's nothing in it, you think?"

"Nothing at all," Caroline said. "I should be surprised if he found Mervyn Hogarth at the Abbey. And more surprised if his suspicions were true."

"It would be dreadful if they were true," Helena said. "But why should Willi Stock be troubled if they were; does he intend to expose the man?"

213

"No, he intends to write a monograph."

Caroline put the palms of her hands out to the sun.

"He thinks he is aloof from the subject of black magic, merely inter-ested. Whereas he is passionately attracted to it. 'My nature,'" she quoted, "'is subdued to what it works in, like the dyer's hand. Pity me then. . . .'"

"Willi always has been eccentric," Helena remarked.

"Part of his cultivated Englishness," said Laurence.

"It will be interesting," Helena said, "to hear what he says when he comes back."

"Don't mention what I've told you," Caroline said, "he's touchy, poor Willi."

She felt a sweet pleasure in her words, "Poor Willi!" They soothed her resentment of the Baron's "Poor Caroline!" with which he must have ended many an afternoon's session at Charing Cross Road. Especially with Helena was she pleased to discredit the Baron. Sometimes Helena would enquire gently of Caroline if she was quite happy— nothing worrying her? From which Caroline was sensitive to assume that the Baron had been talking. In fact, Helena had discouraged the Baron's gossip. One day in the early spring he had asked her plainly,

"Is it all off between Laurence and Caroline?"

"No, I don't think so. They are waiting."

"For what? My dear, they are not chicks," said the Baron.

"I suppose Caroline wants to get her book off her hands. But I don't know their business at all really. I wish they would do something definite, but there it is."

"Caroline's 'book,'" he said; "do you mean the book she is writing or the one in which she lives?"

"Now, Willi! Caroline is not a silly girl. She did have a little upset and imagined things, I know. And then there was the accident. But since that time she's recovered wonderfully."

"*My* dear Helena, I do assure you that Caroline has been receiving communications from her Typing Spooks continuously since that time."

"Nonsense. Caroline is perfectly sane. What's going to win the Lincoln, do you think, Willi?"

And so, occasionally, when Helena asked Caroline, "Quite happy now, dear?" or "Nothing worrying you?" Caroline would be unhappy and worrying about these enquiries.

So, on the day of the picnic she was especially happy to discuss the Baron's latest fantasy with Helena.

"He must have built up a theory," said Helena, "on rumours and suspicions. I hate," she said with unusual force, "doubt and suspicion."

Caroline thought, "She is worried about Mrs. Hogg. The affair in the car is pressing on her mind. Poor Helena! Perhaps she would not at all like to know things clearly."

Laurence lay listening to their voices, contentedly oblivious of what they said. He was too somnolent in the warmth of the sun to take part in the conversation and too enchanted by his sense of the summer day to waste it in sleep. He watched the movements of a young fat woman on a houseboat moored nearby. Every now and then she would disappear into the cabin to fetch something. First a bright scarf to protect her head from the sun. Then a cushion. Next she went below for so long a time, as it seemed to Laurence, that he thought she was never coming back. But she did emerge again, with a cup of tea. She drank it propped tubbily on the tiny bridge of the boat. Laurence spent his pleasurable idleness of long meaningless moments in following every sip. He wished the houseboat were his. He wondered where the man of the house could be, for he was sure there must be a man, referred to by

Tubby as "my friend." Laurence wished it were possible for him to go on lying drowsily by the river and at the same time to poke about in the cabin of the boat, to pry into the cooking arrangements, the bunks, the engine. A little rowing boat which lay alongside caught Laurence's fancy.

It came home to him that Caroline was saying, "I'll start the kettle for tea."

She had lit the spirit stove when Helena said,

"Thunder."

"No," said Laurence. "Couldn't be. I was just thinking," he said, "we might be able to borrow that little boat and row over to the other side."

"*I* thought I heard a rumble," Caroline said.

"No."

"It's quarter past four," Helena said. "I wonder where Georgina has got to?"

"Spirited away," said Laurence remarkably.

Helena roused him to scout round for Georgina.

"I'm sure it's going to rain," she said.

The sky had clouded, and in spite of Laurence's protests the barking of distant thunder was undeniable.

"The thunder's miles away over the downs," Laurence said, "it will miss the valley." Nevertheless, he went off in search of Mrs. Hogg, pausing on the way to look more closely at the houseboat. The plump girl had gone inside.

Caroline and Helena started to move their rugs and tea-cups into the cars.

"Even if we miss the storm," Helena said, "it will certainly set in to rain within the next ten minutes."

Suddenly they caught sight of the Baron on the opposite bank. He shouted something, but he was too far from them to be heard. With his hands describing a circuit he conveyed that he was coming back by the bridge.

"He'll get soaked," Caroline said. "Poor Willi!" But before he set off again she waved him to stop.

"I'll ask for the boat," she said, "and row him over."

"That *would* be nice," Helena said. "Sure you can manage it?"

But Caroline, with Laurence's raincoat over her shoulders, was away to the houseboat. The Baron stood perplexed for a moment. He saw Caroline bend down and knock at the little window. He understood the plan, then, and waited. In a few moments Caroline signed to him that she had the owner's permission to use the boat.

The rain had started, but it was light and the river calm. Caroline reached him within a few moments. He climbed into the boat and took the oars from her.

"I got a sight of Hogarth," he said immediately, "alias Hogg, but he was in disguise. Quite a different appearance from the man I saw conducting the Black Mass. In the circumstances I did not address him, it was too frightening."

"How did you know it was Mervyn Hogarth, then?"

"I asked one of the lay-brothers. He confirmed that Mervyn Hogarth was staying there, and pointed him out. *They* believe he is come to the Abbey for the fishing."

"What fishing?"

"Apparently the Abbey rents out a strip of fishing ground. They put up the anglers in the Abbey," said the Baron. "Little do they know whom they are harbouring. Hogarth alias Hogg," he said.

"I think you are mixed up, Willi." Caroline pulled the raincoat over her head and patted her hair beneath it. "The man at the Black Mass must have been a different Hogarth."

"Oh no, *he* was named Hogg. Hogarth is the daytime name. I know for a fact that Mervyn Hogarth was born

Mervyn Hogg."

"The man at the Black Mass must have been a different Hogg."

"I have the whole picture, which you have not," the Baron said. "This afternoon, as I was leaving the Abbey grounds I saw the witch, Mrs. Hogg, entering them. I turned back and followed her. I *saw*—actually saw, Caroline—Mrs. Hogg approaching Hogarth. He was doing something to a fishing rod at the time. He recognised her of course. He looked very miserable. They exchanged a few words. Soon, he walked away and left her. The couple are clearly known to each other."

They had landed. Caroline thanked the woman while the Baron tied up the boat.

"There's no sign of Georgina," Helena said as they reached her car. "Laurence has been back and he's gone off again to search for her. What a nuisance."

"She was over at the Abbey," said the Baron. "I left her there half an hour ago."

"How vexing. Well, we shall have to wait. Let's try and continue some tea in the back of the car."

The thunder was still distant. The storm that was raging some miles away seemed unlikely to reach them, but now the rain was heavy.

"Which way did Laurence go?" the Baron said.

"Towards the bridge."

"I'll take his car and meet him. I daresay I shall pick up Mrs. Hogg on her way back. She must be at the bridge by now."

He drove off. Every few minutes Helena poked her head out of the back window of her car. "I hope they don't miss each other," she said, "Laurence only has his jacket. Oh, there's Georgina!"

Mrs. Hogg was coming down to the riverside by a track

through the trees on the opposite bank. She saw **Helena** **and** raised her hand in recognition.

Helena made a frantic dumb-show at her. Mrs. **Hogg** stood waiting and stupid-looking.

"Caroline," said Helena, "be an angel."

"You want me to fetch her in the boat," Caroline stated.

"Put the mac over your head, do." Helena was **nervy.** "We shall be kept waiting here for ages if she has to plod round by the bridge. It's two miles each way. I'm dying **to** get home."

When Caroline did not reply, Helena seemed aware **of** having asked more than an ordinary favour.

"I'll go, dear," said Helena at once. "Give me the mac. I'm sure I can manage the boat."

Caroline was sure she couldn't. She jumped out of **the** car and was off like someone taking a plunge **against** nature.

In spite of the rain, with only a cardigan over her sum-mer dress, Helena followed. She caught up Caroline **at** the houseboat, and added her gracious thanks to the owner. As Caroline unmoored she said,

"This really is charitable, Caroline. Poor Georgina would be drenched if she had to walk round to cross the bridge."

Caroline gave her an amiable smile, for she was **too** proud to reveal her neurotic dread. Her dread was on ac-count of a very small thing. She knew she would have **to** give Mrs. Hogg a hand into the boat. The anticipation **of** this physical contact, her hand in Mrs. Hogg's only **for** a moment, horrified Caroline. It was a very small thing, but it was what she constitutionally dreaded.

"Step down here, Mrs. Hogg. On to that stone. **Give** me your hand. Take care, the river's deep here."

The bank had grown muddy but there were several **firm**

footholds. Caroline, standing astride in the boat, reached out and grasped Mrs. Hogg's hand firmly. Step there, now there. "I'm doing fine," Caroline thought, gripping the woman's hand tightly in her own. She was filled with the consciousness of hand.

Mrs. Hogg had rubber-soled shoes which had picked up a good deal of mud. In spite of all her care she slipped on her heels, she tottered backwards with her hand still gripped in Caroline's so that the boat rocked wildly. In an instant she was loudly in the water and Caroline, still grasping the hand by the first compulsive need to overcome her horror of it, went with her. Mrs. Hogg lashed about her in a screaming panic. Caroline freed herself and gripped the side of the boat. But she was wrenched away, the woman's hands were on her neck—"I can't swim!"

Caroline struck her in the face. "Hold on to my shoulders," she shouted. "I can swim." But the woman in her extremity was intent on Caroline's throat. Caroline saw the little boat bobbing away downstream. Then her sight became blocked by one of Mrs. Hogg's great hands clawing across her eyes, the other hand tightening on her throat. Mrs. Hogg's body, and even legs, encompassed Caroline so that her arms were restricted. She knew then that if she could not free herself from Mrs. Hogg they would both go under.

They were under water and out of sight for a while. Helena said later that it was only a matter of seconds before Caroline's head emerged. But in that space of time it was a long breath-holding contest between them. Caroline had practised underwater swimming. Not so, Mrs. Hogg. The woman clung to Caroline's throat until the last. It was not until Mrs. Hogg opened her mouth finally to the inrush of water that her grip slackened and Caroline was free, her lungs aching for the breath of life. Mrs. Hogg subsided away from her. God knows where she went.

Caroline had the sense of being hauled along a bumpy surface, of being landed with a thud like a gasping fish, before she passed out.

"Jolly good luck I had my friend here. I can't swim myself."

Caroline lay in the bunk of the houseboat, without a sense or even a care of where she was. She recognised Helena, then the plump woman of the houseboat and a strange man who was taking off all his dripping wet clothes. Caroline had a sense of childhood, and she closed her eyes.

"There was no sign of the other," the man was saying. "She's had it. Any relation?"

"No," said Helena's voice.

"She gave this one a rough time," said the man. "Just look at her face. I'll bet she's been trained to hold her breath under water. If she hadn't, she'd have had it too, this one."

The woman of the houseboat helped Caroline to sip from a warm beaker.

"Have you anything to put on the scratches?" That was Helena.

Presently Caroline felt something soft being smoothed over her face and throat. Her neck was hurting. And again she was sipping something warm and sweet, her shoulders supported by Helena.

The man said, "I had a look for the other, best I could. It's deep in that spot. I daresay we'll get the body. There was a tragedy five summers back and we got the body two days after."

Helena murmured, "You've been marvellous."

Before she went off to sleep, Caroline heard Laurence's

221

voice from somewhere outside, then the Baron's, **then** Helena again,

"Here they are with the doctor."

Sir Edwin Manders was making his autumn retreat. October 24th, the Feast of St. Raphael the Archangel; he had arrived at the monastery during the afternoon in time for Benediction.

The window of his room looked down on a green courtyard over which the leaves were scattering. Fixing his eye on this sunlit square of leaves and grass, he gave himself to think about his surprising family affairs.

Usually when he was in retreat this man would give his time, under a spiritual director, to regarding the state of his soul. In the past few months he had been given cause to wonder if he did not make his retreats too frequently. Amazing things occurred at home; extraordinary events which he never heard of till later.

"Why didn't you inform me at the time, Helena?"

"You were in retreat, Edwin."

He had misgivings then, about his retreats. He told his spiritual director, "I might have done better to spend the time at home. My family have had to cope with difficulties . . . my son . . . my brother . . . my mother-in-law . . . one of our old servants . . . I might have done better had I not made so many retreats."

"You might have done worse," said the shrewd old priest, and sounded as if he meant it. It was a humiliating thought, which in turn was good for the soul.

"They manage admirably without me," Edwin Manders admitted.

And so he was in retreat again. Really on this occasion he had not wanted to come. But Helena insisted. Ernest even, in his shy way, had said, "Someone has got to pray for us, Edwin." Laurence had said, "Cancel your autumn

222

retreat? Oh you can't do that," without giving any reasons. Caroline Rose had driven him to the station.

For years he had felt drawn to the contemplative life. To partake more fully of it he had retired, all but nominally, from Manders' Figs. Helena took pride in his frequent recourse to monasteries. In fact he was embarrassed at this moment to realise how effectively she had fostered the legend of his "certain sanctity." More and more he had felt attracted by the ascetic formalities. Only this autumn, in his hesitation before leaving home, did he feel he was being pushed into it.

He had no more qualms after his arrival at the monastery. The charm began to work on him. His austere cell was like a drug. The rise and fall of plainsong from the Chapel invited him into its abiding pure world. The noiseless, timeless lay-brothers moved amenably about their business, causing Edwin Manders to feel pleasurably humble in the presence of this profound elect. The fact that there was a big upset going on in the monastic quarters of the buildings due to half the bedrooms being flooded by a burst pipe, that one of the lay-brothers was sick to death of his life, that the Abbot was worried about an overdraft, was mercifully concealed from Edwin at that moment. And so he was sufficiently unhampered by material distractions to see his spiritual temptation plain, which being so, he found it after all resistable, that luxurious nostalgia, that opium daze of devotion, for he knew, more or less, that he never would have made a religious. He gave his mind to reviewing his family affairs.

There were two items in the embarrassing category, for both had reached the newspapers. He was in doubt which was the more distressing, Louisa Jepp's case or Georgina Hogg's. He decided, on the whole, Georgina's. And for a good half-hour he concentrated on Georgina, now lodged, it was believed, in the mud of the Medway, for her body was never recovered. There was a piece in the London evening papers, mentioning by name Helena, Laurence, Caroline, Baron Stock, and the couple on the houseboat. There was an inquest. Poor Helena. In former days, he recalled, their name for Georgina in the household was Manders' Mortification.

As he heard afterwards, for he was in retreat at the time, Helena got Laurence to make enquiries for poor Mrs. Hogg's son. He turned out to be an unfortunate person. The father a bigamist. Helena dropped her enquiries as soon as she learned that Eleanor Hogarth was involved in the bigamy; innocently no doubt, but she was in partnership with his brother Ernest, another embarrassment . . . Helena hushed it up. Helena was marvellous.

"We had a sort of forewarning of Mrs. Hogg's death. Willi Stock and I were on our way to the picnic, with Georgina at the back. . . ."

Women were rather fanciful, of course. Edwin often wondered if there was any truth in the story that Mrs. Hogg's son was miraculously cured. Helena was convinced of it. There had been nothing official on the subject. The man in question had been taken under the wing of a wealthy woman, a Theist or Theosophist, something like that. Anyway, the later news was that he had left that woman's house and departed for Canada to lecture there about his cure.

"In spite of which," Edwin thought, "young Hogarth may be a worthier man than me."

Likewise, when he turned to Baron Stock, he murmured, "Miserere mei, Deus." The Baron, probably a better man than himself, was having treatment in a private mental home and, according to accounts, loving it. He thought of his brother Ernest, so worldly and yet so short of money and not perhaps really keen on that dancing girl. He forced himself to consider Eleanor. . . . "All these people have suffered while I have fattened on fasting." He meant what he said, and so truly he was not as limited as he seemed.

And to think of his mother-in-law! He reflected, now, unflinchingly on the question of Louisa Jepp. There again he could not quite grasp . . . smuggling diamonds, a gang, it sounded like an adventure story. Then there was Louisa's real folly and it was quite embarrassing. Heroically he forced his mind to that moment in September when, at breakfast, Helena limply passed him a letter. The letter was from Louisa. With it was a press cutting from a local paper. The press cutting was headed "Sunset Wedding." It was a long piece. It began "In the sunset of their lives two of the old folks of Ladylees have come together in Holy Matrimony. At All Saints' on Saturday last, Mrs. Louisa Jepp, 78, of Smugglers' Retreat, Ladylees, gave her hand in marriage to Mr. J. G. L. Webster, 77, of the Old Mill, Ladylees. . . . The bride promised to 'obey'. . . ." This was followed by a substantial account of Webster and his career in the Merchant Navy, and the column ended, "Mrs. Jepp (now Webster) has one daughter, Lady Manders, wife of Sir Edwin Manders, head of the famous firm, Manders' Figs in Syrup. The Rev. R. Socket who conducted the ceremony stated, 'This is a very happy and unique occasion. Though not a regular churchgoer, Mrs. Jepp is a figure much loved and respected in the district.' "

The accompanying letter was brief. In it Louisa remarked, "It is not strictly accurate to say that I am not a regular churchgoer as I go to church regularly on Remembrance Day."

"It isn't for us to judge her wisdom," Helena said glumly.

Edwin stared out at the green quadrangle, the blown leaves. Miserere nobis. . . . Have mercy.

Laurence and Caroline had been high-spirited about

Louisa's marriage. That was to be expected of Laurence. He had always adored his grandmother; and indeed she was charming, indeed.

Edwin wondered if Caroline herself was really interested in marriage.

"She's waiting for Laurence to return to the Church," Helena said.

He wondered. Caroline was an odd sort of Catholic, very little heart for it, all mind.

"That dreadful experience with poor Georgina in the river hasn't had any harmful effects on Caroline," Helena said. "She must have a strong constitution. In fact, since then she's been much more light-hearted. She seems to be amused by something, I don't know what."

Caroline had finished her book about novels. Now she announced she was going away on a long holiday. She was going to write a novel.

"I don't call that a holiday," said Helena, "not if you mean to spend it writing a novel."

"This is a holiday of obligation," Caroline replied.

"What is the novel to be about?"

Caroline answered, "Characters in a novel."

Edwin himself had said, "Make it a straight old-fashioned story, no modern mystifications. End with the death of the villain and the marriage of the heroine."

Caroline laughed and said, "Yes, it would end that way."

A few weeks later the character called Laurence Manders was snooping around in Caroline Rose's flat. She was away in Worcestershire writing her novel, and he had gone to the flat to collect some books which she had asked to be sent to her.

He took his time. In fact, the books were the last things he looked for.

He thought, "What am I looking for?" and flicked the dresses in her wardrobe.

He found the books that Caroline wanted, but before he left he sat down at Caroline's desk and wrote her a letter.

"I have spent 2 hours 28 mins. in your flat," he wrote. "I have found those books for you, and had a look round. Why did you lock the right hand drawer in the wall cupboard? I had difficulty in getting it open, and then the hair curlers in one box and the scarves in another, and the white gloves were all I found. I can't lock it again. I have just found myself wondering what I was looking for.

"I found an enormous sheaf of your notes for your novel in the cupboard in that carton marked Keep in a Cool Place. Why did you leave them behind? What's the point of making notes if you don't use them while you are writing the book?

"Do you want me to send the notes to you?

"I wonder if you left them on purpose, so that I should read them?

"But I remember your once saying you always made a lot of notes for a book, then never referred to them. I feel very niggled.

"I will tell you what I think of your notes:

(1) You misrepresent all of us.

(2) Obviously you are the martyr-figure. 'Martyrdom by misunderstanding.' But actually you yourself understand nobody, for instance the Baron, my father, myself, we are martyred by your misunderstanding.

(3) I love you. I think you are hopelessly selfish.

(4) I dislike being a character in your novel. How is it all going to end?"

Laurence wrote a long letter, re-read it, then folded and sealed it. He put it in his pocket, stacked away Caroline's notes in their place in the carton in the cupboard.

227

The autumn afternoon was darkening as he turned into Hampstead Heath. Religion had so changed Caroline. At one time he had thought it would make life easier for her, and indirectly for himself. "You have to be involved personally," Caroline had said on one occasion, infuriating him by the know-all assumption of the words. At least, he thought, I am honest; I misunderstand Caroline. His letter had failed to express his objections. He took it out of his pocket and tore it up into small pieces, scattering them over the Heath where the wind bore them away. He saw the bits of paper come to rest, some on the scrubby ground, some among the deep marsh weeds, and one piece on a thorn-bush; and he did not then foresee his later wonder, with a curious rejoicing, how the letter had got into the book.

The Ballad
of
Peckham Rye

For
ROBIN
with love

Chapter One

"Get away from here, you dirty swine," she said.

"There's a dirty swine in every man," he said.

"Showing your face round here again," she said.

"Now, Mavis, now, Mavis," he said.

She was seen to slam the door in his face, and he to press the bell, and she to open the door again.

"I want a word with Dixie," he said. "Now, Mavis, be reasonable."

"My daughter," Mavis said, "is not in." She slammed the door in his face.

All the same, he appeared to consider the encounter so far satisfactory. He got back into the little Fiat and drove away along the Grove and up to the Common where he parked outside the Rye Hotel. Here he lit a cigarette, got out, and entered the saloon bar.

Three men of retired age at the far end turned from the television and regarded him. One of them nudged his friend. A woman put her hand to her chin and turned to her companion with a look.

His name was Humphrey Place. He was that fellow that walked out on his wedding a few weeks ago. He walked across to the White Horse and drank one bitter.

Next he visited the Morning Star and the Heaton Arms. He finished up at the Harbinger.

The pub door opened and Trevor Lomas walked in. Trevor was seen to approach Humphrey and hit him on the mouth. The barmaid said, "Outside, both of you."

"It wouldn't have happened if Dougal Douglas hadn't come here," a woman remarked.

He was standing at the altar with Trevor, the best man, behind him. Dixie came up the aisle on the arm of Arthur Crewe, her stepfather. There must have been thirty-odd guests in the church. Arthur Crewe was reported in the papers next day as having said: "I had a feeling the wedding wouldn't come off." At the time he stepped up the aisle with Dixie, tall in her flounces, her eyes dark and open, and with a very little trace round the nose of a cold.

She had said, "Keep away from me. You'll catch my cold, Humphrey. It's bad enough me having a cold for the wedding."

But he said, "I want to catch your cold. I like to think of the germs hopping from you to me."

"I know where you got all these disgusting ideas from. You got them from Dougal Douglas. Well, I'm glad he's gone and there won't be him at the wedding to worry about in case he starts showing off the lumps on his head or something."

"I liked Dougal," Humphrey said.

Here they were, kneeling at the altar. The vicar was reading from the prayer book. Dixie took a lacy handkerchief from her sleeve and gently patted her nose. Humphrey noticed the whiff of scent which came from the handkerchief.

The vicar said to Humphrey, "Wilt thou have this woman to thy wedded wife?"

"No," Humphrey said, "to be quite frank I won't."

He got to his feet and walked straight up the aisle. The guests in the pews rustled as if they were all women. Humphrey got to the door, into his Fiat, and drove off by himself to Folkestone. It was there they had planned to spend their honeymoon.

He drove past the Rye, down Rye Lane round-about to Lewisham, past the Dutch House and on to Swanley, past Wrotham Hill and along the A20 to Ditton, where he stopped for a drink. After Maidstone he got through the Ashford by-pass and stopped again at a pub. He drove on to Folkestone, turning left at the Motel Lympne, where yellow headlamps of the French cars began to appear on the road as they had done before. He stayed in the hotel on the front in the double room booked for the honeymoon, and paid double without supplying explanations to the peering, muttering management.

"Outside," said the barmaid. Humphrey rose, finished his drink with a flourish, regarded his handsome hit face in the mirror behind the barmaid, and followed Trevor Lomas out into the autumn evening, while a woman behind them in the pub remarked, "It wouldn't have happened if Dougal Douglas hadn't come here."

Trevor prepared for a fight, but Humphrey made no move to retaliate; he turned up towards the Rye where his car was parked and where, beside it, Trevor had left his motor-scooter.

Trevor Lomas caught him up. "And you can keep away from round here," he said.

Humphrey stopped. He said, "You after Dixie?"

"What's that to you?"

Humphrey hit him. Trevor hit back. There was a fight. Two courting couples returning from the dusky scope of the Rye's broad lyrical acres stepped to the opposite pavement, leant on the railings by the swimming baths, and watched. Eventually the fighters, each having suffered equal damage to different features of the face, were parted by onlookers to save the intervention of the police.

After Humphrey had been sent away from the door, and the matter had been discussed, Dixie Morse, aged seventeen, daughter of the first G.I. bride to have departed from Peckham and returned, stood in her little room on the upper floor of 12 Rye Grove and scrutinised her savings book. As she counted she exercised her pretty hips, jerking them from side to side to the rhythm of *Pickin' a Chicken,* which tune she hummed.

Her mother came up the stairs. Dixie closed the book and said to her mother through the closed door, "Quite definitely I'm not taking up with him again. I got my self-respect to think of."

"Quite right," Mavis replied from the other room.

"He wasn't ever the same after he took up with Dougal Douglas," Dixie said through the wall.

"I liked Dougal," Mavis replied.

"I didn't like him. Trevor didn't like him," Dixie said.

Hearing the front-door bell, Dixie stood attentively. Her mother went down and said something to her stepfather. They were arguing as to who should go and answer the door. Dixie went out on the landing and saw her stepbrother Leslie walking along the ground-floor passage in the wrong direction.

"Leslie, open that door," Dixie said.

The boy looked up at Dixie. The bell rang again. Dixie's mother burst out of the dim-lit sitting-room.

"If it's him again I'll give him something to remember me by," she said, and opened the door. "Oh, Trevor, it's you, Trevor," she said.

"Good evening, Mavis," Trevor said.

Dixie returned rapidly to her room to comb her black hair and put on lipstick. When she came down to the sitting-room, Trevor was seated under the standard lamp, between Mavis and her stepfather, waiting for the television play to come to an end. Trevor had a strip of plaster on his face, close to the mouth.

The play came to an end. Mavis rose in her quick way and switched on the central light. Her husband, Arthur Crewe, smiled at everyone, adjusted his coat and offered Trevor a cigarette. Dixie set one leg across the other, and watched the toe of her shoe, which she wriggled.

"You'll never guess who came to the door this evening."

"Humphrey Place," said Trevor.

"You've seen him?"

"Seen him—I've just knocked his head off."

Dixie's stepfather switched off the television altogether, and pulled round his chair to face Trevor.

"I suppose," he said, "you did right."

"*Did* right," said Dixie.

"I *said* did. I didn't say done. Keep your hair on, girl."

Mavis opened the door and called, "Leslie, put the kettle on." She returned with her quick little steps to her chair. "You could have knocked me over," she said. "I

237

was just giving Dixie her tea; it was, I should say, twenty past five and there was a ring at the bell. I said to Dixie, 'Whoever can that be?' So I went to the door, and lo and behold there he was on the doorstep. He said, 'Hallo, Mavis,' he said. I said, 'You just hop it, you.' He said, 'Can I see Dixie?' I said, 'You certainly can't,' I said. I said, 'You're a dirty swine. You remove yourself,' I said, 'and don't show your face again,' I said. He said, 'Come on, Mavis.' I said, 'Mrs. Crewe to you,' and I shut the door in his face." She turned to Dixie and said, "What about making a cup of tea?"

Dixie said, "If he thinks I would talk to him again, he's making a great mistake. What did he say to you, Trevor?"

Mavis got up and left the room, saying, "If you want anything done in this house you've got to do it yourself."

"Help your mother," said Arthur Crewe absently to Dixie.

"Did he say whether he's gone back to the same job?" Dixie said to Trevor.

Trevor put a hand on each knee and gave a laugh.

Dixie looked from the broad-faced Trevor to the amiable bald head of her stepfather, and started to weep.

"Well, he's come back again," Arthur said. "What you crying for?"

"Don't cry, Dixie," Trevor said.

Dixie stopped crying. Mavis came in with the tea.

Dixie said, "He's common. You only have to look at his sister. Do you know what Elsie did at her first dance?"

"No," said Mavis.

"Well, a fellow came up to her and asked her for a dance. And Elsie said, 'No, I'm sweating.' "

"Well, you never told me that before," Mavis said.

"I only just heard it. Connie Weedin told me."

Trevor gave a short laugh. "We'll run him out of Peckham like we run Dougal Douglas."

"Dougal went of his own accord, to my hearing," Arthur said.

"With a black eye," Trevor said.

Round at the old-fashioned Harbinger various witnesses of the fight were putting the story together. The barmaid said: "It was only a few weeks ago. You saw it in the papers. That chap who left the girl at the altar, that's him. She lives up the Grove. Crewe by name."

One landlady out of a group of three said, "No, she's a Dixie Morse. Crewe's the stepfather. I know because she works at Meadows Meade in poor Miss Coverdale's pool that was. Miss Coverdale told me about her. The fellow had a good position as a refrigerator engineer."

"Who was the chap that hit him?"

"Some friend of the girl's, I daresay."

"Old Lomas's boy. Trevor by name. Electrician. He was best man at the wedding."

"There was I," sang out an old man who was visible with his old wife on the corner bench over in the public bar, "waiting at the church, waiting at the church."

His wife said nothing nor smiled.

"Now then, dad," the barmaid said.

The old man took a draught of his bitter with a tremble of the elbow and a turn of the wrist.

Before closing time the story had spread to the surrounding public bars, where it was established that Humphrey had called at 12 Rye Grove earlier in the evening.

Even in one of the saloon bars, Miss Connie Weedin heard of the reappearance of Humphrey Place, and the subsequent fight; and she later discussed this at length with her father who was Personnel Manager of Meadows, Meade & Grindley, and at present recovering from a nervous breakdown.

"Dixie's boy has come back," she said.

"Has the Scotch man come back?" he said.

"No, he's gone."

Outside the pub at closing time Nelly Mahone, who had lapsed from her native religion on religious grounds, was at her post on the pavement with her long grey hair blown by the late summer wind. There she commented for all to hear, "Praise be to God who employs the weak to confound the strong and whose ancient miracles we see shining even in our times."

Humphrey and Dixie were widely discussed throughout the rest of the week. The reappearance of the bridegroom was told to Collie Gould, aged eighteen, unfit for National Service, who retold it to the gang at the Elephant; and lastly by mid-morning break at Meadows Meade the occurrence was known to all on the floor such as Dawn Waghorn, cone-winder, Annette Wren, trainee-seamer, Elaine Kent, process-controller, Odette Hill, uptwister, Raymond Lowther, packer, Lucille Potter, gummer; and it was revealed also to the checking department and many of the stackers, the sorters, and the Office.

Miss Merle Coverdale, lately head of the typing pool, did not hear of it. Mr. Druce, lately Managing Director, did not hear of it. Neither did Dougal Douglas, the former Arts man, nor his landlady Miss Belle Frierne who had known all Peckham in her youth.

But in any case, within a few weeks, everyone forgot the details. The affair is a legend referred to from time to time in the pubs when the conversation takes a matrimonial turn. Some say the bridegroom came back repentant and married the girl in the end. Some say, no, he married another girl, while the bride married the best man. It is wondered if the bride had been carrying on with the best man for some time past. It is sometimes told that the bride died of grief and the groom shot himself on the Rye. It is generally agreed that he answered "No" at his wedding, that he went away alone on his wedding day and turned up again later.

Chapter Two

Dixie had just become engaged to marry Humphrey when Dougal Douglas joined the firm of Meadows, Meade & Grindley, manufacturers of nylon textiles, a small but growing concern, as Mr. V. R. Druce described it.

At the interview Mr. Druce said to Dougal, "we feel the time has come to take on an Arts man. Industry and the Arts must walk hand in hand."

Mr. Druce had formerly been blond, he was of large build. Dougal, who in the University Dramatics had taken the part of Rizzio in a play about Mary, Queen of Scots, leaned forward and put all his energy into his own appearance; he dwelt with a dark glow on Mr. Druce, he raised his right shoulder, which was already highly crooked by nature, and leaned on his elbow with a becoming twist of the body. Dougal put Mr. Druce through the process of his smile, which was wide and full of white young teeth; he made movements with the alarming bones of his hands. Mr. Druce could not keep his eyes off Dougal, as Dougal perceived.

"I feel I'm your man," Dougal said. "Something told me so when I woke first thing this morning."

"Is that so?" Mr. Druce said. "Is that so?"

"Only a hunch," said Dougal. "I may be wrong."

"Now look," said Mr. Druce, "I must tell you that we feel we have to see other candidates and can't come to any decision straight away."

"Quite," said Dougal.

At the second interview Mr. Druce paced the floor, while Dougal sat like a monkey-puzzle tree, only moving his eyes to follow Mr. Druce. "You'll find the world of Industry a tough one," Mr. Druce said.

Dougal changed his shape and became a professor. He leaned one elbow over the back of his chair and reflected kindly upon Mr. Druce.

"We are creating this post," said Mr. Druce. "We already have a Personnel Manager, Mr. Weedin. He needs an assistant. We feel we need a man with vision. We feel you should come under Weedin. But you should largely work on your own and find your own level, we feel. Of course you will be under Mr. Weedin."

Dougal leaned forward and became a television interviewer. Mr. Druce stopped walking and looked at him in wonder.

"Tell me," coaxed Dougal, "can you give me some rough idea of my duties?"

"It's up to you, entirely up to you. We feel there's a place for an Arts man to bring vision into the lives of the workers. Wonderful people. But they need vision, we feel. Motion study did marvels in the factory. We had a man from Cambridge advising on motion study. It speeded up our output thirty per cent. Movements required to do any given task were studied in detail and he worked out the simplest pattern of movement involving the least loss of energy and time."

"The least loss of energy and time!" Dougal commented.

"The least loss of energy and time," said Mr. Druce. "All our workers' movements are now designed to conserve energy and time in feeding the line. You'll see it on the posters all over the factory, 'Conserve energy and time in feeding the line.' "

"In feeding the line!" Dougal said.

"In feeding the line," Mr. Druce said. "As I say, this expert came from Cambridge. But we felt that a Cambridge man in Personnel wouldn't do. What we feel about you is you'll be in touch with the workers, or rather, as we prefer to say, our staff; you'll be in the know, we feel. Of course you'll find the world of Industry a tough one."

Dougal turned sideways in his chair and gazed out of the window at the railway bridge; he was now a man of vision with a deformed shoulder. "The world of Industry," said Dougal, "throbs with human life. It will be my job to take the pulse of the people and plumb the industrial depths of Peckham."

Mr. Druce said: "Exactly. You have to bridge the gap and hold out a helping hand. Our absenteeism," he said, "is a problem."

"They must be bored with their jobs," said Dougal in a split second of absent-mindedness.

"I wouldn't say bored," said Mr. Druce. "Not bored. Meadows Meade are building up a sound reputation with regard to their worker-staff. We have a training scheme, a recreation scheme, and a bonus scheme. We haven't yet got a pension scheme, or a marriage scheme, or a burial scheme, but these will come. Comparatively speaking we are a small concern, I admit, but we are expanding."

"I shall have to do research," Dougal mused, "into their

inner lives. Research into the real Peckham. It will be necessary to discover the spiritual well-spring, the glorious history of the place, before I am able to offer some impetus."

Mr. Druce betrayed a little emotion. "But no lectures on Art," he said, pulling himself together. "We've tried them. They didn't quite come off. The workers, the staff, don't like coming back to the building after working hours. Too many outside attractions. Our aim is to be one happy family."

"Industry is by now," declared Dougal, "a great tradition. Is that not so? The staff must be made conscious of that tradition."

"A great tradition," said Mr. Druce. "That is so, Mr. Douglas. I wish you luck, and I want you to meet Mr. Weedin while you're here." He pressed a button on his desk and, speaking into an instrument, summoned Mr. Weedin.

"Mr. Weedin," he said to Dougal, "is not an Arts man. But he knows his job inside out. Wonderful people, Personnel staff. If you don't tread on his toes you'll be all right with Personnel. Then of course there's Welfare. You'll have some dealings with Welfare, bound to do. But we feel you must find your own level and the job is what you make it—— Come in, Mr. Weedin, and meet Mr. Douglas, M.A., who has just joined us. Mr. Douglas has come from Edinburgh to take charge of human research."

If you look inexperienced or young and go shopping for food in the by-streets of Peckham it is as different from shopping in the main streets as it is from shopping in

Kensington or the West End. In the little shops in the Peckham by-streets, the other customers take a deep interest in what you are buying. They concern themselves lest you are cheated. Sometimes they ask you questions of a civil nature, such as: Where do you work? Is it a good position? Where are you stopping? What rent do they take off you? And according to your answer they may comment that the money you get is good or the rent you have to pay is wicked, as the case may be. Dougal, who had gone to a small grocer on a Saturday morning, and asked for a piece of cheese, was aware of a young woman with a pram, a middle-aged woman and an old man accumulating behind him. The grocer came to weigh the cheese.

"Don't you give him that," said the young woman; "it's sweating."

"Don't let him give you that, son," said the old man.

The grocer removed the piece of cheese from the scales and took up another.

"You don't want as much as all that," said the older woman. "Is it just for yourself?"

"Only for me," Dougal said.

"Then you want to ask for two ounces," she said. "Give him two ounces," she said. "You just come from Ireland, son?"

"No, Scotland," said Dougal.

"Thought he was Irish from his voice," commented the old man.

"Me too," said the younger woman. "Irish sounds a bit like Scotch like, to hear it."

The older woman said, "You want to learn some experience, son. Where you stopping?"

246

"I've got temporary lodgings in Brixton. I'm looking for a place round here."

The grocer forgot his grievances and pointed a finger at Dougal.

"You want to go to a lady up on the Rye, name of Frierne. She's got nice rooms; just suit you. All gentlemen. No ladies, she won't have."

"Who's she?" said the young woman. "Don't know her."

"Don't know Miss Frierne?" said the old man.

The older woman said, "She's lived up there all her life. Her father left her the house. Big furniture removers they used to be."

"Give me the address," said Dougal, "and I'll be much obliged."

"I think she charges," said the older woman. "You got a good position, son?"

Dougal leaned on the counter so that his high shoulder heaved higher still. He turned his lean face to answer. "I've just started at Meadows, Meade & Grindley."

"I know them," said the younger woman. "A nice firm. The girl Waghorn works there."

"Miss Frierne's rooms go as high as thirty, thirty-five shillings," remarked the older woman to the grocer.

"Inclusive heat and light," said the grocer.

"Excuse me," said the older woman. "She had meters put in the rooms, that I do know. You can't do inclusive these days."

The grocer looked away from the woman with closed eyes and opened them again to address Dougal.

"If Miss Frierne has a vacancy you'll be a lucky chap," he said. "Mention my name."

"What department you in?" said the old man to Dougal.

"The Office," said Dougal.

"The Office don't get paid much," said the man.

"That depends," the grocer said.

"Good prospects?" said the older woman to Dougal.

"Yes, fine," Dougal said.

"Let him go up Miss Frierne's," said the old man.

"Just out of National Service?" said the older woman.

"No, they didn't pass me."

"That would be his deformity," commented the old man, pointing at Dougal's shoulder.

Dougal nodded and patted his shoulder.

"You was lucky," said the younger woman and laughed a good deal.

"Could I speak to Miss Fergusson?" Dougal said.

The voice at the other end of the line said, "Hold on. I'll see if she's in."

Dougal stood in Miss Frierne's wood-panelled entrance hall, holding on and looking around him.

At last she came. "Jinny," Dougal said.

"Oh, it's you."

"I've found a room in Peckham. I can come over and see you if you like. How——"

"Listen, I've left some milk boiling on the stove. I'll ring you back."

"Jinny, are you feeling all right? Maria Cheeseman wants me to write her autobiography."

"It will be boiling over. I'll ring you back."

"You don't know the number."

But she had rung off.

Dougal left fourpence on the telephone table and went

up to his new room at the very top of Miss Frierne's house.

He sat down among his belongings, which were partly in and partly out of his zipper bag. There was a handsome brass bedstead with a tall railed head along which was gathered a muslin curtain. It was the type of bed which was becoming fashionable again, but Miss Frierne did not know this. It was the only item of furniture in the room for which she had apologised; she had explained it was only temporary and would soon be replaced by a new single divan. Dougal detected in this little speech a good intention, repeated to each newcomer, which never came off. He assured her that he liked the brass bed with its railings and knobs. Could he remove, perhaps, the curtain? Miss Frierne said, no, it needed the bit of curtain, and before long would be replaced by a single divan. But no, Dougal said, I like the bed. Miss Frierne smiled to herself that she had found such an obliging tenant. "Really, I do like it," Dougal said, "more than anything else in the room."

The two windows in the room pleased him, looking out on a lot of sky and down to Miss Frierne's long lawn and those of her neighbours; beyond them lay the back gardens belonging to the opposite street of houses, but these were neglected, overgrown and packed with junk and sheds for motor-bicycles, not neat like Miss Frierne's and the row of gardens on the near side, with their borders and sometimes a trellis bower.

He saw a little door, four feet high, where the attic ceiling met the wall. He opened it, and found a deep long cupboard using up the remainder of the roof-slope. Having stooped to enter the cupboard, Dougal found he could almost walk in it. He came out, pleased with his fairly useless cave, and started putting away his shirts in the dark painted chest of drawers. He stroked the ceiling, that part of it which sloped down within reach. Some white powdery distemper came off on his fingers. He went downstairs to telephone to Jinny. Her number was engaged.

The linoleum in his room was imitation parquetry and shone with polish. Two small patterned mats and one larger one made islands on the wide floor. Dougal placed a pile of his clothes on each island, then hauled it over the polished floor to the wardrobe. He unlocked his typewriter and arranged his belongings, as all his student-life in Edinburgh Jinny used to do for him. One day in their final year, at Leith docks, watching the boats, she had said: "I must bend over the rails. I've got that indigestion." Already, at this first stage in her illness, he had shown no sympathy. "Jinny, everyone will think you're drunk. Stand up." In the course of her illness she stopped calling him a crooked fellow, and instead became bitter, calling him sometimes a callous swine or a worm. "I hate sickness, not you," he had said. Still, at that time he had forced himself to visit her sometimes in the Infirmary. He got his degree, and was thought of as frivolous in the pubs, not being a Nationalist. Jinny's degree was delayed a year, he meanwhile spending that year in France and finally London, where he lived in Earl's Court and got through his money waiting for Jinny.

For a few weeks he spent much of his time in the flat of the retired actress and singer, Maria Cheeseman, in Chelsea, who had once shared a stage with an aunt of Jinny's.

He went to meet Jinny at last at King's Cross. She had bright high cheek-bones and brown straight hair. They could surely be married in six months' time. "I've to go into hospital again," said Jinny. "I've to have an operation this time. I've a letter to a surgeon in the Middlesex Hospital.

"You'll come and visit me there?" she said.

"No, quite honestly, I won't," Dougal said. "You know how I feel about places of sickness. I'll write to you every day."

She got a room in Kensington, went into hospital two weeks later, was discharged on a Saturday and wrote to tell Dougal not to meet her at the hospital and she was glad he had got the job in Peckham, and was writing Miss Cheeseman's life, and she hoped he would do well in life.

"Jinny, I've found a room in Peckham. I can come over and see you if you like."

"I've left some milk on the stove. I'll ring you back."

Dougal tried on one of his new white shirts and tilted the mirror on the dressing-table to see himself better. Already it seemed that Peckham brought out something in him that Earl's Court had overlooked. He left the room and descended the stairs. Miss Frierne came out of her front room.

"Have you got everything you want, Mr. Douglas?"

"You and I," said Dougal, "are going to get on fine."

"You'll do well at Meadows Meade, Mr. Douglas. I've had fellows before from Meadows Meade."

"Just call me Dougal," said Dougal.

"Douglas," she said, pronouncing it "Dooglass."

"No, *Dougal*—Douglas is my surname."

"Oh, Dougal Douglas. Dougal's the first name."

"That's right, Miss Frierne. What buses do you take for Kensington?"

"It's my one secret weakness," he said to Jinny.

"I can't help it," he said. "Sickness kills me."

"Be big," he said, "be strong. Be a fine woman, Jinny."

"Understand me," he said, "try to understand my fatal flaw. Everybody has one."

"It's time I had my lie-down," she said. "I'll ring you when I'm stronger."

"Ring me tomorrow."

"All right, tomorrow."

"What time?"

"I don't know. Some time."

"You would think we had never been lovers, you speak so coldly," he said. "Ring me at eleven in the morning. Will you be awake by then?"

"All right, eleven." He leaned one elbow on the back of his chair. She was unmoved. He smiled intimately. She closed her eyes.

"You haven't asked for my number," he said.

"All right, leave your number."

He wrote it on a bit of paper and returned south of the river to Peckham. There, as Dougal entered the saloon bar of the Morning Star, Nelly Mahone crossed the road in her rags crying, "Praise be to the Lord, almighty and eternal, wonderful in the dispensation of all his works, the glory of the faithful and the life of the just." As Dougal bought his drink, Humphrey Place came up and spoke to him. Dougal recalled that Humphrey Place, refrigerator engineer of Freeze-eezy's, was living in the room below his and had been introduced to him by Miss Frierne that morning. Afterwards Miss Frierne had told Dougal, "He is clean and go-ahead."

Chapter Three

"What d'you mean by different?" Mavis said.

"I don't know. He's just different. Says funny things. You have to laugh," Dixie said.

"He's just an ordinary chap," Humphrey said. "Nice chap. Ordinary."

But Dixie could see that Humphrey did not mean it. Humphrey knew that Douglas was different. Humphrey had been talking a good deal about Douglas during the past fortnight and how they sat up talking late at Miss Frierne's.

"Better fetch him here to tea one night," said Dixie's stepfather. "Let's have a look at him."

"He's too high up in the Office," Mavis said.

"He's on research," Dixie said. "He's brainy, supposed to be. But he's friendly, I'll say that."

"He's no snob," said Humphrey.

"He hasn't got nothing to be a snob about," said Dixie.

"*Anything*, not *nothing*."

"Anything," said Dixie, "to be a snob about. He's no better than us just because he's twenty-three and got a good job."

"But he's got to do his overtime for nothing," Mavis said.

"He's the same as what we are," Dixie said.

"You said he was different."

"Well, but no better than us. I don't know why you sit up talking at nights with him."

Humphrey sat up late in Dougal's room.

"My father's in the same trade. He puts himself down as a fitter. Same job."

"It is right and proper," Dougal said, "that you should be called a refrigerator engineer. It brings lyricism to the concept."

"I don't trouble myself about that," Humphrey said. "But what you call a job makes a difference to the Unions. My dad doesn't see that."

"Do you like brass bedsteads?" Dougal said. "We had them at home. We used to unscrew the knobs and hide the fag ends inside."

"By common law," Humphrey said, "a trade union has no power to take disciplinary action against its members. By common law a trade union cannot fine, suspend, or expel its members. It can only do so contractually. That is, by its rules."

"Quite," said Dougal, who was lolling on his brass bed.

"You can use your imagination," Humphrey said. "If a member is expelled from a union that operates a closed shop. . . ."

"Ghastly," said Dougal, who was trying to unscrew one of the knobs.

"But all that won't concern you much," Humphrey said. "What you want to know about for your human research is arbitration in trade disputes. There's the Conciliation Act 1896 and the Industrial Courts Act 1919, but you wouldn't need to go into those. You might study the Industrial Disputes Order 1951. But you aren't likely to have a dispute at Meadows, Meade & Grindley. You might have an issue, though."

"Is there a difference?"

"Oh, a vast difference. Sometimes they take it to law to decide whether an issue or a dispute has arisen. It's been as far as the Court of Appeal. I'll let you have the books. Issue is whether certain employers should observe certain terms of employment. Dispute is any dispute between employer and employee as to terms of employment or conditions of labour."

"Terrific," Dougal said. "You must have given your mind to it."

"I took a course. But you'll soon get to know what's what in Industrial Relations."

"Fascinating," Dougal said. "Everything is fascinating, to me, so far. Do you know what I came across the other day? An account of the fair up the road at Camberwell Green."

"Fair?"

"According to Colburn's Calendar of Amusements 1840," Dougal said. He reached for his notebook, leaned on his elbow, heaved his high shoulder and read:

There is here, and only here, to be seen what you can see nowhere else, the lately caught and highly accomplished young mermaid, about whom the continental journals have written so ably. She combs her hair in the manner practised in China, and admires herself in a glass in the manner practised everywhere. She has had the best instructors in every peculiarity of education, and can argue on any given subject, from the most popular way of preserving plums, down to the necessity of a change of Ministers. She plays the harp in the new effectual style prescribed by Mr. Bocha, of whom we wished her to take lessons, but, having some mermaiden scruples, she begged to be provided with a less popular master. Being so clever and accomplished, she can't bear to be contradicted, and lately leaped out of her tub and floored a distinguished fellow of the Royal Zoological Society, who was pleased to be more curious and cunning than she was pleased to think agreeable. She has composed various poems for the periodicals, and airs with variations for the harp and piano, all very popular and pleasing.

Dougal gracefully cast his book aside. "How I should like to meet a mermaid!" he said.

"Terrific," Humphrey said. "You make it up?" he asked.

"No, I copied it out of an old book in the library. My research. Mendelssohn wrote his *Spring Song* in Ruskin Park. Ruskin lived on Denmark Hill. Mrs. Fitzherbert lived in Camberwell Grove. Boadicea committed suicide on Peckham Rye probably where the bowling green is now, I should imagine. But, look here, how would you like to be engaged to marry a mermaid that writes poetry?"

"Fascinating," Humphrey said.

Dougal gazed at him like a succubus whose mouth is its eyes.

Humphrey's friend, Trevor Lomas, had said Dougal was probably pansy.

"I don't think so," Humphrey had replied. "He's got a girl somewhere."

"Might be versatile."

"Could be."

Dougal said, "The boss advised me to mix with everybody in the district, high and low. I should like to mix with that mermaid."

Dougal put a record on the gramophone he had borrowed from Elaine Kent in the textile factory. It was a Mozart quartet. He slid the rugs aside with his foot and danced to the music on the bare linoleum, with stricken movements of his hands. He stopped when the record stopped, replaced the rugs, and said, "I must get to know some of the youth clubs. Dixie will be a member of a youth club, I expect."

"She isn't," Humphrey said rather rapidly.

Dougal opened a bottle of Algerian wine. He took his time, and with a pair of long tweezers fished out a bit of cork that had dropped inside the bottle. He held up the pair of tweezers.

"I use these," he said, "to pluck out the hairs which grow inside my nostrils, and which are unsightly. Eventually, I lose the tweezers, then I buy another pair."

He placed the tweezers on the bed. Humphrey lifted them, examined them, then placed them on the dressing table.

"Dixie will know," Dougal said, "about the youth clubs."

"No, she won't. She doesn't have anything to do with youth clubs. There are classes within classes in Peckham."

"Dixie would be upper-working," said Dougal. He poured wine into two tumblers and handed one to Humphrey.

"Well, I'd say middle class. It's not a snob business, it's a question of your type."

"Or lower-middle," Dougal said.

Humphrey looked vaguely as if Dixie was being insulted. But then he looked pleased. His eyes went narrow, his head lolled on the back of the chair, copying one of Dougal's habitual poses.

"Dixie's saving up," he said. "It's all she can think of, saving up to get married. And now what does she say? We can't go out more than one night a week so that I can save up too."

"Avarice," Dougal said, "must be her fatal flaw. We all have a fatal flaw. If she took sick, how would you feel, would she repel you?"

Dougal had taken Miss Merle Coverdale for a walk across the great sunny common of the Rye on a Saturday afternoon. Merle Coverdale was head of the typing pool at Meadows, Meade & Grindley. She was thirty-seven.

Dougal said, "My lonely heart is deluged by melancholy and it feels quite nice."

"Someone might hear you talking like that."

"You are a terror and a treat," Dougal said. "You look to me like an okapi," he said.

"A what?"

"An okapi is a rare beast from the Congo. It looks a little like a deer, but it tries to be a giraffe. It has stripes and it stretches its neck as far as possible and its ears are like a donkey's. It is a little bit of everything. There are only a few in captivity. It is very shy."

"Why do you say I'm like it?"

"Because you're so shy."

"Me shy?"

"Yes. You haven't told me about your love affair with Mr. Druce. You're too shy."

259

"Oh, that's only a friendship. You've got it all wrong. What makes you think it's a love affair? Who told you that?"

"I've got second sight."

He brought her to the gate of the park and was leading her through it, when she said,

"This doesn't lead anywhere. We'll have to go back the same way."

"Yes, it does," Dougal said, "it leads to One Tree Hill and two cemeteries, the Old and the New. Which would you prefer?"

"I'm not going into any cemetery," she said, standing with legs apart in the gateway as if he might move her by force.

Dougal said, "There's a lovely walk through the New Cemetery. Lots of angels. Beautiful. I'm surprised at you. Are you a free woman or are you a slave?"

She let him take her through the cemetery, eventually, and even pointed out to him the tower of the crematorium when it came into sight. Dougal posed like an angel on a grave which had only an insignificant headstone. He posed like an angel-devil, with his hump shoulder and gleaming smile, and his fingers of each hand widespread against the sky. She looked startled. Then she laughed.

"Enjoying yourself?" she said.

On the way back along the pastoral streets of trees and across the Rye she told him about her six years as mistress of Mr. Druce, about Mr. Druce's wife who never came to the annual dinners and who was a wife in name only.

"How they bring themselves to go on living together I don't know," she said. "There's no feeling between them. It's immoral."

260

She told Dougal how she had fallen out of love with Mr. Druce yet could not discontinue the relationship, she didn't know why.

"You've got used to him," Dougal said.

"I suppose so."

"But you feel," Dougal said, "that you're living a lie."

"I do," she said. "You've put my very thoughts into words.

"And then," she said, "he's got some funny ways with him."

Dougal slid his eyes to regard her without moving his face. He caught her doing the same thing to him.

"What funny ways? Come on, tell me," Dougal said. "There's no good telling the half and then stopping."

"No," she said. "It wouldn't be right to discuss Mr. Druce with you. He's your boss and mine, after all."

"I haven't seen him," Dougal said, "since the day he engaged me. He must have forgotten about me."

"No, he talked a lot about you. And he sent for you the other day. You were out of the office."

"What day was that?"

"Tuesday. I said you were out on research."

"So I was," said Dougal. "I was out on research."

"Nobody gets forgotten at Meadows Meade," she said. "He'll want to know about your research in a few weeks' time."

Dougal put his long cold hand down the back of her coat. She was short enough for his hand to reach quite a long way. He tickled her.

She wriggled and said, "Not in broad daylight, Dougal."

"In dark midnight," Dougal said, "I wouldn't be able to find my way."

261

She laughed from her chest.

"Tell me," Dougal said, "what is the choicest of Mr. Druce's little ways?"

"He's childish," she said. "I don't know why I stick to him. I could have left Meadows Meade many a time. I could have got into a big firm. You don't think Meadows Meade's a big firm, do you, by any chance? Because, if you do, let me tell you, Meadows Meade is by comparison very small. Very small."

"It looks big to me," Dougal said. "But perhaps it's the effect of all that glass."

"We used to have open-plan," she said. "So that you could see everyone in the office without the glass, even Mr. Druce. But the bosses wanted their privacy back, so we had the glass partitions put up."

"I like those wee glass houses," Dougal said. "When I'm in the office I feel like a tomato, getting ripe."

"*When* you're in the office."

"Merle," he said, "Merle Coverdale, I'm a hard-working fellow. I've got to be out and about on my human research."

They were moving up to the Rye where the buses blazed in the sun. Their walk was nearly over.

"Oh, we're soon here," she said.

Dougal pointed to a house on the right. "There's a baby's pram," he said, "stuck out on a balcony which hasn't any railings."

She looked and sure enough there was a pram perched on an open ledge only big enough to hold it, outside a second-floor window. She said, "They ought to be prosecuted. There's a baby in that pram, too."

"No, it's only a doll," Dougal said.

262

"How do you know?"

"I've seen it before. The house is a baby-carriage works. The pram is only for show."

"Oh, it gave me a fright."

"How long have you lived in Peckham?" he said.

"Twelve and a half years."

"You've never noticed the pram before?"

"No, can't say I have. Must be new."

"From the style of the pram, it can't be new. In fact the pram has been there for twenty-five years. You see, you simply haven't noticed it."

"I don't hardly ever come across the Rye. Let's walk round a bit. Let's go into the Old English garden."

"Tell me more," Dougal said, "about Mr. Druce. Don't you see him on Saturdays?"

"Not during the day. I do in the evening."

"You'll be seeing him tonight?"

"Yes, he comes for supper."

Dougal said, "I suppose he's been doing his garden all day. Is that what he does on Saturdays?"

"No. As a matter of fact, believe it or not, on Saturday mornings he goes up to the West End to the big shops. He goes up and down in the lifts. He rests in the afternoons. Childish."

"He must get some sexual satisfaction out of it."

"Don't be silly," she said.

"A nice jerky lift," said Dougal. "Not one of the new smooth ones but the kind that go yee-oo at the bottom." And Dougal sprang in the air and dipped with bent knees to illustrate his point, so that two or three people in the Old English garden turned to look at him. "It gives me," Dougal said, "a sexual sensation just to think of it. I can quite see the attraction those old lifts have for Mr. Druce. Yee-oo."

She said, "For God's sake lower your voice." Then she laughed her laugh from the chest, and Dougal pulled that blond front lock of her otherwise brown hair, while she gave him a hefty push such as she had not done to a man for twenty years.

He walked down Nunhead Lane with her; their ways parted by the prefabs at Costa Road.

"I'm to go to tea at Dixie's house tonight," he said.

"I don't know what you want to do with that lot," she said.

"Of course, I realise you're head of the typing pool and Dixie's only a wee typist," he said.

"You're taking me up wrong."

"Let's go for another walk if it's nice on Monday morning," he said.

"I'll be at work on Monday morning. I'll be down to work, not like you."

"Take Monday off, my girl," Dougal said. "Just take Monday off."

"Hallo. Come in. Pleased to see you. There's your tea," Mavis said.

The family had all had theirs, and Dougal's tea was set on the table. Cold ham and tongue and potato salad with bread and butter, followed by fruit cake and tea. Dougal sat down and tucked in while Mavis, Dixie and Humphrey Place sat round the table. When he had finished eating, Mavis poured the tea and they all sat and drank it.

"That Miss Coverdale in the pool," said Mavis, "is

working Dixie to death. I think she's trying to get Dixie out. Ever since Dixie got engaged she's been horrible to Dixie, hasn't she, Dixie?"

"It was quarter to four," said Dixie, "and she came up with an estimate and said 'priority'—just like that—priority. I said, 'Excuse me, Miss Coverdale, but I've got two priorities already.' She said, 'Well, it's only quarter to four.' '*Only*,' I said, '*only* quarter to four. Do you realise how long these estimates take? I'm not going without my tea-break, if that's what you're thinking, Miss Coverdale.' She said, 'Oh, Dixie, you're impossible,' and turned away. I jumped up and I said, 'Repeat that,' I said. I said——"

"You should have reported her to Personnel," Humphrey said. "That was your correct procedure."

"A disappointed spinster," Mavis said, "that's what she is."

"She's immoral with Mr. Druce, a married man, that I know for a fact," Dixie said. "So she's covered. You can't touch her, there's no point in reporting her to Personnel. It gets you down."

"Take Monday off," said Dougal. "Take Tuesday off as well. Have a holiday."

"No, I don't agree to that," Humphrey said. "Absenteeism is downright immoral. Give a fair week's work for a fair week's pay."

Dixie's stepfather, who had been watching the television in the sitting-room and who suddenly felt lonely, put his head round the door.

"Want a cup of tea, Arthur?" said Mavis. "Meet Mr. Douglas. Mr. Douglas, Mr. Crewe."

"Where's Leslie?" said Arthur Crewe.

"Well, he ought to be in. I let him go out," Mavis said.

"Because there's something going on out the front," Arthur said.

They all trooped through to the sitting-room and peered into the falling dusk, where a group of young people in their teens were being questioned by an almost equal number of policemen.

"The youth club," Mavis said.

Dougal immediately went out to investigate. As he opened the street door, young Leslie slid in as if from some concealment; he was breathless.

Dougal returned presently to report that the tyres of a number of cars parked up at the Rye had been slashed. The police were rounding up the teenage suspects. Young Leslie was chewing bubble-gum. Every now and then he pulled a long strand out of his mouth and let it spring back into his mouth.

"But it seems to me the culprits may have been children," Dougal said, "as much as these older kids."

Leslie stopped chewing for an instant and stared back at Dougal in such disgust that he seemed to be looking at Dougal through his nostrils rather than his eyes. Then he resumed his chewing.

Dougal winked at him. The boy stared back.

"Take that muck out of your mouth, son," said his father.

"You can't stop him," said his mother. "He won't listen to you. Leslie, did you hear what your father said?"

Leslie shifted the gum to the other side of his cheek and left the room.

Dougal looked out of the window at the group who were still being questioned.

"Two girls there come from Meadows Meade," he said. "Odette Hill, uptwister, and Lucille Potter, gummer."

"Oh, the factory lot are always mixed up in the youth club trouble," Mavis said. "You don't want anything to do with that lot." As she spoke she moved her hand across her perm, nipping each brown wave in turn between her third and index fingers.

Dougal winked at her and smiled with all his teeth.

Mavis said to Dixie in a whisper, "Has *he* gone?"

"Yup," said Dixie, meaning, yes, her stepfather had gone out for his evening drink.

Mavis went to the sideboard and fetched out a large envelope.

"Here we are again," Dixie said.

"She always says that," Mavis said.

"Well, Mum, you keep on pulling them out; every new person that comes to the house, out they come."

Mavis had extracted three large press cuttings from the envelope and handed them to Dougal.

Dixie sighed, looking at Humphrey.

"Why you two not go on out? Go on out to the pictures," Mavis said.

"We went out last night."

"But you didn't go to the pictures, I bet. Saving and pinching to get married, you're losing the best time of your life."

"That's what I tell her," said Humphrey. "That's what I say."

"Where'd you go last night?" Mavis said.

Dixie looked at Humphrey. "A walk," she said.

"What you make of these?" Mavis said to Dougal.

The cuttings were dated June, 1942. Two of them bore

large photographs of Mavis boarding an ocean liner. All announced that she was the first of Peckham's G.I. brides to depart these shores.

"You don't look a day older," Dougal said.

"Oh, go on," Dixie said.

"Not a day," said Dougal. "Anyone can see your mother's had a romantic life."

Dixie took her nail file out of her bag, snapped the bag shut and started to grate at her nails

Humphrey bent forward in his chair, one hand on each knee, as if, by affecting intense interest in Mavis's affair, to compensate for Dixie's mockery.

"Well, it was romantic," Mavis said, "and it wasn't. It was both. Glub—that was my first husband—Glub was wonderful at first." Her voice became progressively American. "Made you feel like a queen. He sure was gallant. *And* romantic, as you say. But then . . . Dixie came along . . . everything sorta wenna pieces. We were living a lie," Mavis said, "and it was becoming sorta immoral to live together, not loving each other." She sighed for a space. Then pulling herself together she said, "So I come home."

"*Came* home," Dixie said.

"And got a divorce. And then I met Arthur. Old Arthur's a good sort."

"Mum's had her moments," Dixie said. "She won't let you forget that."

"More than what you'll have, if you go on like you do, putting every penny in the bank. Why, at your age I was putting all my wages what I had left over after paying my keep on my back."

"My own American dad pays my keep," Dixie said.

"He thinks he do, but it don't go far."

"Does. Doesn't," Dixie said.

"I better put the kettle on," Mavis said.

Dougal said then to Dixie, "I didn't never have no money of my own at your age." He heaved his shoulder and glittered his eyes at her, and she did not dare to correct him. But when Humphrey laughed she turned to him and said, "What's the joke?"

"Dougal here," he said, "he's your match."

Mavis came back and switched on the television to a cabaret. Her husband returned to find Dougal keeping the cabaret company with a dance of his own in the middle of their carpet. Mavis was shrieking with joy. Humphrey was smiling with closed lips. Dixie sat also with closed lips, not smiling.

On Saturday mornings, as on Sundays, the gentlemen in Miss Frierne's establishment were desired to make their own beds. On his return at eleven o'clock on Saturday night Dougal found at note in his room.

To-day's bed was a landlady's delight. Full marks in your end-of-term report!

Dougal stuck it up on the mirror of his dressingtable and went downstairs to see if Miss Frierne was still up. He found her in the kitchen, sitting primly up to the table with half a bottle of stout.

"Any letters for me?"

"No, Dougal."

"There should have been a letter."

"Never mind. It might come on Monday."

"Tell me some of your stories."

"You've heard them all, I'm sure." He had heard about the footpads on the Rye in the old days; about the minstrels in the street, or rather carriageway as Miss Frierne said it was called then. She sipped her stout and told him once more of her escapade with a girl called Flo, how they had hired a cab at Camberwell Green and gone up to the Elephant for a drink and treated the cabby to two-penn'orth of gin, and returned without anyone at home being the wiser.

"You must have had some courting days," Dougal said. But her narrow old face turned away in disdain at the suggestion, for these were early days in their friendship, and it was a full month before Miss Frierne, one evening when she had finished her nourishing stout with a sigh and got out the gin bottle, told Dougal how the Gordon Highlanders were stationed at Peckham during the First War; how it was a question among the young ladies whether the soldiers wore anything underneath their kilts; how Miss Frierne at the ripe age of twenty-seven went walking with one of the Highlanders up to One Tree Hill; how he turned to her and said, "My girl, I know you're all bloody curious as to what we have beneath the kilt, and I forthwith propose to satisfy your mind on the subject"; how he then took her hand and thrust it under his kilt; and how she then screamed so hard, she had a quinsy for a week.

But in the meantime when Dougal, at the end of his second week at Miss Frierne's, said, "You must have had some courting days," she turned her narrow pale face away from him and indicated by various slight movements of her bony body that he had gone too far.

Eventually she said, "Did Humphrey come in with you?"

"No, I left him round at Dixie's."

"I wanted to ask his private advice about something."

"Anything I can do? I give rare advice."

She was still offended. "No, thank you. I wish to ask Humphrey privately. Do I hear rain?"

Dougal went to bed and the rain danced on the roof above his head. A key clicked in the front door and Humphrey's footsteps, climbing carefully, rose to the first landing. Humphrey paused on the landing, a long pause, as if he were resting from some effort. Then Humphrey's steps fumbled up on the second flight. Either he was drunk or carrying a heavy weight, for he staggered at the top, just outside Dougal's door.

The long cupboard in Dougal's bedroom gave out a loud tom-tom as the rain beat on the low roof within, and together with this sound was discernible that of Humphrey staggering along the short passage to his own room.

Dougal woke again at the very moment, it seemed, that the rain stopped. And at this very moment a whisper and a giggle came from the direction of his cupboard. He switched on his light and got up. The cupboard was empty. Just as he was going to shut the small door again, there was a slight scuffle. He opened the door, put his head in, and found nothing. He returned to bed and slept.

On Monday morning Dougal got his letter. Jinny had finished with him. He went into the offices of Meadows, Meade & Grindley and typed out some of his notes. Then, at the morning tea-break, he walked over to the long, long factory canteen and asked especially for Odette Hill and Lucille Potter. He was told they were not at work that morning. "Taking the day off. Foreman's mad. Absenteeism makes him mad." He had a bun and a cup of tea, then another bun. A bell rang to mark the end of the tea-break. The men disappeared rapidly. A few girls loitered, as on principle, talking with three of the women who served the canteen. Dougal put his head on his arms in full view of these few girls, and wept.

"What's the matter with him?"

"What's the matter, son?" said a girl of about sixteen whom Dougal, on looking up, found to be Dawn Waghorn, one of the cone-winders whose movements when winding the cone, as laid down by the Cambridge expert, had seemed to Dougal, when he had been taken round the floors, very appealing. Dougal put down his head and resumed his weeping.

Dawn patted his poor shoulder. He slightly raised his head and shook it sadly from side to side. A woman came round from the canteen bar with a clean-folded oven cloth which she held out to him. "Here, dry your eyes before anyone sees you," she said.

"What's the matter, mate?" said another girl. She said, "Here's a hanky." She was Annette Wren who was in training for seaming. She was giggling most heartlessly.

"I've lost my girl," Dougal said, as he blew his nose on the oven cloth.

Elaine Kent, who was well on in her twenties, an experienced controller of process, turned on Annette Wren and told her to shut her mouth, what was there to laugh at?

The two other canteen women came round to Dougal, and he was now surrounded by women. Elaine Kent opened her bag and took out a comb. With it she combed

Dougal's hair as it moved with his head slowly from side to side.

"You'll get another girl," said one of the canteen women, Milly Lloyd by name.

Annette giggled again. Dawn slapped her face and said, "You're ignorant. Can't you see he's handicapped?"

Whereupon Annette burst into tears.

"Keep your head still," said Elaine. "How can I comb you if you keep moving your head?"

"It calms you down, a good comb," remarked one of the canteen.

Milly Lloyd was looking for a fresh handkerchief for Annette whose sobs were tending towards the hysterical.

"How did you lose your girl?" said Dawn.

"I've got a fatal flaw," Dougal said.

Dawn assumed this to be his deformed shoulder, which she now stroked. "It's a shame," she said. "Little no-good bitch I bet she is."

Suddenly Merle Coverdale appeared at the door in the long distance and started walking towards the group.

"Office," whispered Milly, "typing pool," and returned behind the canteen bar.

Merle shouted along the length of the canteen as she approached. "Tea for Mr. Druce, please. He was out. Now he's come in. He wants some tea." Then she saw the group round Dougal. "What the hell's going on?" she said.

"Migraine," Dougal said sadly. "A headache."

"You should all be back on the floor," Merle said to the girls. "There's going to be trouble."

"Who you to talk to us like that?"

"Who's she, coming it over us?"

And so Merle could do nothing with them. She said meaningfully to Dougal,

"I had a headache myself this morning. Came into work late. I went for a brisk walk on the Rye. All by myself."

"I dimly recall arranging to meet you there," Dougal said. "But I was prevented."

Merle gave him a hostile look and said to the canteen women, "What about that tea?"

Milly Lloyd put a cup of tea into Dougal's hand. Merle walked off, bearing Mr. Druce's tea, moving her neck slightly back and forth as she walked all the long length of the canteen. Annette took a cup of tea and, as she gulped it, tried also to express her rage against the girl who had slapped her. As Dougal sipped his tea, young Dawn stroked his high shoulder and said, never mind, it was a shame, while Elaine combed his hair. It was curly hair but cut quite short. Nevertheless she combed it as if it had been as long as the Laughing Cavalier's.

Dixie sat with Humphrey, Dougal and Elaine Kent in Costa's Café. Dixie yawned. Her eyes were sleepy. The only reason she had denied herself an early night was that Dougal was paying for the supper.

"I've felt tired all day," she said. She addressed the men, ignoring Elaine as she had done all evening, because Elaine was factory, even though Elaine was high up in process-control. After a trial period Elaine likewise confined her remarks to the men.

"Look what's just come in," Elaine said. Tall Trevor Lomas had just come in. He sat at the nearest table, with his head and shoulders turned away from Dougal's party, and stared out of the window. Trevor Lomas was at this time employed as an electrician by the Borough.

Trevor turned his head sleepily and permitted an eye to rest on Humphrey for a small second. Humphrey said "Hallo." Trevor did not reply.

Trevor's girl arrived presently, tall and copper-tinted, with a tight short black skirt and much green eye-shadow. "Hi, snake," said Trevor. "Hi," said the girl, and sat down beside him.

Dixie and Elaine stared at the girl as she slid out of her coat and let it fall on the back of her chair. They stared as if by duty, and watched every detail. The girl was aware of this, and seemed to expect it.

Then Trevor pushed back his chair, still seated, so that he half-faced Humphrey's party. He said to his girl in a loud voice: "Got your lace hanky on you, Beauty?"

Beauty did not reply. She was holding up a small mirror, putting on lipstick with care.

"Because," said Trevor, "I'm going to cry." He took his large white handkerchief out of his top pocket and flourished it before each eye in turn. "Going to cry my eyes out, I am," said Trevor, "because I've lost me girl. Hoo, I've lost me girl."

Beauty laughed a great deal. The more she laughed the more noisily did Trevor continue. He laid his head on the table and affected to sob. The girl rocked in her chair, her newly-painted lips open wide apart.

Then Dixie started to laugh.

Dougal shoved his chair back and stood up. Elaine jumped up and held his arm.

"Let be," she said.

Humphrey, whom the story of Dougal's weeping in the

canteen had not yet reached, said to Dixie, "What's up?"

Dixie could not tell him for laughing.

"Let be, mate," Elaine said to Dougal.

Dougal said to Trevor, "I'll see you up on the Rye outside the tennis court."

Elaine walked over to Trevor and gave him a push. "Can't you see he's deformed?" she said. "Making game of a chap like that, it's ignorant."

Dougal, whose deformed shoulder had actually endowed him with a curious speciality in the art of fighting, in that he was able to turn his right wrist at an extraordinary back-hand outward angle and to get a man by the throat as with a claw, did not at that moment boast of the fact.

"Cripple as I am," he merely said, "I'll knock his mean wee sex-starved conceited low and lying L.C.C. electrician's head off."

"Who's sex-starved?" Trevor said, standing up.

Two youths who had been sitting by the window moved over the better to see. A Greek in an off-white coat appeared, and pointed to a telephone receiver which stuck out of the wall behind him in the passageway to the dim kitchen.

"I'll use that phone," he said.

Trevor gave him one of his long sleepy looks. Then he gave one of them to Dougal.

"Who's sex-starved?" he said.

"You are," Dougal said, while counting his money to pay the bill. "And I'll see you on the Rye within the quarter hour."

Trevor walked out of the café and Beauty hastily wriggled herself into her coat and tripped out after him. After them both went the Greek, but Trevor's motor-scooter had just moved off.

"Hasn't paid for coffee," said the Greek, returning. "What name and address he is, please?"

"No idea," Dougal said. "I don't mix with him."

The Greek turned to Humphrey. "I seen you here before with that fellow."

Humphrey threw half-a-crown on the table, and, as the four departed, the Greek slammed his glass doors behind them as hard as he judged the glass would stand up to.

The two girls got into Humphrey's car, but he at first refused to drive them up to the Rye. Dougal stood and argued on the pavement.

Humphrey said, "No, not at all. Don't go. Don't be a fool, Dougal. Let it pass. He's ignorant."

"All right, I'll walk," Dougal said.

"I'm going to send Trevor Lomas home," Humphrey said. He left Dougal and started up the car and drove off with the girls, Dixie in front and Elaine behind agitating, too late, to be let out.

Dougal arrived at the tennis courts six minutes later. Some seconds before he arrived he had heard a sound as of women screaming.

Between two distant lamp-posts, in their vague oblique light, a group was gathered. Dougal discerned Humphrey and Trevor with a strange youth called Collie who was without a coat and whose shirt was unbuttoned, exposing his chest to the night air. These figures were apparently molesting three further figures who turned out to be Dixie, Elaine, and Beauty, who were screaming. Soon it appeared that the men were not molesting but restraining them. Dixie had a long-strapped shoulder bag with which she was attempting to lay about her, largely in the direction of Elaine. Elaine, who was at present in the grip of Trevor, managed to dig Beauty's leg with her steel stiletto heel. Beauty wailed and struggled in Humphrey's grip.

"What's going on?" Dougal said.

Nobody took any notice of him. He went and hit Trevor in the face. Trevor let go of Elaine so that she fell heavily against Beauty. Meanwhile Trevor hit out at Dougal, who staggered backwards into Humphrey. Beauty wailed louder, and struggled harder. Elaine recovered herself and used her freedom to kick with her stiletto heel at Trevor. Dixie, meanwhile, was attempting to release herself from the grasp of that strange youth, Collie, with the bared chest, by biting the arm that held her. The screams grew louder. Dougal's eyes were calculating his chance of coming to adequate terms with Trevor Lomas amidst the confusion when a curious thing happened.

The confusion stopped. Elaine started to sing in the same tone as her screaming, joylessly, and as if in continuation of it. The other girls, seeming to take a signal from her, sidled their wails into a song,

> Sad to say I'm on my way,
> I got a little girl in Kingston Town

meanwhile casting their eyes fitfully over the Rye beyond the trees.

The strange youth let go of Dixie and began to jive with Elaine. In a few seconds everyone except Dougal was singing, performing the twisting jive, merging the motions of the fight into those of the frantic dance. Dougal saw Humphrey's face as his neck swooped upwards. It was frightened. Dixie's expression was, with a decided effort, bright. So was Elaine's. A one-sided smile on the face of the strange boy, and the fact that, as he bent and twisted in the jive, he buttoned up his shirt, made Dougal look round outside the group for the cause of this effect. He saw it immediately. Two policemen were quite close to them now. They must have been observed at a distance of three minutes' police-pace when Elaine had started to sing and the signal had gone round.

"What you think this is—a dance hall?"

"No, constable. No, inspector. Just having a dance with the girls. Just going home, mate."

"Well, *go* home. Get a move on. Out of the park, the lot of you."

"It was Dixie," said Humphrey to Dougal on the way home, "that started the fight. She was over-tired and worked up. She said that tart of Trevor's was giving her looks. She went up to the girl and said, 'Who you looking at?' and then the girl *did* give her a look. Then Dixie let fly with her handbag. That's how it all began."

Rain started to fall as they turned up past the old Quaker cemetery. Nelly Mahone took a green-seeming scarf from a black bag and placed it over her long grey hair. She cried: "The meadows are open and the green herbs have appeared, and the hay is gathered out of the mountain. The wicked man fleeth when no man pursueth, but the just, bold as a lion, shall be without dread."

"Pleasant evening, though a bit wet," Dougal said.

Nelly looked round after him.

Up in his room Dougal poured Algerian wine and remarked as he passed a glass to Humphrey,

"The cupboards run the whole length of the attic floor."

Humphrey put the glass on the floor at his feet and looked up at Dougal.

"There was a noise in the cupboard," Dougal said, "the night before last. It went creak-oop, creak-oop. I thought it came from my cupboard here, but I think maybe it didn't. I think maybe it came from your cupboard through the wall. Creak-oop." Dougal bent his knees apart, then sprang up in the air. He repeated this several times. "Creak-oop," he said.

Humphrey said, "It's only on wet Saturday nights when we can't go up on the Rye."

"Isn't she heavy to carry upstairs?" Dougal said.

Humphrey looked alarmed. "Did it sound as if I was carrying her upstairs?"

"Yes. Better to let her walk up in her stocking feet."

"No, she did that once. The old woman came out and nearly caught us."

"Better to lie in the bed than in the creaky cupboard," Dougal said. "The chap in the room below will hear it."

"No, the old woman came up one night when we were in the bed. We were nearly caught. Dixie had to run and hide in the cupboard."

Humphrey lifted his glass of wine from the floor by his feet and drank it in one gulp.

"Don't worry yourself," Dougal said.

"It's a worry what to do. All right on fine Saturday nights; we can go up on the Rye and Dixie gets home about half-past eleven. But if it starts to rain we come back here. I don't see why not, I pay for the room. But there's the difficulty of getting her up, then down again in the morning while the old woman's at early church. Then she has to pay her brother Leslie five shillings a time to let her in quietly. And she worries about that, does Dixie. She's a great saver, is Dixie."

"It's a tiring occupation, is saving," Dougal said. "Dixie's looking tired."

"Yes, as a matter of fact she does lie awake worrying. And there's no need to worry. Terrible at seventeen. I said, 'What you think you'll be like in ten years' time?'"

"When are you getting married?" Dougal said.

"September. Could do before. But Dixie wants a certain sum. She has her mind set to a certain sum. It keeps her awake at night."

"I advised her to take Monday morning off," Dougal said. "Everyone should take Mondays off."

"Now I don't agree to that," Humphrey said. "It's immoral. Once you start absenting yourself you lose your self-respect. *And* you lose the support of your unions; they won't back you. Of course the typists haven't got a union. As yet."

"No?" said Dougal.

"No," Humphrey said, "but it's a question of principle."

Dougal bent his knees apart as before and leapt into the air. "Creak-oop, creak-oop," he said.

Humphrey laughed deeply with his head thrown back. He stopped when a series of knocks started up from the floor.

"Chap downstairs," Dougal said, "knocks on his ceiling with a broom handle. He doesn't like my wee dances." He performed his antic three times more, shouting, "Creakoop."

Humphrey cast his head back and laughed, so that Dougal could see the whole inside of his mouth.

"I have a dream at nights," Dougal said, pouring the

281

wine, "of girls in factories doing a dance with only the movements of their breasts, bottoms and arms as they sort, stack, pack, check, cone-wind, gum, uptwist, assemble, seam and set. I see the Devil in the guise of a chap from Cambridge who does motion-study, and he's the choreographer. He sings a song that goes, 'We study in detail the movements requisite for any given task and we work out the simplest pattern of movement involving the least loss of energy and time.' While he sings this song, the girls are waggling and winding, like this——" and Dougal waggled his body and wove his arms intricately. "Like Indian dancing, you know," he said.

"And," said Dougal, "of course this choreographer is a projection of me. I was at the University of Edinburgh myself, but in the dream I'm the Devil and Cambridge."

Humphrey smiled, looked wise, and said, "Inhuman"; which three things he sometimes did when slightly at a loss.

Chapter Four

Miss Merle Coverdale opened the door of her flat on Denmark Hill, and admitted Mr. Druce in the early evening of midsummer's day. He took off his hat and hung it on a peg in her entrance-hall which was the shape and size of a small kitchen table, and from the ceiling of which hung a crystal chandelier. Mr. Druce followed Merle into the sitting-room. So far he had not spoken, and still without a word, while Merle took up her knitting by the two-bar electric heater, he opened the door of a small sideboard and extracted a bottle of whisky which he lifted up to the light. Opening another compartment of the sideboard he took out a glass. He poured some whisky into it and from a syphon which stood on a tray on the sideboard splashed soda-water into his drink. Then, "Want some?" he said.

"No, thanks."

He sighed and brought his drink to a large chair opposite Merle's smaller one.

"No," she said, "I've changed my mind. I think I feel like a whisky and ginger."

He sighed and went to the sideboard, where, opening a drawer, he extracted a bottle-opener. He stooped to the cupboard and found a bottle of ginger ale.

"No, I'll have gin and tonic. I think I feel like a gin and tonic."

He turned, with the bottle-opener in his hand, and looked at her.

"Yes, I feel like a gin and tonic."

And so he prepared the mixture and brought it to her. Then, sitting down, he took off his shoes and put on a pair of slippers which lay beside the chair.

Presently he looked at his watch. At which Merle put down her knitting and switched on the television. A documentary travel film was in progress, and in accompaniment to this they talked.

"Drover Willis's," he said, "have started on their new extension."

"Yes, you told me the other day."

"I see," he said, "they are advertising for automatic weaver instructors and hands. They are going to do made-up goods as well. They are advertising for ten twin-needle flat-bed machinists, also flat-lock machinists and instructors. They must be expanding."

"Four, five, six," she said, "purl two, seven, eight."

"I see," he said, "they are advertising for an Arts man."

"Well, what do you expect? It was recommended at the Conference, wasn't it?"

"Yes, but remember, Merle, we were the first in the area to adopt that recommendation. Did he come into the office today?"

"No."

"Tell him I want to see him, it's time we had a report. I've only seen him three times since he started. Weedin wants a report."

"Remind me in the morning on the business premises,

Vincent," she said. "I don't bring the office into my home, as you know."

"Weedin hasn't seen him for a week. Neither Welfare nor Personnel can get word of him."

She went to clatter dishes in the scullery. Mr. Druce got up and began to lay the table with mats, knives and forks which he took out of the sideboard. Then he went out into the hall and from his coat pocket took a bottle of stomach tablets which he placed on the table together with the pepper and salt.

Merle brought in some bread. Mr. Druce took a bread-knife from the drawer and looked at her. Then he placed the knife beside the bread on the board.

"The Brussels are not quite ready," she said, and she sat in her chair and took up her knitting. He perched on the arm. She pushed him with her elbow in the same movement as she was using for her knitting. He tickled the back of her neck, which she put up with for a while. But suddenly he pinched the skin of her neck. She screamed.

"Sh-sh," he said.

"You hurt me," she said.

"No, I was only doing this." And he pinched her neck again.

She screamed and jumped from the chair.

"The Brussels are ready," she said.

He turned off the television when she brought in the meal. "Bad for the digestion while you're eating," he said.

They did not speak throughout the meal.

Afterwards he stood with her in the red-and-white scullery, and looked on while she washed up. She placed the dishes in a red drying-rack while he dried the knives and forks. These he carried into the living-room and put away in their separate compartments in the drawer of the sideboard. As he put away the last fork he watched Merle bring in a tray with coffee cups.

Merle switched on the television and found a play far advanced. They watched the fragment of the play as they drank their coffee. Then they went into the bedroom and took off their clothes in a steady rhythm. Merle took off her cardigan and Mr. Druce took off his coat. Merle went to the wardrobe and brought out a green quilted silk dressing-gown. Mr. Druce went to the wardrobe and found his blue dressing-gown with white spots. Merle took off her blouse and Mr. Druce his waistcoat. Merle put the dressing-gown over her shoulders and, concealed by it, took off the rest of her clothes, with modest gestures. Mr. Druce slid his braces and emerged from his trousers. These he folded carefully and, padding across the room to the window, laid them on a chair. He made another trip bearing his waistcoat and jacket which he placed over the back of the chair.

They stayed in bed for an hour, in the course of which Merle twice screamed because Mr. Druce had once pinched and once bit her. "I'm covered with marks as it is," she said.

Mr. Druce rose first and put on his dressing-gown. He went to wash and returned very soon, putting a wet irritable hand round the bedroom door. Merle said, "Oh, isn't there a towel?" and taking a towel from a drawer, placed it in his hand.

When he returned she was dressed.

She went into the scullery and put on the kettle while he put on his trousers and went home to his wife.

A western breeze blew over the Rye and it was midsummer night, a Saturday. Humphrey carried the two tartan rugs from his car while Dixie walked by his side, looking to left and right and sometimes turning to see if the path was clear of policemen.

Dixie said, "I'm cold."

He said, "It's a warm night."

She said, "I'm cold."

He said, "We've got two rugs."

She walked on beside him until they came to their usual spot under a tree behind the hedge of the Old English garden.

Humphrey spread a rug and she sat down upon it. She lifted the fringe and started to pull at it, separating the matted threads.

He spread the other rug over her legs and lay leaning on his elbow beside her.

"My mum got suspicious the other night," she said. "Leslie told her I was stopping over Camberwell after the dance with Connie Weedin, but she got suspicious. And when I got in she asked me all sorts of questions about the dance. I had to make them up."

"Sure you can trust Leslie?"

"Well, I give him five shillings a week. I think it should be three shillings weeks when I don't stop out all night. But he's greedy, Leslie is."

Humphrey pulled her towards him, and started to unbutton her coat. She buttoned it up again. "I'm cold," she said.

287

"Oh, come on, Dixie," he said.

"Connie Weedin got an increment," she said. "I've got to wait for my increment till August. I only found out through the girl that does the copy die-stamp operation and had the staff salaries' balance sheet to do. Connie Weedin does the same job as what I do and she's only been there six months longer. It's only because her father's Personnel. I'm going to take it up with Miss Coverdale."

Humphrey pulled her down towards him again and kissed her face.

"What's the matter?" he said. "There's something the matter with you."

"I'm going to take Monday off," she said. "They appreciate you more if you stop away now and again."

"Well, frankly and personally," Humphrey said, "I think it's an immoral thing to do."

"Fifteen shilling rise, less tax, nine and six in Connie Weedin's packet," she said, "and I've got to wait to August. And they're all in it together. And if I don't get satisfaction from Miss Coverdale, who is there to go to? Only Personnel, and that's *Mr.* Weedin. Naturally he's going to cover up for his daughter. And if I go above him to Mr. Druce he'll only send me back to Miss Coverdale, because you know what's between *them*."

"When we're married you won't have to worry about any of them. We can get married Saturday week if you like."

"No, I don't like. What about the house? There's got to be money down for the house."

"There's money down for the house," he said.

"What about my spin-dryer?"

"Oh, to hell with your spin-dryer."

"That fifteen shillings less tax that's due to me," she said, "could have gone in the bank. If it's due to her it's due to me. Fair's fair."

He pulled the top rug up to her chin and under it started to unbutton her coat.

She sat up.

"There's something wrong with you," he said. "We should have gone dancing instead. It wouldn't have cost much."

"You're getting too sexy," she said. "It's through you having to do with Dougal Douglas. He's a sex maniac. I was told. He's immoral."

"He isn't," Humphrey said.

"Yes he is, he talks about sex quite open, any time of the day. Girls and sex."

"Why don't you relax like you used to do?" he said.

"Not unless you give up that man. He's putting ideas in your head."

"You've done plenty yourself to put ideas in my head," he said. "I didn't used to need to look far to get ideas, when you were around. Especially up in the cupboard."

"Repeat that, Humphrey."

"Lie down and relax."

"Not after what you said. It was an insult."

"I know what's the matter with you," he said. "You're losing all your sex. It's all this saving up to get married and looking to the lolly all the time, it takes the sex out of a girl. It stands to reason, it's only psychological."

"You must have been talking it over with Dougal Douglas," she said. "You wouldn't have thought of that by yourself."

She stood up and brushed down her coat. He folded up the rugs.

"I won't be talked about, it's a let-down," she said.

"Who's talked about you?" he said.

"Well, if you haven't talked about me, you've been listening to *him* talking."

"Let me tell you something," he said. "Dougal Douglas is an educated man."

"My mum's uncle's a teacher and he doesn't act like him. He doesn't cry his eyes out like Dougal did in our canteen." Dixie laughed. "He's a pansy."

"That's just his game. You don't know Dougal. I bet he wasn't crying really."

"Yes, he was. He only just lost his girl, and he cried like anything. Make you laugh."

"Then he can't be a pansy, or he wouldn't cry over a girl."

"He must be or he wouldn't cry at all."

On midsummer night Trevor Lomas walked with a somnambulistic sway into Findlater's Ballroom and looked round for Beauty. The floor was expertly laid and polished. The walls were pale rose, with concealed lighting. Beauty stood on the girls' side, talking to a group of very similar and lustrous girls. They had prepared themselves for this occasion with diligence, and as they spoke together, they did not smile much nor attend to each other's words. As an accepted thing, any of the girls might break off in the middle of a sentence, should a young man approach her, and, turning to him, might give him her entire and smiling regard.

Most of the men looked as if they had not properly

woken from deep sleep, but glided as if drugged, and with half-closed lids, towards their chosen partner. This approach found favour with the girls. The actual invitation to dance was mostly delivered by gesture; a scarcely noticeable flick of the man's head towards the dance floor. Whereupon the girl, with an outstretched movement of surrender, would swim into the hands of the summoning partner.

Trevor Lomas so far departed from the norm as to indicate to Beauty his wish by word of mouth, which he did not, however, open more than a sixteenth of an inch.

"Come and wriggle, snake," he said through this aperture.

Findlater's rooms were not given to rowdy rock but concentrated instead upon a more cultivated jive, cha-cha and variants. Beauty wriggled with excellence, and was particularly good at shrugging her shoulders and lifting forward her small stomach; while Trevor's knee-work was easy. Dougal, who had just entered with blond Elaine, looked round with approval.

During the next dance—forward half a step, one fall and a dip, back half a step, one fall and a dip—Beauty flicked her lashes towards the bandleader who was then facing the dancers, a young pale man with a thin neck which sprouted from a loose jacket of sky-blue. He acknowledged the gesture with one swift rise-and-drop of the eyebrows. Trevor looked round at the man who had now turned to his band and was flicking his limp wrists very slightly. Trevor's teeth said, "Who's your friend?"

"Whose friend?"

The crown of Trevor's head briefly indicated the bandleader.

Beauty shrugged in her jive and expressed her reply, both in the same movement.

Dougal was dancing with Elaine. He leapt into the air, he let go of her hands and dangled his arms in front of his hunched body. He placed his left hand on his hip and raised his right while his feet performed the rapid movements of the Highland Fling, heel to instep, then to knee. Elaine bowed her body and straightened it again and again in her laughter. The jiving couples slowed down like an unwound toy roundabout, and gathered beside Dougal. A tall stout man in evening dress walked over to the band; he said something to the band-leader who looked over his shoulder, observed the crowd round Dougal, and stopped the band.

"Hooch!" cried Dougal as the band stopped.

Everyone was talking or laughing. Those who were talking were all saying the same thing. They either said, "Tell him to take more water in it," or "Shouldn't be allowed," or "He's all right. Leave him alone." Some clapped their hands and said, " 'Core." The tall stout manager came over to Dougal and said with a beaming face, "It's all right, son, but no more, please."

"Don't you like Highland dancing?" Dougal said.

The manager beamed and walked away. The band started up. Dougal left the hall followed by Elaine. He reappeared shortly with Elaine tugging his arm in the opposite direction. However, he pressed into the midst of the dancers, bearing before him the lid of a dust-bin, which he had obtained from the back premises. Then he placed the lid upside down on the floor, sat cross-legged inside it, and was a man in a rocking boat rowing for his life. The band stopped, but nobody noticed the fact, owing to the many different sounds of mirth, protest, encouragement and rage. The dancers circled slowly around him while he performed a Zulu dance with the lid for a shield.

Two West Indians among the crowd started to object. "No, man."

"We don't take no insults, man."

But two other tall, black and shining dancers cheered him on, bending at the knees and clapping. These were supported by their woolly-cropped girls who laughed loud above the noise, rolling their bodies from the waist, rolling their shoulders, heads and eyes.

Dougal bowed to the black girls.

Next, Dougal sat on his haunches and banged a message out on a tom-tom. He sprang up and with the lid on his head was a Chinese coolie eating melancholy rice. He was an ardent cyclist, crouched over handlebars and pedalling uphill with the lid between his knees. He was an old woman with an umbrella; he stood on the upturned edges of the lid and speared fish from his rocking canoe; he was the man at the wheel of a racing car; he did many things with the lid before he finally propped the dust-bin lid up on his high shoulder, beating this cymbal rhythmically with his hand while with the other hand he limply conducted an invisible band, being, with long blank face, the band-leader.

The manager pushed through the crowd, still beaming. And, still beaming, he pointed out that the lid was scratching and spoiling the dance floor, and that Dougal had better leave the premises. He took Dougal, who still bore the dust-bin lid, by the elbow.

"Don't you get rough with him," Elaine shouted. "Can't you see he's deformed?"

Dougal disengaged his elbow from the manager's grasp and himself took the manager by the elbow.

"Tell me," Dougal said, as he propelled the manager through the door, "have you got a fatal flaw?"

"It's the best hall in South London and we don't want it mucked up, see? If we put on a cabaret we do it properly."

"Be kind enough," Dougal said, "to replace this lid on the dust-bin out yonder while I return to the scene within."

Elaine was standing behind him. "Come and leap, leopard," Dougal said, and soon they were moving with the rest.

They were passed by Trevor and Beauty. Trevor regarded Dougal from under his lids, letting the corners of his mouth droop meaningfully.

"Got a pain, panda?" Dougal said.

"Now, don't start," Elaine said.

Beauty laughed up and down the scale as she wriggled. When Trevor passed again he said to Dougal, "Got your lace hanky on you?"

Dougal put out his foot. Trevor stumbled. The band started playing the National Anthem. Trevor said, "You ought to get a surgical boot and lift your shoulder up to line."

"Have respect for the National Anthem," Beauty said. Her eyes were on the band-leader who, as he turned to face the floor, raised his eyebrows slightly in her direction.

"See you up on the Rye," Dougal said.

Elaine said, "Oh, no, you don't. You're seeing me home."

Trevor said, "You girls got to go home together. I've got a date with a rat on the Rye."

Several of the dancers, as they left the hall, called out to Dougal various words of gratitude, such as, "Thanks a lot for the show" and "You was swell, boy."

Dougal bowed.

Beauty, on her way to the girls' cloakroom, loitered a little behind the queue. The band-leader passed by her and moved his solemn lips very slightly. Trevor, close by, heard him say, "Come and frolic, lamb."

Beauty moved her eyes to indicate the presence of Trevor, who observed the gesture.

"She's going straight home," Trevor said through his nose, putting his face close to that of the band-leader. He gave Beauty a shove in the direction of the queue.

Beauty immediately turned back to the band-leader.

"No man," she said to Trevor, "lays hands on me."

The band-leader raised his eyebrows and dropped them sadly.

"You're coming home with me," Trevor told her.

"Thought you got a date on the Rye."

"He'll keep," Trevor said.

Beauty took a mirror from her bag and carefully applied her lipstick, turning her bronze head from side to side as she did so. Meanwhile her eyes traced the band-leader's departure from the hall.

"Elaine and I's going home together," she said.

"No, you don't," Trevor said. He peered out to the crowded entrance and there saw Elaine hanging on to Dougal. He caught her attention and beckoned to her by moving his forefinger twice very slowly. Elaine disengaged her arm from Dougal's, opened her bag, took out a cigarette, lit it, puffed slowly, then ambled over to Trevor.

"If you know what's good for your friend you'll take him home," Trevor said.

Elaine blew a puff of smoke in his face and turned away.

"The fight's off," she said to Dougal when she rejoined him. "He wants to keep an eye on his girl, he don't trust her. She got no morals."

As Trevor and Beauty emerged from the hall, Dougal, on the pavement, said to him, "Feeling frail, nightingale?"

Trevor shook off Beauty's arm and approached Dougal.

"Now don't start with him," Elaine shrieked at Dougal, "he's ignorant."

Beauty walked off on her own, with her high determined heels and her model-girl sway, placing her feet confidently and as on a chalk line.

Trevor looked round after her, then ran and caught her up.

Dougal walked with Elaine to Camberwell Green where, standing under the orange lights, he searched his pockets. When he had found a folded sheet of paper he opened it and read, " 'I walked with her to Camberwell Green, and we said goodbye rather sorrowfully at the corner of New Road; and that possibility of meek happiness vanished for ever.' This is John Ruskin and his girl Charlotte Wilkes," Dougal said, "my human research. But you and I will not say goodbye here and now. No. I'm taking you the rest of the way home in a taxi, because you're the nicest wee process-controller I've ever met."

"One thing about you I'll admit," she said, "you're different. If I didn't know you were Scotch I'd swear you were Irish. My mother's Irish."

She said they could not take a taxi up to her door because her mother didn't like her coming home with men in taxis. They dropped off at the Canal Head at Brixton.

"I'm leaving Meadows Meade," Elaine said, "Saturday week. Starting on the Monday at Drover Willis's. It's advancement."

"I saw they were advertising," Dougal said, "for staff at Drover Willis's."

They walked along by the Canal a little way, watching the quiet water.

Chapter Five

Mr. Druce said with embarrassment, "I feel I should just mention the fact that absenteeism has increased in the six weeks you've been with us. Eight per cent to be precise. Not that I'm complaining. I'm not complaining. Rome can't be built in a day. I'm just mentioning a factor that Personnel keep stressing. Weedin's a funny sort of fellow. How do you find Weedin?"

"Totally," Dougal said, "lacking in vision. It is his fatal flaw. Otherwise quite sane." He bore on his uneven shoulders all the learning and experience of the world as he said it. Mr. Druce looked away, looked again at Dougal, and looked away.

"Vision," said Mr. Druce.

"Vision," Dougal said, and he was a confessor in his box, leaning forward with his insidious advice through the grille, "is the first requisite of sanity."

"Sanity," Mr. Druce said.

Dougal closed his eyes and slowly smiled with his wide mouth. Dougal nodded his head twice and slowly, as one who understands all. Mr. Druce was moved to confess, "Sometimes I wonder if I'm sane myself, what with one thing and another." Then he laughed and said, "Fancy

298

the Managing Director of Meadows, Meade & Grindley saying things like this."

Dougal opened his eyes. "Mr. Druce, you are not as happy as you might be."

"No," Mr. Druce said, "I am not. Mrs. Druce, if I may speak in confidence . . ."

"Certainly," Dougal said.

"Mrs. Druce is not a wife in any real sense of the word." Dougal nodded.

"Mrs. Druce and I have nothing in common. When we were first married thirty-two years ago I was a travelling salesman in rayon. Times were hard, then. But I got on." Mr. Druce looked pleadingly at Dougal. "I was a success. I got on."

Dougal tightened his lips prudishly, and nodded, and he was a divorce judge suspending judgment till the whole story was heard out.

"You can't get on in business," Mr. Druce pleaded, "unless you've got the fibre for it.

"You can't get on," Mr. Druce said, "unless you've got the moral fibre. *And* you don't have to be narrow-minded. That's one thing you don't have to be."

Dougal waited.

"You have to be broad-minded," Mr. Druce protested. "In this life." He laid his elbow on the desk and, for a moment, his forehead on his hand. Then he shifted his chin to his hand and continued, "Mrs. Druce is not broad-minded. Mrs. Druce is narrow-minded."

Dougal had an elbow on each arm-rest of his chair, and his hands were joined under his chin. "There is some question of incompatibility, I should say," Dougal said.

"I should say," he said, "you have a nature at once deep and sensitive, Mr. Druce."

"Would you really?" Druce enquired of the analyst.

"And a sensitive nature," Dougal said, "requires psychological understanding."

"My wife," Druce said, ". . . it's like living a lie. We don't even speak to each other. Haven't spoken for nearly five years. One day, it was a Sunday, we were having lunch. I was talking away quite normally; you know, just talking away. And suddenly she said, 'Quack, quack.' She said, 'Quack, quack.' She said, 'Quack, quack,' and her hand was opening and shutting like this——" Mr. Druce opened and shut his hand like a duck's bill. Dougal likewise raised his hand and made it open and shut. "Quack, quack," Dougal said. "Like that?"

Mr. Druce dropped his arm. "Yes, and she said, 'That's how *you* go on—quack, quack.' "

"Quack," Dougal said, still moving his hand, "quack."

"She said to me, my wife," said Mr. Druce, "she said, 'That's how *you* go quacking on.' Well, from that day to this I've never opened my mouth to her. I can't, Dougal, it's psychological, I just can't—you don't mind me calling you Dougal?"

"Not at all, Vincent," Dougal said. "I feel I understand you. How do you communicate with Mrs. Druce?"

"Write notes," said Mr. Druce. "Do you call that a marriage?" Mr. Druce bent to open a lower drawer of his desk and brought out a book with a bright yellow wrapper. Its title was *Marital Relational Psychology*. Druce flicked over the pages, then set the book aside. "It's no use to me," he said. "Interesting case histories but it doesn't cover my case. I've thought of seeing a psychiatrist, and

300

then I think, why should I? Let *her* see a psychiatrist."

"Take her a bunch of flowers," Dougal said, looking down at the back of his hand, the little finger of which was curling daintily. "Put your arms around her," he said, becoming a lady-columnist, "and start afresh. It frequently needs but one little gesture from one partner——"

"Dougal, I can't. I don't know why it is, but I can't." Mr. Druce placed a hand just above his stomach. "Something stops me."

"You two must separate," Dougal said, "if only for a while."

Mr. Druce's hand abruptly removed from his stomach. "No," he said, "oh, no, I can't leave her." He shifted in his chair into his business-like pose. "No, I can't do that. I've got to stay with her for old times' sake."

The telephone rang. "I'm engaged," he said sharply into it. He jerked down the receiver and looked up to find Dougal's forefinger pointing into his face. Dougal looked grave, lean and inquisitorial. "Mrs. Druce," Dougal said, "has got money."

"There are interests in vital concerns which we both share," Mr. Druce said with his gaze on Dougal's finger, "Mrs. Druce and I."

Dougal shook his outstretched finger a little. "She won't *let* you leave her," he said, "because of the money."

Mr. Druce looked frightened.

"And there is also the information which she holds," Dougal said, "against you."

"What are you talking about?"

"I'm fey. I've got Highland blood." Dougal dropped his hand. "You have my every sympathy, Vincent," he said.

Mr. Druce laid his head on his desk and wept.

Dougal sat back and lit a cigarette out of Mr. Druce's box. He heaved his high shoulder in a sigh. He sat back like an exhausted medium of the spiritualist persuasion. "Does you good," Dougal said, "a wee greet. A hundred years ago all chaps used to cry regardless."

Merle Coverdale came in with the letters to be signed. She clicked her heels together as she stopped at the sight.

"Thank you, Miss Coverdale," Dougal said, putting out a hand for the letters.

Meanwhile Mr. Druce sat up and blew his nose.

"Got a comb on you?" Dougal said, squeezing Merle's hand under the letters.

She said, "This place is becoming chaos."

"What was that, Miss Coverdale?" Mr. Druce said with as little moisture as possible.

"Mr. Druce has a bad head," Dougal said as he left the room with her.

"Come and tell me what happened," said Merle.

Dougal looked at his watch. "Sorry, can't stop. I've got an urgent appointment in connection with my human research."

Dougal sat in the cheerful waiting-room looking at the tulips in their earthy bowls.

"Mr. Douglas Dougal?"

Dougal did not correct her. On the contrary he said, "That's right."

"Come this way, please."

He followed her into the office of Mr. Willis, managing director of Drover Willis's, textile manufacturers of Peckham.

"Good afternoon, Mr. Dougal," said the man behind the desk. "Take a seat."

On hearing Mr. Willis's voice Dougal changed his manner, for he perceived that Mr. Willis was a Scot.

Mr. Willis was looking at Dougal's letter of application.

"Graduate of Edinburgh?" said Mr. Willis.

"Yes, Mr. Willis."

Mr. Willis's blue eyes stared out of his brick-coloured small-featured face. They stared and stared at Dougal.

"Douglas Dougal," the man read out from Dougal's letter, and asked with a one-sided smile, "Any relation to Fergie Dougal the golfer?"

"No," Dougal said. "I'm afraid not."

Mr. Willis smiled by turning down the sides of his mouth.

"Why do you want to come into Industry, Mr. Dougal?"

"I think there's money in it," Dougal said.

Mr. Willis smiled again. "That's the correct answer. The last candidate answered, 'Industry and the Arts must walk hand in hand,' when I put that question to him. His answer was wrong. Tell me, Mr. Dougal, why do you want to come to us?"

"I saw your advertisement," Dougal said, "and I wanted a job. I saw your advertisements, too, for automatic weaver instructors and hands, and for twin-needle flat-bed machinists and flat-lock machinists and instructors. I gathered you're expanding."

"You know something about textiles?"

"I've seen over a factory. Meadows, Meade & Grindley."

"Meadows Meade are away behind us."

"Yes. So I gathered."

"Now I'll tell you what we're looking for, what we want. . . ."

Dougal sat upright and listened, only interrupting when Mr. Willis said, "The hours are nine to five-thirty."

"I would need time off for research."

"Research?"

"Industrial relations. The psychological factors behind the absenteeism, and so on, as you've been saying——"

"You could do an evening course in industrial psychology. And of course you'd have access to the factory."

"The research I have in mind," Dougal said, "would need the best part of the day for at least two months. Two months should do it. I want to look into the external environment. The home conditions. Peckham must have a moral character of its own."

Mr. Willis's blue eyes photographed every word. Dougal sat out these eyes, he went on talking, reasonably, like a solid steady Edinburgh boy, all the steadier for the hump on his shoulder.

"I'll have to speak to Davis. He is Personnel. We have to talk over the candidates and we may ask to see you again, Mr. Dougal. If we decide on you, don't fear you'll be hampered in your research."

The factory was opening its gates as Dougal came down the steps from the office into the leafy lanes of Nun Row. Some of the girls were being met by their husbands and boy friends in cars. Others rode off on motor-scooters. A number walked down to the station. "Hi, Dougal," called one of them, "what you doing here?"

It was Elaine, who had now been over a week at Drover Willis's.

"What you doing here, Dougal?"

"I'm after a job," he said. "I think I've got it."

"You leaving Meadows Meade too?"

"No," he said, "oh, no, not on your life."

"What's your game, Dougal?"

"Come and have a drink," he said, "and my Christian name is Douglas on this side of the Rye, mind that. Dougal Douglas at Meadows Meade and Douglas Dougal at Willis's, mind. Only a formality for the insurance cards and such."

"I better call you Doug, and be done with it."

Dixie sat at her desk in the typing pool and, without lifting her eyes from her shorthand book or interrupting the dance of her fingers on the keyboard, spoke out her reply to her neighbour.

"He's all one-sided at the shoulders. I don't know how any girl could go with him."

Connie Weedin, daughter of the Personnel Manager, typed on and said, "My dad says he's nuts. But I say he's got something. Definitely."

"Got something, all right. Got a good cheek. My young brother doesn't like him. My mum likes him. My dad likes him so-so. Humphrey likes him. I don't agree to that. The factory girls like him—what can you expect? I don't like him, he's got funny ideas." She stopped typing with her last word and took the papers out of her typewriter. She placed them neatly on a small stack of papers in a tray, put an envelope in her typewriter, typed an address, put more papers in her typewriter, turned over the page of her shorthand notes, and started typing again. "My dad doesn't mind him, but Leslie can't stand him. I tell you who else doesn't like him."

"Who?"

"Trevor Lomas. Trevor doesn't like him."

"I don't like Trevor, never did," Connie said. "Definitely ignorant. He goes with that girl from Celia Modes that's called Beauty. Some beauty!"

"He's a good dancer. He doesn't like Dougal Douglas and, boy, I'll say he's got something there," Dixie said.

"My dad says he's nuts. Supposed to be helping my dad to keep the factory sweet. But my dad says he don't do much with all his brains and his letters. But you can't help but like him. He's different."

"He goes out with the factory girls. He goes out with Elaine Kent that was process-controller. She's gone to Drover Willis's. He goes out with her ladyship too."

"You don't say?"

"I do say. He better watch out for Mr. Druce if it's her ladyship he's after."

"Watch out—her ladyship's looking this way."

Miss Merle Coverdale, at her supervisor's seat at the top of the room, called out, "Is there anything you want, Dixie?"

"No."

"If there's anything you want, come and ask. Is there anything you want, Connie?"

"No."

"If there's anything you want, come up here and ask for it."

Dougal came in just then, and walked with his springy step all up the long open-plan office, bobbing as he walked as if the plastic inlay flooring was a certain green and paradisal turf.

"Good morning, girls."

"You'd think he was somebody," Dixie said.

Connie opened a drawer in her small desk in which she kept a mirror, and looking down into it, tidied her hair.

Dougal sat down beside Merle Coverdale.

"There was a personal call for you," she said, handing him a slip of paper, "from a lady. Will you ring this number?"

He looked at it, put the paper in his pocket and said, "One of my employers."

Merle gave one of her laughs from the chest. "Employers—that's a good name for them. How many you got?"

"Two," Dougal said, "and a possible third. Is Mr. Weedin in?"

"Yes, he's been asking for you."

Dougal jumped up and went in to Mr. Weedin where he sat in one of the glass offices which extended from the typing pool.

"Mr. Douglas," said Mr. Weedin, "I want to ask you a personal question. What do you mean exactly by vision?"

"Vision?" Dougal said.

"Yes, vision, that's what I said."

"Do you speak literally as concerning optics, or figuratively, as it might be with regard to an enlargement of the total perceptive capacity?"

"Druce is complaining we haven't got vision in this department. I thought perhaps maybe you had been having one of your long chats with him."

"Mr. Weedin," Dougal said, "don't tremble like that. Just relax." He took from his pocket a small square silver vinaigrette which had two separate compartments. Dougal opened both lids. In one compartment lay some small white tablets. In the other were a number of yellow ones.

Dougal offered the case to Mr. Weedin. "For calming down you take two of the white ones and for revving up you take one of the yellow ones."

"I don't want your drugs. I just want to know——"

"The yellow ones make you feel sexy. The white ones, being of a relaxing nature, ensure the more successful expression of such feelings. But these, of course, are mere by-effects."

"Do you want my job? Is that what you're wanting?"

"No," Dougal said.

"Because if you want it you can have it. I'm tired of working for a firm where the boss listens to the advice of any young showpiece that takes his fancy. I've had this before. I had it with Merle Coverdale. She told Druce I was inefficient at relationship-maintenance. She told Druce that everything in the pool goes back to me through my girl Connie. She——"

"Miss Coverdale is a sensitive girl. Like an okapi, you know. You spell it O K A P I. A bit of all sorts of beast. Very rare, very nervy. You have to make allowances."

"And now you come along and you tell Druce we lack vision. And Druce calls me in and I see from the look on his face he's got a new idea. Vision, it is, this time. Try to take a tip or two, he says, from the Arts man. I said, he never hardly puts a foot inside the door does your Arts man. Nonsense, Weedin, he says, Mr. Douglas and I have many a long session. He says, watch his manner, he has a lovely manner with the workers. I said, yes, up on the Rye Saturday nights. That is unworthy of you, Weedin, he says. Is it coincidence, says I, that absenteeism has risen eight per cent since Mr. Douglas came here and is still rising? Things are bound to get worse, he says, before they get better. If you had the vision, Weedin, he says, you would comprehend my meaning. Study Douglas, he says, watch his methods."

"Funny thing I've just found out," Dougal said, "we have five cemeteries up here round the Rye within the space of a square mile. We have Camberwell New, Camberwell Old—that's full up. We have Nunhead, Deptford and Lewisham Green. Did you know that Nunhead reservoir holds twenty million gallons of water? The original title that Mendelssohn gave his *Spring Song* was *Camberwell Green*. It's a small world."

Mr. Weedin laid his head in his hand and burst into tears.

Dougal said, "You're a sick man, Mr. Weedin. I can't bear sickness. It's my fatal flaw. But I've brought a comb with me. Would you like me to comb your hair?"

"You're unnatural," said Mr. Weedin.

"All human beings who breathe are a bit unnatural," Dougal said. "If you try to be too natural, see where it gets you."

Mr. Weedin blew his nose, and shouted at Dougal: "It isn't possible to get another good position in another firm at my age. Personnel is a much-coveted position. If I had to leave here, Mr. Douglas, I would have to take a subordinate post elsewhere. I have my wife and family to think of. Druce is impossible to work for. It's impossible to leave this firm. Sometimes I think I'm going to have a breakdown."

"It would not be severe in your case," Dougal said. "It is at its worst when a man is a skyscraper. But you're only a nice wee bungalow."

"We live in a flat," Mr. Weedin managed to say.

"Do you know," Dougal said, "up at the police station they are excavating an underground tunnel which starts in the station yard and runs all the way to Nunhead. You should ponder sometimes about underground tunnels. Did you know Boadicea was broken and defeated on the Rye? She was a great beefy soldier. I think you should take Mr. Druce's advice and study my manner, Mr. Weedin. I could give you lessons at ten and six an hour."

Mr. Weedin rose to hit him, but since the walls of his office were made mostly of glass, he was prevented in the act by an overwhelming sense of being looked at from all sides.

Dougal sat in Miss Frierne's panelled hall on Saturday morning and telephoned to the Flaxman number on the little slip of paper which Merle Coverdale had handed to him the previous day.

"Miss Cheeseman, please," said Dougal.

"She isn't in," said the voice from across the water. "Who shall I say it was?"

"Mr. Dougal-Douglas," Dougal said, "spelt with a hyphen. Tell Miss Cheeseman I'll be at home all morning."

He next rang Jinny.

"Hallo, are you better?" he said.

"I've got soup on the stove. I'll ring you back."

Miss Frierne was ironing in the kitchen. She said to Dougal, "Humphrey is going to see to the roof this afternoon. It's creaking. It isn't a loose slate, it must be one of the beams loose in his cupboard."

"Funny thing," Dougal said, "it only creaks at night. It goes Creak-oop!" The dishes rattled in their rack as he leapt.

"It's the cold makes it creak, I daresay," she said.

The telephone rang. Dougal rushed out to the hall. It was not Jinny, however.

"Doug dear," said Miss Maria Cheeseman from across the river.

"Oh, it's you, Cheese."

"We really must get down to things," Miss Cheeseman said. "All this about my childhood in Peckham, it's all wrong, it was Streatham."

"There's the law of libel to be considered," Dougal said. "A lot of your early associates in Streatham are still alive. If you want to write the true story of your life you can't place it in Streatham."

"But Doug dear," she said, "that bit where you make me say I played with Harold Lloyd and Ford Sterling at the Golden Domes in Camberwell, it isn't true, dear. I *was* in a show with Fatty Arbuckle but it was South Shields."

"I thought it was a work of art you wanted to write," Dougal said, "now was that not so? If you only want to write a straight autobiography you should have got a straight ghost. I'm crooked."

"Well, Doug dear, I don't think this story about me and the Gordon Highlander is quite nice, do you? I mean to say, it isn't true. Of course it's funny about the kilt, but it's a little embarrassing——"

"Well, write your own autobiography," Dougal said.

"Oh, Doug dear, do come over to tea."

"No, you've hurt my feelings."

"Doug dear, I'm thrilled with my book. I'm sure it's going to be marvellous. I can't say I'm quite happy about all of chapter three but——"

"What's wrong with chapter three?"

"Well, it's only that last bit you wrote, it isn't *me*."

"I'll see you at four o'clock," he said, "but understand, Cheese, I don't like crossing the water when I'm in the middle of a work of art. I'm giving all my time to it."

Dougal said to Humphrey, "I was over the other side of the river on business this afternoon, and while I was over that way I called in to see my girl."

"Oh, you got a girl over there?"

"Used to have. She's got engaged to somebody else."

"Women have no moral sense," Humphrey said. "You see it in the Unions. They vote one way then go and act another way."

"She was nice, Jinny," Dougal said, "but she was too delicate in health. Do you believe in the Devil?"

"No."

"Do you know anyone that believes in the Devil?"

"I think some of those Irish——"

"Feel my head," Dougal said.

"What?"

"Feel these little bumps up here." Dougal guided Humphrey's hand among his curls at each side. "I had it done by a plastic surgeon," Dougal said.

"What?"

"He did an operation and took away the two horns. They had to shave my head in the nursing home before the operation. It took a long time for my hair to grow again."

Humphrey smiled and felt again among Dougal's curls.

"A couple of cysts," he said. "I've got one myself at the back of my head. Feel it."

Dougal touched the bump like a connoisseur.

"You supposed to be the Devil, then?" Humphrey asked.

"No, oh, no, I'm only supposed to be one of the wicked spirits that wander through the world for the ruin of souls. Have you mended those beams in the roof yet, that go Creak-oop?"

"I have," Humphrey said. "Dixie refuses to come any more."

Chapter Six

"What strikes me as remarkable," Dougal said, "is how he manages to get in so much outside his school hours."

Nelly Mahone nodded, trod out her cigarette-end, and looked at the packet of cigarettes which Dougal had placed on the table.

"Help yourself," Dougal said, and he lit the cigarette for her.

"Ta," said Nelly. She looked round her room. "It's all *clean* dirt," she said.

"You would think," Dougal said, "his parents would have some control over him."

Nelly inhaled gratefully. "Up the Elephant, that's where they all go. What was name?"

"Leslie Crewe. Thirteen years of age. The father's manager of Beverly Hills Outfitters at Brixton."

"Where they live?"

"Twelve Rye Grove."

Nelly nodded. "How much you paid him?"

"A pound the first time, thirty bob the second time. But now he's asking five quid a week flat."

Nelly whispered, "Then there's a gang behind him, surely. Can't you give up one of the jobs for a month or two?"

"I don't see why I should," Dougal said, "just to please a thirteen-year-old blackmailer."

Nelly made signs with her hands and moved her mouth soundlessly, and swung her eyes to the wall between her room and the next, to show that the walls had ears.

"A thirteen-year-old blackmailer," Dougal said, more softly. But Nelly did not like the word blackmailer at all; she placed her old fish-smelling hand over Dougal's mouth, and whispered in his ear—her grey long hair falling against his nose—"A lousy fellow next door," she said. "A slob that wouldn't do a day's work if you paid him gold. So guard your mouth." She released Dougal and started to draw the curtains.

"And here's me," Dougal said, "willing to do three, four, five men's jobs, and I get blackmailed on grounds of false pretences."

She ran with her long low dipping strides to his side and gave him a hard poke in the back. She returned to her window, which was as opaque as sackcloth and not really distinguishable from the curtain she pulled across it. On the floorboards were a few strips of very worn-out matting of a similar colour. The bed in the corner was much of the same hue, lumpy and lopsided. "But I'm charmed to see you, all the same," Nelly said for the third time, "and will you have a cup of tea?"

Dougal said, no thanks, for the third time.

Nelly scratched her head, and raising her voice, declared, "Praise be to God, who rewards those who meditate the truths he has proposed for their intelligence."

"It seems to me," Dougal said, "that my course in life has much support from the Scriptures."

"Never," Nelly said, shaking her thin body out of its

ecstasy and taking a cigarette out of Dougal's packet.

"Consider the story of Moses in the bullrushes. That was a crafty trick. The mother got her baby back and all expenses paid into the bargain. And consider the parable of the Unjust Steward. Do you know the parable of——"

"Stop," Nelly said, with her hand on her old blouse. "I get that excited by Holy Scripture I'm afraid to get my old lung trouble back."

"Were you born in Peckham?" Dougal said.

"No, Galway. I don't remember it though. I was a girl in Peckham."

"Where did you work?"

"Shoe factory I started life. Will you have a cup of tea?"

Dougal took out ten shillings.

"It's not enough," Nelly said.

Dougal made it a pound.

"If I got to follow them fellows round between here and the Elephant you just think of the fares alone," Nelly said. "I'll need more than that to go along with."

"Two quid, then," Dougal said. "And more next week."

"All right," she said.

"Otherwise it's going to be cheaper to pay Leslie."

"No it isn't," she said. "They go on and on wanting more and more. I hope you'll remember me nice if I get some way to stop their gobs."

"Ten quid," said Dougal.

"All right," she said. "But suppose one of your bosses finds out in the meantime? After all, rival firms is like to get nasty."

"Tell me," Dougal said, "how old are you?"

"I should say I was sixty-four. Have a cup of tea." She looked round the room. "It's all clean dirt."

"Tell me," Dougal said, "what it was like to work in the shoe factory."

She told him all of her life in the shoe factory till it was time for her to go out on her rounds proclaiming. Dougal followed her down the sour dark winding stairs of Lightbody Buildings, and they parted company in the passage, he going out before her.

"Good night, Nelly."

"Good night, Mr. Doubtless."

"Where's Mr. Douglas?" said Mr. Weedin.

"Haven't seen him for a week," Merle Coverdale replied. "Would you like me to ring him up at home and see if he's all right?"

"Yes, do that," Mr. Weedin said. "No, don't. Yes, I don't see why not. No, perhaps, though, we'd——"

Merle Coverdale stood tapping her pencil on her notebook, watching Mr. Weedin's hands shuffling among the papers on his desk.

"I'd better ask Mr. Druce," Mr. Weedin said. "He probably knows where Mr. Douglas is."

"He doesn't," Merle said.

"Doesn't he?"

"No, he doesn't."

"Wait till tomorrow. See if he comes in tomorrow."

"Are you feeling all right, Mr. Weedin?"

"Who? Me? I'm all right."

Merle went in to Mr. Druce. "Dougal hasn't been near the place for a week."

"Leave him alone. The boy's doing good work."

She returned to Mr. Weedin and stood in his open door

with an exaggerated simper. "We are to leave him alone. The boy's doing good work."

"Come in and shut the door," said Mr. Weedin.

She shut the door and approached his desk.

"I'm not much of a believer," Mr. Weedin said, quivering his hands across the papers before him. "But there's something Mr. Douglas told me that's on my mind." He craned upward to look through the glass panels on all sides of his room.

"They're all out at tea-break," Merle said.

Mr. Weedin dropped his head on his hands. "It may surprise you," he said, "coming from me. But it's my belief that Dougal Douglas is a diabolical agent, if not in fact the Devil."

"Mr. Weedin," said Miss Coverdale.

"Yes, I know what you're thinking. Yes, yes, you're thinking I'm going wrong up here." He pointed to his right temple and screwed it with his finger. "Do you know," he said, "that Douglas himself showed me bumps on his head where he had horns removed by plastic surgery?"

"Don't get excited, Mr. Weedin. Don't shout. The girls are coming up from the canteen."

"I felt those bumps with these very hands. Have you looked, have you ever properly looked at his eyes? That shoulder——"

"Keep calm, Mr. Weedin, you aren't getting yourself anywhere, you know."

Mr. Weedin pointed with a shaking arm in the direction of the managing director's office. "He's bewitched," he said.

Merle took tiny steps backward and got herself out of

318

the door. She went in to Mr. Druce again.

"Mr. Weedin will be wanting a holiday," she said.

Mr. Druce lifted his paper-knife, toyed with it in his hand, pointed it at Merle, and put it down. "What did you say?" he said.

Drover Willis's was humming with work when Dougal reported on Friday morning to the managing director.

"During my first week," Dougal told Mr. Willis, "I have been observing the morals of Peckham. It seemed to me that the moral element lay at the root of all industrial discontents which lead to absenteeism and the slackness at work which you described to me."

Mr. Willis looked with his blue eyes at his rational compatriot sitting before him with a shiny brief-case on his lap.

Mr. Willis said at last, "That would seem to be the correct approach, Mr. Dougal."

Dougal sat easily in his chair and continued his speech with half-closed, detached and scholarly eyes.

"There are four types of morality observable in Peckham," he said. "One, emotional. Two, functional. Three, puritanical. Four, Christian."

Mr. Willis opened the lid of a silver cigarette-box and passed it over to Dougal.

"No, thank you," Dougal said. "Take the first category, Emotional. Here, for example, it is considered immoral for a man to live with a wife who no longer appeals to him. Take the second, Functional, in which the principal factor is class solidarity such as, in some periods and places, has also existed amongst the aristocracy, and of which the main manifestation these days is the trade union movement. Three, Puritanical, of which there are several modern variants, monetary advancement being the most prevalent gauge of the moral life in this category. Four, Traditional, which accounts for about one per cent of the Peckham population, and which in its simplest form is Christian. All moral categories are of course intermingled. Sometimes all are to be found in the beliefs and behaviour of one individual."

"Where does this get us?"

"I can't say," Dougal said. "It is only a preliminary analysis."

"Please embody all this in a report for us, Mr. Dougal."

Dougal opened his brief-case and took out two sheets of paper. "I have elaborated on the question here. I have included case histories."

Mr. Willis smiled with one side of his mouth and said, "Which of these four moral codes would you say was most attractive, Mr. Dougal?"

"Attractive?" Dougal said with a trace of disapproval.

"Attractive to us. Useful, I mean, useful."

Dougal pondered seriously until Mr. Willis's little smile was forced, for dignity's sake, to fade. Then, "I could not decide until I had further studied the question."

"We'll expect another report next week?"

"No, I'll need a month," Dougal stated. "A month to work on my own. I can't come in here again for a month if you wish me to continue research on this line of industrial psychology."

"You must see round the factory," said Mr. Willis. "Peckham is a big place. We're concerned with our own works first of all."

"I've arranged to be shown round this afternoon," Dougal said. "And at the end of a month I hope to spend some time with the workers in the recreation halls and canteens."

Mr. Willis looked silently at Dougal who then permitted himself a slight display of enthusiasm. He leaned forward.

"Have you observed, Mr. Willis, the frequency with which your employees use the word 'immoral'? Have you noticed how equally often they use the word 'ignorant'? These words are significant," Dougal said, "psychologically and sociologically."

Mr. Willis smiled, as far as he was able, into Dougal's face. "Take a month and see what you can do," he said. "But bring us a good plan of action at the end of it. Drover, my partner, is anxious about absenteeism. We want some moral line that will be both commendable by us and acceptable to our staff. You've got some sound ideas, I can see that. And method. I like method."

Dougal nodded and took his long serious face out of the room.

Miss Frierne said, "That boy Leslie Crewe has been here. He was looking for you. Wants to go your errands and make a bob like a good kid. Perhaps his mother's a bit short."

"Anyone with him?"

"No. He came to the back door this time."

"Oh," Dougal said, "did you get rid of him quickly?"

"Well, he wouldn't go for a long time. He kept saying when would Mr. Douglas be home, and could he do anything for you. He was very polite, I will say that. Then he asked the time and then he said his Dad used to live up this road in number eight. So I took him in the kitchen.

I thought, well, he's only a boy, and gave him a doughnut. He said his sister was looking forward to marrying Humphrey in September. He said she saves all her wages and the father in America dresses her. He said——"

"He must have kept you talking a long time," Dougal said.

"Oh, I didn't mind. It was a nice break in the afternoon. A nice lad, he is. He goes out Sundays with the Rover Scouts. I'd just that minute come in and I was feeling a bit upset because of something that happened in the street, so——"

"Did he ask if he could go up and wait in my room?"

"No, not this time. I wouldn't have let him in your room, especially after you said nobody was to be let in there. Don't you worry about your room. Nobody wants to go into your room, I'm sure."

Dougal said, "You are too innocent for this wicked world."

"Innocent I always was," Miss Frierne said, "and that was why I was so taken aback that day by the Gordon Highlander up on One Tree Hill. Have a cup of tea."

"Thanks," Dougal said. "I'll just pop upstairs a minute first."

His room had, of course, been disturbed. He unlocked a drawer in his dressing-table and found that two notebooks were missing. His portable typewriter had been opened and clumsily shut. Ten five-pound notes were, however, untouched in another drawer by the person who had climbed to his room while Leslie had engaged Miss Frierne in talk.

He came down to the kitchen where Miss Frierne sighed into her tea.

"Next time that Leslie comes round to the back door have a look, will you, to see who he's left at the front door. His father's worried about his companions after school hours, I happen to know."

"He only wanted to know if you had any errands to run. I daresay to help his mother, like a good kid. I told him I thought you're short of bacon for your breakfast. He'll be back. There's no harm in that boy, I know it by instinct, and instinct always tells. Like what happened to me in the street to-day." She sipped her tea, and was silent.

Dougal sipped his. "Go on," he said, "you're dying to tell me what happened."

"As true as God is my judge," she said, "I saw my brother up at Camberwell Green that left home in nine-teen-nineteen. We never heard a word from him all those years. He was coming out of Lyons."

"Didn't you go and speak to him?"

"No," she said, "I didn't. He was very shabby, he looked awful. Something stopped me. It was an instinct. I couldn't do it. He saw me, too."

She took a handkerchief out of her sleeve and patted beneath her glasses.

"You should have gone up to him," Dougal said. "You should have said, 'Are you . . .' —what was his name?"

"Harold," she said.

"You should have said, 'Are you Harold?', that's what you ought to have done. Instead of which you didn't. You came back here and gave a doughnut to that rotten little Leslie."

"Don't you point your finger at me, Dougal. Nobody does that in my house. You can find other accommodation *if* you like, any *time* you like and when you like."

Dougal got up and shuffled round the kitchen with a slouch and an old ill look. "Is that what your old brother looked like?" he said.

She laughed in high-pitched ripples.

Dougal thrust his hands into his pockets and looked miserably at his toes.

She started to cry all over her spectacles.

"Perhaps it wasn't your brother at all," Dougal said.

"That's what I'm wondering, son."

"Just feel my head," Dougal said, "these two small bumps here."

"There are four types of morality in Peckman," Dougal said to Mr. Druce. "The first category is——"

"Dougal," he said, "are you doing anything tonight?"

"Well, I usually prepare my notes. You realise, don't you, that Oliver Goldsmith taught in a school in Peckham? He used to commit absenteeism and spent a lot of his time in a coffeehouse at the Temple instead of in Peckham. I wonder why?"

"I need your advice," Mr. Druce said. "There's a place in Soho——"

"I don't like crossing the river," Dougal said, "not without my broomstick."

Mr. Druce made double chins and looked lovingly at Dougal.

"There's a place in Soho——"

"I could spare a couple of hours," Dougal said. "I could see you up at Dulwich at the Dragon at nine."

"Well, I was thinking of making an evening of it, Dougal; some dinner at this place in Soho——"

"Nine at the Dragon," Dougal said.

"Mrs. Druce knows a lot of people in Dulwich."

"All the better," Dougal said.

Dougal arrived at the Dragon at nine sharp. He drank gin and peppermint while he waited. At half-past nine two girls from Drover Willis's came in. Dougal joined them. Mr. Druce did not come. At ten o'clock they went on a bus to the Rosemary Branch in Southampton Way. Here, Dougal expounded the idea that everyone should take every second Monday morning off their work. When they came out of the pub, at eleven, Nelly Mahone crossed the street towards them.

"Praise be to the Lord," she cried, "whose providence in all things never fails."

"Hi, Nelly," said one of the girls as she passed.

Nelly raised up her voice and in the same tone proclaimed, "Praise be to God who by sin is offended, Trevor Lomas, Collie Gould up the Elephant with young Leslie, and by penance appeased, the exaltation of the humble and the strength of the righteous."

"Ah, Nelly," Dougal said.

Chapter Seven

"Yes, Cheese?" Dougal said.

"Look, Doug, I think I can't have this story about the Dragon at Dulwich, it's indecent. Besides, it isn't true. And I never went to Soho at that age. I never went out with any managing director——"

"It will help to sell the book," Dougal said. He breathed moistly on the oak panel of Miss Frierne's hall, and with his free hand drew a face on the misty surface where he had breathed.

"And Doug dear," said the voice from across the river, "how did you know I started life in a shoe factory? I mean to say, I didn't tell you that. How did you know?"

"I didn't know, Cheese," Dougal said.

"You must have known. You've got all the details right, except that it wasn't in Peckham, it was Streatham. It all came back to me as I read it. It's uncanny. You've been checking up on me, haven't you, Doug?"

"Aye," Dougal said. He breathed on the panel, wrote in a word, then rubbed it off.

"Doug, you mustn't do that. It makes me creepy to think that people can find out all about you," Miss Cheeseman said. "I mean, I don't want to put in about the shoe factory and all that. Besides, the period. It dates me."

"It only makes you sixty-eight, Cheese."

"Well, Doug, there must be a way of making me not even that. I want you to come over, Doug. I've been feeling off colour."

"I've got a fatal flaw," Dougal said, "to the effect that I can't bear anyone off colour. Moreover, Saturday's my day off and it's a beautiful summer day."

"Dear Doug, I promise to be well. Only come over. I'm *worried* about my book. It's rather . . . rather too . . ."

"Rambling," Dougal said.

"Yes, that's it."

"I'll see you at four," Dougal said.

At the back of Hollis's Hamburgers at Elephant and Castle was a room furnished with a fitted grey carpet, a red upholstered modern suite comprising a sofa and two cubic armchairs, a television receiver on a light wood stand, a low glass-topped coffee table, a table on which stood an electric portable gramophone and a tape recorder, a light wood bureau desk, a standard lamp and several ash-trays on stands. Two of the walls were papered with a wide grey stripe. The other two were covered with a pattern of gold stars on red. Fixed to the walls were a number of white brackets containing pots of indoor ivy. The curtains, which were striped red and white, were drawn. This cheerful interior was lit by a couple of red-shaded wall-lamps. In one chair sat Leslie Crewe, with his neck held rigidly and attentively. He was dressed in a navy-blue suit of normal cut, and a peach-coloured tie, and looked older than thirteen. In another chair lolled Collie Gould who was eighteen and had been found unfit for National Service; Collie suffered from lung trouble for which he was constantly under treatment and was at present on probation for motor stealing. He wore a dark-grey draped jacket with narrow black trousers. Trevor Lomas, dressed in blue-grey, lay between them on the sofa. All smoked American cigarettes. All looked miserable, not as an expression of their feelings, but as if by an instinctive pre-arrangement, to convey a decision on all affairs whatsoever.

Trevor held in his hand one of the two thin exercise books he had stolen from Dougal's drawer. The other lay on the carpet beside him.

"Listen to this," Trevor said. "It's called 'Phrases suitable for Cheese.'"

"Suitable for what?" said Collie.

"Cheese, it says. Code word, obvious. Listen to this what you make of it. There's a list.

"I thrilled to his touch

"I was too young at the time to understand why my mother was crying

"As he entered the room a shudder went through my frame

"In that moment of silent communion we renewed our shattered faith

"She was to play a vital role in my life

"Memory had not played me false

"He was always an incurable romantic

"I became the proud owner of a bicycle

"He spoke to me in desiccated tones

"Autumn again. Autumn. The burning of leaves in the park

328

"He spelt disaster to me
"I revelled in my first tragic part
"I had no eyes for any other man
"We were living a lie
"She proved a mine of information
"Once more fate intervened
"Munificence was his middle name
"I felt a grim satisfaction
"They were poles apart
"I dropped into a fitful doze."

"Read us it again, Trev," Leslie said. "It sounds like English Dictation. Perhaps he's a teacher as well."

Trevor ignored him. He tapped the notebook and addressed Collie.

"Code," he said. "It's worth lolly."

An intensified expression of misery on Collie's face expressed his agreement.

"In with a gang, he is. It's bigger than I thought. Question now, to find out what his racket is."

"Sex," Leslie said.

"You don't say so?" Trevor said. "Well, that's helpful, son. But we happen to have guessed all that. Question is, what game of sex? Question is, national or international?"

Collie blew out his smoke as if it were slow poison. "Got to work back from a clue," he said in his sick voice. "Autumn's a clue. Wasn't there something about autumn?"

"How dumb can you get?" Trevor enquired through his nose. "It's a code. Autumn means something else. Everything means something." He dropped the notebook and painfully picked up the other. He read:

329

"Peckham. Modes of communication.

"Actions more effective than words. Enact everything. Depict.

"Morality. Functional. Emotional. Puritanical. Classical.

"Nelly Mahone. Lightbody Buildings.

"Tunnel. Meeting-house Lane Excavations police station yard. Order of St. Bridget. Nuns decamped in the night."

Trevor turned the pages.

Entry Parish Register 1658. May 5.
    Rose, wife of Wm. Hathaway buried
    Aged 103, who boare a sonn at the age
    of 63.

Trevor said, "Definitely a code. Look how he spells 'son.' And this about bearing at the age of sixty-three."

Collie and Leslie came over to see the book.

"There's a clue here," Collie said, "that we could follow up."

"No," said Trevor, "you don't say so? Come on, kids, we got to look up Nelly Mahone."

"If we're going to have a row," Mavis said, "turn on the wireless loud."

"We're not going to have a row," said her husband, Arthur Crewe, in a voice trembling with patience. "I only ask a plain question, what you mean you can't ask him where he's going when he goes out?"

Mavis switched on the wireless to a roar. Then she herself shouted above it.

"If you want to know where he goes, ask him yourself."

"If you can't ask him how can I ask him?" Arthur said in competition with the revue on the wireless.

"What's it matter where he goes? You can't keep running about after him like he was a baby. He's thirteen now."

"You ought to a kept some control of him. Of course it's too late now——"

"Why didn't you keep some control——"

"How can I be at my work and control the kids same time? If you was——"

"There's no need to swear," Mavis said.

"I didn't swear. But I bloody well will, and there's no need to shout." He turned off the wireless and silence occurred, bringing a definite aural sensation.

"Turn on that wireless. If we're going to have a row I'm not letting the neighbours get to know," Mavis said.

"Leave it be," Arthur said, effortful with peace. "There's not going to be any row."

Dixie came downstairs. "What's all the row?" she said.

"Your step-dad's on about young Leslie. Expects me to ask him where he's going when he goes out. I say, why don't *he* ask if he wants to know. I haven't got eyes the back of my head, have I?"

"Sh-sh-sh. Don't raise your voice," Arthur said.

"He's afraid to say a word to Leslie," Dixie said.

"That's just about it," said her mother.

"Who's afraid?" Arthur shouted.

"You are," Mavis shouted.

"I'm not afraid. You're afraid. . . ."

"Keep time," said Trevor. "All keep in time. It's psychological."

331

And so they all three trod in time up the stone stairs of Lightbody Buildings. Twice, a door opened on a landing, a head looked out, and the door shut quickly again. Trevor and his followers stamped louder as they approached Nelly Mahone's. Trevor beat like a policeman thrice on her door, and placed his ear to the crack.

There was a shuffling sound, a light switch clicked, then silence.

Trevor beat again.

"Who is it?" Nelly said from immediately on the other side of the door.

"Police agents," Trevor said.

The light switch clicked again, and Nelly opened the door a fragment.

Trevor pushed it wide open and walked in, followed by Collie and Leslie.

Leslie said, "I'm not stopping in this dirty hole," and made to leave.

Trevor caught him by the coat and worked him to a standstill.

"It's all clean dirt," Nelly said.

"Sit over there," Trevor said to Nelly, pointing to a chair beside the table. She did so.

He sat himself on the edge of the table and pointed to the edge of the bed for Leslie and the lopsided armchair for Collie.

"We come to talk business," Trevor said, "concerning a Mr. Dougal Douglas."

"Never heard of him," Nelly said.

"No?" Trevor said, folding his arms.

"Supposed to be police agents, are you? Well, you can be moving off if you don't want trouble. There's a gentleman asleep next door. I only got to raise me voice and——"

Collie and Leslie looked at the wall towards which Nelly pointed.

"Nark it," Trevor said. "He's gone to football this afternoon. Now, about Mr. Dougal Douglas——"

"Never heard of him," Nelly said.

Trevor leaned forward slightly towards her and, taking a lock of her long hair in his hand, twitched it sharply.

"Help! Murder! Police!" Nelly said.

Trevor put his big hand over her mouth and spoke to her.

"Listen, Nelly, for your own good. We got money for you."

Nelly struggled, her yellow eyeballs were big.

"I get my boys to rough you up if you won't listen, Nelly. Won't we, boys?"

"That's right," Collie said.

"Won't we, boys?" Trevor said, looking at Leslie.

"Sure," said Leslie.

Trevor removed his hand, now wet, from Nelly's mouth, and wiped it on the side of his trousers. He took a large wallet from his pocket, and flicked through a pile of bank notes.

"He's at Miss Frierne's up the Rye," Nelly said.

Trevor laid his wallet on the table and folding his arms, looked hard at Nelly.

"He got a job at Meadows Meade," Nelly said.

Trevor waited.

"He got another job at Drover Willis's under different name. No harm in him, son."

Trevor waited.

"That's all, son," Nelly said.

333

"What's cheese?" Trevor said.

"What's what?"

Trevor pulled her hair, so that she toppled towards him from her chair.

"I'll find out more. I only seen him once," Nelly said.

"What he want with you?"

"Huh?"

"You heard me."

Nelly looked at the two others, then back at Trevor.

"The boys is under age," she remarked, and her eyes flicked a little to reveal that her brain was working.

"I ask you a question," Trevor said. "What Mr. Dougal Douglas come to you for?"

"About the girl," she said.

"What girl?"

"He's after Beauty," she said. "He want me to find out where she live and that. You better go and see what he's up to. Probable he's with her now."

"Who's his gang?" Trevor enquired, reaching for Nelly's hair.

She jumped away from him. Leslie's nerve gave way and he ran to Nelly and hit her on the face.

"Murder!" Nelly screamed.

Trevor put his hand over her mouth, and signalled with his eyes to Collie, who went to the door, opened it a little way, listened, then shut it again. Collie then struck Leslie, who backed on to the bed.

Trevor, with his big hand on Nelly's mouth, whispered softly in her ear,

"Who's his gang, Nelly? What's the code key? Ten quid to you, Nelly."

She squirmed and he took his moist hand from her mouth. "Who's his gang?"

"He goes with Miss Coverdale sometimes. He goes with that fair-haired lady controller that's gone to Drover Willis's. That's all I know of his company."

"Who are the fellows?"

"I'll find out," she said, "I'll find out, son. Have a heart."

"Who's Rose Hathaway?"

"Never heard of her."

Trevor took Dougal's rolled-up exercise book from an inside pocket and spreading it out at the page read out the bit about that Rose Hathaway who was buried at a hundred and three. "That mean anything to you?" Trevor said.

"It sounds all wrong. I'll ask him."

"You won't. You'll find out your own way. Not a word we been here, get that?"

"It's only his larks. He's off his nut, son."

"Did he by any chance bring Humphrey Place here with him?"

"Who?"

Trevor twisted her arm.

"Humphrey Place. Goes with Dixie Morse."

"No, never seen him but once at the Grapes."

"You'll be seeing *us* again," Trevor said.

He went down the dark stone stairs followed by Leslie and Collie.

"Killing herself," Merle said, "that's what she is, for money. Then she comes in to the pool dropping tired next day, not fit for the job. I said to her, 'Dixie,' I said, 'what time did you go to bed last night?' 'I consider that a personal question, Miss Coverdale,' she says. 'Oh,' I says, 'well, if it isn't a personal question will you kindly type these two reports over again? There's five mistakes on one and six on the other.' 'Oh!' she said, 'what mistakes?' Because she won't own up to her mistakes till you put them under her nose. I said, 'These mistakes as marked.' She said 'Oh!' I said, 'You've been doing nothing but yawn yawn yawn all week.' Well, at tea-break when Dixie was out Connie says to me, 'Miss Coverdale, it's Dixie's evening job making her tired.' 'Evening job?' I said. She said, 'Yes, she's an usherette at the Regal from six-thirty to ten-thirty, makes extra for her wedding savings.' 'Well,' I said, 'no wonder she can't do her job here!' "

Dougal flashed an invisible cinema-torch on to the sprightly summer turf of the Rye. "Mind the step, Madam. Three-and-sixes on the right."

Merle began to laugh from her chest. Suddenly she sat down on the Rye and began to cry. "God!" she said. "Dougal, I've had a rotten life."

"And it isn't over yet," Dougal said, sitting down beside her at a little distance. "There might be worse ahead."

"First my parents," she said. "Too possessive. They're full of themselves. They don't think anything of me myself. They like to be able to say 'Merle's head of the pool at Meadows Meade,' but that's about all there is to it. I broke away and of course like a fool took up with Mr. Druce. Now I can't get away from him, somehow. You've unsettled me, Dougal, since you came to Peckham. I shall have a nervous breakdown, I can see it coming."

"If you do," Dougal said, "I won't come near you. I can't bear sickness of any sort."

"Dougal," she said, "I was counting on you to help me to get away from Mr. Druce."

"Get another job," he said, "and refuse to see him any more. It's easy."

"Oh, everything's easy for you. You're free."

"Aren't you free?" Dougal said.

"Yes, as far as the law goes."

"Well, stop seeing Druce."

"After six years, going on seven, Dougal, I'm tied in a sort of way. And what sort of job would I get at thirty-eight?"

"You would have to come down," Dougal said.

"After being head of the pool," she said, "I couldn't. I've got to think of my pride. And there's the upkeep of my flat. Mr. Druce puts a bit towards it."

"People are looking at you crying," Dougal said, "and they think it's because of me."

"So it is in a way. I've had a rotten life."

"Goodness, look at that," Dougal said.

She looked upward to where he was pointing.

"What?" she said.

"Up there," Dougal said; "trees in the sky."

"What are you talking about? I don't see anything."

"Look properly," Dougal said, "up there. And don't look away because Mr. Druce is watching us from behind the pavilion."

She looked at Dougal.

"Keep looking up," he said, "at the trees with red tassels in the sky. Look, where I'm pointing."

Several people who were crossing the Rye stopped to

337

look up at where Dougal was pointing. Dougal said to them, "A new idea. Did you see it in the papers? Planting trees and shrubs in the sky. Look there—it's a tip of a pine."

"I think I *do* see something," said a girl.

Most of the crowd moved sceptically away, still glancing upward now and then. Dougal brought Merle to her feet and drifted along with the others.

"Is he still there?" Merle said.

"Yes. He must be getting tired of going up and down in lifts."

"Oh, he only does that on Saturday mornings. He usually stays at home in the afternoons. He comes to me in the evenings. I've got a rotten life. Sometimes I think I'll swallow a bottle of aspirins."

"That doesn't work," Dougal said. "It only makes you ill. And the very thought of illness is abhorrent to me."

"He's keen on you," Merle said.

"I know he is, but *he* doesn't."

"He must do if he's keen——"

"Not at all. I'm his first waking experience of an attractive man."

"You fancy yourself."

"No, Mr. Druce does that."

"With your crooked shoulder," she said, "you're not all that much cop."

"Advise Druce on those lines," he said.

"He doesn't take my advice any more."

"How long would you give him with the firm?"

"Well, since he's started to slip, I've debated that question a lot. The business is on the decline. It's a worry, I mean about my flat, if Mr. Druce loses his job."

"I'd give him three months," Dougal said.

Merle started to cry again, walking towards the streets with Dougal. "Is he still there?" she said. Dougal did a dancer's pirouette, round and round, and stopped once more by Merle's side.

"He's walking away in the other direction."

"Oh, I wonder where he's going?"

"Home to Dulwich, I expect."

"It's immoral," Merle said, "the way he goes back to that woman in that house. They never say a word to each other."

"Stop girning. You look awful with your red eyes. It detracts from the okapi look. But all the same, what a long neck you've got!"

She put her hand up to her throat and moved it up her long neck. "Mr. Druce squeezed it tight the other day," she said, "for fun, but I got a fright."

"It looks like a maniac's delight, your neck," Dougal said.

"Well, you've not got much of one, with your shoulder up round your ear."

"A short neck denotes a good mind," Dougal said. "You see, the messages go quicker to the brain because they've shorter to go." He bent and touched his toes. "Suppose the message starts down here. Well, it come up here——"

"Watch out, people are looking."

They were in the middle of Rye Lane, flowing with shopping women and prams. A pram bumped into Dougal as he stood upright, causing him to barge forward into two women who stood talking. Dougal embraced them with wide arms. "Darlings, watch where you're going," he said. They beamed at each other and at him.

339

"Charming, aren't you?" Merle said. "There's a man leaning out of that car parked outside Higgins and Jones, seems to be watching you."

Dougal looked across the road. "Mr. Willis is watching me," he said. "Come and meet Mr. Willis." He took her arm to cross the road.

"I'm not dressed for an introduction," Merle said.

"You are only an object of human research," Dougal said, guiding her obliquely through the traffic towards Mr. Willis.

"I'm just waiting for my wife. She's shopping in there," Mr. Willis explained. Now that Dougal had approached him he seemed rather embarrassed. "I wasn't sure it was you, Mr. Dougal," he explained. "I was just looking to see. A bit short-sighted."

"Miss Merle Coverdale, one of my unofficial helpers," Dougal said uppishly. "Interesting," he said, "to see what Peckham does on its Saturday afternoons."

"Yes, quite." Mr. Willis pinkly took Merle's hand and glanced towards the shop door.

Dougal gave a reserved nod and, as dismissing Mr. Willis from his thoughts, led Merle away.

"Why did he call you Mr. Dougal?" Merle said.

"Because he's my social inferior. Formerly a footman in our family."

"What's he now?"

"One of my secret agents."

"You'd send me mad if I let you. Look what you've done to Weedin. You're driving Mr. Druce up the wall."

"I have powers of exorcism," Dougal said, "that's all."

"What's that?"

"The ability to drive devils out of people."

340

"I thought you said you were a devil yourself."

"The two states are not incompatible. Come to the police station."

"Where are we going, Dougal?"

"The police station. I want to see the excavation."

He took her into the station yard where he had already made himself known as an interested archaeologist. By the coal-heap was a wooden construction above a cavity already some feet deep. Work had stopped for the week-end. They peered inside.

"The tunnel leads up to Nunhead," Dougal said, "the nuns used to use it. They packed up one night over a hundred years ago, and did a flit, and left a lot of debts behind them."

A policeman came up to them with quiet steps and, pointing to the coal-heap, said, "The penitential cell stood in that corner. Afternoon, sir."

"Goodness, you gave me a fright," Merle said.

"There's bodies of nuns down there, miss," the police-man said.

Merle had gone home to await Mr. Druce. Dougal walked up to Costa's Café in the cool of the evening. Eight people were inside, among them Humphrey and Dixie, seated at a separate table eating the remains of sausage and egg. Humphrey kicked out a chair at their table for Dougal to sit down upon. Dixie touched the corners of her mouth with a paper napkin, and carefully picking up her knife and fork, continued eating, turning her head a little obliquely to receive each small mouthful. Humphrey had just finished. He set down his knife and fork on the plate and pushed the plate away. He rubbed

the palms of his hands together twice and said to Dougal,
"How's life?"

"It exists," Dougal said, and looked about him.

"You had a distinguished visitor this afternoon. But
you'd just gone out. The old lady was out and I answered
to him. He wouldn't leave his name. But of course I knew
it. Mr. Druce of Meadows Meade. Dixie pointed him out
to me, once, didn't you, Dixie?"

"Yes," Dixie said.

"He followed me all over the Rye, so greatly did Mr.
Druce wish to see me," Dougal said.

"If I was you," Humphrey said, "I'd keep to normal
working hours. Then he wouldn't have any call on you
Saturday afternoons—would he, Dixie?"

"I suppose not," Dixie said.

"Coffee for three," Dougal said to the waiter.

"You had another visitor, about four o'clock," Humphrey said. "I'll give you a clue. She had a pot of flowers
and a big parcel."

"Elaine," Dougal said.

The waiter brought three cups of coffee, one in his right
hand and two—one resting on the other—in his left. These
he placed carefully on the table. Dixie's slopped over in
her saucer. She looked at the saucer.

"Swap with me," Humphrey said.

"Have mine," Dougal said.

She allowed Humphrey to exchange his saucer with
hers. He tipped the contents of the saucer into his coffee,
sipped it, and set it down.

"Sugar," he said.

Dougal passed the sugar to Dixie.

She said, "Thank you." She took two lumps, dropped

342

them in her coffee, and stirred it, watching it intently.

Humphrey put three lumps in his coffee, stirred it rapidly, tasted it. He pushed the sugar bowl over to Dougal, who took a lump and put it in his mouth.

"I let her go up to your room," Humphrey said. "She said she wanted to put in some personal touches. There was the pot of flowers and some cretonne cushions. The old lady was out. I thought it nice of Elaine to do that—wasn't it nice, Dixie?"

"Wasn't what nice?"

"Elaine coming to introduce feminine touches in Dougal's room."

"I suppose so."

"Feeling all right?" Humphrey said to her.

"I suppose so."

"Do you want to go on somewhere else or do you want to stay here?"

"Anything you like."

"Have a cake."

"No, thank you."

"Why does your brother go hungry?" Dougal said to her.

"Whose brother goes hungry?"

"Yours. Leslie."

"What you mean, goes hungry?"

"He came round scrounging doughnuts off my land-lady the other day," Dougal said.

Humphrey rubbed the palms of his hands together and smiled at Dougal. "Oh, kids, you know what they're like."

"I won't stand for him saying anything against Leslie," Dixie said, looking round to see if anyone at the other tables was listening. "Our Leslie isn't a scrounger. It's a lie."

"It is not a lie," Dougal said.

"I'll speak to my step-dad," Dixie said.

"I should," Dougal said.

"What's a doughnut to a kid?" Humphrey said to them both. "Don't make something out of nothing. Don't *start*."

"Who started?" Dixie said.

"You did, a matter of fact," Humphrey said, "with your bad manners. You could hardly say hallo to Dougal when he came in."

"That's right, take his part," she said. "Well, I'm not staying here to be insulted."

She rose and picked up her bag. Dougal pulled her down to her chair again.

"Take your hand off me," she said, and rose.

Humphrey pulled her down again.

She remained seated, looking ahead into the far distance.

"There's Beauty just come in," Dougal said.

Dixie turned her head to see Beauty. Then she resumed her fixed gaze.

Dougal whistled in Beauty's direction.

"I shouldn't do that," Humphrey said.

"My God, he's supposed to be a professional man," Dixie said, "and he opens his mouth and whistles at a girl."

Dougal whistled again.

Beauty raised her eyebrows.

"You'll have Trevor Lomas in after us," Humphrey said. The waiter and Costa himself came and hovered round their table.

"Come on up to the Harbinger," Dougal said, "and we'll take Beauty with us."

"Now look. I quite *like* Trevor," Humphrey said.

"He's to be best man at our wedding," Dixie said. "He's got a good job with prospects and sticks in to it."

Dougal whistled. Then he called across two tables to Beauty, "Waiting for somebody?"

Beauty dropped her lashes. "Not in particular," she said.

"Coming up to the Harbinger?"

"Don't mind."

Dixie said, "Well, *I* do. I'm fussy about my company."

"What she say?" Beauty said, jerking herself upright in support of the question.

"I said," said Dixie, "that I've got another appointment."

"Beauty and I will be getting along then," Dougal said. He went across to Beauty who was preparing to comb her hair.

Humphrey said, "After all, Dixie, we've got nothing else to do. It might look funny if we don't go with Dougal. If Trevor finds out he's been to a pub with his girl——"

"You're bored with me—*I* know," Dixie said. "My company isn't good enough for you as soon as Dougal comes on the scene."

"Such compliments as you pay me!" Dougal said across to her.

"I was not aware I was addressing you," Dixie said.

"All right, Dixie, we'll stop here," Humphrey said.

Dougal was holding up a small mirror while the girl combed her long copper-coloured hair over the table.

Dixie's eyes then switched over to Dougal. She gave a

long sigh. "I suppose we'd better go to the pub with them," she said, "or you'll say I spoiled your evening."

"No necessity," Beauty said as she put away her comb and patted her handbag.

"We might enjoy ourselves," Humphrey said.

Dixie got her things together rather excitedly. But she said, "Oh, it isn't my idea of a night out."

And so they followed Dougal and Beauty up Rye Lane to the Harbinger. Beauty was halfway through the door of the saloon bar, but Dougal had stopped to look into the darkness of the Rye beyond the swimming baths, from which came the sound of a drunken woman approaching; and yet as it came nearer, it turned out not to be a drunken woman, but Nelly proclaiming.

Humphrey and Dixie had reached the pub door. "It's only Nelly," Humphrey said, and he pushed Dougal towards the doorway in which Beauty stood waiting.

"I like listening to Nelly," Dougal said, "for my human research."

"Oh, get inside for goodness' sake," Dixie said as Nelly appeared in the street light.

"Six things," Nelly declaimed, "there are which the Lord hateth, and the seventh his soul detesteth. Haughty eyes, a lying tongue, hands that shed innocent blood. See me in the morning. A heart that deviseth wicked plots, feet that are swift to run into mischief. Ten at Paley's yard. A deceitful witness that uttereth lies. Meeting-house Lane. And him that soweth discord among brethren."

"Nelly's had a few," Humphrey said as they pushed into the bar. "She's a bit shaky on the pins tonight."

A bright spiky chandelier and a row of glittering crystal

lamps set against a mirror behind the bar—though in fact these had been installed since the war—were designed to preserve in theory the pub's vintage fame in the old Camberwell Palace days. The chief barmaid had a tiny nose and a big chin; she was a middle-aged woman of twenty-five. The barman was small and lithe. He kept swinging to and fro on the balls of his feet.

Beauty wanted a martini. Dixie, at first under the impression that Humphrey was buying the round, asked for a ginger ale, but when she perceived that Dougal was to pay for the drinks, she said, "Gin and ginger ale." Humphrey and Dougal carried to a table the girls' drinks and their own half-pints of mild which glittered in knobbly-moulded glass mugs like versions of the chandelier. Round the wall were hung signed photographs of old-time variety actors with such names, meaningless to most but oddly suggestive, as Flora Finch and Ford Sterling, who were generally assumed to be Edwardian stars. An upright piano placed flat against a wall caused Tony the pianist to see little of the life of the house, except when he turned round for a rest between numbers. Tony's face was not merely pale, but quite bloodless. He wore a navy-blue coat over a very white shirt, the shirt buttoned up to the neck with no tie. His half-pint mug, constantly replenished by the customers, stood on an invariable spot on the right-hand side of the piano-top. As he played, he swung his shoulders from side to side and bent over the piano occasionally to stress his notes. He might, from this back view, have been in an enthusiastic mood, but when he turned round it was obvious he was not. It was Tony's lot to play tunes of the nineteen-tens and -twenties, to the accompaniment of slightly jeering comments from the customers, and as he stooped over to execute *Charmaine*, Beauty said to him, "Groove in, Tony." He ignored this as he had ignored all remarks for the past nineteen months. "Go, man, go," someone suggested. "Leave him alone," the barmaid said. "You just show up your ignorance. He's a beautiful player. It's period stuff. He got to play it like that." Tony finished his number, took down his beer and turned his melancholy front to the company.

"Got any rock and cha-cha on your list, Tony?"

"Rev up to it, son. Groove in."

Tony turned, replaced his beer on the top of the piano, and rippled his hands over *Ramona*.

"Go, man, go."

"Any more of that," said the barmaid, "and you go man go outside."

"Yes, that's what *I* say. Tony's the pops."

"Here's a pint, Tony. Cheer up, son, it may never happen."

At ten past nine Trevor Lomas entered the pub followed by Collie Gould. Trevor edged in to the bar and stood with his back to it, leaning on an elbow and surveying as it were the passing scene.

"Hallo, Trevor," Dixie said.

"Hi, Dixie," Trevor replied severely.

"Hi," Collie Gould said.

Beauty, who was on her fourth martini, bowed graciously, and had some difficulty in regaining her upright posture.

The barmaid said, "Are you ordering, sir?"

Trevor said over his shoulder, "Two pints bitter." He lit a cigarette and blew out the smoke very very slowly.

"Trev," Collie said in a low voice, "Trev, don't muck it up."

"I'm being patient," Trevor said through half-closed lips. "I'm being very very patient. But if——"

"Trev," Collie said, "Trev, think of the lolly. Them notebooks."

Trevor threw half-a-crown backwards on to the counter.

"Manners," the barmaid said as she rang the till. She banged his change on the counter, where Trevor let it lie.

Dougal and Humphrey approached the bar with four empty glasses. "Ginger ale only," Dixie called after them, since it was Humphrey's turn.

"One martini. Two half milds. One *gin* and ginger ale," Humphrey said to the barman. And he invited Trevor to join them by pointing to their table with his ear.

Trevor did not move. Collie was watching Trevor.

Dougal got out some money.

"My turn," Humphrey said, fishing out his money.

Dougal picked half-a-crown from his money and, leaning his back against the bar, tossed it over his shoulder to the counter. He then lit a cigarette and blew out the smoke very slowly, pulling his face to a grave length and batting his eyelashes.

Beauty shouted, "Doug, you're a boy! Dig Doug! He's got you, Trev. He does Trevor to a T." Tony was playing the *St. Louis Blues.*

"Trev," Collie said, "don't, Trev, don't."

Trevor raised his sparkling pint glass and smashed the top on the edge of the counter. In his hand remained the bottom half with six spikes of glass sticking up from it. He lunged it forward at Dougal's face. At the same swift moment Dougal leaned back, back, until the crown of his head touched the bar. The spikes of glass went full into one side of Humphrey's face which had been turned in profile. Dougal bent and caught Trevor's legs while another man pulled Trevor's collar until presently he lay pinned by a number of hands to the floor. Humphrey was being attended by another number of hands, and was taken to the back premises, the barmaid holding to his face a large thick towel which was becoming redder and redder.

The barman shouted above the din, "Outside, all."

Most of the people were leaving in any case lest they should be questioned. To those who lingered the barman shouted, "Outside, all, or I'll call the police."

Trevor found himself free to get to his feet and he left, followed by Collie and Beauty, who was seen to spit at Trevor before she clicked her way up Rye Lane.

Dixie remained behind with Dougal. She was saying to him, "It was meant for *you*. Dirty swine you were to duck."

"Outside or I call the police," the barman said, bouncing up and down on the balls of his feet.

"We were with the chap that's hurt," Dougal said, "and if we can't collect him *I'll* call the police."

"Follow me," said the barman.

Humphrey was holding his head over a bowl while cold water was being poured over his wounds by Tony, who seemed to take this as one of his boring evening duties.

"Goodness, you look terrible," Dougal said. "It must be my fatal flaw, but I doubt if I can bear to look."

"Dirty swine, he is," Dixie said, "letting another fellow have it instead of himself."

"Shut up, will you?" Humphrey seemed to say.

They got into Humphrey's car, speedily assisted by the

barman. Dougal drove, first taking Dixie home. She said to him, "I could spit at you," and slammed the car door.

"Oh, shut up," Humphrey said, as well as he could.

Dougal next drove Humphrey to the outpatient department of St. George's Hospital. "Though it pains me to cross the river," Dougal said, "I think we'd better avoid the southern region for tonight."

He told a story about Humphrey's having tripped over a milk-bottle as he got out of his car, the milk-bottle having splintered and Humphrey fallen on his face among the splinters. Humphrey nodded agreement as the nurse dressed and plastered his wounds. Dougal gave Humphrey's name as Mr. Dougal-Douglas, care of Miss Cheeseman, 14 Chelsea Rise, S.W.3. Humphrey was told to return within a week. They then went home to Miss Frierne's.

"And I won't even see her again till next Saturday night on account of her doing week-nights as an usherette at the Regal," Humphrey said to Dougal at a quarter to twelve that night. He sat up in bed in striped pyjamas, talking as much as possible; but the strips of plaster on his cheek caused him to speak rather out of the opposite side of his mouth. "And she won't think of taking one day off on her holidays this year on account of the honeymoon in September. It's nothing but save, save, save. You'd think I wasn't earning good money the way she goes on. And result, she's losing her sex."

Dougal crouched over the gas-ring with a fork, pushing the bacon about in the frying-pan. He removed the bacon on to a plate, then broke two eggs into the pan.

"I wouldn't marry her," Dougal said, "if you paid me."

"My sister Elsie doesn't like her," Humphrey said out of the side of his mouth.

Dougal stood up and took the plate of bacon in his hand. He held this at some way from his body and looked at it, moving it slightly back and forth towards him, as if it were a book he was reading, and he short-sighted.

Dougal read from the book: "Wilt thou take this woman," he said with a deep ecclesiastical throb, "to be thai wedded waif?"

Then he put the plate aside and knelt; he was a sinister goggling bridegroom. "No," he declared to the ceiling, "I won't, quite frankly."

"Christ, don't make me laugh, it pulls the plaster."

Dougal dished out the eggs and bacon. He cut up the bacon small for Humphrey.

"You shouldn't have any scars if you're careful and get your face regularly dressed, they said."

Humphrey stroked his wounded cheek.

"Scars wouldn't worry me. Might worry Dixie."

"As a qualified refrigerator engineer and a union man you could have your pick of the girls."

"I know, but I want Dixie." He put the eggs and bacon slowly away into the side of his mouth.

The rain of a cold summer morning fell on Nelly Mahone as she sat on a heap of disused lorry tyres in the yard of Paley's, scrap merchants of Meeting-house Lane. She had been waiting since ten past nine although she did not expect Dougal to arrive until ten o'clock. He came at five past ten, bobbing up and down under an umbrella.

"They come to see me Saturday," she said at once.

"Trevor Lomas, Collie Gould, Leslie Crewe. They treated me bad."

"You've got wet," Dougal said. "Why didn't you take shelter?"

She looked round the yard. "Got to be careful where you go, son. Stand up in the open, they can only tell you to move on. But go inside a place, they can call the cops." Her nose thrust forward towards the police station at the corner of the lane.

Dougal looked round the yard for possible shelter. The bodies of two lorries, bashed in from bad accidents, stood lopsided in a corner. On a low wooden cradle stood a house-boat. "We'll go into the boat."

"Oh, I couldn't get up there."

Dougal kicked a wooden crate over and over till it stood beneath the door of the boat. He pulled the door-handle. Eventually it gave way. He climbed in, then out again, and took Nelly by the arm.

"Up you go, Nelly."

"What if the cops come?"

"I'm in with them," Dougal said.

"Jesus, that's not your game?"

"Up you go."

He heaved her up and settled in the boat beside her on a torn upholstered seat. Some sad cretonne curtains still drooped in the windows. Dougal drew them across the windows as far as was possible.

"I feel that ill," Nelly said.

"I'm not too keen on illness," Dougal said.

"Nor me. They come to ask after you," Nelly said. "They found out you was seeing me. They got your code. They want to know what's cheese. They want to know

353

what's your code key, they offer me ten quid. They want to know who's your gang."

"I'm in with the cops, tell them."

"That I would never believe. They want to know who's Rose Hathaway. They'll be back again. I got to tell them something."

"Tell them I'm paid by the police to investigate certain irregularities in the industrial life of Peckham in the first place. See, Nelly? I mean crime at the top in the wee factories. And secondly——"

Her yellowish eyes and wet grey hair turned towards him in a startled way.

"If I thought you was a nark——"

"Investigator," Dougal said. "It all comes under human research. And secondly my job covers various departments of youthful terrorism. So you can just tell me, Nelly, what they did to you on Saturday afternoon."

"Ah, they didn't do nothing out of the way."

"You said they treated you roughly."

"No, not so to get them in trouble."

Dougal took out an envelope. "Your ten pounds," he said.

"You can keep it," Nelly said. "I'm going on my way."

"Feel my head, Nelly." He guided her hand to the two small bumps among his curls.

"Cancer of the brain a-coming on," she said.

"Nelly, I had a pair of horns like a goat when I was born. I lost them in a fight at a later date."

"Holy Mary, let me out of here. I don't know whether I'm coming or going with you."

Dougal stood up and found that by standing astride in the middle of the boat he could make it rock. So he rocked

354

it for a while and sang a sailor's song to Nelly.

Then he helped her to climb down from the boat, put up his umbrella and tried to catch up with her as she hurried out of the scrap yard. A policeman, coming out of the station, at the corner, nodded to Dougal.

"I'll be going into the station then, Nelly," Dougal said. "To see my chums."

She stared at him, then spat on the rainy pavement.

"And I don't mind," Dougal said, "if you tell Trevor Lomas what I'm doing. You can tell him if he returns my notebooks to me there will be nothing further said. We policemen have got to keep our records and our secret codes, you realise."

She moved sideways away from him, watching the traffic so that she could cross at the earliest moment.

"You and I," Dougal said, "won't be molested from that quarter for a week or two if you give them the tip-off."

He went into the station yard to see how the excavations were getting on. He discovered that the tunnel itself was now visible from the top of the shaft.

Dougal pointed out to his policemen friends the evidence of the Thames silt in the under-soil. "One time," he said, "the Thames was five miles wide, and it covered all Peckham."

So they understood, they said, from other archaeologists who were interested in the excavation.

"Hope I'm not troubling you if I pop in like this from time to time?" Dougal said.

"No, sir, you're welcome. We get people from the papers sometimes as well as students. Did you read of the finds?"

Towards evening a parcel was delivered at Miss Frierne's

addressed to Dougal. It contained his notebooks.

"I hope to remain with you," Dougal said to Miss Frierne, "for at least two months. For I see no call upon me to remove from Peckham as yet."

"If I'm still alive . . ." Miss Frierne said. "I saw that man again this morning. I could swear it was my brother."

"You didn't speak to him?"

"No. Something stopped me." She began to cry.

"Who put the pot of indoor creeping ivy in my room?" Dougal said. "Was it my little dog-toothed blond process-controller?"

"Yes, it was a scraggy little blonde. Looks as if she could do with a good feed. They all do."

Mr. Druce whispered, "I couldn't manage it the other night. Things were difficult."

"I sat at the Dragon in Dulwich from nine till closing time," Dougal said, "and you didn't come."

"I couldn't get away. Mrs. Druce was on the watch. If you'd come to that place in Soho——"

Dougal consulted his pocket diary. He shut it and put it away. "Next month it would have to be. This month my duties press." He rose and walked up and down Mr. Druce's office as with something on his mind.

"I called for you last Saturday," Mr. Druce said. "I thought you would care for a spin."

"So I understand," Dougal said absently. "I believe I was researching on Miss Coverdale that afternoon." Dougal smiled at Mr. Druce. "Interrogating her, you know."

"Oh, yes."

"Her devotion to you is quite remarkable," Dougal said. "She spoke of you continually."

356

"As a matter of interest, what did you say? Look, Dougal, you can't trust everyone——"

Dougal looked at his watch. "Goodness," he said, "the time. What I came to see you about—the question of my increase in salary."

"It's going through," Mr. Druce said. "I put it to the Board that, since Weedin's breakdown, a great deal of extra work falls on your shoulders."

Dougal massaged both his shoulders, first his high one, then his low one.

"Dougal," said Mr. Druce.

"Vincent," said Dougal, and departed.

Chapter Eight

Joyce Willis said, "Quite frankly, the first time Richard invited you to dinner I knew we'd found the answer. Richard didn't see it at first, quite frankly, but I think he's beginning to see it now."

She crossed the room, moving her long hips, and looked out of the bow window into the August evening. "Richard should be in any moment," she said. She touched her throat with her fine fingers. She put to rights a cushion in the window-seat.

Still standing, she lifted her glass, and sipped, and put it down on a low table. She crossed the room and sat on a chair upholstered in deep pink brocade.

"I feel I can really *talk* to you now," she said. "I feel we've known each other for years."

She said, "The Drovers *were* getting the upper hand. Richard was, well, quite frankly, being pushed into the position of subordinate partner.

"The nephew, Mark Bewlay—that's *her* nephew, of course—came to the firm two—was it two?—no, it was three years ago, imagine it, in October. And he was supposed to go through the factory from A to Z. Well, quite frankly he was sitting on the Board within six

358

months. Then the son John came straight down from Oxford last year, and same thing again. The Board's reeking with Drovers.

"One of Richard's great mistakes—I'm speaking to you quite frankly," she said, "was insisting on our *living* in Peckham. Well, the house is all right—but I mean, the environment. There are simply no people in the place. Our friends always get lost finding the way here; they drive round for hours. And there are blacks at the other end of the Avenue, you know. I mean, it's so silly.

"Richard's a Scot, of course," she said, "and in a way that's why I think you understand his position. He's so scrupulously industrious and patho*log*ically honest. And it's rather sweet in a way. Yes, I must say that. He simply doesn't see that the Drovers living in Sussex in a Georgian rectory gives them a big advantage. A big advantage. It's psychological."

She said, "Yes, Richard insists on living near the job, as he says. And quite frankly, I have to put up with a good deal of condescension from Queenie Drover, although she's sweet in a way. She knows of course that Richard's a bit old-fashioned and prides himself on being a *real merchant,* they both know, the Drovers. They know it only too well."

She filled both glasses with sherry, turning the good bones of her wrists and holding the glasses at the ends of her long fingers with their lacquered nails and the bright emerald. She looked at herself, before she sat down, in the gilt-framed glass and turned back a wisp of her short dark-gold hair. Her face was oval; she posed it to one side; she said, "Of course it has been a disappointment that we had no children. If there had been a son to support Richard on the Board . . . Sometimes I feel, quite frankly, the firm should be called Drover, Drover, Drover Willis, not just Drover Willis.

"Richard was touched a few weeks ago," she said, "he told me so, when he met you one Saturday afternoon while he was waiting for me outside the shop, and he saw you working away on your Saturday afternoon, spending your Saturday afternoon with a Peckham girl, trying to get to know the types. Richard thinks you are brilliant, you know. A fine brain and a sound moral sense, he told me, quite frankly, and he thinks you're absolutely wasted in the personnel research job. The thing about you—and I saw it long before Richard and I'm not just saying it because you're here—you're so young and energetic, and yet so *steady*. I suppose it's being a Scot.

"Not many young fellows of your age," she said, "—I'm not flattering you—and of your qualifications and ability would be prepared to settle down as you have done in a place like Peckham where the scope for any kind of gaiety is so limited, there's nothing to do and there are no young people for you to meet. I'm speaking quite frankly, as I would to my own son if I had one.

"I feel towards you," she said, "as to a son. I hope—I would always hope—to count you as one of the family although, as you know, there are only Richard and me. I was so interested in your conversation the other night about so many things I didn't quite frankly know existed in this area. The Camberwell Art Gallery I knew of course; but the excavations of the tunnel—I had only read of its progress in the *South London Observer*—I didn't dream there was anything so serious and learned behind it."

She turned and plumped out the cushion behind her. She looked at her pointed toes. "You must sometimes come to town with us. We go to the theatre at least once a week," she said.

She said, "The idea that you should come on the Board with Richard in the autumn is an excellent one. It will almost be like having a Willis in the firm. Your way of speaking is so like Richard's—I mean, not just the accent, but well, quite frankly, I mean, you don't say *much*, but when you say something it's the right thing. Richard needs you and I think I'm right in saying it's an ideal prospect for a young man of your temperament, and it means serious responsibility and an established position within a matter of five or six years. You have this way of approaching life seriously, not just here to-day and gone tomorrow, and it appeals to Richard. Richard is a judge of character. One day the firm might be Drover, Willis & Dougal. Just a moment——"

She went over to the window, smoothing her waist, and glanced through the window as a car drew up in the small curved drive. "Here's Richard," she said. "He's been looking forward to having a serious chat with you this evening, and getting things settled before we go abroad."

"Is that you, Jinny?"
"Yes."
"Have you got any milk on the stove?"
"No."
"When can I come and see you?"
"I'm getting married next week."
"No, Jinny."
"I'm in love with him. He was sweet when I was ill."

"Just when I'm getting on my feet and drawing two pays for nothing," Dougal said, "you tell me——"

"It wouldn't have worked between us, Dougal. I'm not strong in health."

"Well, that's that," Dougal said.

"Miss Cheeseman's thrilled with her autobiography so far," Jinny said. "You'll do well, Dougal."

"You've changed. You are using words like 'sweet' and 'thrilled.'"

"Oh, get away. Miss Cheeseman said she was pleased."

"She doesn't tell me that."

"Well, she has some tiny reservations about the Peckham bits, but on the whole——"

"I'm coming over to see you, Jinny."

"No, Dougal, I mean it."

Dougal went in to Miss Frierne's kitchen and wept into his large pocket handkerchief.

"Are you feeling all right?" she said.

"No. My girl's getting married to another chap."

She filled the kettle and put it down on the draining board. She opened the back door and shut it again. She took up a duster and dusted a kitchen chair, back and legs.

"You're better off without her," she said.

"I'm not," Dougal said, "but I've got a fatal flaw."

"You're not drinking at nights, Dougal?"

"No more than usual."

She lifted the kettle and put it down again.

"Calm down," Dougal said.

"Well, it upsets me inside to see a man upset."

"Light the gas and put the kettle on it," he said.

362

She did this, then stood and looked at him. She took off her apron.

"Sit down," Dougal said.

She sat down.

"Stand up," he said, "and fetch me a tot of your gin."

She brought two glasses and the gin bottle. "It's only quarter-past five," she said. "It's early to start on gin. Here's to you, son. You'll soon get over it."

The front-door bell rang. Miss Frierne caused the bottle and glasses to disappear. The bell rang again. She went to answer it.

"Name of Frierne?" said a man's voice.

"Yes, what do you want?"

"Could I have a private word with you?"

Miss Frierne returned to the kitchen followed by a policeman.

"A man aged about seventy-nine was run over by a bus this morning on the Walworth Road. Sorry, madam, but he had the name Frierne in his pocket written on a bit of paper. He died an hour ago. Any relation you know of, madam?"

"No, I don't know of him. Must be a mistake. You can ask my neighbours if you like. I'm the only one left in the world."

"Very good," said the policeman, making notes. "Did he have any other papers on him?"

"No, nothing. A pauper, poor devil."

The policeman left.

"Well, there wasn't anything I could do if he's dead, was there?" Miss Frierne said to Dougal. She started crying. "Except pay for the funeral. And it's hard enough keeping going and that."

Dougal fetched out the gin again and poured two glasses. Presently he placed a kitchen chair to face the chair on which he sat. He put up his feet on it and said, "Ever seen a corpse?" He lolled his head back, closed his eyes and opened his mouth so that the bottom jaw was sunken and rigid.

"You're callous, that's what you are," Miss Frierne said. Then she screamed with hysterical mirth.

Humphrey sat with Mavis and Arthur Crewe in their sitting-room, touching, every now and then, two marks on his face.

"Well, if by any chance you don't have her, it's your luck," Mavis said. "I say it though she's my own daughter. When I was turned seventeen, eighteen, I was out with the boys every night, dancing and so forth. You wouldn't have caught me doing no evening work just for a bit of money. And there aren't so many boys willing to sit round waiting like you. She'll learn when it's too late."

"It isn't as if she parts with any of her money," Arthur Crewe said. "You don't get the smell of an oil-rag out of Dixie. The more she's got the meaner she gets."

"What's that got to do with it?" Dixie's mother said. "You don't want anything from her, do you?"

"I never said I did. I was only saying——"

"Dixie has her generous side," Mavis said. "You must hand it to her, she's good to Leslie. She's always slipping him five bob here and five bob there."

"Pity she does it," Arthur said. "The boy's ruined. He's money mad."

"What you know about kids? There's nothing wrong

364

with Leslie. He's no different from the rest. They all like money in their pockets."

"Where's Leslie now, anyway?"

"Gone out."

"Where?"

"How do I know? You ask him."

"He's with Trevor Lomas," Humphrey said. "Up at Costa's."

"There you are, Arthur. There's no harm in Trevor Lomas."

"He's a bit old company for Leslie."

"Grumble, grumble, grumble," Mavis said, and switched on the television.

Leslie came in at eleven. He looked round the sitting-room.

"Hallo, Les," Humphrey said.

Leslie did not speak. He went upstairs.

At half-past eleven Dixie came home. She kicked off her shoes in the sitting-room and flopped on to the sofa. "You been here long?" she said to Humphrey.

"An hour or two."

"Nice to be able to sit down of a summer evening," Dixie said.

"Yes, why don't you try it?"

"Trevor Lomas says there's plenty of overtime at Freeze-eezy if anyone wants it."

"Well, I don't want it," Humphrey said.

"Obvious."

"Who wants to do overtime all their lives?" Mavis said.

"I was just remarking," Dixie said, "what Trevor Lomas told me."

"Overtime should be avoided except in cases of necessity," Humphrey said, "because eventually it reduces the normal capacity of the worker and in the long run leads to under-production, resulting in further demands for overtime. A vicious circle. Where did you see Trevor Lomas?"

"It *is* a case of necessity," Dixie said, "because we need all the money we can get."

"That's how she goes on," Mavis said. "Why she can't be content to settle down with a man's good wages like other people I don't know. With a bungalow earmarked for October——"

"I want it to be a model bungalow," Dixie said.

"You'll have your model bungalow," Humphrey said.

"She wants a big splash wedding," Mavis said. "Well, Arthur and I will do what we can but *only* what we can."

"That's right," Arthur said.

"Dixie's entitled to the best," Mavis said. "She's got a model dress in view."

"Where did you see Trevor Lomas?" Humphrey said to Dixie.

"Up at Costa's. I went in for a Coke on the way home. Any objections?"

"No, dear, no," Humphrey said.

"Nice of you. Well, I'm going to bed, I'm tired out. You still got your scars."

"They'll go away in time."

"I don't mind. Trevor's got a scar."

"I better keep my eye on Trevor Lomas," Humphrey said.

"You better keep your eye on your friend Dougal Douglas. Trevor says he's a dick."

"I don't believe it," Mavis said.

"Nor do I," said Arthur.

366

"No more do I," said Humphrey.

"I know you think he's perfect," Dixie said. "He can do no wrong. But I'm just telling you what Trevor said. So don't say I didn't tell you."

"Trevor's having you on," Humphrey said. "He doesn't like Dougal."

"I like him," Arthur said.

"I like him," Mavis said. "Our Leslie don't like him. Dixie don't like him."

"I like him," Humphrey said. "My sister Elsie doesn't like him."

"Is Mr. Douglas at home?"

"Well, he's up in his room playing the typewriter at the moment," said Miss Frierne, "as you can hear."

"Can I go up?"

"No, I must enquire. Come inside, please. What name?"

"Miss Coverdale."

Miss Frierne left Miss Coverdale in that hall which was lined with wood like a coffin. The sound of the typewriter stopped. Dougal's voice called down from the second landing, "Come up." Miss Frierne frowned in the direction of his voice. "Top floor," she said to Merle.

"I'm miserable. I had to see you," Merle said to Dougal. "What a nice little room you've got here!"

"Why are you not at work?" Dougal said.

"I'm too upset to work. Mr. Druce is talking of leaving the country for good. What should I do?"

"What do you want to do?" Dougal said.

"I want to go with him but he won't take me."

"Why not?"

367

"He knows I don't like him."

Dougal stretched himself out on the top of his bed.

"Does Mr. Druce mention any date for his departure?"

"No, there's nothing settled. Perhaps it's only a threat. But I think he's frightened of something."

Dougal sat up and placed one hand within the other. He shortened his eyesight and peered at Merle with sublime appreciation. "Dougal," he said, "there is a little place in Soho, would you not come to spend the evening and have a chat? Mrs. Druce is just a bit difficult, she watches——"

"Oh, don't," Merle said. "It brings everything back to me. I can't tell you how I hate the man. I can't bear him to be near me. And now, after all these years, the best years of my life, the swine talks of leaving me."

Dougal lay back with his arms behind his head. "What's he frightened of?" he said.

"You," Merle said. "He's got hold of the idea that you're spying on him."

"In what capacity?"

"Oh, I couldn't say."

"Yes, you could."

"If you're working for the police, Dougal, please tell me. Think of my position. After all, I told you about Mr. Druce in all innocence and if I'm going to be dragged into anything——"

"I'm not working for the police," Dougal said.

"Well, of course, I knew you wouldn't admit it."

"What guilty wee consciences you've all got," Dougal said.

"Don't do anything about Mr. Druce, will you? The Board are just waiting for an excuse, and if they get to know about his deals and all that it will only come back on me. Where will I stand if he emigrates?"

"Who tipped Druce off? Was it Trevor Lomas?"

"No, it was Dixie, the little bitch. She's been going in and out to Mr. Druce a lot behind my back."

"Ah well. Take some shorthand dictation, will you, as you're here?" He got up and fetched her a notebook and a Biro pen.

"Dougal, I'm upset."

"There's nothing like work to calm your emotions. After all, you should be working at this moment. Are you ready? Tell me if I'm going too fast:

" 'Peckham was fun exclamation mark but the day inevitably dawned when I realised that I and my beloved pals at the factory were poles apart full stop The great throbbing heart of London across the river spelt fame comma success comma glamour to me full stop I was always an incurable romantic exclamation mark New para The poignant moment arrived when I bade farewell to my first love full stop Up till now I had had eyes for no others but fate—capital F—had intervened full stop We kissed dot dot dot a shudder went through my frame dot dot dot every fibre of my being spoke of gratitude and grief but the budding genius within me cried out for expression full stop And so we parted for ever full stop New para I felt a grim satisfaction as the cab which bore me and my few poor belongings bowled across Vauxhall Bridge and into the great world—capital G capital W—ahead full stop Yes comma Peckham had been fun exclamation mark' Now, leave a space, please, and——"

"What's all this about?" Merle said.

"Don't fuss, you're putting me off."

"God, if Mr. Druce thought I was working in with you, he'd kill me."

"Leave a space," Dougal said, "then a row of dots. That denotes a new section. Now continue. 'Throughout all the years of my success I have never forgotten those early comma joyful comma innocent days in Peckham full stop Only the other day I came across the following paragraph in the paper——' Hand me the paper," Dougal said, "till I find the bit."

She passed him the newspaper. "Dougal," she said, "I'm going."

"Surely not till you've typed it out for me?" he said. "There isn't much more to take down."

He found the paragraph and said, "Put this bit in quotation marks. Are you ready? 'The excavations on the underground tunnel leading from the police station yard at Peckham are now nearing completion full stop The tunnel comma formerly used by the nuns of the Order of St. Bridget comma stretches roughly six hundred yards from the police station bracket formerly the site of the priory unbracket to Gordon Road and not comma as formerly supposed comma to Nunhead. Archaeologists have reported some interesting finds and human remains all of which will be removed before the tunnel is open to the public quite shortly full stop end quotes.' "

"Is this a police report?" Merle said. "Because if so I don't want to do it, Dougal. Mr. Druce would——"

"Only a few more words," Dougal said. "Ready? New paragraph 'When I read the above tears started to my eyes full stop How well did I recall every detail of that station yard two exclamation marks The police in my day were far from——"

"I can't go on," Merle said. "This is putting me in a difficult position."

"All right, dear," Dougal said. He sat up and stroked her long neck till she started to cry.

"Type it out," Dougal said, "and forget your troubles. It's a nice typewriter. You'll find the paper on the table."

She sat up to the table and typed from her shorthand notes.

Dougal lay back on his bed. "There is no more beautiful sight," he said, "than to see a fine woman bashing away at a typewriter."

"Is Mr. Douglas in?"

"He's up in his room writing out his reports. He's busy."

"Can I go up?"

"I'll see if it's convenient. But he's busy. Come inside, please. What name?"

"Elaine Kent."

"Come up," Dougal called from the second landing.

"You may go up," Miss Frierne said. "Top floor." Miss Frierne stood and watched her climbing out of sight.

"You've been putting too much water in the plant," Elaine said, feeling the soil round the potted ivy. "You should water it once a week only."

"People come here to cry," Dougal said, "which accounts for an excess of moisture in this room."

She took a crumpled brown-paper bag from her shopping basket. They were Dougal's socks which had been washed and darned.

"There's talk going round about you," Elaine said.

371

"Makes me laugh. They say you're in the pay of the cops."

"What's funny about it?"

"Catch the Peckham police boys spending their money on you."

"Oh, I would make an excellent informer. I don't say plain-clothes policeman, exactly, but for gathering information and having no scruples in passing it on you could look farther than me and fare worse."

"There's a gang watching out for you," Elaine said. "So be careful where you go at nights. I shouldn't go out alone much."

"Terrifying, isn't it? I mean, say this is the street and there's Trevor over there. And say here's Collie Gould crossing the road. And young Leslie comes up to me and asks the time and I look at my watch. Then out jumps Trevor with a razor—rip, rip, rip. But Collie whistles loud on his three fingers. Leslie gives me a parting kick where I lie in the gutter and slinks after Trevor away into the black concealing night. Up comes the copper and finds me. The cop takes one look, turns away and pukes on the pavement. He then with trembling fingers places a whistle to his lips."

"Sit down and stop pushing the good furniture about," she said.

"I've gone and worked myself up with my blether," Dougal said. "I feel that frightened."

"Leslie was waiting for Mr. Willis at five o'clock the day before he went on his holidays. I saw him standing behind Mr. Willis's car. So I hung on just to see. And then Mr. Willis came out. And then Leslie came forward. And then Leslie said something and Mr. Willis said something. So I walked past. I heard Mr. Willis say, 'Have you left school?' and Leslie said, 'What's that to you?' and Mr. Willis said, 'I should want to know a good deal more about you before I took notice of what you say'— or it was something like that, Mr. Willis said. And then Mr. Willis drove away."

"Ah well," Dougal said, "I expect to be leaving here next month. Will you cry when I'm gone?"

"I'd watch it."

"Come on out to the pictures," Dougal said, "for fine evening though it is I am inclined for a bit of darkness." On the way out he picked up a letter postmarked from Grasse. He read it going down the street with Elaine.

Dear Douglas,

We arrived on Saturday night. The weather is perfect and this is quite a pleasant hotel with delightful view. The food is quite good. The people are very pleasant, at least so far! We have had one or two pleasant drives along the coast. Quite frankly, Richard needs a rest. You know yourself how he forces himself and is so conscientious.

Richard is very pleased with the arrangements we came to the other evening. It will be so much better to have someone to support him as there are so many Drovers in the firm now. (I almost think, quite frankly, the firm should be called Drover, Drover, Drover Willis instead of Drover Willis!) I hope you yourself are satisfied with the new arrangements. Richard instructed the accountant before he left about your increase and it will be back-dated from the date of your joining the firm as arranged.

I feel I ought to tell you of an incident which occurred just before we left, although, quite frankly, Richard decided not to mention it to you (in case it put you off!). A young boy in his teens waylaid Richard and told him you were a paid police informer employed apparently to look into the industries of Peckham in case of irregularities. Of course, Richard took no notice, and as I said to Richard, there would hardly be any reason for the police to suspect any criminal activities at Drover Willis's! Quite frankly, I thought I would tell you this to put you on your guard, as I feel I can talk to you, Douglas, as to a son. You have obviously made one or two enemies in the course of your research. That is always the trouble, they are so ungrateful. Before the war these boys used to be glad of a meal and a night's shelter, but now quite frankly . . .

Dougal put away the letter. "I am as melancholy a young man as you might meet on a summer's day," he said to Elaine, "and it feels quite nice."

They came out of the pictures at eight o'clock. Nelly Mahone was outside the pub opposite, declaiming, "The words of the double-tongued are as if they were harmless, but they reach even to the inner part of the bowels. Praise be to the Lord, who distinguishes our cause and delivers us from the unjust and deceitful man."

Dougal and Elaine crossed the road. As they passed, Nelly spat on the pavement.

Chapter Nine

Merle Coverdale said to Trevor Lomas, "I've only been helping him out with a few private things. He's good company and he's different. I don't have much of a life."

"Only a few private things," Trevor said. "Only just helping him out."

"Well, what's wrong with that?"

"Typing out his nark information for him."

"Look," Merle said, "he isn't anything to do with the police. I don't know where that story started, but it isn't true."

"What's this private business you do for him?"

"No business of yours."

"We got to carve up that boy one of these days," Trevor said. "D'you want to get carved alongside of him?"

"Christ, I'm telling you the truth," Merle said. "It's only a story he's writing for someone he calls Cheese that had to do with Peckham in the old days. You don't understand Dougal. He's got no harm in him. He's just different."

"Cheese," Trevor said. "That's what you go there every Tuesday and every Friday night to work on."

"It's not real cheese," Merle said. "Cheese is a person, it isn't the real name."

"You don't say so," Trevor said. "And what's the real name?"

"I don't know, Mr. Lomas, truly."

"You won't go back there," Trevor stated.

"I'll have to explain to him, then. He's just a friend, Mr. Lomas."

"You don't see him again. Understand. We got plans for him."

"Mr. Lomas, you'd better go. Mr. Druce will be along soon. I don't want Mr. Druce to find you here."

"He knows I'm here."

"You never told him of me going to Dougal's, week-nights?"

"He knows, I said."

"It's you's the informer, not Dougal."

"Re-member. Any more work you do for him's going to go against you."

Trevor trod down the stairs from her flat with the same deliberate march as when he had arrived, and she watched him from her window taking Denmark Hill as if he owned it.

Mr. Druce arrived twelve minutes later. He took off his hat and hung it on the peg in her hall. He followed her into the sitting-room and opened the door of the side-board. He took out some whisky and poured himself a measure, squirting soda into it.

Merle took up her knitting.

"Want some?" he said.

"I'll have a glass of red wine. I feel I need something red, to buck me up."

He stooped to get the bottle of wine and, opening a drawer, took out the corkscrew.

"I just had a visitor," she said.

He turned to look at her with the corkscrew pointing from his fist.

"I daresay you know who it was," she said.

"Certainly I do. I sent him."

"My private life's my private life," she said. "I've never interfered with yours. I've never come near Mrs. Druce though many's the time I could have felt like telling her a thing or two."

He handed over her glass of wine. He looked at the label on the bottle. He sat down and took his shoes off. He put on his slippers. He looked at his watch. Merle switched on the television. Neither looked at it. "I've been greatly taken in by that Scotch fellow. He's in the pay of the police *and* of the board of Meadows Meade. He's been watching me for close on three months and putting in his reports."

"No, you're wrong there," Merle said.

"And you've been in with him this last month." He pointed his finger at her throat, nearly touching it.

"You're wrong there. I've only been typing out some stories for him."

"What stories?"

"About Peckham in the old days. It's about some old lady he knows. You've got no damn right to accuse me and send that big tough round here threatening me."

"Trevor Lomas," Mr. Druce said, "is in my pay. You'll do what Trevor suggests. We're going to run that Dougal Douglas, so-called, out of Peckham with something to remember us by."

"I thought you were going to emigrate."

"I am."

"When?"

"When it suits me."

He crossed his legs and attended to the television.

"I don't feel like any supper tonight," she said.

"Well, I do."

She went into the kitchen and made a clatter. She came back crying. "I've had a rotten life of it."

"Not since Dougal Douglas, so-called, joined the firm, from what I hear."

"He's only a friend. You don't understand him."

Mr. Druce breathed in deeply and looked up at the lampshade as if calling it to witness.

"You can have a chop with some potatoes and peas," she said. "I don't want any."

She sat down and took up her knitting, weeping upon it.

He leaned forward and tickled her neck. She drew away. He pinched the skin of her long neck, and she screamed.

"Sh-sh-sh," he said, and stroked her neck.

He went to pour himself some more whisky. He turned and looked at her. "What have you been up to with Dougal Douglas, so-called?" he said.

"Nothing. He's just a friend. A bit of company for me."

The corkscrew lay on the sideboard. He lifted an end, let it drop, lifted it, let it drop.

"I'd better turn the chop," she said and went into the kitchen.

He followed her. "You gave him information about me," he said.

"No, I've told you——"

"And you typed his reports to the Board."

She pushed past him, weeping noisily, to find her hand-kerchief on the chair.

"What else was between you and him?" he said, raising his voice above the roar of the television.

He came towards her with the corkscrew and stabbed it into her long neck nine times, and killed her. Then he took his hat and went home to his wife.

"Doug dear," said Miss Maria Cheeseman.

"I'm in a state," Dougal said, "so could you ring off?"

"Doug, I just wanted to say. You've re-written my early years so beautifully. Those new Peckham stories are absolutely sweet. I'm sure you feel, as I feel, that the extra effort was quite worth it. And now the whole book's perfect, and I'm thrilled."

"Thanks," said Dougal. "I doubt if the new bits were worth all the trouble, but——"

"Doug, come over and see me this afternoon."

"Sorry, Cheese, I'm in a state. I'm packing. I'm leaving here."

"Doug, I've got a little gift for you. Just an appreciation——"

"I'll ring you back," Dougal said. "I've just remembered I've left some milk on the stove."

"You'll let me have your new address, won't you?"

Dougal went into the kitchen. Miss Frierne was seated at the table, but she had slipped down in her chair. She seemed to be asleep. One side of her face was askew. Her eyelid fluttered.

Dougal looked round for the gin bottle to measure the extent of Miss Frierne's collapse. But there was no gin bottle, no bottle at all, no used glass. He took another look at Miss Frierne. Her eyelid fluttered and her lower lip moved on one side of her mouth.

Dougal telephoned to the police to send a doctor. Then he went upstairs and fetched down his luggage comprising his zipper-case, his shiny new brief-case and his typewriter. The doctor arrived presently and went in to Miss Frierne. "A stroke," he said.

"Well, I'll be off," Dougal said.

"Are you a relative?"

"No, a tenant. I'm leaving."

"Right away?"

"Yes," Dougal said. "I was leaving in any case, but I've got a definite flaw where illness is concerned."

"Has she got any relatives?"

"No."

"I'd better ring the ambulance," the doctor said. "She's pretty far gone."

Dougal walked with his luggage up Rye Lane. In the distance he saw a crowd outside the police station yard. He joined it, and pressed through with his bags into the yard.

"Going away?" said one of the policemen.

"I'm leaving the district. I thought, from the crowd, there might be some new find in the tunnel."

The policeman nodded towards the crowd. "We've just arrested a man in connection with the murder."

"Druce," Dougal said.

"That's right."

"Druce is the man," Dougal said.

"He's the chap all right. She might have been left there for days if it hadn't been for the food burning on the gas.

The neighbours thought there was a fire and broke in. The tunnel's open now, as you see; the steps are in. Official opening on Wednesday. Lights are being fixed now."

"Pity I won't be here. I should have liked to go along the tunnel."

"Go down if you like. It's only six hundred yards. Brings you out at Gordon Road. One of our men is on guard at that point. He'll know you. Pity not to see it as you've taken so much interest."

"I'll come," Dougal said.

"I can't take you," the policeman said. "But I'll get you a torch. It's just a straight run. All the coins and the old bronze have been taken away, so there's nothing there except some bones we haven't cleared away as yet. But you can say you've been through."

He went to fetch the torch. A young apprentice electrician emerged from the tunnel with two empty tea-mugs in his hand and went out through the crowd to a café across the road.

The policeman came back with a small torch. "Give this to the constable at the other end. Save you trouble of bringing it back. Well, goodbye. Glad to know you. I've got to go on duty now."

This tunnel had been newly supported in its eight-foot height by wooden props, between which Dougal wound his way. This tunnel—which in a few days' time was to be opened to the public, and in yet a few days more closed down owing to three scandals ensuing from its being frequented by the Secondary Modern Mixed School—was strewn with new gravel, trodden only, so far, by the workmen, and by Dougal as he proceeded with his bags.

About half-way through the tunnel Dougal put his bags

down and started to pick up some bones which were piled in a crevice ready to be taken away before the official opening. Then he held the torch between his teeth and juggled with some carefully chosen shin bones which were clotted with earth. He managed six at a time, throwing and catching, never missing, so that the earth fell away from them and scattered.

He picked up his bags and continued through the hot tunnel which smelt of its new disinfectant. He saw a strong lamp ahead and the figure of the electrician on a ladder cutting some wire in the wall.

The electrician turned. "You been quick, Bobby," he said.

Dougal switched out his torch and set down his bags on the gritty floor of the tunnel. He saw the electrician descend from the ladder with his knife and turn the big lamp towards him.

"Trevor Lomas, watch out for the old bones, they're haunted," Dougal said. He chucked what was once a hip at Trevor's head. Then with his left hand he grabbed the wrist that held the knife. Trevor kicked. Dougal employed that speciality of his with his right hand, clutching Trevor's throat back-handedly with his claw-like grip. Trevor went backward and stumbled over the bags, dropping the knife. Dougal picked it up, grabbed the bags and fled.

Near the end of the tunnel, where the light from the big lamp barely reached, Trevor caught up with him and delivered to Dougal a stab in the eye with a bone. Whereupon Dougal flashed his torch in Trevor's face and leapt at him with his high shoulder raised and elbow sticking out. He applied once more his deformed specialty. Holding Trevor's throat with this right-hand twist, he fetched him a left-hand blow on the corner of the jaw. Trevor sat down. Dougal picked up his bags, pointing his torch to the ground, and emerged from the tunnel at Gordon Road. There he reported to the policeman on duty that the electrician was sitting in a dazed condition among the old nuns' bones, having been overcome by the heat. "I can't stop to assist you," Dougal said, "for, as you see, I have to catch a train. Would you mind returning this torch with my thanks to the police station?"

"You hurt yourself?" the policeman said, looking at Dougal's eye.

"I bumped into something in the dark," Dougal said. "But it's only a bruise. Pity the lights weren't up."

He went into the Merry Widow for a drink. Then he took his bags up to Peckham High Street, got into a taxi and was driven across the river, where he entered a chemist's shop and got a dressing put on his wounded eye.

"I'm glad he's cleared off," Dixie said to her mother. "Humphrey's not glad but I'm glad. Now he won't be coming to the wedding. You never know what he might have done. He might have gone mad among the guests showing the bumps on his head. He might have made a speech. He might have jumped and done something rude. I didn't like him. Our Leslie didn't like him. Humphrey liked him. He was bad for Humphrey. Mr. Druce liked him and look what Mr. Druce has come to. Poor Miss Coverdale liked him. Trevor didn't like him. But I'm not worried now. I've got this bad cold, though."

Chapter Ten

There was Dixie come up to the altar with her wide flouncy dress and her nose, a little red from her cold, tilted up towards the minister.

"Wilt thou have this woman to thy wedded wife?"

"No, to be quite frank," Humphrey said, "I won't."

Dougal never read of it in the newspapers. He was away off to Africa with the intention of selling tape-recorders to all the witch doctors. "No medicine man," Dougal said, "these days can afford to be without a portable tape-recorder. Without the aid of this modern device, which may be easily concealed in the undergrowth of the jungle, the old tribal authority will rapidly become undermined by the mounting influence of modern scepticism."

Much could be told of Dougal's subsequent life. He returned from Africa and became a novice in a Franciscan monastery. Before he was asked to leave, the Prior had endured a nervous breakdown and several of the monks had broken their vows of obedience in actuality, and their other vows by desire; Dougal pleaded his powers as an exorcist in vain. Thereafter, for economy's sake, he gathered together the scrap ends of his profligate experience—for he was a frugal man at heart—and turned them into a lot of cock-eyed books, and went far in the world. He never married.

The night after Humphrey arrived alone at the honeymoon hotel at Folkestone, Arthur Crewe walked into the bar.

"The girl's heart-broken," he said to Humphrey.

"Better soon than late," Humphrey said. "Tell her I'm coming back."

"She's blaming Dougal Douglas. Is he here with you?"

"Not so's you'd notice it," Humphrey said.

"I haven't come here to blame you. I reckon there must be some reason behind it. But it's hard on the girl, in her wedding dress. My Leslie's been put on probation for robbing a till."

Some said Humphrey came back and married the girl in the end. Some said, no, he married another girl. Others said, it was like this, Dixie died of a broken heart and he never looked at another girl again. Some thought he had returned, and she had slammed the door in his face and called him a dirty swine, which he was. One or two recalled there had been a fight between Humphrey and Trevor Lomas. But at all events everyone remembered how a man had answered "No" at his wedding.

In fact they got married two months later, and although few guests were invited, quite a lot of people came to the church to see if Humphrey would do it again.

Humphrey drove off with Dixie. She said, "I feel as if I've been twenty years married instead of two hours."

He thought this a pity for a girl of eighteen. But it was a sunny day for November, and, as he drove swiftly past the Rye, he saw the children playing there and the women coming home from work with their shopping-bags, the Rye for an instant looking like a cloud of green and gold, the people seeming to ride upon it, as you might say there was another world than this.

Memento Mori

For

TERESA WALSHE

With Love

What shall I do with this absurdity—
O heart, O troubled heart—this caricature,
Decrepit age that has been tied to me
As to a dog's tail?

—W. B. YEATS, The Tower

O what venerable and reverent creatures did
the aged seem! Immortal Cherubims!

—THOMAS TRAHERNE,
Centuries of Meditation

Q. What are the four last things to be ever
   remembered?
A. The four last things to be ever remembered are Death, Judgment, Hell, and
   Heaven.

—The Penny Catechism

Chapter One

Dame Lettie Colston refilled her fountain pen and continued her letter:

One of these days I hope you will write as brilliantly on a happier theme. In these days of cold war I *do* feel we should soar above the murk & smog & get into the clear crystal.

The telephone rang. She lifted the receiver. As she had feared the man spoke before she could say a word. When he had spoken the familiar sentence she said, "Who is that speaking, who is it?"

But the voice, as on eight previous occasions, had rung off.

Dame Lettie telephoned to the Assistant Inspector as she had been requested to do. "It has occurred again," she said.

"I see. Did you notice the time?"

"It was only a moment ago."

"The same thing?"

"Yes," she said, "the same. Surely you have some means of tracing—"

"Yes, Dame Lettie, we will get him, of course."

A few moments later Dame Lettie telephoned to her brother Godfrey.

"Godfrey, it has happened again."

"I'll come and fetch you, Lettie," he said. "You must spend the night with us."

"Nonsense. There is no danger. It is merely a disturbance."

"What did he say?"

"The same thing. And quite matter-of-fact, not really threatening. Of course the man's mad. I don't know what the police are thinking of, they must be sleeping. It's been going on for six weeks now."

"Just those words?"

"Just the same words—'*Remember you must die*'—nothing more."

"He must be a maniac," said Godfrey.

Godfrey's wife, Charmian, sat with her eyes closed, attempting to put her thoughts into alphabetical order which Godfrey had told her was better than no order at all, since she now had grasp of neither logic nor chronology. Charmian was eighty-five. The other day a journalist from a weekly paper had been to see her. Godfrey had subsequently read aloud to her the young man's article:

> . . . By the fire sat a frail old lady, a lady who once set the whole of the literary world (if not the Thames) on fire. . . . Despite her age, this legendary figure is still abundantly alive. . . .

Charmian felt herself dropping off, and so she said to the maid, who was arranging the magazines on the long oak table by the window, "Taylor, I am dropping off to sleep for five minutes. Telephone to St. Mark's and say I am coming."

Just at that moment Godfrey entered the room holding his hat and wearing his outdoor coat. "What's that you say?" he said.

"Oh, Godfrey, you made me start."

394

"Taylor . . ." he repeated, "St. Mark's . . . Don't you realise there is no maid in this room, and furthermore, you are not in Venice."

"Come and get warm by the fire," she said, "and take your coat off"; for she thought he had just come in from the street.

"I am about to go *out*," he said. "I am going to fetch Lettie who is to stop with us to-night. She has been troubled by another of those anonymous calls."

"That was a pleasant young man who called the other day," said Charmian.

"Which young man?"

"From the paper. The one who wrote—"

"That was five years and two months ago," said Godfrey.

"Why can't one be kind to her?" he asked himself as he drove to Lettie's house in Hampstead. "Why can't one be more gentle?" He himself was eighty-seven, and in charge of all his faculties. Whenever he considered his own behaviour he thought of himself not as "I" but as "one."

"One has one's difficulties with Charmian," he told himself.

"Nonsense," said Lettie. "I have no enemies."

"Think," said Godfrey. "Think hard."

"The red lights," said Lettie. "And don't talk to me as if I were Charmian."

"Lettie, if you please, I do not need to be told how to drive. I observed the lights." He had braked hard, and Dame Lettie was jerked forward.

She gave a meaningful sigh which, when the green lights came on, made him drive all the faster.

"You know, Godfrey," she said, "you are wonderful for your age."

"So everyone says." His driving pace became moderate;

her sigh of relief was inaudible, her patting herself on the back invisible.

"In your position," he said, "you must have enemies."

"Nonsense."

"I say *yes*." He accelerated.

"Well, perhaps you're right." He slowed down again, but Dame Lettie thought, I wish I hadn't come.

They were at Knightsbridge. It was only a matter of keeping him happy till they reached Kensington Church Street and turned into Vicarage Gardens where Godfrey and Charmian lived.

"I have written to Eric," she said, "about his book. Of course, he has something of his mother's former brilliance, but it did seem to me that the subject-matter lacked the joy and hope which was the mark of a good novel in those days."

"I couldn't *read* the book," said Godfrey. "I simply could not go on with it. A motor salesman in Leeds and his wife spending a night in a hotel with that communist librarian . . . Where does it all lead you?"

Eric was his son. Eric was fifty-six and had recently published his second novel.

"He'll never do as well as Charmian did," Godfrey said. "Try as he may."

"Well, I can't quite agree with that," said Lettie, seeing that they had now pulled up in front of the house. "Eric has a hard streak of realism which Charmian never—"

Godfrey had got out and slammed the door. Dame Lettie sighed and followed him into the house, wishing she hadn't come.

"Did you have a nice evening at the pictures, Taylor?" said Charmian.

"I am not Taylor," said Dame Lettie, "and in any case, you always called Taylor Jean during her last twenty or so years in your service."

Mrs. Anthony, their daily housekeeper, brought in the milky coffee and placed it on the breakfast table.

"Did you have a nice evening at the pictures, Taylor?" Charmian asked her.

"Yes, thanks, Mrs. Colston," said the housekeeper.

"Mrs. Anthony is not Taylor," said Lettie. "There is no one by name of Taylor here. And anyway you used to call her Jean latterly. It was only when you were a girl that you called Taylor Taylor. And, in any event, Mrs. Anthony is not Taylor."

Godfrey came in. He kissed Charmian. She said, "Good morning, Eric."

"He is not Eric," said Dame Lettie.

Godfrey frowned at his sister. Her resemblance to himself irritated him. He opened *The Times*.

"Are there lots of obituaries to-day?" said Charmian.

"Oh, don't be gruesome," said Lettie.

"Would you like me to read you the obituaries, dear?" Godfrey said, turning the pages to find the place in defiance of his sister.

"Well, I should like the war news," Charmian said.

"The war has been over since nineteen forty-five," Dame Lettie said. "If indeed it is the last war you are referring to. Perhaps, however, you mean the First World War? The Crimean perhaps . . . ?"

"Lettie, please," said Godfrey. He noticed that Lettie's hand was unsteady as she raised her cup, and the twitch on her large left cheek was pronounced. He thought in how much better form he himself was than his sister, though she was the younger, only seventy-nine.

Mrs. Anthony looked round the door. "Someone on the phone for Dame Lettie."

"Oh, who is it?"

"Wouldn't give a name."

"Ask who it is, please."

"Did ask. Wouldn't give—"

"I'll go," said Godfrey.

Dame Lettie followed him to the telephone and overheard the male voice. "Tell Dame Lettie," it said, "to remember she must die."

"Who's there?" said Godfrey. But the man had hung up.

"We must have been followed," said Lettie. "I told no one I was coming over here last night."

She telephoned to report the occurrence to the Assistant Inspector.

He said, "Sure you didn't mention to anyone that you intended to stay at your brother's home?"

"Of course I'm sure."

"Your brother actually heard the voice? Heard it himself?"

"Yes, as I say, he took the call."

She told Godfrey, "I'm glad you took the call. It corroborates my story. I have just realised that the police have been doubting it."

"Doubting your word?"

"Well, I suppose they thought I might have imagined it. Now, perhaps, they will be more active."

Charmian said, "The police . . . What are you saying about the police? Have we been robbed?"

"I am being molested," said Dame Lettie.

Mrs. Anthony came in to clear the table.

"Ah, Taylor, how old are you?" said Charmian.

"Sixty-nine, Mrs. Colston," said Mrs. Anthony.

"When will you be seventy?"

"Twenty-eighth November."

"That will be splendid, Taylor. You will then be one of us," said Charmian.

Chapter Two

There were twelve occupants of the Maud Long Medical Ward (aged people, female). The ward sister called them the Baker's Dozen, not knowing that this is thirteen, but having only heard the phrase; and thus it is that a good many old sayings lose their force.

First came a Mrs. Emeline Roberts, seventy-six, who had been a cashier at the Odeon in the days when it *was* the Odeon. Next came Miss or Mrs. Lydia Reewes-Duncan, seventy-eight, whose past career was uncertain, but who was visited fortnightly by a middle-aged niece, very bossy towards the doctors and staff, very uppish. After that came Miss Jean Taylor, eighty-two, who had been a companion-maid to the famous authoress Charmian Piper after her marriage into the Colston Brewery family. Next again lay Miss Jessie Barnacle who had no birth certificate but was put down as eighty-one, and who for forty-eight years had been a newsvendor at Holborn Circus. There was also a Madame Trotsky, a Mrs. Fanny Green, a Miss Doreen Valvona, and five others, all of known and various careers, and of ages ranging from seventy to ninety-three. These twelve old women were known variously as Granny Roberts, Granny Duncan, Granny Taylor, Grannies Barnacle, Trotsky, Green, Valvona, and so on.

Sometimes, on first being received into her bed, the patient would be shocked and feel rather let down by being called Granny. Miss or Mrs. Reewes-Duncan threatened for a whole week to report anyone who called her Granny Duncan. She threatened to cut them out of her will and to write to her M.P. The nurses provided writing-paper and a pencil at her urgent request. However, she changed her mind about informing her M.P. when they promised not to call her Granny any more. "But," she said, "you shall never go back into my will."

"In the name of God that's real awful of you," said the ward sister as she bustled about. "I thought you was going to leave us all a packet."

"Not now," said Granny Duncan. "Not now, I won't. You don't catch me for a fool."

Tough Granny Barnacle, she who had sold the evening paper for forty-eight years at Holborn Circus, and who always said, "Actions speak louder than words," would send out to Woolworth's for a will-form about once a week; this would occupy her for two or three days. She would ask the nurse how to spell words like "hundred" and "ermine."

"Goin' to leave me a hundred quid, Granny?" said the nurse. "Goin' to leave me your ermine cape?"

The doctor on his rounds would say, "Well, Granny Barnacle, am I to be remembered or not?"

"You're down for a thousand, Doc."

"My word, I must stick in with you, Granny. I'll bet you've got a long stocking, my girl."

Miss Jean Taylor mused upon her condition and upon old age in general. Why do some people lose their memories, some their hearing? Why do some talk of their youth and others of their wills? She thought of Dame Lettie Colston who had all her senses intact, and yet played a real will-game, attempting to keep the two nephews in suspense, enemies of each other. And Charmian . . . Poor Charmian, since her stroke. How muddled she was about most things, and yet perfectly sensible when she discussed the books she had written. Quite clear on just that one thing, the subject of her books.

A year ago, when Miss Taylor had been admitted to the ward, she had suffered misery when addressed as Granny Taylor, and she thought she would rather die in a ditch than be kept alive under such conditions. But she was a woman practised in restraint; she never displayed her resentment. The lacerating familiarity of the nurses' treatment merged in with her arthritis, and she bore them both as long as she could without complaint. Then she was forced to cry out with pain during a long haunted night when the dim ward lamp made the beds into grey-white lumps like terrible bundles of laundry which muttered and snored occasionally. A nurse brought her an injection.

"You'll be better now, Granny Taylor."

"Thank you, nurse."

"Turn over, Granny, that's a good girl."

"Very well, nurse."

The arthritic pain subsided, leaving the pain of desolate humiliation, so that she wished rather to endure the physical nagging again.

After the first year she resolved to make her suffering a voluntary affair. If this is God's will then it is mine. She gained from this state of mind a decided and visible dignity, at the same time as she lost her stoical resistance to pain. She complained more, called often for the bed pan, and did not hesitate, on one occasion when the nurse was dilatory, to wet the bed as the other grannies did so frequently.

Miss Taylor spent much time considering her position. The doctor's "Well, how's Granny Taylor this morning? Have *you* been making your last will and test—" would falter when he saw her eyes, the intelligence. She could not help hating these visits, and the nurses giving her a hair-do, telling her she looked like sixteen, but she volunteered mentally for them, as it were, regarding them as the Will of God. She reflected that everything could be worse, and was sorry for the youngest generation now being born into the world, who in their old age, whether of good family or no, educated or no, would be forced by law into Chronic Wards; she dared say every citizen in the Kingdom would take it for granted; and the time would surely come for everyone to be a government granny or grandpa, unless they were mercifully laid to rest in their prime.

Miss Doreen Valvona was a good reader, she had the best eyes in the ward. Each morning at eleven she read aloud everyone's horoscope from the newspaper, holding it close to her brown nose and, behind her glasses, to the black eyes which came from her Italian father. She knew by heart everyone's Zodiacal sign. "Granny Green—Virgo," she would say. " 'A day for bold measures. Close partnerships are beneficial. A wonderful period for entertaining.' "

"Read us it again. My hearing aid wasn't fixed."

"No, you'll have to wait. Granny Duncan's next. Granny Duncan—Scorpio. 'Go all out for what you want to-day. Plenty of variety and gaiety to keep you on your toes.' "

Granny Valvona remembered everyone's horoscope all the day, checking up to see the points where it came true, so that, after Dame Lettie Colston had been to visit Granny Taylor, the old family servant, a cry arose from Granny Valvona: "What did I tell you in your horoscope? Listen while I read it out again. Granny Taylor—Gemini. 'You are in wonderful form to-day. Exceptionally bright social potents are indicated.' "

" 'Portents,' " said Miss Taylor. "Not potents."

Granny Valvona looked again. She spelt it out. "Potents," she said. Miss Taylor gave it up, murmuring, "I see."

"Well?" said Granny Valvona. "Wasn't that a remarkable forecast? 'You are in wonderful form to-day. Ex-

402

ceptionally bright social' . . . Now isn't that your visitor foretold, Granny Taylor?"

"Yes indeed, Granny Valvona."

"Some dame!" said the littlest nurse, who could not make out why Granny Taylor had so seriously called her visitor "Dame Lettie." She had heard of dames as jokes, and at the pictures.

"Wait, nurse, I'll read your horoscope. What's your month?"

"I've to go, Granny Valvoni. Sister's on the hunt."

"Don't call my name Valvoni, it's Valvona. It ends with an *ah*."

"*Ah*," said the little nurse, and disappeared with a hop and a skip.

"Taylor was in wonderful form to-day," Dame Lettie told her brother.

"You've been to see Taylor? You are really very good," said Godfrey. "But you look tired, I hope you haven't tired yourself."

"Indeed, I felt I could have changed places with Taylor. Those people are so fortunate these days. Central heating, everything they want, plenty of company."

"Is she in with nice people?"

"Who—Taylor? Well they all look splendid and clean. Taylor always says she is perfectly satisfied with everything. So she should be."

"Got all her faculties still?" Godfrey was obsessed by the question of old people and their faculties.

"Certainly. She asked for you and Charmian. She cries a little of course at the mention of Charmian. Of course she was fond of Charmian."

Godfrey looked at her closely. "You look ill, Lettie."

"Utter nonsense. I'm in wonderful form to-day. I've never felt more fit in my life."

"I don't think you should return to Hampstead," he said.

"After tea. I've arranged to go home after tea, and after tea I'm going."

"There was a telephone call for you," said Godfrey.

"Who was it?"

"That chap again."

"Really? Have you rung the C.I.D.?"

"Yes. In fact, they're coming round to-night to have a talk with us. They are rather puzzled about some aspects of the case."

"What did the man say? What did he say?"

"Lettie, don't upset yourself. You know very well what he said."

"I go back to Hampstead after tea," said Lettie.

"But the C.I.D.—"

"Tell them I have returned to Hampstead."

Charmian came unsteadily in. "Ah, Taylor, have you enjoyed your walk? You look in wonderful form to-day."

"Mrs. Anthony is late with tea," said Dame Lettie, moving her chair so that her back was turned to Charmian.

"You must not sleep alone at Hampstead," said Godfrey. "Call on Lisa Brooke and ask her to stop with you for a few days. The police will soon get the man."

"Lisa Brooke be damned," said Dame Lettie, which would have been an alarming statement if intended seriously, for Lisa Brooke was not many moments dead, as Godfrey discovered in *The Times* obituary the next morning.

Chapter Three

Lisa Brooke died in her seventy-third year, after her second stroke. She had taken nine months to die, and in fact it was only a year before her death that, feeling rather ill, she had decided to reform her life, and reminding herself how attractive she still was, offered up the new idea, her celibacy, to the Lord to whom no gift whatsoever is unacceptable.

It did not occur to Godfrey as he marched into a pew in the crematorium chapel that anyone else present had ever been Lisa's lover except himself. It did not even come to mind that he had been Lisa's lover, for he had never been her lover in any part of England, only Spain and Belgium, and at the moment he was busy with statistics. There were sixteen people present. On first analysis it emerged that five were relatives of Lisa. Next, among the remaining eleven, Godfrey elicited Lisa's lawyer, her housekeeper, the bank manager. Lettie had just arrived. Then there was himself. That left six, only one of whom he recognised, but all of whom were presumably Lisa's hangers-on, and he was glad their fountain of ready cash had dried up. All those years of daylight robbery; and many a time he had told Lisa, "A child of six could do better than that," when she displayed one of the paintings, outrages committed by one of her pets. "If he hasn't made his way in the world by now," he had said, time and again, of old Percy Mannering the poet, "he never will. You are a fool, Lisa, letting him drink your gin and shout his poetry in your ears."

Percy Mannering, almost eighty, stood with his lean stoop as the coffin was borne up the aisle. Godfrey stared hard at the poet's red-veined hatchet cheekbones and thin nose. He thought, I bet he's regretting the termination of his income. They've all bled poor Lisa white. . . . The poet was, in fact, in a state of excitement. Lisa's death had filled him with thrilling awe, for though he knew the general axiom that death was everyone's lot he could never realise the particular case; each new death gave him something fresh to feel. It came to him as the service began that within a few minutes Lisa's coffin would start sliding down into the furnace, and he saw as in a fiery vision her flame-tinted hair aglow as always, competing with the angry tresses of the fire below. He grinned like an elated wolf and shed tears of human grief as if he were half-beast, half-man, instead of half-poet, half-man. Godfrey watched him and thought, He must be senile. He has probably lost his faculties.

The coffin began to slide slowly down the slope towards a gap in the wall while the organ played something soft and religious. Godfrey, who was not a believer, was profoundly touched by this ensemble, and decided once and for all to be cremated when his time came. "There goes Lisa Brooke," he said to himself as he saw the last tilt of the coffin. The prow, thought the poet, lifts, and the ship goes under with the skipper on board. . . . No, that's too banal, Lisa herself as the ship is a better idea. Godfrey looked round him and thought, She should have been good for another ten years, but what can you expect with all that drink and all these spongers? So furiously did he glare about him that he startled the faces which caught his eye.

Tubby Dame Lettie caught up with her brother in the aisle as he moved with the others to the porch. "What's the matter with you, Godfrey?" Lettie breathed.

The chaplain was shaking doleful hands with everyone at the door. As Godfrey gave his hand he said over his shoulder to Lettie, "The matter with *me?* What d'you mean what's the matter with me? What's the matter with *you?*"

Lettie, as she dabbed her eyes, whispered, "Don't talk so loud. Don't glare so. Everyone's looking at you."

On the floor of the long porch was a muster of flowers done up, some in tasteful bunches, one or two in old-fashioned wreaths. These were being inspected by Lisa's relatives, her middle-aged nephew and his wife, her parched elder sister Janet Sidebottome who had been a missionary in India at a time when it *was* India, her brother Ronald Sidebottome who had long since retired from the City and Ronald's Australian wife who had been christened Tempest. Godfrey did not immediately identify them, for he saw only the row of their several behinds as they stooped to examine the cards attached to each tribute.

"Look, Ronald, isn't this sweet? A tiny bunch of violets —oh, see, it says, 'Thank you, Lisa dear, for all those wonderful times, with love from Tony.' "

"Rather odd words. Are you sure—"

"Who's Tony, I wonder?"

"See, Janet, this huge yellow rose wreath here from Mrs. Pettigrew. It must have cost her a fortune."

"What did you say?" said Janet who did not hear well.

"A wreath from Mrs. Pettigrew. It must have cost a fortune."

"Sh-sh-sh," said Janet, looking round. True enough, Mrs. Pettigrew, Lisa's old housekeeper, was approaching in her well-dressed confident manner. Janet, cramped from the card-inspection, straightened painfully and turned to meet Mrs. Pettigrew. She let the woman grip her hand.

"Thank you for all you have done for my sister," said Janet sternly.

"It was a pleasure." Mrs. Pettigrew spoke in a surprisingly soft voice. It was understood Janet was thinking of the will. "I loved Mrs. Brooke, poor soul."

Janet inclined her head graciously, firmly withdrew her hand and rudely turned her back.

"Can we see the ashes?" loudly enquired Percy Mannering as he emerged from the chapel. "Is there any hope of *seeing* them?" At the noise he made, Lisa's nephew and wife jumped nervily and looked round.

"I want to see those ashes if possible." The poet had cornered Dame Lettie, pressing his hungry demand. Lettie felt there was something unhealthy about the man. She moved away.

"That's one of Lisa's artists," she whispered to John Sidebottome, not meaning to prompt him to say "Oh!" and lift his hat in Percy's direction, as he did.

Godfrey stepped backwards and stood on a spray of pink carnations. "Oh—sorry," he said to the carnations, stepping off them quickly, and then was vexed at his folly, and knew that in any case no one had seen him after all. He ambled away from the trampled flowers.

"What's that fellow want with the ashes?" he said to Lettie.

"He wants to see them. Wants to see if they've gone grey. He is quite disgusting."

"Of course they will be grey. The fellow must have lost his faculties. *If* he ever had any."

"I don't know about faculties," said Lettie. "Certainly he has no feelings."

Tempest Sidebottome, blue-haired and well corseted was saying in a voice which carried away out to the Garden of Remembrance, "To some people there's just nothing that's sacred."

"Madam," said Percy, baring his sparse green teeth in a smile, "the ashes of Lisa Brooke will always be sacred to

me. I desire to see them, kiss them if they are cool enough. Where's that cleric? He'll have the ashes."

"Do you see over there—Lisa's housekeeper?" Lettie said to Godfrey.

"Yes, yes, I wonder—"

"That's what *I'm* wondering," said Lettie, who was wondering if Mrs. Pettigrew wanted a job, and if so would agree to undertake the personal care of Charmian.

"But I think we would need a younger woman. That one must be getting on," said Godfrey, "if I remember aright."

"Mrs. Pettigrew has a constitution like a horse," said Dame Lettie, casting a horse-dealer's glance over Mrs. Pettigrew's upright form. "And it is impossible to get younger women."

"Has she got all her faculties?"

"Of course. She had poor Lisa right under her thumb."

"I hardly think Charmian would want—"

"Charmian needs to be bullied. What Charmian needs is a firm hand. She will simply go to pieces if you don't keep at her. Charmian needs a firm hand. It's the only way."

"But what about Mrs. Anthony?" said Godfrey. "The woman might not get on with Mrs. Anthony. It would be tragic if we lost her."

"If you don't find someone soon to look after Charmian you will certainly lose Mrs. Anthony. Charmian is too much of a handful for Mrs. Anthony. You will lose Mrs. Anthony. Charmian keeps calling her Taylor. She is bound to resent it. Who are you staring at?"

Godfrey was staring at a short bent man walking with the aid of two sticks round a corner of the chapel. "Who is that man?" said Godfrey. "He looks familiar."

Tempest Sidebottome fussed over to the little man who beamed up at her with a fresh face under his wide black hat. He spoke in a shrill boyish tone. "Afraid I'm late," he said. "Is the party over? Are you all Lisa's sinisters and bothers?"

"That's Guy Leet," said Godfrey, at once recognising him, for Guy had always used to call sisters and brothers sinisters and bothers. "The little rotter," said Godfrey, "he used to be after Charmian. It must be thirty-odd years since last I saw him. He can't be more than seventy-five and just see what he's come to."

Tables at a tea-shop near Golders Green had been reserved for Lisa's post-crematorial party. Godfrey had intended to miss the tea party but the arrival of Guy Leet had changed his mind. He was magnetized by the sight of the clever little man doubled over his sticks, and could not keep his eyes off the arthritic hobbling of Guy making his way among the funeral flowers.

"Better join them for tea," he said to Lettie, "hadn't we?"

"What for?" said Lettie, looking round the company. "We can have tea at home. Come back with me for tea, we can have it at home."

"I think we'd better join them," said Godfrey. "We might have a word with Mrs. Pettigrew about her taking on Charmian."

Lettie saw Godfrey's gaze following the hunched figure of Guy Leet who, on his sticks, had now reached the door of his taxi. Several of the party helped Guy inside, then joined him. As they drove off, Godfrey said, "Little rotter. Supposed to be a critic. Tried to take liberties with all the lady novelists, and then he was a theatre critic and he was after the actresses. You'll remember him, I daresay."

"Vaguely," said Lettie. "He never got much change out of *me*."

"He was never after you," said Godfrey.

At the tea-shop Dame Lettie and Godfrey found the

mourners being organised into their places by Tempest Sidebottome, big and firm in her corsets, aged seventy-five, with that accumulated energy which strikes despair in the hearts of jaded youth, and which now fairly intimidated even the two comparative youngsters in the group, Lisa's nephew and his wife who were not long past fifty.

"Ronald, sit down here and stay put," Tempest said to her husband, who put on his glasses and sat down.

Godfrey was casting about for Guy Leet, but in the course of doing so his sight was waylaid by the tables on which were set silver-plate cakestands with thin bread and butter on the bottom tier, cut fruitcake above that, and on the top, a pile of iced cakes wrapped in cellophane paper. Godfrey began to feel a passionate longing for his tea, and he pushed past Dame Lettie to stand conspicuously near the organiser, Tempest. She did notice him right away and allotted him a seat at a table. "Lettie," he called then, "come over here. We're sitting here."

"Dame Lettie," said Tempest over his head, "you must come and sit with us, my dear. Over here beside Ronald."

Damned snob, thought Godfrey. I suppose she thinks Lettie is somebody.

Someone leant over to offer him a cigarette which was a filter-tip. However, he said, "Thanks, I'll keep it for after tea." Then looking up, he saw the wolf grin on the face of the man who was offering him the packet with a trembling hand. Godfrey plucked out a cigarette and placed it beside his plate. He was angry at being put beside Percy Mannering, not only because Percy had been one of Lisa's spongers, but also because he must surely be senile with that grin and frightful teeth, and Godfrey felt the poet would not be able to manage his teacup with those shaking hands.

He was right, for Percy spilled a lot of his tea on the cloth. He ought to be in a home, thought Godfrey. Tempest glanced at their table every now and then and tut-

tutted a lot, but she did this all round, as if it were a children's beanfeast. Percy was oblivious of the mess he was making or of anyone's disapproval. Two others sat at their table, Janet Sidebottome and Mrs. Pettigrew. The poet had taken it for granted that he was the most distinguished and therefore the leader of conversation.

"One time I fell out with Lisa," he roared, "was when she took up Dylan Thomas." He pronounced the first name Dye-lan. "Dylan Thomas," he said, "and Lisa good to him. Do you know, if I was to go to Heaven and find Dylan Thomas there, I'd prefer to go to HELL. *And* I wouldn't be surprised if Lisa hasn't gone to Hell for aiding and abetting him in his poetry, so-called."

Janet Sidebottome bent her ear closer to Percy. "What did you say about poor Lisa? I don't hear well."

"I say," he said, "I wonder if Lisa's gone to Hell because of her—"

"From respect to my dear sister," said Janet, with a hostile look, "I don't think we will discuss—"

"Dye-lan Thomas died from D.T." said the old poet, becoming gleeful. "You see the coincidence? His initials were D. T. and he *died* from D.T. Hah!"

"In respect for my late sister—"

"Poetry!" said Percy. "Dylan Thomas didn't know the meaning of the word. As I said to Lisa, I said, 'You're making a bloody fool of yourself supporting that charlatan. It isn't poetry, it's a leg-pull.' She didn't see it, nobody saw it, but I'm telling you his verse was all a HOAX."

Tempest turned round in her chair. "Hush, Mr. Mannering." she said, tapping Percy on the shoulder.

Percy looked at her and roared, "Ha! Do you know what you can tell Satan to do with Dye-lan Thomas's poetry?" He sat back to observe, with his two-fanged gloat, the effect of this question, which he next answered in unprintable terms, causing Mrs. Pettigrew to say, "Gracious!" and to wipe the corners of her mouth with her

412

handkerchief. Meanwhile various commotions arose at the other tables and the senior waitress said, "Not in *here*, sir!"

Godfrey's disgust was arrested by fear that the party might now break up. While everyone's attention was still on Percy he hastily took a couple of the cellophane-wrapped cakes from the top tier of the cakestand, and stuffed them into his pocket. He looked round and felt sure no one had noticed the action.

Janet Sidebottome leaned over to Mrs. Pettigrew. "What did he say?" she said.

"Well, Miss Sidebottome," said Mrs. Pettigrew, meanwhile glancing at herself sideways in a glass on the wall, "as far as I could comprehend, he was talking about some gentleman indelicately."

"Poor Lisa," said Janet. Tears came to her eyes. She kissed her relatives and departed. Lisa's nephew and his wife sidled away, though before they had reached the door they were summoned back by Tempest because the nephew had left his scarf. Eventually, the couple were permitted to go. Percy Mannering remained grinning in his seat.

To Godfrey's relief Mrs. Pettigrew refilled his cup. She also poured one for herself, but when Percy passed his shaking cup she ignored it. Percy said, "Hah! That was strong meat for you ladies, wasn't it?" He reached for the teapot. "I hope it wasn't me made Lisa's sister cry," he said solemnly. "I'd be sorry to have made her cry." The teapot was too heavy for his quivering fingers and fell from them on to its side, while a leafy brown sea spread from the open lid over the tablecloth and on to Godfrey's trousers.

Tempest rose, pushing back her chair as if she meant business. She was followed to the calamitous table by Dame Lettie and a waitress. While Godfrey was being sponged, Lettie took the poet by the arm and said, "Please go." Tempest, busy with Godfrey's trousers, called over her shoulder to her husband, "Ronald, you're a man. Give Dame Lettie a hand."

"What? Who?" said Ronald.

"Wake up, Ronald. Can't you see what has to be done? Help Dame Lettie to take Mr. Mannering outside."

"Oh," said Ronald, "why, someone's spilt their tea!" He ogled the swimming tablecloth.

Percy shook off Dame Lettie's hand from his arm and, grinning to right and left, buttoning up his thin coat, departed.

A place was made for Godfrey and Mrs. Pettigrew at the Sidebottomes' table. "Now we shall have a fresh pot of tea," said Tempest. Everyone gave deep sighs. The waitresses cleaned up the mess. The room was noticeably quiet.

Dame Lettie started to question Mrs. Pettigrew about her future plans. Godfrey was anxious to overhear this conversation. He was not sure that he wanted Lisa Brooke's housekeeper to look after Charmian. She might be too old or too expensive. She looked a smart woman, she might have expensive ideas. And he was not sure that Charmian would not have to go into a home.

"There's no definite offer, of course," he interposed.

"Well, Mr. Colston, as I was saying," said Mrs. Pettigrew, "I can't make any plans, myself, until things are settled."

"What things?" said Godfrey.

"Godfrey, please," said Lettie, "Mrs. Pettigrew and I are having a chat." She slumped her elbow on the table and turned to Mrs. Pettigrew, cutting off her brother from view.

"What is your feeling about the service?" said Tempest.

Godfrey looked round at the waitresses. "Very satisfactory," he said. "That older one handled that Mannering very well, I thought."

Tempest closed her eyes as one who prays for grace. "I mean," she said, "poor Lisa's rites at the crematorium."

"Oh," said Godfrey, "you should have said funeral service. When you said the service, naturally I thought—"

"What do you feel about the cremation service?"

"First rate," said Godfrey. "I've quite decided to be cremated when my time comes. Cleanest way. Dead bodies under the ground only contaminate our water supplies. You should have said cremation service in the first place."

"I thought it was cold," said Tempest. "I do wish the minister had read out poor Lisa's obituary. The last cremation I was at—that was Ronald's poor brother Henry—they read out his obituary from the *Nottingham Guardian*, all about his war service and his work for SSAFA and Road Safety. It was so very moving. Now why couldn't they have read out Lisa's? All that in the papers about what she did for the Arts, he should have read it out to us."

"I quite agree," said Godfrey. "It was the least he could have done. Did you make a special request for it?"

"No," she sighed. "I left the arrangements to Ronald. Unless you do everything yourself . . ."

"They always get very violent about other poets," said Ronald. "You see, they feel very personal about poetry."

"Whatever is he talking about?" said Tempest. "He's talking about Mr. Mannering, that's what he's on about. We aren't talking about Mr. Mannering, Ronald. Mr. Mannering's left, it's a thing of the past. We've gone on to something else."

As they rose to leave Godfrey felt a touch on his arm. Turning round he saw Guy Leet behind him, his body crouched over his sticks and his baby face raised askew to Godfrey's.

"Got your funeral-baked meats all right?" said Guy.

"What?" said Godfrey.

Guy nodded his head towards Godfrey's pocket which bulged with the cakes. "Taking them home to Charmian?"

"Yes," said Godfrey.

"And how is Charmian?"

Godfrey had partly regained his poise. "She's in wonderful form," he said. "I'm sorry," he said, "to see you having such a difficult time. Must be terrible not being able to get about on your own pins."

Guy gave a high laugh. He came close to Godfrey and breathed into his waistcoat, "But I *did* get about, dear fellow. At least I did."

On the way home Godfrey threw the cakes out of his car window. Why did one pocket those damned things? he thought. One doesn't need them, one could buy up every cake-shop in London and never miss the money. Why did one do it? It doesn't make sense.

"I have been to Lisa Brooke's funeral," he said to Charmian when he got home, "or rather, cremation."

Charmian remembered Lisa Brooke; she had cause to remember her. "Personally, I'm afraid," said Charmian, "that Lisa was a little spiteful to me sometimes, but she had her better side. A generous nature when dealing with the right person, but—"

"Guy Leet was there," said Godfrey. "He's nearly finished now, bent over two sticks."

Charmian said, "Oh, and what a clever man he was!"

"Clever?" said Godfrey.

Charmian, when she saw Godfrey's face, giggled squeakily through her nose.

"I have quite decided to be cremated when my time comes," said Godfrey. "It is the cleanest way. The cemeteries only pollute our water supplies. Cremation is best."

"I do so agree with you," said Charmian sleepily.

"No, you do *not* agree with me," he said. "R.C.'s are not allowed to be cremated."

"I mean, I'm sure you are right, Eric dear."

"I am not Eric," said Godfrey. "You are not sure I'm right. Ask Mrs. Anthony, she'll tell you that R.C.'s are against cremation." He opened the door and bawled for Mrs. Anthony. She came in with a sigh.

"Mrs. Anthony, you're a Roman Catholic, aren't you?" said Godfrey.

"That's right. I've got something on the stove."

"Do you believe in cremation?"

"Well," she said, "I don't really much like the idea of being shoved away quick like that. I feel somehow it's sort of—"

"It isn't a matter of how you feel, it's a question of what your Church says you've not got to do. Your Church says you must not be cremated, that's the point."

"Well, as I say, Mr. Colston, I don't really fancy the idea—"

"'*Fancy the idea*' . . . It is not a question of what you fancy. You have no choice in the matter, do you see?"

"Well, I always like to see a proper burial, I always like—"

"It's a point of discipline in your Church," he said, "that you mustn't be cremated. You women don't know your own system."

"I see, Mr. Colston. I've got something on the stove."

"*I* believe in cremation, but you don't—Charmian, you disap*prove* of cremation, you understand."

"Very well, Godfrey."

"And you too, Mrs. Anthony."

"O.K., Mr. Colston."

"On principle," said Godfrey.

"That's right," said Mrs. Anthony and disappeared.

Godfrey poured himself a stout whisky and soda. He took from a drawer a box of matches and a razor blade and set to work, carefully splitting the slim length of each match, so that from one box of matches he would eventually make two boxfuls. And while he worked he sipped his drink with satisfaction.

Chapter Four

The reason Lisa Brooke's family arranged her post-funeral party at a tea-shop rather than at her small brick studio-house at Hampstead was this. Mrs. Pettigrew, her housekeeper, was still in residence there. The family had meanwhile discovered that Lisa had bequeathed most of her fortune to Mrs. Pettigrew whom they had long conceived as an unfortunate element in Lisa's life. They held this idea in the way that people often are obscurely right, though the suspicions that lead up to their conclusions are faulty. Whatever they suspected was the form that Mrs. Pettigrew's influence over Lisa took, they hoped to contest Lisa's will if possible, on the grounds that Lisa, when she made it, was not in her right mind, and probably under undue influence of Mrs. Pettigrew.

The very form of the will, they argued, proved that Lisa had been unbalanced when she made it. The will had not been drafted by a lawyer. It was a mere sheet of writing paper, witnessed by the charwoman and her daughter a year before Lisa's death, bequeathing her entire fortune "to my husband if he survives me, and thereafter to my housekeeper, Mabel Pettigrew." Now Lisa, so her relatives believed, had no husband alive. Old Brooke was long dead, and moreover Lisa had been divorced from him during the Great War. She must have been dotty, they argued, even to mention a husband. The sheet of paper, they insisted, must be invalid. Alarmingly, their lawyers saw nothing invalid on the face of it; Mrs. Pettigrew was apparently the sole beneficiary.

Tempest Sidebottome was furious. "Ronald and Janet," she said, "should inherit by rights. We'll fight it. Lisa would never have mentioned a husband had she been in her right mind. Mrs. Pettigrew must have had a hold on Lisa."

"Lisa was always liable to say foolish things," Ronald Sidebottome remarked.

"You're a born obstructionist," Tempest said.

Hence, they had felt it cautious to avoid the threshold of Harmony Studio for the time being, and had felt it equally cautious to invite Mrs. Pettigrew to the tea-shop.

Dame Lettie was explaining this to Miss Taylor, who had seen much in her long service with Charmian. Dame Lettie had, unawares, in the past few months, slipped into the habit of confiding in Miss Taylor. So many of Lettie's contemporaries, those who knew her world and its past, had lost their memories or their lives, or were away in private homes in the country; it was handy having Miss Taylor available in London to discuss things with.

"You see, Taylor," said Dame Lettie, "they never did like Mrs. Pettigrew. Now, Mrs. Pettigrew is an admirable woman. I was hoping to persuade her to take on Charmian. But of course with Lisa's money in prospect, she does not intend to work any longer. She must be over seventy, although of course she says . . . Well, you see, with Lisa's money—"

"She would never do for Charmian," said Miss Taylor.

"Oh really, I feel Charmian needs a firm hand if we are to keep her at home. Otherwise she will have to go into a nursing home. Taylor, you have no conception how irritated poor Godfrey gets. He tries his best." Dame Lettie lowered her voice. "And then, Taylor, there is the lavatory question. Mrs. Anthony can't be expected to take her every time. As it is, Godfrey attends to the chamber pots in the morning. He isn't used to it, Taylor, he's not used to that sort of thing."

In view of the warm September afternoon Miss Taylor had been put out on the balcony of the Maud Long Ward where she sat with a blanket round her knees.

"Poor Charmian," she said, "darling Charmian. As we get older these affairs of the bladder and kidneys do become so important to us. I hope she has a commode by her bedside, you know how difficult it is for old bones to manage a pot."

"She has a commode," said Dame Lettie. "But that doesn't solve the daytime problem. Now Mrs. Pettigrew would have been admirable in that respect. Think what she did for poor Lisa after the first stroke. However, Mrs. Pettigrew is out of the question because of this inheritance from Lisa. It was ridiculous of Lisa."

Miss Taylor looked distressed. "It would be tragic," she said, "for Mrs. Pettigrew to go to the Colstons'. Charmian would be most unhappy with the woman. You must not think of such a thing Dame Lettie. You don't know Mrs. Pettigrew as I do."

Dame Lettie's yellow-brown eyes focused as upon an exciting scene as she bent close to Miss Taylor. "Do you think," she enquired, "there was anything peculiar, I mean not right, between Mrs. Pettigrew and Lisa Brooke?"

Miss Taylor did not pretend not to know what she meant. "I cannot say," she said, "what were the habits of their relationship in former years. I only know this, and you yourself know, Dame Lettie, Mrs. Pettigrew was very domineering towards Mrs. Brooke in the last eight or nine years. She is not suitable for Charmian."

"It is precisely because she is domineering," said Lettie, "that I wanted her for Charmian. Charmian *needs* a bully. For her own good. But anyway, that's beside the point, Mrs. Pettigrew does not desire the job. I understand Lisa has left her practically everything. Now Lisa was very comfortable as you know, and—"

"I would not be sure that Mrs. Pettigrew will in fact inherit," insisted Miss Taylor.

"No, Taylor," said Dame Lettie, "I'm afraid Lisa's family do not stand a chance. I doubt if their advisers will let them take it to court. There is no case. Lisa was perfectly sane to the day she died. It is true Mrs. Pettigrew had an undesirable influence over Lisa, but Lisa was in her right mind to the end."

"Yes, it is true Mrs. Pettigrew had a hold on her."

"I wouldn't say a hold, I would say an influence. If Lisa was fool enough—"

"Quite, Dame Lettie. Was Mr. Leet at the funeral, by any chance?"

"Oh, Guy Leet was there. I shouldn't think he will last long. Rheumatoid arthritis with complications." Dame Lettie recalled, as she spoke, that rheumatoid arthritis was one of Miss Taylor's afflictions, but, she thought, after all she must face the facts. "Very advanced case," said Dame Lettie, "he was managing with great difficulty on two sticks."

"It is like wartime," Miss Taylor remarked.

"What do you say?"

"Being over seventy is like being engaged in a war. All our friends are going or gone and we survive amongst the dead and the dying as on a battlefield."

She is wandering in her mind and becoming morbid, thought Dame Lettie.

"Or suffering from war nerves," said Miss Taylor.

Dame Lettie was annoyed, because she had intended to gain some advice from Miss Taylor.

"Come now, Taylor," she said. "You are talking like Charmian."

"I must," said Miss Taylor, "have caught a lot of her ways of thought and speech."

"Taylor," said Lettie, "I want to ask your advice." She looked at the other woman to see if she was alert. "Four months ago," she said, "I began to receive anonymous telephone calls from a man. I have been receiving them ever since. On one occasion when I was staying with Godfrey, the man, who must have traced me there, gave a message for me to Godfrey."

"What does he say?" said Miss Taylor.

Dame Lettie leant to Miss Taylor's ear and, in a low tone, informed her.

"Have you told the police?"

"Of course we have told the police. They are useless. Godfrey had an interview with them too. Useless. They seem to think we are making it up."

"You will have thought of consulting Chief Inspector Mortimer who was such a fan of Charmian's?"

"Of course I have not consulted Mortimer. Mortimer is retired, he is close on seventy. Time passes, you know. You are living in the past, Taylor."

"I only thought," said Miss Taylor, "that Inspector Mortimer might act privately. He might at least be helpful in some way. He always struck me as a most unusual—"

"Mortimer is out of the question. We want a young, active detective on this job. There is a dangerous lunatic at large. I know not how many people besides myself are endangered."

"I should not answer the telephone, Dame Lettie, if I were you."

"My dear Taylor, one can't be cut off perpetually. I still have my Homes to consider, I am not entirely a back number, Taylor. One must be on the phone. But I confess, I am feeling the strain. Imagine for yourself every time one answers the telephone. I never know if one is going to hear that distressing sentence. It *is* distressing."

" 'Remember you must die,' " said Miss Taylor.

"Hush," said Dame Lettie, looking warily over her shoulder.

"Can you not ignore it, Dame Lettie?"

"No, I cannot. I have tried, but it troubles me deeply. It *is* a troublesome remark."

"Perhaps you might obey it," said Miss Taylor.

"What's that you say?"

"You might, perhaps, try to remember you must die."

She is wandering again, thought Lettie. "Taylor," she said, "I do not wish to be advised how to think. What I hoped you could suggest is some way of apprehending the criminal, for I see that I must take matters into my own hands. Do you understand telephone wires? Can you follow the system of calls made from private telephone boxes?"

"It's difficult," said Miss Taylor, "for people of advanced years to start remembering they must die. It is best to form the habit while young. I shall think of some plan, Dame Lettie, for tracing the man. I did once know something about the telephone system, I will try to recall what I knew."

"I must go." Lettie rose, and added, "I expect you are keeping pretty well, Taylor?"

"We have a new ward sister here," said Miss Taylor. "She is not so pleasant as the last. I have no complaint personally, but some of my companions are inclined to be touchy, to imagine things."

Lettie cast her eye along the sunny verandah of the Maud Long Ward where a row of old women sat out in their chairs.

"They are fortunate," said Dame Lettie and uttered a sigh.

"I know it," said Miss Taylor. "But they are discontented and afraid."

"Afraid of what?"

"The sister in charge," said Miss Taylor.

"But what's wrong with her?"

"Nothing," said Miss Taylor, "except that she is afraid of these old people."

"*She* is afraid? I thought you said the patients were afraid of *her*."

"It comes to the same thing," said Miss Taylor.

She is wandering, thought Lettie, and she said, "In the Balkan countries, the peasants turn their aged parents out of doors every summer to beg their keep for the winter."

"Indeed?" said Miss Taylor. "That is an interesting system." Her hand, when Dame Lettie lifted it to say goodbye, was painful at the distorted joints.

"I hope," said Miss Taylor, "you will think no more of employing Mrs. Pettigrew."

Dame Lettie thought, She is jealous of anyone else's having to do with Charmian.

Perhaps I am, thought Miss Taylor who could read Dame Lettie's idea.

And as usual after Dame Lettie had left, she pondered and understood more and more why Lettie came so frequently to visit her and seemed to find it pleasant, and at the same time seldom spoke or behaved pleasantly. It was the old enmity about Miss Taylor's love affair in 1907 which in fact Dame Lettie had forgotten—had dangerously forgotten; so that she retained in her mind a vague fascinating enmity for Jean Taylor without any salutary definition. Whereas Miss Taylor herself, until quite recently, had remembered the details of her love affair, and Dame Lettie's subsequent engagement to marry the man, which came to nothing after all. But recently, thought Miss Taylor, I am beginning to feel as she does. Enmity is catching. Miss Taylor closed her eyes and laid her hands loosely on the rug which covered her knees. Soon the nurses would come in to put the grannies to bed. Meanwhile she thought with a sleepy pleasure, I enjoy Dame Lettie's visits, I look forward to them, in spite of which

I treat her with my asperity. Perhaps it is because I have now so little to lose. Perhaps it is because these encounters have an exhilarating quality. I might sink into a torpor were it not for fat old Lettie. And perhaps, into the bargain, I might use her in the matter of the ward sister, although that is unlikely.

"Granny Taylor—Gemini. 'Evening festivities may give you all the excitement you want. A brisk day for business enterprises,' " Granny Valvona read out for the second time that day.

"There," said Miss Taylor.

The Maud Long Ward had been put to bed and was now awaiting supper.

"It comes near the mark," said Miss Valvona. "You can always know by your horoscope when your visitors are coming to see you, Granny Taylor. Either your Dame or that gentleman that comes; you can always tell by the stars."

Granny Trotsky lifted her wizened head with low brow and pug nose, and said something. Her health had been degenerating for some weeks. It was no longer possible to hear exactly what she said. Miss Taylor was the quickest in the ward at guessing what Granny Trotsky's remarks might be, but Miss Barnacle was the most inventive.

Granny Trotsky repeated her words, whatever they were.

Miss Taylor replied, "All right, Granny."

"What did she say?" demanded Granny Valvona.

"I am not sure," said Miss Taylor.

Mrs. Reewes-Duncan who claimed to have lived in a bungalow in former days, addressed Miss Valvona. "Are you aware that the horoscope you have just read out to us specifies evening festivities, whereas Granny Taylor's visitor came at three-fifteen this afternoon?"

Granny Trotsky again raised her curiously shaped head

and spoke, emphasising her statement with vehement nods of this head which was so fearfully and wonderfully made. Whereupon Granny Barnacle ventured, "She says festivities my backside. What's the use of the stars foretell with that murderous bitch of a sister outside there, she says, waiting to finish off the whole ward in the winter when the lot goes down with pneumonia. You'll be reading your stars, she says all right when they need the beds for the next lot. That's what she says—don't you, Granny Trotsky?"

Granny Trotsky, raising her head, made one more, and very voluble effort, then drooped exhausted on her pillow, closing her eyes.

"That's what she said," said Granny Barnacle. "And right she is, too. Come the winter them that's made nuisances of theirselves don't last long under that sort."

A ripple of murmurs ran up the rows of beds. It ceased as a nurse walked through the ward, and started again when she had gone.

Miss Valvona's strong eyes stared through her spectacles into the past, as they frequently did in the autumn, and she saw the shop door open on a Sunday afternoon, and the perfect ices her father manufactured, and heard the beautiful bellow of his accordion after night had fallen, on and on till closing time. "Oh, the parlour and the sundaes and white ladies we used to serve," she said, "and my father with the Box. The white ladies stiff on your plate, they were hard, and made from the best-quality products. And the fellows who would say to me, 'How do, Doreen,' even if they had another girl with them after the pictures. And my father got down the Box and played like a champion. It cost him fifty pounds, in those days, mind you it was a lot."

Granny Duncan addressed Miss Taylor, "Did you ask that Dame to do something for us, at all?"

"Not exactly," said Miss Taylor, "but I mentioned that

426

we were not so comfortable now as we have been previously."

"She goin' to *do* something for us?" demanded Granny Barnacle.

"She is not herself on the management committee," Miss Taylor explained. "It is a friend of hers who is on the committee. Now, it will take time. I can't, you know, press her. She is very easily put off. And then, you know, in the meantime, we must try to make the best of this." The nurse walked back through the ward among the grannies, all sullen and silent but for Granny Trotsky who had now fallen noisily asleep with her mouth open.

It was true, thought Miss Taylor, that the young nurses were less jolly since Sister Burstead had taken over the ward. Of course it was but two seconds before she had become "Sister Bastard" on the lips of Granny Barnacle. The associations of her name, perhaps, in addition to her age—Sister Burstead was well over fifty—had affected Granny Barnacle with immediate hostile feelings. "Over fifty they got the workhouse mind. You can't never trust a ward sister over fifty. They don't study that there's new ways of goin' on since the war, by law." These sentiments in turn had affected the other occupants of the ward. But the ground had been prepared the week before by their knowledge of the departure of the younger sister: "A change, hear that?—there's to be a change. What's the stars say, Granny Valvona?" Then, on the morning that Sister Burstead took over, she being wiry, bespectacled and middle-aged with a bad-tempered twitch at one side of her face between lip and jaw, Granny Barnacle declared she had absolutely placed her. "The workhouse mind. You see what'll happen now. Anyone that's a nuisance or can't contain themselves like me with Bright's disease, they won't last long in this ward. You get pneumonia in the winter, can't help but do, and that's her chance."

"What you think she'll do, Granny Barnacle?"

"Do? It's what she won't do. You wait to the winter, you'll be lyin' there and nothin' done for you. Specially if you got no relations or that to raise enquiries."

"The other nurses is all right, Granny, though."

"You'll see a difference in *them*."

There had been a difference. The nurses were terrified of their new superior, that was all. But as they became more brisk and efficient so did the majority of the grannies behold them with hostile thoughts and deadly suspicions. When the night staff came on duty the ward relaxed, and this took the form of much shouting throughout the night. The grannies shouted in their sleep and half-waking restlessness. They accepted their sedative pills fearfully, and in the morning would ask each other, "Was I all right last night?" not quite remembering whether they or another had made the noise.

"It all goes down in the book," said Granny Barnacle. "Nothing happens during the night but what it goes into the book. And Sister Bastard sees it in the morning. You know what that'll mean, don't you, when the winter comes?"

At first, Miss Taylor took a frivolous view of these sayings. It was true the new sister was jittery and strict, and over fifty years of age, and frightened. It will all blow over, thought Miss Taylor, when both sides get used to the change. She was sorry for Sister Burstead and her fifty-odd years. Thirty years ago, thought Miss Taylor, I was into my fifties, and getting old. How nerve-racking it is to be getting old, how much better to be old! It had been touch and go, in those days, whether she would leave the Colstons and settle down with her brother in Coventry while she had the chance. It was such a temptation to leave them, she having been cultivated by twenty-five years' association with Charmian. By the time she was fifty it really seemed absurd for her to continue her service with Charmian, her habits and tastes were so superior to those of the maids she met on her travels with Charmian, she was so much more intelligent. She had been all on edge for the first two years of her fifties, not knowing whether to go to look after the widowed brother in Coventry and enjoy some status or whether to continue waking Charmian up every morning, and observing in silence Godfrey's infidelities. For two years while she made up her mind she had given Charmian hell, threatening to leave every month, folding Charmian's dresses in the trunk so that they were horribly creased, going off to art galleries while Charmian rang for her in vain.

"You're far worse now," Charmian would tell her, "than when you were going through the menopause."

Charmian plied her with bottles of tonic medicine which she had poured down the lavatory with a weird joy. At last, after a month's holiday with her brother in Coventry, she found she could never stand life with him and his ways, the getting him off to his office in the morning, the keeping him in clean shirts, and the avaricious whist parties in the evening. At the Colstons' there was always some exotic company, and Charmian's sitting-room had been done out in black and orange. All the time she was at Coventry Miss Taylor had missed the exciting scraps of conversation which she had been used to hearing on Charmian's afternoons.

"Charmian darling, don't you think, honestly, I should have Boris bumped off?"

"No, I rather like Boris."

And those telephone messages far into the nights.

"Is that you, Taylor darling? Get Charmian to the phone, will you? Tell her I'm in a state. Tell her I want to read her my new poem." That was thirty years ago.

Ten years before that, the telephone messages had been different again, "Taylor, tell Mrs. Colston I'm in London. Guy Leet. Not a word, Taylor to *Mr.* Colston." These were messages which Miss Taylor sometimes did not deliver. Charmian herself was going through her difficult age at that time, and was apt to fly like a cat at any man who made approaches to her, even Guy who had previously been her lover.

At the age of fifty-three Miss Taylor had settled down. She could even meet Alec Warner without any of the old feelings. She went everywhere with Charmian, sat for hours while Charmian read aloud her books, while still in manuscript, gave judgment. As gradually the other servants became difficult and left, so Jean Taylor took charge. When Charmian had her hair bobbed, so did Miss Taylor. When Charmian entered the Catholic Church Miss Taylor was received, really just to please Charmian.

She rarely saw her brother from Coventry, and when she did, counted herself lucky to have escaped him. On one occasion she told Godfrey Colston to watch his step. The disappointed twitch at the side of her mouth which had appeared during her forties, now gradually disappeared.

So it will be, thought Miss Taylor, in the case of Sister Burstead, once she settles down. The twitch will go.

Presently, however, Miss Taylor began to feel there was very little chance of the new sister's twitch disappearing. The grannies were so worked up about her, it would not be surprising if she did indeed let them die of pneumonia should she ever get the chance.

"You must speak to the doctor, Granny Barnacle," said Miss Taylor, "if you really feel you aren't getting the right treatment."

"The doctor my backside. They're hand-in-glove. What's a old woman to them? I ask you."

The only good that could be discerned in the arrival of the new sister was the fact that the ward was now more alert. Everyone's wits had improved, as if the sister were a sort of shock treatment. The grannies had forgotten their will-making, and no longer threatened to disinherit each other or the nurses.

Mrs. Reewes-Duncan, however, made the great mistake of threatening the sister with her solicitor one dinner-time when the meat was tough or off, Miss Taylor could not recall which. "Fetch the ward sister to me," Mrs. Reewes-Duncan demanded. "Fetch her here to me."

The sister marched in purposefully when thus summoned.

"Well, Granny Duncan, what's the matter? Hurry up now, I'm busy. What's the matter?"

"This meat, my good woman . . ." The ward felt at once that Granny Duncan was making a great mistake. "My niece will be informed. . . . My solicitor—"

For some reason, the word "solicitor" set fire to Sister Burstead. That one word did the trick. You could evidently threaten the doctor, the matron, or your relations, and she would merely stand there glaring angrily with her twitch, she would say no more than, "You people don't know you're born," and, "Fire ahead, tell your niece, *my dear*." But the word solicitor fairly turned her, as Granny Barnacle recounted next day, arse over tit. She gripped the bedrail and yelled at Granny Duncan for a long time, it might have been ten minutes. Words, in isolation and grouped in phrases, detached themselves like sparks from the fiery scream proceeding from Sister Burstead's mouth. "Old beast . . . dirty old beast . . . food . . . grumble and grouse . . . I've been on since eight o'clock this morning . . . I've been on and on . . . work, work, work, day after day, for a lot of useless old, filthy old . . ."

Sister Burstead went off duty immediately assisted by a nurse. If only, thought Miss Taylor, we could try to be sweet old ladies, she would be all right. It's because we aren't sweet old things. . . .

"Scorpio," Granny Valvona had declared four hours later, although like everyone else in the ward she was shaken-up. "Granny Duncan—Scorpio. 'You can sail ahead with confidence. The success of another person could affect you closely.' " Granny Valvona put down the paper. "You see what I mean?" she said. "The stars never let you down. 'The success of another person . . .' A remarkable forecast."

The incident was reported to the matron and the doctor. The former made enquiries next morning of a kind which clearly indicated she was hoping against hope Sister Burstead could be exonerated, for she would be difficult to replace.

The matron bent over Miss Taylor and spoke quietly and exclusively. "Sister Burstead is having a rest for a few days. She has been overworking."

"Evidently," said Miss Taylor, whose head ached horribly.

"Tell me what you know of the affair. Sister Burstead was provoked, I believe?"

"Evidently," said Miss Taylor, eyeing the bland face above her and desiring it to withdraw.

"Sister Burstead was cross with Granny Duncan?" said the matron.

"She was nothing," said Miss Taylor, "if not cross. I suggest the sister might be transferred to another ward where there are younger people and the work is lighter."

"All the work in this hospital," said the matron, "is heavy."

Most of the grannies felt too upset to enjoy the few days' absence from duty of Sister Burstead, for whenever the general hysteria showed signs of waning, Granny Barnacle applied the bellows: "Wait till the winter. When you get pneumonia . . ."

During those days it happened that Granny Trotsky had her second stroke. An aged male cousin was summoned to her bedside, and a screen was put round her bed. He emerged after an hour still wearing the greenish-black hat in which he had arrived, shaking his head and hat, and crying all over his blotchy foreign face.

Granny Barnacle, who was up in her chair that day, called to him, "Pssst!"

Obediently he came to her side.

Granny Barnacle flicked her head towards the screened-in bed.

"She gone?"

"Nah. She breathe, but not speak."

"D'you know who done it?" said Granny Barnacle. "It was the sister that brought it on."

"She have no sister. I am next of kin."

A nurse came and hurried him away.

Granny Barnacle declared once more to the ward, "Sister Bastard done for Granny Trotsky."

"Ah but Granny, it was her second stroke. There's always a second, you know."

"Sister done it with her bad temper."

On learning that Sister Burstead had neither been dismissed nor transferred to another ward but was to return on the following day, Granny Barnacle gave notice to the doctor that she refused further treatment, was discharging herself next day, and that she would tell the world why.

"I know my bloody rights as a patient," she said. "Don't think I don't know the law. *And* what's more, I can get the phone number of the newspaper. I only got to ring up and they come along and want to know what's what."

"Take it easy, Granny," said the doctor.

"If Sister Bastard comes back, I go," said Granny Barnacle.

"Where to?" said the nurse.

Granny Barnacle glared. She felt that the nurse was being sarcastic, must know that she had spent three months in Holloway prison thirty-six years ago, six months twenty-two years ago, and subsequently various months. Granny Barnacle felt the nurse was referring to her record when she said "Where to?" in that voice of hers.

The doctor frowned at the nurse and said to Granny

Barnacle, "Take it easy, Granny. Your blood pressure isn't too good this morning. What sort of a night did you have? Pretty restless?"

This speech unnerved Granny Barnacle who had indeed had a bad night.

Granny Trotsky, who had so far recovered that the bed-screen had been removed, had been uttering slobbery mutters. The very sight of Granny Trotsky, the very sound of her trying to talk as she did at this moment, took away Granny Barnacle's nerve entirely.

She looked at the doctor's face, to read it. "Ah doc, I don't feel too bloody good," she said. "And I just don't feel easy with that bitch in charge. I just feel anything might happen."

"Come, come, the poor woman's overworked," he recited. "We all like to be of help if we can and in any way we can. We are trying to help you, Granny."

When he had gone Granny Barnacle whispered over to Miss Taylor, "Do I look bad, love?"

"No, Granny, you look fine." In fact, Granny Barnacle's face was blotched with dark red.

"Did you hear what doc said about my blood pressure? Do you think it was a lie, just so's I wouldn't make a fuss?"

"Perhaps not."

"For two pins, Granny Taylor, I'd be out of that door and down them stairs if it was the last thing I did and—"

"I shouldn't do that," said Miss Taylor.

"Could they certify me, love?"

"I don't know," said Miss Taylor.

"I'll tell the priest."

"You know what he'll say to you," said Miss Taylor.

"Offer it bloodywell up for the Holy Souls."

"I daresay."

"It's a hard religion, Granny Taylor. If it wasn't that my mother was R.C. I would never of—"

"I know a lady—" It was then Miss Taylor had said,

434

rashly, "I know a lady who knows another lady who is on the management committee of this hospital. It may take some time but I will see what I can do to get them to transfer Sister Burstead."

"God bless you, Granny Taylor."

"I can't promise. But I'll try. I shall have to be tactful."

"You hear that?" said Granny Barnacle to everyone in the ward. "You hear what Granny Taylor's goin' to do?"

Miss Taylor was not very disappointed with her first effort at sounding Dame Lettie. It was a beginning. She would keep on at Dame Lettie. There was also, possibly, Alec Warner. He might be induced to speak to Tempest Sidebottome who sat on the management committee of the hospital. It might even be arranged without blame to dreary Sister Burstead.

"Didn't your Dame promise nothing definite then?" said Granny Barnacle.

"No, it will take time."

"Will it be done before the winter?"

"I hope so."

"Did you tell her what she done to Granny Duncan?"

"Not exactly."

"You should of. Strikes me you're not on our side entirely, Granny Taylor. I seem to remember that face somehow."

"Whose face?"

"That Dame's face."

The difficulty was, Miss Taylor reflected, she could not feel the affair to be pre-eminently important. Sometimes she would have liked to say to the grannies, "What if your fears were correct? What if we died next winter?" Sometimes she did say to them, "Some of us may die next winter in any case. It is highly probable." Granny Valvona would reply, "I'm ready to meet my God, any time." And Granny Barnacle would stoutly add, "But not before time."

"You must keep on at your friend, Granny Taylor," said Granny Duncan, who, among all the grannies, most irritated Sister Burstead. Granny Duncan had cancer. Miss Taylor often wondered if the sister was afraid of cancer.

"I seem to remember that Dame's face," Granny Barnacle kept on. "Was she ever much round Holborn way of an evening?"

"I don't think so," said Miss Taylor.

"She might be an old customer of mine," said Granny Barnacle.

"I think she had her papers sent."

"Did she go out to work, this Dame?"

"Well, not to a job. But she did various kinds of committee work. That sort of thing."

Granny Barnacle turned over the face of Dame Lettie in her mind. "Was it charity work you said she did?"

"That kind of thing," said Miss Taylor. "Nothing special."

Granny Barnacle looked at her suspiciously, but Miss Taylor would not be drawn, nor say that Dame Lettie had been a Prison Visitor at Holloway from her thirtieth year until it became too difficult for her, with her great weight and breathlessness, to climb the stairs.

"I will keep on at Dame Lettie," she promised.

It was Sister Burstead's day off, and a nurse whistled as she brought in the first supper tray.

Granny Barnacle commented in a hearty voice,

"A whistling woman, a crowing hen,
Is neither fit for God nor man."

The nurse stopped whistling and gave Granny Barnacle a close look, dumped the tray and went to fetch another.

Granny Trotsky attempted to raise her head and say something.

436

"Granny Trotsky wants something," said Granny Duncan.

"What you want, Granny?"

"She is saying," said Miss Taylor, "that we shouldn't be unkind to the nurses just because—"

"Unkind to the nurses! What they goin' to do when the winter—"

Miss Taylor prayed for grace. Is there no way, she thought, for them to forget the winter? Can't they go back to making their wills every week?

In the course of the night Granny Trotsky died as the result of the bursting of a small blood-vessel in her brain, and her spirit returned to God who gave it.

Chapter Five

Mrs. Anthony knew instinctively that Mrs. Pettigrew was a kindly woman. Her instinct was wrong. But the first few weeks after Mrs. Pettigrew came to the Colstons' to look after Charmian she sat in the kitchen and told Mrs. Anthony of her troubles.

"Have a fag," said Mrs. Anthony, indicating with her elbow the packet on the table while she poured strong tea. "Everything might be worse."

Mrs. Pettigrew said, "It couldn't very well be worse. Thirty years of my life I gave to Mrs. Lisa Brooke. Everyone knew I was to get that money. Then this Guy Leet turns up to claim. It wasn't any marriage, that wasn't. Not a proper marriage." She pulled her cup of tea towards her and thrusting her head close to Mrs. Anthony's, told her in what atrocious manner and for what long-ago reason, Guy Leet had been incapable of consummating his marriage with Lisa Brooke.

Mrs. Anthony swallowed a large sip of her tea, the cup of which she held in both hands, and breathed back into the cup while the warm-smelling steam spread comfortingly over her nose. "Still," she said, "a husband's a husband. By law."

"Lisa never recognised him as such," said Mrs. Pettigrew. "No one knew about the marriage with Guy Leet, until she died, the little swine."

"I thought you says she was all right," said Mrs. Anthony.

"Guy Leet," said Mrs. Pettigrew. "He's the little swine."

"Oh, I see. Well the courts will have something to say to that, dear, when it comes up. Have a fag."

"You're making me into a smoker, Mrs. Anthony. Thanks, I will. But you should try to cut them down, they aren't too good for you."

"Twenty a day since I was twenty-five and seventy yesterday," said Mrs. Anthony.

"Seventy! Gracious, you'll be—"

"Seventy years of age yesterday."

"Oh, seventy. Isn't it time you had a rest then? I don't envy you with this lot," Mrs. Pettigrew indicated with her head the kitchen door, meaning the Colstons residing beyond it.

"Not so bad," said Mrs. Anthony. *"He's* a bit tight, but *she's* nice. I like *her."*

"He's tight with the money?" said Mrs. Pettigrew.

Mrs. Anthony said, "Oh very," swivelling her eyes towards her companion to fix the remark.

Mrs. Pettigrew patted her hair which was thick, dyed black and well cut, as Lisa had made her wear it. "How old," she said, "would you say I was Mrs. Anthony?"

Mrs. Anthony, still sitting, pushed back in her chair the better to view Mrs. Pettigrew. She looked at the woman's feet in their suède black shoes, her tight good legs—no veins, her encased hips and good bust. Mrs. Anthony then put her head sideways to regard, from an angle of fifteen degrees, Mrs. Pettigrew's face. There were lines from nose to mouth, a small cherry-painted mouth. Only the beginnings of one extra chin. Two lines across the brow. The eyes were dark and clear, the nose firm and broad. "I should say," said Mrs. Anthony, folding her arms, "you was sixty-four abouts."

439

The unexpectedness of Mrs. Pettigrew's gentle voice was due to her heavily-marked appearance. It was gentler still as she said to Mrs. Anthony, "Add five years."

"Sixty-nine. You don't look it," said Mrs. Anthony. "Of course you've had the time and money to look after yourself and powder your face. You should of been in business."

In fact, Mrs. Pettigrew was seventy-three, but she did not at all look the age under her make-up.

She drew her hand across her forehead, however, and shook her head slowly. She was worried about the money, the court case which would probably drag on and on. Lisa's family were claiming their rights too.

Mrs. Anthony had started washing up.

"Old Warner still in with *her*," she said, "I suppose?"

"Yes," said Mrs. Pettigrew. "He is."

"It takes her off my hands for a while," said Mrs. Anthony.

"I must say," Mrs. Pettigrew said, "when I was with Lisa Brooke I used to be asked in to meet the callers. I mixed with everyone."

Mrs. Anthony started peeling potatoes and singing.

"I'm going in," said Mrs. Pettigrew, rising and brushing down her neat skirt. "Whether she likes it or whether she doesn't, I'd better keep my eye on her in any case, that's what I'm here for."

When Mrs. Pettigrew entered the drawing-room she said, "Oh, Mrs. Colston, I was just wondering if you were tired."

"You may take the tea-things away," said Charmian.

Instead Mrs. Pettigrew rang for Mrs. Anthony, and, as she piled plates on the tray for the housekeeper to take away, she knew Charmian's guest was looking at her.

Charmian said to Mrs. Anthony, "Thank you, Taylor."

Mrs. Pettigrew had met Alec Warner sometimes at Lisa

Brooke's. He smiled at her and nodded. She sat down and took a cigarette out of her black suède bag. Alec lit it. The clatter of Mrs. Anthony's tray faded out as she receded to the kitchen.

"You were telling me . . . ?" Charmian said to her guest.

"Oh yes." He turned his white head and grey face to Mrs. Pettigrew. "I was explaining the rise of democracy in the British Isles. Do you miss Mrs. Brooke?"

"Very much," said Mabel Pettigrew, blowing out a long puff of smoke. She had put on her social manner. "Do continue about democracy," she said.

"When I went to Russia," said Charmian, "the Tsarina sent an escort to—"

"No, Mrs. Colston, just a moment, while Mr. Alec Warner tells us about democracy."

Charmian looked about her strangely for a moment, then said, "Yes, continue about democracy, Eric."

"Not Eric—Alec," said Mrs. Pettigrew.

Alec Warner soothed the air with his old, old steady hand.

"The real rise of democracy in the British Isles occurred in Scotland by means of Queen Victoria's bladder," he said. "There had, you know, existed an idea of democracy, but the real thing occurred through this little weakness of Queen Victoria's."

Mabel Pettigrew laughed with a backward throw of her head. Charmian looked vague. Alec Warner continued slowly as one filling in the time with his voice. His eyes were watchful.

"Queen Victoria had a little trouble with the bladder, you see. When she went to stay at Balmoral in her latter years a number of privies were caused to be built at the backs of little cottages which had not previously possessed privies. This was to enable the Queen to go on her morning drive round the countryside in comfort, and to descend from her carriage from time to time, ostensibly to visit the humble cottagers in their dwellings. Eventually, word went round that Queen Victoria was exceedingly democratic. Of course it was all due to her little weakness. But everyone copied the Queen and the idea spread, and now you see we have a great democracy."

Mrs. Pettigrew laughed for a long time. Alec Warner was gazing like a bird-watcher at Charmian, who plucked at the rug round her knees, waiting to tell her own story.

"When I went to Russia," said Charmian, looking up at him like a child, "the Tsarina sent an escort to meet me at the frontier, but did not send an escort to take me back. That is so like Russia, they make resolutions then get bored. The male peasants lie on the stove all winter. All the way to Russia my fellow-passengers were opening their boxes and going over their belongings. It was spring and . . ."

Mrs. Pettigrew winked at Alec Warner. Charmian stopped and smiled at him. "Have you seen Jean Taylor lately?" she said.

"Not for a week or two. I have been away to Folkestone on my research work. I shall go to see her next week."

"Lettie goes regularly. She says Jean is very happy and fortunate."

"Lettie is—" He was going to say she was a selfish fool, then remembered Mrs. Pettigrew's presence. "Well, you know what I think of Lettie's opinions," he said and waved away the topic with his hand.

And as if the topic had landed on Charmian's lap, she stared at her lap and continued, "If only you had discovered Lettie's character a little sooner. If only . . ."

He rose to leave, for he knew how Charmian's memory was inclined to wake up in the past, in some arbitrary year. She would likely fix on those events, that year 1907, and bring them close up to her, as one might bring a book close to one's eyes. The time of his love affair with Jean Taylor when she was a parlour-maid at the Pipers' before Charmian's marriage, would be like last week to Charmian. And her novelist's mind by sheer habit still gave to those disjointed happenings a shape which he could not accept, and in a way which he thought dishonest. He had been in love with Jean Taylor, he had decided after all to take everyone's advice. He had therefore engaged himself to Lettie. He had broken the engagement when he came to know Lettie better. These were the facts in 1907. By 1912 he had been able to contemplate them without emotion. But dear Charmian made the most of them. She saw the facts as a dramatic sequence reaching its fingers into all his life's work. This interested him so far as it reflected Charmian, though not at all so far as it affected himself. He would, nevertheless, have liked to linger in his chair on that afternoon, in his seventy-ninth year, and listen to Charmian recalling her youth. But he was embarrassed by Mrs. Pettigrew's presence. Her intrusion had irritated him, and he could not, like Charmian, talk on as if she were not present. He looked at Mrs. Pettigrew as she helped him on with his coat in the hall, and thought, An irritating woman. Then he thought, A fine-looking woman, and this was associated with her career at Lisa's as he had glimpsed it at intervals over twenty-six years. He thought about Mabel Pettigrew all the way home across two parks, though he had meant to think about Charmian on that walk. And he reflected upon himself, amazed, since he was nearly eighty and Mrs. Pettigrew a good, he supposed, sixty-five. "Oh," he said to himself, "these erotic throes that come like thieves in the night to steal my High Churchmanship!" Only, he was not a High Churchman— it was no more than a manner of speaking to himself.

He returned to his rooms—which, since they were officially described as "gentleman's chambers," he always denied were a flat—off St. James's Street. He hung his coat, put away his hat and gloves, then stood at the large bow window gazing out as at an imposing prospect, though in reality the window looked down only on the side entrance to a club. He noted the comings and goings of the club porter. The porter of his own chambers came up the narrow street intently reading the back page of an evening paper. With his inward eye, Dr. Warner, the old sociologist, at the same time contemplated Old Age which had been his study since he had turned seventy. Nearly ten years of inquisitive work had gone into the card indexes and files encased in two oak cabinets, one on either side of the window. His approach to the subject was unique; few gerontologists had the ingenuity or the freedom to conduct their investigations on the lines he had adopted. He got about a good deal; he employed agents; his work was, he hoped, valuable; or would be, one day.

His wide desk was bare, but from a drawer he took a thick bound notebook and sat down to write.

Presently he rose to fetch the two boxes of index cards which he used constantly when working at his desk. One of these contained the names of those of his friends and acquaintances, who were over seventy, with details of his relationship to them, and in the case of chance encounters, the circumstances of their meeting. Special sections were devoted to St. Aubrey's home for mental cases in Folkestone where, for ten years, he had been visiting certain elderly patients by way of unofficial research.

Much of the information on this first set of cards was an aid to memory, for, although his memory was still fairly good, he wished to ensure against his losing it: he had envisaged the day when he might take up a card, read the name and wonder, for instance, "Colston—Charmian,— who is Charmian Colston? Charmian Colston . . . I know the name but I can't for the moment think who . . ." Against this possibility was inscribed "Née Piper. Met 1907. *Vide* Ww page . . ." "Ww," stood for *Who's Who*. The page number was inserted in pencil, to be changed every four years when he acquired a new *Who's Who*.

Most of the cards in this category were filled in with small writing on both sides. All of them were, by his instruction, to be destroyed at his death. At the top left-hand corner of each card was a reference letter and number in red ink. These cross-referred to a second set of cards which bore pseudonyms invented by Dr. Warner for each person. (Thus, Charmian was, in the second set of cards, "Gladys.") All these cards in the second set were his real working cards, for these bore the clues to the case-histories. On each was marked a neat network of codes and numbers relating to various passages in the books around the walls, on the subjects of gerontology and senescence, and to the ten years' accumulation of his thick notebooks.

Alec Warner lifted the house phone and ordered grilled turbot. He sat to his desk, opened a drawer and extracted a notebook; this was his current diary which would also be destroyed at his death. In it he noted his afternoon observations of Charmian, Mrs. Pettigrew and himself. "Her mind," he wrote, "has by no means ceased to function, as her husband makes out. Her mind works associatively. At first she went off into a dream, making plucking movements at the rug on her knees. She appeared to be impatient. She did not follow my story at all, but apparently the words 'Queen Victoria' had evoked some other regal figure. As soon as I had finished she embarked upon a reminiscence (which is likely to be true in detail) of her visit to Petrograd to see her father in 1908. (As she spoke, I myself recalled, for the first time since 1908, Charmian's preparations for her journey to Russia. This has been dormant in my memory since then.) I observed that Charmian did not, however, mention the meeting with her father nor the other diplomat whose name I forget, who later committed suicide on her account. Nor did she mention that she was accompanied by Jean Taylor. I have no reason to doubt the accuracy of her memory on the habits of Russian travellers. So far as I recall her actual words were . . ."

He wrote on till his turbot came up.

My Aunt Marcia, he reflected as he ate, was ninety-two, that is seven years older than Charmian, and was still playing a brilliant game of chess to the time of her death. Mrs. Flaxman, wife of the former Rector of Pineville, was seventy-three when she lost her memory completely; twelve years younger than Charmian. Charmian's memory is not completely gone, it is only erratic. He rose from the table and went to his desk to make a note in the margin of his diary where he had written his day's account of Charmian: "*Vide* Mrs. Flaxman."

He returned to his turbot. Ninon de Lenclos of the seventeenth century died at ninety-nine, in full reason and reputed for wit, he reflected.

His wine glass rested a moment on his lip. Goethe, he mused, was older than me when he was writing love poems to young girls. Renoir at eighty-six . . . Titian, Voltaire. Verdi composed *Falstaff* at the age of eighty. But artists are perhaps exceptions.

He thought of the Maud Long Ward where Jean Taylor lay, and wondered what Cicero would make of it. He looked round his shelves. The great Germans on the subject: they were either visionaries or pathologists, largely. To understand the subject, one had to befriend the people, one had to use spies and win allies.

He ate half of what he had been sent. He drank part of half a bottle of wine. He read over what he had written, the account of the afternoon from the time of his arrival at the Colstons' to his walk back across the park with the thoughts, which had taken him by surprise, of Mrs. Pettigrew whose intrusive presence, as he had noted in his diary, had excited him with both moral irritability and erotic feelings. The diary would go into the fire, but his every morning's work was to analyse and abstract from it

446

the data for his case-histories, entering them in the various methodical notebooks. There Charmian would become an impersonal, almost homeless, "Gladys." Mabel Pettigrew "Joan" and he himself "George."

Meantime he put away his cards and his journal and read, for an hour, from one of the fat volumes of Newman's *Life and Letters*. Before he put it down he marked a passage with a pencil:

> I wonder, in old times what people died of. We read, "After this, it was told Joseph that his father was sick." "And the days of David drew nigh that he should die." What were they sick, what did they die, of? And so of the great Fathers. St. Athanasius died past seventy—was his a paralytic seizure? We cannot imitate the Martyrs in their death—but I sometimes feel it would be a comfort if we could associate ourselves with the great Confessor Saints in their illnesses and decline: Pope St. Gregory had the gout, St. Basil had a liver complaint, but St. Gregory Nazianzen? St. Ambrose? St. Augustine and St. Martin died of fevers, proper to old age. . . .

At nine-thirty he took a packet of ten cigarettes from a drawer and went out. He turned into Pall Mall where the road was up and a nightwatchman on duty whom Alec Warner had been visiting each night for a week past. He hoped to get sufficient consistent answers to construct a history. "How old are you? Where do you live? What do you eat? Do you believe in God? Any religion? Did you ever go in for sport? How do you get on with your wife? How old is she? Who? What? Why? How do you feel?"

"Evening," said the man as Alec approached. "Thanks," he said, as he took the cigarettes. He shifted up on the plank by the brazier to let Alec sit down beside him.

Alec warmed his hands.

"How you feeling to-night?" he said.

"Not so bad! How's yourself, guv?"

"Not so bad. How old did you say . . . ?"

"Seventy-five. Sixty-nine to the Council."

"Of course," said Alec.

"Doesn't do to let on too much."

"I'm seventy-nine," coaxed Alec.

"Don't look a day over sixty-five."

Alec smiled into the fire knowing the remark was untrue, and that he did not care how old he looked, and that most people cared. "Where were you born?" said Alec.

A policeman passed and swivelled his eyes towards the two old men without changing the rhythm of his tread. He was not surprised to see the nightwatchman's superior-looking companion. He had seen plenty of odd old birds.

"That young copper," said Alec, "is wondering what we're up to."

The watchman reached for his bottle of tea, and pulled out the cork.

"Got any tips for to-morrow?"

"Gunmetal for the two-thirty. They say Out of Reach for the four-fifteen. Tell me—"

"Gunmetal's even money," said the watchman. "Not worth your trouble."

"How long," said Alec, "do you sleep during the day?"

Charmian had been put to bed. Rough physical handling made her mind more lucid in some ways, more cloudy in others. She knew quite well at this moment that Mrs. Anthony was not Taylor, and Mabel Pettigrew was Lisa Brooke's former housekeeper, whom she disliked.

She lay and resented, and decided against, Mrs. Pettigrew. The woman had had three weeks' trial and had proved unsatisfactory.

Charmian also lay and fancied Mrs. Pettigrew had wronged her, long ago in the past. This was not the case. In reality, it was Lisa Brooke who had blackmailed Char-

448

mian, so that she had been forced to pay and pay, although Lisa had not needed the money; she had been forced to lie awake worrying throughout long night hours, and in the end she had been forced to give up her lover Guy Leet, while Guy had secretly married Lisa to satisfy and silence her for Charmian's sake. All this Charmian blamed upon Mrs. Pettigrew, forgetting for the moment that her past tormentor had been Lisa; so bitter was the particular memory and so vicious was her new tormentor. For Mrs. Pettigrew had wrenched Charmian's arm while getting her dress off, had possibly bruised the arm with her hard impatient grasp. "What you need," Mrs. Pettigrew had said, "is a nurse. I am not a nurse."

Charmian felt indignant at the suggestion that she needed a nurse.

She decided to give Mrs. Pettigrew a month's money in the morning and tell her to go. Before Mrs. Pettigrew had switched out the light, Charmian had spoken sharply. "I think, Mrs. Pettigrew—"

"Oh do call me Mabel and be friendly."

"I think, Mrs. Pettigrew, it will not be necessary for you to come in to the drawing-room when I have visitors unless I ring."

"Good*night*," said Mrs. Pettigrew and switched out the light.

Mrs. Pettigrew descended to her sitting-room and switched on the television which had been installed at her request. Mrs. Anthony had gone home. She took up her knitting and sat working at it while watching the screen. She wanted to loosen her stays but was not sure whether Godfrey would look in to see her. During the three weeks of her stay at the Colstons' he had been in to see her on five evenings. He had not come in last night. Perhaps he would come to-night, and she did not wish to be caught untidy-looking. There was indeed a knock at the door, and she bade him come in.

On the first occasion it had been necessary for him to indicate his requirements to her. But now, she perfectly understood. Godfrey, with his thin face outstanding in the dim lamplight, and his excited eyes, placed on the low coffee table a pound note. He then stood, arms dangling and legs apart, like a stage rustic, watching her. Without shifting her posture she raised the hem of her skirt at one side until the top of her stocking and the tip of her garter were visible. Then she went on knitting and watching the television screen. Godfrey gazed at the stocking-top and the glittering steel of the garter-tip for the space of two minutes' silence. Then he pulled back his shoulders as if recalling his propriety, and still in silence, walked out.

After the first occasion Mrs. Pettigrew had imagined, almost with alarm, that his request was merely the preliminary to more daring explorations on his part, but by now she knew with an old woman's relief that this was all he would ever desire, the top of her stocking and the tip of her garter. She took the pound note off the table, put it in her black suède handbag and loosened her stays. She had plans for the future. Meantime a pound was a pound.

Chapter Six

Miss Jean Taylor sat in the chair beside her bed. She never knew, when she sat in her chair, if it was the last time she would be able to sit out of bed. Her arthritis was gradually spreading and digging deep. She could turn her head slowly. So, and with difficulty, she did. Alec Warner shifted his upright chair a little to face her.

She said, "Are you tormenting Dame Lettie?"

The thought crossed his mind, among other thoughts, that Jean's brain might be undergoing a softening process. He looked carefully at her eyes and saw the grey ring round the edge of the cornea, the *arcus senilis*. Nevertheless, it surrounded the main thing, a continuing intelligence amongst the ruins.

Miss Taylor perceived his scrutiny and thought, It is true he is a student of the subject but he is in many ways the same as the rest. How we all watch each other for signs of failure!

"Come, Alec," she said, "tell me."

"Tormenting Lettie?" he said.

She told him about the anonymous telephone calls, then said, "Stop *studying* me, Alec. I am not soft in the brain as yet."

"Lettie must be so," he said.

"No, she isn't, Alec."

"And supposing," he said, "she really has been receiving

451

these telephone calls. Why do you suggest I am the culprit? I ask as a matter of interest."

"It seems to me likely, Alec. I may be wrong, but it is the sort of thing, isn't it, that you would do for purposes of study? An experiment—"

"It is the sort of thing," he said, "but in this case I doubt if I am the culprit."

"You *doubt*."

"Of course I doubt. In a court of law, my dear, I would with complete honesty deny the charge. But you know, I can't affirm or deny anything that is within the range of natural possibility."

"Alec, are you the man, or not?"

"I don't know," he said. "If so, I am unaware of it. But I may be a Jekyll and Hyde, may I not? There was a recent case—"

"Because," she said, "if you are the culprit the police will get you."

"They would have to prove the deed. And if they proved it to my satisfaction I should no longer be in doubt."

"Alec," she said, "are you the man behind those phone calls?"

"Not to my knowledge," he said.

"Then," she said, "you are not the man. Is it someone employed by you?"

He did not seem to hear the question, but was watching Granny Barnacle like a naturalist on holiday. Granny Barnacle accepted his attention with obliging submission, as she did when the doctor brought the medical students round her bed, or when the priest brought the Blessed Sacrament.

"Ask her how she is keeping," said Miss Taylor, "since you are staring at her."

"How are you keeping?" said Alec.

"Not too good," said Granny Barnacle. She jerked her

head to indicate the ward dispensaries just beyond the door. "Time there was a change of management," she said.

"Indeed yes," said Alec, and, inclining his head in final acknowledgment, which included the whole of the Maud Long Ward, returned his attention to Jean Taylor.

"Someone," she said, "in your employ?"

"I doubt it."

"In that case," she said, "the man is neither you nor your agent."

When she had first met him, nearly fifty years ago, she had been dismayed when he had expressed these curious "doubts." She had thought him perhaps a little mad. It had not occurred to her till many years later that this was a self-protective manner of speech which he used exclusively when talking to women whom he liked. He never spoke so to men. She had discerned, after these many years, that this whole approach to the female mind, his only way of coping with it, was to seem to derive amusement from it. When Miss Taylor had made this discovery she was glad they had never been married. He was too much masked behind his mocking, paternal attitude—now become a habit—for any proper relationship with a grown woman.

She recalled an afternoon years ago in 1928—long after the love affair—when she had been attending Charmian on a week-end party in the country and Alec Warner was a fellow-guest. One afternoon he had taken Jean Taylor off for a walk—Charmian had been amused—"to question her, as Jean was so reliable in her evidence." Most of their conversation she had forgotten, but she recalled his first question.

"Do you think, Jean, that other people exist?"

She had not at once understood the nature of the question. For a moment she had wondered if his words might in some way refer to that love affair twenty-odd years earlier, and his further words, "I mean, Jean, do you consider that people—the people around us—are real or illusory?" had possibly some personal bearing. But this did not fit with her knowledge of the man. Even at the time of their love relationship he was not the type to proffer the conceit: there is no one in the world but we two; we alone exist. Besides, she who was now walking beside this middle-aged man was herself a woman in her early fifties.

"What do you mean?" she said.

"Only what I say." They had come to a beech wood which was damp from a last night's storm. Every now and then a little succession of raindrops would pelt from the leaves on to his hat or her hat. He took her arm and led her off the main path, so that for all his sober sense, it rapidly crossed her mind that he might be a murderer, a maniac. But she had, the next instant, recalled her fifty years and more. Were they not usually young women who were strangled in woods by sexual maniacs? No, she thought again, sometimes they were women of fifty-odd. The leaves squelched beneath their feet. Her mind flashed messages to itself back and forth. But I know him well, he's Alec Warner. Do I know him, though?—he is odd. Even as a lover he was strange. But he is known everywhere, his reputation . . . Still, some eminent men have secret vices. No one ever finds them out; their very eminence is a protection.

"Surely," he was saying, as he continued to draw her into the narrow, dripping shadows, "you see that here is a respectable question. Given that you believe in your own existence as self-evident, do you believe in that of others? Tell me, Jean, do you believe that I for instance, at this moment, exist?" He peered down at her face beneath the brim of her brown felt hat.

"Where are you taking me?" she said, stopping still.

"Out of these wet woods," he said, "by a short cut. Tell

me, now, surely you understand what I am asking? It's a plain question. . . ."

She looked ahead through the trees and saw that their path was indeed a short cut to the open fields. She realised at once that his question was entirely academic and he was not contemplating murder with indecent assault. And what reason, after all, had she to suspect this? How things do, she thought, come and go through a woman's mind. He was an unusual man.

"I agree," she then said, "that your question can be asked. One does sometimes wonder, perhaps only half-consciously, if other people are real."

"Please," he said, "wonder more than half-consciously about this question. Wonder about it with as much consciousness as you have, and tell me what is your answer."

"Oh," she said, "I think in that case, other people do exist. That's my answer. It's only common sense."

"You have made up your mind too quickly," he said. "Take time and think about it."

They had emerged from the wood and took a path skirting a ploughed field which led to the village. There the church with its steep sloping graveyard stood at the top of the street. Miss Taylor looked over the wall at the graveyard as they passed it. She was not sure now if his words had been frivolous or serious or both; for, even in their younger days—especially during that month of July 1907 at the farmhouse—she had never really known what to make of him, and had sometimes felt afraid.

She looked at the graveyard and he looked at her. He noted dispassionately that her jaw beneath the shade of the hat was more square than it had ever been. As a young woman she had been round-faced and soft; her voice had been extremely quiet, like the voice of an invalid. In middle age she had begun to reveal, in appearance, angular qualities; her voice was deeper; her jaw-line nearly masculine. He was interested in these factors; he supposed he approved of them; he liked Jean. She stopped and leaned over the low stone wall looking at the gravestones.

"This graveyard is a kind of evidence," she said, "that other people exist."

"How do you mean?" he said.

She was not sure. Having said it, she was not sure why. The more she wondered what she had meant the less she knew.

He tried to climb over the wall, and failed. It was a low wall, but still he was not up to it. "I am going on fifty," he said to her without embarrassment, not even with a covering smile, and she remembered how, at the farmhouse in 1907, when he had chanced to comment that they were both past their prime, he being twenty-eight and she thirty-one, she had felt hurt and embarrassed till she realised he meant no harm by it, meaning only to point a fact. And she, catching this habit and tone, had been able to state quite levelly, "We are not social equals," before the month was over.

He brushed the dust of the graveyard wall from his trousers. "I am going on fifty. I should like to look at the gravestones. Let's go in by the gate."

And so they had walked among the graves, stooping to read the names on the stones.

"They are, I quite see, they are," he said, "an indication of the existence of others, for there are the names and times carved in stone. Not a proof, but at least a large testimony."

"Of course," she said, "the gravestones might be hallucinations. But I think not."

"There is that to be considered," he said so courteously that she became angry.

"But the graves are at least reassuring," she said, "for why bother to bury people if they don't exist?"

"Yes, oh precisely," he said.

They ambled up the short drive to the house where Lettie, who sat writing at the library window, glanced towards them and then away again. As they entered, Lisa Brooke with her flaming bobbed head, came out. "Hallo, you two," she said, looking sweetly at Jean Taylor. Alec went straight to his room while Miss Taylor went in search of Charmian. On the way, various people encountered and said "Hallo" to her. This party was composed of a progressive set; they would think nothing of her walk with Alec that summer of 1928 even though some remembered the farmhouse affair of 1907 which had been a little scandal in those days. Only a brigadier, a misfit in the party who had been invited because the host wanted his advice on dairy herds, and who had passed the couple on their walk, later enquired of Lettie in Miss Taylor's hearing, "Who was that lady I passed with Alec? Has she just arrived?" And Lettie, loathing Jean as she did, but wishing to be broad-minded, replied, "Oh, she's Charmian's maid."

"Say what you like about that sort of thing, the other domestics won't like it," commented the brigadier, which was, after all, true.

And yet, Jean Taylor reflected as she sat with Alec in the Maud Long Ward, perhaps it was not all mockery. He may have half-meant the question.

"Be serious," she said, looking down at her twisted arthritic hands.

Alec Warner looked at his watch.

"Must you be going?" she said.

"Not for another ten minutes. But it'll take me three-quarters of an hour across the parks. I have to keep fairly strictly to my times, you know. I am going on eighty."

"I'm relieved it's not you, Alec—the telephone calls . . ."

"My dear, this has come from Lettie's imagination, surely that is obvious."

"Oh no. The man has twice left a message with Godfrey. 'Tell Dame Lettie,' he said, 'to remember she must die.' "

"Godfrey heard it too?" he said. "Well, I suppose, in that case, it must be a lunatic. How did Godfrey take it? Did he get a fright?"

"Dame Lettie didn't say."

"Oh, do find out what their reactions were. I hope the police don't catch the fellow too soon. One might get some interesting reactions." He rose to leave.

"Oh, Alec—before you go—there was something else I wanted to ask you."

He sat down again and replaced his hat on her locker.

"Do you know Mrs. Sidebottome?"

"Tempest? Ronald's wife. Sister-in-law of Lisa Brooke. Now in her seventy-first year. I first met her on a boat entering the Bay of Biscay in 1930. She was—"

"That's right. She is on the Management Committee of this hospital. The sister in charge of this ward is unsuitable. We all here desire her to be transferred to another ward. Do you want me to go into details?"

"No," he said. "You wish me to talk to Tempest."

"Yes. Make it plain that the nurse in question is simply overworked. There was a fuss about her some time ago, but nothing came of it."

"I cannot speak to Tempest just yet. She went into a nursing home for an operation last week."

"A serious one?"

"A tumour on the womb. But at her age it is, in itself, less serious than in a younger woman."

"Oh well, then you can't do anything for us at present."

"I shall think," he said, "if I know anyone else. Have you approached Lettie on the subject?"

"Oh, yes."

He smiled, and said, "Approach her no more. It is a waste of time. You must seriously think, Jean, of going to that home in Surrey. The cost is not high. Godfrey and I can manage it. I think Charmian would be joining you there soon. Jean, you should have a room of your own."

"Not now," said Miss Taylor. "I shan't move from here. I've made friends here, it's my home."

"See you next Wednesday, my dear," he said, taking his hat and looking round the ward, sharply, at each of the grannies in turn.

"All being well," she said.

Two years ago, when she first came to the ward, she had longed for the private nursing home in Surrey about which there had been too much talk. Godfrey had made a fuss about the cost, he had expostulated in her presence, and had quoted a number of their friends of the progressive set on the subject of the new free hospitals, how superior they were to the private affairs. Alec Warner had pointed out that these were days of transition, that a person of Jean Taylor's intelligence and habits might perhaps not feel at home among the general aged of a hospital.

"If only," he said, "because she is partly what we have made her, we should look after her."

He had offered to bear half the cost of keeping Jean in Surrey. But Dame Lettie had finally put an end to these arguments by coming to Jean with a challenge, "Would you not really, my dear, *prefer* to be independent? After all, you are the public. The hospitals are *yours*. You are entitled . . ." Miss Taylor had replied, "I prefer to go to hospital, certainly." She had made her own arrangements and had left them with the daily argument still in progress concerning her disposal.

Alec Warner had not liked to see her in this ward. The first week he had wanted her to move. In misery she had vacillated. Her pains were increasing, she was not yet resigned to them. There had been further consultations and talking things over. Should she be moved to Surrey? Might not Charmian join her there eventually?

Not now, she thought, after Alec Warner had departed. Granny Valvona had put on her glasses and was searching for the horoscopes. Not now, thought Miss Taylor. Not now that the worst is over.

At first, in the morning light, Charmian forgave Mrs. Pettigrew. She was able, slowly, to walk downstairs by herself. Other movements were difficult and Mrs. Pettigrew had helped her to dress quite gently.

"But," said Mabel Pettigrew to her, "you should get into the habit of breakfast in bed."

"No," said Charmian cheerfully as she tottered round the table, grasping the backs of chairs, to her place. "That would be a bad habit. My morning cup of tea in bed is all that I desire. Good morning, Godfrey."

" 'Lydia May,' " said Godfrey, reading from the paper, " 'died yesterday at her home in Knightsbridge six days before her ninety-second birthday.' "

"A Gaiety Girl," said Charmian. "I well remember."

"You're in good form this morning," Mrs. Pettigrew remarked. "Don't forget to take your pills." She had put the bottle beside Charmian's plate. She now unscrewed the cap and extracted two pills which she laid before Charmian.

"I have had my pills already," said Charmian. "I had them with my morning tea, don't you remember?"

"No," said Mrs. Pettigrew, "you are mistaken, dear. Take your pills."

"She made a fortune," Godfrey remarked. "Retired in 1893 and married money both times. I wonder what she has left?"

"She was before my time, of course," said Mabel Pettigrew.

"Nonsense," said Godfrey.

460

"I beg your pardon, Mr. Colston, she was before my time. If she retired in 1893 I was only a child in 1893."

"*I* remember her," said Charmian. "She sang most expressively—in the convention of those times you know."

"At the Gaiety?" said Mrs. Pettigrew. "Surely—"

"No, I heard her at a private party."

"Ah, you would be quite a grown girl, then. Take your pills dear." She pushed the two white tablets towards Charmian. Charmian pushed them back and said, "I have already taken my pills this morning. I recall quite clearly. I usually do take them with my early tea."

"Not always," said Mrs. Pettigrew. "Sometimes you forget and leave them on your tray, as you did this morning, actually."

" 'She was the youngest of fourteen children,' " Godfrey read out from the paper, " 'of a strict Baptist family. It was not till her father's death, that, at the age of eighteen she made her début in a small part at the Lyceum. Trained by Ellen Terry and Sir Henry Irving, she left them however for The Gaiety where she became the principal dancer. The then Prince of Wales—' "

"She was introduced to us at Cannes," said Charmian, gaining confidence in her good memory that morning, "wasn't she?"

"That's right," said Godfrey, "it would be about 1910."

"And she stood up on a chair and looked round her and said, 'Gad! The place is stinking with royalty.' Remember we were terribly embarrassed, and—"

"No, Charmian, no. You've got it wrong there. It was one of the Lilly Sisters who stood on a chair. And that was much later. There was nothing like that about Lydia May, she was a different class of girl."

Mrs. Pettigrew placed the two pills a little nearer to Charmian, but said no more about them. Charmian said, "I mustn't exceed my dose," and shakily replaced them in the bottle.

"Charmian, take your pills, my dear," said Godfrey and took a noisy sip from his coffee.

"I have taken two pills already. I remember quite clearly doing so. Four might be dangerous."

Mrs. Pettigrew cast her eyes to the ceiling and sighed.

"What is the use," said Godfrey, "of me paying big doctor's bills if you won't take his stuff?"

"Godfrey, I do not wish to be poisoned by an overdose. Moreover, my own money pays for the bills."

" 'Poisoned,' " said Mrs. Pettigrew, laying down her napkin as if tried beyond endurance. "I ask you."

"Or merely upset," said Charmian. "I do not wish to take the pills, Godfrey."

"Oh well," he said, "if that's how you feel, I must say it makes life damned difficult for all of us, and we simply can't take responsibility if you have an attack through neglecting the doctor's instructions."

Charmian began to cry. "I know you want to put me away in a home."

Mrs. Anthony had just come in to clear the table.

"There," she said. "Who wants to put you in a home?"

"We are a little upset, what with one thing and another," said Mrs. Pettigrew.

Charmian stopped crying. She said to Mrs. Anthony, "Taylor, did you see my early tea-tray when it came down?"

Mrs. Anthony seemed not to grasp the question, for though she had heard it, for some reason she felt it was more complicated than it really was.

Charmian repeated, "Did you see—"

"Now, Charmian," said Godfrey, foreseeing some possible contradiction between Mrs. Anthony's reply and Mrs. Pettigrew's previous assertion. In this, he was concerned overwhelmingly to prevent a conflict between the two women. His comfort, the whole routine of his life, depended on retaining Mrs. Anthony. Otherwise he might

462

have to give up the house and go to some hotel. And Mrs. Pettigrew having been acquired, she must be retained; otherwise Charmian would have to go to a home. "Now, Charmian, we don't want any more fuss about your pills," he said.

"What did you say about the tea-tray, Mrs. Colston?"

"Was there anything on it when it came down from my room?"

Mrs. Pettigrew said, "Of course there was nothing on the tray. I replaced the pills you had left on it in the bottle."

"There was a cup and saucer on the tray. Mrs. Pettigrew brought it down," said Mrs. Anthony, contributing what accuracy she could to questions which still confused her.

Mrs. Pettigrew started noisily loading the breakfast dishes on to Mrs. Anthony's tray. She said to Mrs. Anthony, "Come, my dear, we've work to do."

Mrs. Anthony felt she had somehow failed Charmian, and so, as she followed Mrs. Pettigrew out of the door she pulled a face at her.

When they were gone Godfrey said, "See the fuss you've caused. Mrs. Pettigrew was quite put out. If we lose her—"

"Ah," said Charmian, "you are taking your revenge, Eric."

"I am not Eric," he said.

"But you are taking your revenge." Fifteen years ago, in her seventy-first year, when her memory had started slightly to fail, she had realised that Godfrey was turning upon her as one who had been awaiting his revenge. She did not think he was himself aware of this. It was an instinctive reaction to the years of being a talented, celebrated woman's husband, knowing himself to be reaping continually in her a harvest which he had not sown.

Throughout her seventies Charmian had not reproached him with his bullying manner. She had accepted his new domination without comment until her weakness had become so marked that she physically depended on him more and more. It was then, in her eighties, that she started frequently to say what, in the past, she would have considered unwise: "You are taking your revenge."

And on this occasion, as always, he replied, "What revenge for *what?*" He really did not know. He saw only that she was beginning to look for persecution: poison, revenge; what next? "You are getting into a state of imagining that all those around you are conspiring against you," he said.

"Whose fault is it," she said with a jolting sharpness, "if I am getting into such a state?"

This question exasperated him, partly because he sensed a deeper sanity in it than in all her other accusations, and partly because he could not answer it. He felt himself to be a heavily burdened man.

Later in the morning, when the doctor called, Godfrey stopped him in the hall.

"She is damn difficult to-day, Doctor."

"Ah well," said the doctor, "it's a sign of life."

"Have to see about a home if she goes on like this."

"It might be a good idea, if only she can be brought round to liking it," said the doctor. "The scope for regular attention is so much better in a nursing home, and I have known cases far more advanced than your wife's which have improved tremendously once they have been moved to a really comfortable home. How are you feeling yourself?"

"Me? Well, what can you expect with all the domestic worries on my shoulders?" said Godfrey. He pointed to the door of the garden-room where Charmian was waiting. "You'd better go on in," he said, being disappointed of the sympathy and support he had hoped for, and vaguely put out by the doctor's talk of Charmian's possible improvement in health, should she be sent to a home.

The doctor's hand was on the door knob. "I shouldn't worry too much about domestic matters," he said. "Go out as much as possible. Your wife, as I say, may buck up tremendously if we have to move her. It sometimes proves a stimulus. Of course, at her age . . . her resistance . . . but there's a chance that she may still get about again. It is largely neurasthenia. She has extraordinary powers of recovery, almost as if she had some secret source. . . ."

Godfrey thought: This is his smarm. Charmian has a secret source, and I pay the bills. He said explosively, "Well sometimes I feel she deserves to be sent away. Take this morning for instance—"

"Oh *deserves*," said the doctor, "we don't recommend nursing-homes as a punishment, you know."

"Bloody man," said Godfrey in the doctor's hearing and before he had properly got into the room where Charmian waited.

Immediately the doctor had entered through the door so did Mrs. Pettigrew through the french windows. "Pleasant for the time of year," she said.

"Yes," said the doctor. "Good morning, Mrs. Colston. How do you feel to-day?"

"We wouldn't," said Mrs. Pettigrew, "take our pills this morning, Doctor, I'm afraid."

"Oh, that doesn't matter," he said.

"I did take them," said Charmian. "I took them with my early tea, and they tried to force me to take more at breakfast. I know I took them with my early tea, and just suppose I had taken a second dose—"

"It wouldn't really have mattered," he said.

"But surely," said Mrs. Pettigrew, "it is always danger-ous to exceed a stated dose."

"Just try to keep a careful check—a set routine for medicines in future," he said to Mrs. Pettigrew. "Then neither of you will make a mistake."

"There was no mistake on my part," said Mrs. Pettigrew. "There is nothing wrong with my memory."

"In that case," said Charmian, "we must question your *intentions* in trying to give me a second dose. Taylor knows I took my pills as I always do. I did not leave them on the tray."

The doctor said as he took her pulse, "Mrs. Pettigrew, if you would excuse us for a moment . . ."

She went out with a deep loud weary sigh, and, in the kitchen, stood and berated Mrs. Anthony for "taking that mad-woman's part this morning."

"She isn't," said Mrs. Anthony, "a mad-woman. She's always been good to me."

"No, she isn't mad," said Mrs. Pettigrew, "you are right. She's cunning and sly. She isn't as feeble as she makes out, let me tell you. I've watched her when she didn't know I was watching. She can move about quite easily when she likes."

"Not when she likes," said Mrs. Anthony, "but when she feels up to it. After all, I've been here nine years, haven't I? Mrs. Colston is a person who needs a lot of understanding, she has her off days and her on days. No one understands her like I do."

"It's preposterous," said Mrs. Pettigrew, "a woman of my position being accused of attempts to poison. Why, if I was going to do that I should go about it a very different way, I assure you, to giving her overdoses in front of everybody."

"I bet you would," said Mrs. Anthony. "Mind out my way," she said, for she was sweeping the floor unnecessarily.

"Mind how you talk to me, Mrs. Anthony."

"Look," said Mrs. Anthony, "my husband goes on at me about this job now he's at home all day, he doesn't like me being out. I only do it for that bit of independence and it's what I've always done my married life. But we can do on the pension now I'm seventy and the old man sixty-eight, and any trouble from you, let me tell you I'm leaving here. I managed *her* myself these nine years and we got on without you interfering and making trouble."

"I shall speak to Mr. Colston," said Mrs. Pettigrew, "and inform him of what you say."

"Him," said Mrs. Anthony. "Go on and speak to him. I don't reckon much of him. She's the one that I care for, not *him*." Mrs. Anthony followed this with an insolent look.

"What do you mean by that exactly?" said Mrs. Pettigrew. "What exactly do you mean?"

"You work it out for yourself," said Mrs. Anthony. "I'm busy with their luncheon."

Mrs. Pettigrew went in search of Godfrey who was, however, out. She went by way of the front door round to the french windows, and through them. She saw that the doctor had left and Charmian was reading a book. She was filled with a furious envy at the thought that, if she herself were to take the vapours, there would not be any expensive doctor to come and give her a kind talk and an injection no doubt, and calm her down so that she could sit and read a book after turning the household upside down.

Mrs. Pettigrew went upstairs to look round the bedrooms, to see if they were all right and tidy, and in reality to simmer down and look round. She was annoyed with herself for letting go at Mrs. Anthony. She should have kept aloof. But it had always been the same—even when she had been with Lisa Brooke—when she had to deal with lower domestics she became too much one of them. It was kindness of heart, but it was weak. She reflected that she had really started off on the wrong foot with Mrs. Anthony; that, when she had first arrived, she should have kept her distance with the woman and refrained from confidences. And now she had lowered herself to an argument with Mrs. Anthony. These thoughts overwhelmed Mrs.

Pettigrew with that sense of having done a foolish thing against one's interests, which in some people stands for guilt. And in this frame of heart she repented, and decided, as she stood by Charmian's neatly-made bed, to establish her position more solidly in the household, and from now on to treat Mrs. Anthony with remoteness.

A smell of burning food rose up the well of the stairs and into Charmian's bedroom. Mrs. Pettigrew leaned over the banister and sniffed. Then she listened. No sound came from the kitchen, no sound of hurried removal of pots from the gas jets. Mrs. Pettigrew came half-way down the stairs and listened. From the small garden-room where Charmian had been sitting came voices. Mrs. Anthony was in there, recounting her wrongs to Charmian while the food was burning in the oven and the potatoes burning dry and the kettle burning on the stove. Mrs. Pettigrew turned back up the stairs, and up one more flight to her own room. There she got from a drawer a box of keys. She selected four and putting them in the black suède handbag which, perhaps by virtue of her office, she always carried about the house, descended to Charmian's bedroom. Here, she tried the keys one by one in the lid of Charmian's bureau. The third fitted. She did not glance within the desk, but locked the lid again. With the same key she tried the drawers. It did not fit them. She placed the key carefully in a separate compartment of her handbag and tried the other keys. None fitted the drawers. She went to the landing, where the smell of burning had become alarming, and listened. Mrs. Anthony had not yet left Charmian, and it was clear to Mrs. Pettigrew that when she did, there would be enough to keep her busy for ten minutes more. She took from her bag a package of chewing gum, and unwrapped it. There were five strips of gum. She put the paper with three of the pieces back in her bag and two pieces of gum in her mouth. She sat on a chair near the open door and chewed for a few

468

seconds. Then she wet the tips of her fingers with her tongue, took the soft gum from her mouth and flattened it. She next wet the surface of the gum with her tongue and applied it to the keyhole of one of the drawers. She withdrew it quickly and put it on Charmian's bedside table to set. She took two more pieces of gum, and having chewed them as before, moistened the lump and applied it to the keyhole of another drawer. She slung back her bag up to her wrist and holding the two pieces of gum with their keyhole impressions, between the finger and thumb of each hand, walked up the flight of stairs to her bedroom. She placed the hardened gum carefully in a drawer, locked the drawer, and set off downstairs, through the houseful of smoke and smell.

Mrs. Anthony came rushing out of the garden-room just as Mrs. Pettigrew appeared on the first flight of stairs.

"Do I," said Mrs. Pettigrew, "smell burning?"

By the time she reached the foot of the stairs Mrs. Anthony was already in the kitchen holding the smoking raging saucepan under the tap. A steady blue cloud was pouring through the cracks of the oven door. Mrs. Pettigrew opened the door of the oven, and was driven back by a rush of smoke. Mrs. Anthony dropped her potato saucepan and ran to the oven.

"Turn off the gas," she said to Mrs. Pettigrew. "Oh, the pie!"

Mrs. Pettigrew, spluttering, approached the oven and turned off the gas taps, then she ran coughing from the kitchen and went in to Charmian.

"Do I smell burning?" said Charmian.

"The pie and potatoes are burned to cinders."

"Oh, I shouldn't have kept Taylor talking," said Charmian. "The smell is quite bad, isn't it? Shall we open the windows?"

Mrs. Pettigrew opened the french windows and like a

ghost, a stream of blue smoke obligingly wafted out into the garden.

"Godfrey," said Charmian, "will be so cross. What is the time?"

"Twenty past," said Mrs. Pettigrew.

"Eleven?"

"No, twelve."

"Oh, dear. Do go and see how Mrs. Anthony is getting on. Godfrey will be in any moment."

Mrs. Pettigrew remained by the french windows. "I expect," she said, "Mrs. Anthony is losing her sense of smell. She is quite aged for seventy, isn't she? What I would call an *old* seventy. You would have thought she could have smelt the burning long before it got to this stage." A sizzling sound came round the back of the house from the kitchen where Mrs. Anthony was drenching everything with water.

"*I* smelt nothing," said Charmian. "I'm afraid I kept her talking. Poor soul, she is—"

"There's Mr. Colston," said Mrs. Pettigrew, "just come in " She went out to the hall to meet him.

"What the hell is burning?" he said. "Have you had a fire?"

Mrs. Anthony came out of the kitchen and gave him an account of what had happened, together with accusations, complaints, and a fortnight's notice.

"I shall go and make an omelette," said Mrs. Pettigrew, and casting her eyes to heaven for Godfrey to see behind Mrs. Anthony's back, disappeared into the kitchen to cope with the disorder.

But Godfrey would eat nothing. He told Charmian, "This is all your fault. The household is upside down just because you argued about your pills this morning."

"An overdose may have harmed me, Godfrey. I was not to know the pills were harmless."

"There was no question of overdose. I should like to

470

know *why* the pills were harmless. I mean to say, if the fellow prescribes two and you may just as well take four, what sort of a prescription is that, what good are the pills to you? I'm going to pay the bill and tell him not to come back. We'll get another doctor."

"I shall refuse to see another doctor."

"Mrs. Anthony has given notice, do you realise what that means?"

"I shall persuade her to stay," said Charmian. "She has been under great strain this morning."

He said, "Well, I'm going out again. This place is stinking." He went to get his coat and returned to say, "Be sure to get Mrs. Anthony to change her mind." From past experience, he knew that only Charmian could do it. "It's the least you can do after all the trouble. . . ."

Mrs. Pettigrew and Mrs. Anthony sat eating their omelette with their coats on, since it was necessary to have all windows open. In the course of the meal Mrs. Pettigrew quarrelled with Mrs. Anthony again, and was annoyed with herself afterwards for it. If only, she thought guiltily, I could keep a distance, that would be playing my cards.

Mrs. Anthony sat with Charmian all afternoon, while Mrs. Pettigrew, with the sense of performing an act of reparation, took her two pieces of chewing gum, each marked with a clear keyhole impression, to a person she knew at Camberwell Green.

Chapter Seven

There was a chill in the air, but Godfrey walked on the sunny side of the street. He had parked his car in a turning off King's Road outside a bombed building, so that anyone who recognised it would not be able to guess particularly why it was there. Godfrey had, for over three years now, been laboriously telling any of his acquaintance who lived near Chelsea, that his oculist was in Chelsea, his lawyer was in Chelsea, and that he frequently visited a chiropodist in Chelsea. The more alert of his acquaintance had sometimes wondered why he stated these facts emphatically and so often—almost every time they met him. But he was, after all, over eighty and, one supposed, inclined to waffle about the merest coincidences.

Godfrey himself was of the feeling that one can never be too careful. Having established an oculist, a lawyer and a chiropodist in the neighbourhood to account for his frequent appearances in Chelsea, he still felt it necessary to park his car anonymously, and walk the rest of the way, by routes expressly devious, to Tite Street where, in a basement flat, Olive Mannering, grand-daughter of Percy Mannering, the poet, resided.

He looked to right and left at the top of the area steps. The coast was clear. He looked to right again, and descended. He pushed the door open and called, "Hello, there."

"Mind the steps," Olive called from the front room on

472

the left. There were three more steps to descend within the doorway. Godfrey walked down carefully, and found his way along the passage into a room of many lights. Olive's furnishings were boxy and modern, coloured with a predominance of yellow. She herself was fairly drab in comparison. She was twenty-four. Her skin was pale with a touch of green. She had a Spanish look, with slightly protruding, large eyes. Her legs, full at the calves, were bare. She sat on a stool and warmed these legs by a large electric fire while reading the *Manchester Guardian*.

"Goodness, it's you," she said, as Godfrey entered. "Your voice is exactly like Eric's. I thought it was Eric."

"Is he in London, then?" said Godfrey, looking round the room suspiciously, for there had been an afternoon when he had called on Olive and met his son Eric there. Godfrey, however, had immediately said to Olive,

"I wonder if you have your grandfather's address? I wish to get in touch with him."

Olive had started to giggle. Eric had said "Ha—hum" very meaningly and, as Olive told him later, disrespectfully.

"I wish to get in touch with him in connection with," said Godfrey, glaring at his son, "some poetry."

Olive was a fair-minded girl in so far as she handed over to Eric most of the monthly allowances she obtained from Godfrey. She felt this was only Eric's due, since his father had allowed him nothing for nearly ten years past, Eric being now fifty-six.

"Is Eric in London?" said Godfrey again.

"He is," said Olive.

"I'd better not stop," said Godfrey.

"He won't be coming here to-day," she said. "I'll just go and put my stockings on," she said. "Would you like some tea?"

"Yes, all right," said Godfrey. He folded his coat double and laid it on the divan-bed. On top of it he placed his hat. He looked to see if the curtains were properly drawn across the basement window. He sat down with a thump in one of the yellow chairs which were too low-built for his liking, and picked up the *Manchester Guardian*. Sometimes, while he waited, he looked at the clock.

Olive returned, wearing stockings and carrying a tea-tray.

"Goodness, are you in a hurry?" she said as she saw Godfrey looking at the clock. He was not in a hurry, exactly. He was not yet sure of the cause of his impatience that afternoon.

Olive placed the tray on a low table and sat on her low stool. She lifted the hem of her skirt to the point where her garter met the top of her stockings, and with legs set together almost primly sideways, she poured out the tea.

Godfrey did not know what had come over him. He stared at the garter-tips, but somehow did not experience his usual satisfaction at the sight. He looked at the clock.

Olive, passing him his tea, noticed that his attention was less fixed on her garter-tips than was customary.

"Anything the matter, Godfrey?" she said.

"No," he said, and took his tea. He sipped it, and stared again at the tops of her stockings, evidently trying hard to be mesmerised.

Olive lit a cigarette and watched him. His eyes did not possess their gleam.

"What's the matter?" she said.

He was wondering himself what was the matter. He sipped his tea.

"Running a car," he remarked, "is a great expense."

She burst into a single laugh and said, "Oh, go on."

"Cost of living," he muttered.

She covered up her garter-tops with her skirt and sat hugging her knees, as one whose efforts are wasted. He did not seem to notice.

"Did you see in the paper," she said, "about the preacher giving a sermon on his hundredth birthday?"

"Which paper, where?" he said, reaching out for the *Manchester Guardian*.

"It was the *Mirror*," she said. "I wonder what I've done with it? He said anyone can live to a hundred if they keep God's laws and remain young in spirit. Goodness."

"The government robbers," he said, "won't let you keep young in spirit. Sheer robbery."

Olive was not listening, or she would not have chosen that moment to say, "Eric's in a bad way, you know."

"He's always in a bad way. What's the matter now?"

"The usual," she said.

"What usual?"

"Money," she said.

"I can't do more for Eric. I've done more than enough for Eric. Eric has ruined me."

Then, as in a revelation, he realised what had put him off Olive's garters that afternoon. It was this money question, this standing arrangement with Olive. It had been going on for three years. Pleasant times, of course . . . One had possibly gained . . . but now, Mabel Pettigrew— what a find! Quite pleased with a mere tip, a pound, and a handsome woman, too. All this business of coming over to Chelsea. No wonder one was feeling put out, especially as one could not easily extricate oneself from an arrangement such as that with Olive. Moreover . . .

"I'm not so strong these days," he commented. "My doctor thinks I'm going about too much."

"Oh?" said Olive.

"Yes. Must keep indoors more."

"Goodness," said Olive. "You are wonderful for your age. A man like you could never stay indoors all day."

"Well," he admitted, "there is that to it." He was moved to look longingly at her legs at the point where, beneath her dress, the tip of her garter would meet the top of her stockings, but she made no move to reveal them.

"You tell your doctor," she said, "to go to hell. What did you see the doctor about, anyway?"

"Just aches and pains, my dear, nothing serious of course."

"Many a younger man," she said, "is riddled with aches and pains. Take Eric, for instance—"

"Feeling his age, is he?"

"I'll say he is. Goodness."

Godfrey said, "Only himself to blame. No, I'm wrong, I blame his mother. From the moment that boy was born, she—"

He leaned back in his chair with his hands crossed above his stomach. Olive closed her eyes and relaxed while his voice proceeded into the late afternoon.

Godfrey reached his car outside the bomb site. He had felt cramped when he rose from that frightful modern chair of Olive's. One had talked on, and remained longer than one had intended. He climbed stiffly into the car and slammed the door, suddenly reproached by the more dignified personality he now had to resume.

Why does one behave like this, why? he asked himself as he drove into King's Road and along it. Why does one do these things? he thought, never defining, however, exactly what things. How did it start, at what point in one's life does one find oneself doing things like this? And he felt resentful against Charmian who had been, all her life with him, regarded by everyone as the angelic partner endowed with sensibility and refined tastes. As for oneself, of Colston's Breweries, one had been the crude fellow, tolerated for her sake, and thus driven into carnality, as it were. He felt resentful against Charmian, and raced home to see if she had made everything all right after upsetting Mrs. Anthony and Mrs. Pettigrew. He took out his watch. It was seven and a half minutes to six. Home,

476

home, for a drink. Funny how Olive never seemed to have any drinks in her flat. Couldn't afford it, she said. Funny she couldn't afford it; what did she do with her money, one wondered.

At half-past six Alec Warner arrived at Olive's. She poured him a gin and tonic which he placed on a table beside his chair. He took a hard-covered notebook from his briefcase. "How are things?" he said, leaning his large white head against the yellow chair-back.

"Guy Leet," she said, "has been diagnosed again for his neck. It's a rare type of rheumatism, it sounds like *tortoise*."

"Torticollis?" said Alec Warner.

"That's it."

Alec Warner made a note in his book. "Trust him," he said, "to have a rare rheumatism. How are things otherwise?"

"Dame Lettie Colston has changed her will again."

"Lovely," he said, and made a note. "What way has she changed it?"

"Eric is out again, for one. Martin is put in again. That's the other nephew in Africa."

"She thinks Eric is responsible for the telephone calls, does she?"

"She suspects everyone. Goodness. This is her way of testing Eric. That ex-detective is out."

"Chief Inspector Mortimer?"

"Yes. She thinks it might be him. Funny, it is. She has no sooner got him working privately on the case, than she thinks it might be him."

"How old is Mortimer?" he asked.

"Nearly seventy."

"I know. But when exactly will he be seventy? Did you enquire?"

"I'll find out exactly," said Olive.

"Always find out exactly," he said.

"I think," said Olive, defending her lapse as best she could, "he'll be seventy quite soon—early next year, I think."

"Find out exactly, dear," said Warner. "Meantime he is not one of us. We'll come to *him* next year."

"She thinks you may be the culprit," said Olive. "Are you?"

"I doubt it," he said wearily. He had received a letter from Dame Lettie asking the same question.

"How you talk," she said. "Well, I wouldn't have put it past you."

"Mrs. Anthony," she said, "had a row with Mrs. Pettigrew this morning and is threatening to leave. Charmian accused Mrs. Pettigrew of trying to poison her."

"That's *very* hot news," he said. "Godfrey has been here to-day, I gather?"

"Oh yes. He was rather odd to-day. Something's put him off his stroke."

"Not interested in garters to-day?"

"No, but he was trying hard. He said his doctor doesn't want him to go out and about so much. I didn't know whether to take that as a hint, or—"

"Mrs. Pettigrew—have you thought of *her*?"

"Oh goodness," said Olive, "I haven't." She smiled widely and placed a hand over her mouth.

"Try to find out," he said.

"Oh dear," said Olive, "no more fivers for poor old Eric. I can see it coming. Do you think Mrs. Pettigrew has it in her?"

"I do," said Alec, writing his notes.

"There's a bit in the paper in the kitchen," said Olive, "about a preacher preaching on his hundredth birthday."

"What paper?"

"The *Mirror*."

"My press-cutting agency covers the *Mirror*. It's only

the out-of-the-way papers they sometimes overlook. But thanks all the same. Always tell me of anything like that, just in case. Keep on the look out."

"O.K.," said Olive, and sipped her drink, watching the old veined hand moving its pen steadily, in tiny writing, over the page.

He looked up. "How frequently would you say," he said, "he passes water?"

"Oh goodness, it didn't say anything about that in the *Mirror*."

"You know I mean Godfrey Colston."

"Well, he was here about two hours and he went twice. Of course he had two cups of tea."

"Is twice the average when he comes here?"

"I can't remember. I think—"

"You must try to remember everything exactly, my dear," said Alec. "You must watch, my dear, and pray. It is the only way to be a scholar, to watch and to pray."

"Me a scholar, goodness. He had patches of red on the cheekbones to-day, more so than usual."

"Thank you," said Alec, and made a note. "Notice everything, Olive," he looked up and said, "for only you can observe him in relation to yourself. When I meet him, you understand, he is a different personality."

"I'll bet," she said, and laughed.

He did not laugh. "Be sure to find out all you can on his next visit in case he deserts you for Mrs. Pettigrew. When do you expect to see him again?"

"Friday, I suppose."

"There is someone," he said, "tapping at the window behind me."

"Is there? It must be Granpa, he always does that." She rose to go to the door.

Alec said quickly, "Tell me, does he tap on the window of his own accord or have you asked him to announce himself in that way?"

"He does it of his own accord. He always has tapped at the window."

"Why? Do you know?"

"No—no idea."

Alec bent once more with his pen over his book, and recorded the facts which he would later analyse down to their last, stubborn elements.

Olive fetched in Percy Mannering who, on entering the room, addressed Alec Warner without preliminaries, waving in front of him a monthly magazine of a literary nature, on the cover of which was stamped in bold lettering, "Kinsington Public Libraries."

"Guy Leet," roared Percy, "that moron has published part of his memoirs in which he refers to Ernest Dowson as 'that weak-kneed wailer of Gallic weariness afflicted with an all-too-agonised afflatus.' He is fantastically wrong about Dowson. Ernest Dowson was the spiritual and aesthetic child of Swinburne, Tennyson and Verlaine. You can hear all their voices and Dowson was something of a French scholar and quite obviously under the spell of Verlaine as well as Tennyson and Swinburne, and very much in Arthur Symons' circle. He is fantastically wrong about Ernest Dowson."

"How are you keeping?" said Alec, having risen from his chair.

"Guy Leet was never a good theatre critic, and he was a worse novel critic. He knows nothing about poetry, he has no right to touch the subject. Can't someone stop him?"

"What else," said Alec, "does he say in his memoir?"

"A lot of superficiality about how he attacked a novel of Henry James's and then met James outside the Athenæum one day and James was talking about his conscience as an artist and Guy's conscience as a critic, and that whatever was actually committed to print—"

"Let the fire see the people, Granpa," said Olive, for Percy was standing back-to-fire straddling and monopolising it. Alec Warner had closed and put away his note-book.

The poet did not move.

"That's because Henry James is fashionable to-day, that's why he writes about Henry James. Whereas he jeers at poor Ernest— If you're pouring that brandy for me, Olive, it's too much. Half of that— Ernest Dowson, a supreme lyricist." He took the glass, which he held with a shaky claw-like hand, and while taking his first sip seemed of a sudden to forget Ernest Dowson.

He said to Alec, "I didn't see you at Lisa's funeral."

"Sit down, Granpa," said Olive. She worked him into a chair.

"I missed it," said Alec, watching Percy's lean profile with concentration. "I was in Folkestone at the time."

"It was a fearful and thrilling experience," said Percy.

"In what way?" said Alec.

The old poet smiled. He cackled from the depth of his throat, and the memory of Lisa's cremation seemed to be refracted from his mind's eye to the avid eyes in his head. As he talked, the eyes of Alec feasted on him, in turn.

Percy stayed on with his grand-daughter after Alec Warner had left. She prepared a supper of mushrooms and bacon which they ate off trays perched on their knees. She watched him while he ate. He gnawed with his few teeth at the toasted bread, but got through all of it, even the difficult crusts.

He looked up as he managed the last small rim of crust and saw her watching him. When he had finished all, he remarked, "Final perseverance."

"What you say, Granpa?"

"Final perseverance is the doctrine that wins the eternal victory in small things as in great."

"I say, Granpa, did you ever read any books by Charmian Piper?"

"Oh rather, we all knew her books. She was a fine-looking woman. You should have heard her read poetry from a platform in the days of Poetry. Harold Munro always said—"

"Her son, Eric, has told me there's talk of her novels being reprinted. There's a revival of interest in her novels. There's been an article written, Eric says. But he says the novels all consist of people saying 'touché' to each other, and it's all an affectation, the revival of interest, just because his mother is so old and still alive and was famous once."

"She's still famous. Always has been. Your trouble is, you know nothing, Olive. Everyone knows Charmian Piper."

"Oh no they don't. No one's heard of her except a few old people, but there's going to be a revival. I say there's been an article—"

"You know nothing about literature."

"Touché" she snapped, for Percy himself was always pretending that nobody had forgotten his poetry, really. Then she gave him three pounds to make up for her cruelty, which in fact he had not noticed; he simply did not acknowledge the idea of revival in either case, since he did not recognise the interim death. However, he took the three pounds from Olive, of whose side-line activities he was unaware, for, besides having small private means from her mother's side, she also had occasional jobs as an actress on the B.B.C.

He carried the money by bus and underground to Leicester Square where the post office was open all night, and wrote out, on several telegraph forms, in large slow capitals, a wire to Guy Leet, The Old Stable, Stedrost, Surrey: "You are fantastically wrong in your reference to Ernest Dowson that exceedingly poignant poet who only just steered clear of sentimentality and self-pity stop Ernest Dowson was the spiritual and aesthetic child of Swinburne Tennyson and especially Verlaine by whose verse he was veritably haunted Dowsons verse requires to be read aloud which is more than most verse by later hands can stand up to stop I cried for madder music and for stronger wine new line but when the feast is finished and the lamps expire new line then falls thy shadow. Cynara the night is thine new line and I am desolate and sick of an old passion etcetera stop read it aloud man your cheap alliterative jibe carries no weight you are fantastically wrong—Percy Mannering."

He handed in the sheaf of forms at the counter. The clerk looked closely at Percy, whereupon Percy made visible the three pound notes.

"Are you sure," said the clerk then, "you want to send all this?"

"I am," bawled Percy Mannering. He handed over two of the notes, took his change and went out into the bright-lit night.

Chapter Eight

Dame Lettie Colston had been happier without a resident maid, but the telephone incidents had now forced on her the necessity of having someone in the house to answer the dreadful calls. The mystery of it was, that the man never gave the terrible message to the girl. On the other hand, in the two weeks since her arrival, there had been a series of calls which proved to be someone getting the wrong number. When they had occurred three times in one day Dame Lettie began to bewilder the girl with questions.

"Who was it, Gwen, was it a man?"

"It was a wrong number."

"Was it a man?"

"Yes, but it was a wrong number."

"What did he say exactly? Do answer my question please."

"He said, 'Sorry, it's a wrong number,'" shouted Gwen, "that's what he said."

"What kind of voice was it?"

"Oh mad-um. I said it was a man, didn't I? The lines must be crossed. I know phones like the back of my hand."

"Yes, but was the voice young or old? Was it the same one as got the last wrong number?"

"Well, they're all the same to me, if they're wrong numbers. You better answer the phone yourself and then—"

"I was only asking," said Dame Lettie, "because we

484

seem to be having such a lot of wrong numbers since you've been here. And it always seems to be a man."

"What you mean? What exactly you mean by that, mad-*um*?"

Dame Lettie had not meant whatever the girl thought she meant. It was Gwen's evening out, and Lettie was glad Godfrey was coming to dine with her.

At about eight o'clock, when they were at dinner, the telephone rang.

"Godfrey, you answer it please."

He marched out into the hall. She heard him lift the receiver and give the number. "Yes, that's right," he said next. "Who's that, who is it?" Lettie heard him say. Then he replaced the receiver.

"Godfrey," she said, "that was the man?"

"Yes," he shouted. " 'Tell Dame Lettie to remember she must die.' Then he rang off. Damned peculiar." He sat down and continued eating his soup.

"There is no need to shout, Godfrey. Keep calm." Her own large body was trembling.

"Well, it's damned odd. I say you must have an enemy. Sounds a common little fellow, with his lisp."

"Oh no, Godfrey, he is quite cultured. But sinister."

"I say he's a common chap. This isn't the first time I've heard him."

"There must be something wrong with your hearing, Godfrey. A middle-aged, cultivated man who should know better—"

"A barrow boy, I should say."

"Nonsense. Go and ring the police. They said always to report—"

"What's the use?" he said. And seeing she would argue, he added, "After dinner. I'll ring after dinner."

"That is the first time he has left that message since I took on Gwen a fortnight ago. When Gwen answers the telephone the man says, 'Sorry, wrong number.' He does it two or three times a day."

"It may *be* some fellow getting a wrong number. Your lines must be crossed with someone else's. Have you reported this nuisance to the Exchange?"

"I have," she said. "They tell me the lines are perfectly in order."

"They must be crossed—"

"Oh," she said, "you are as bad as Gwen, going on about crossed lines. I have a good idea who it is. I think it is Chief Inspector Mortimer."

"Nothing like Mortimer's voice."

"Or his accomplice," she said.

"Rubbish. A man in his position."

"That is why the police don't find the culprit. They know, but they won't reveal his identity. He is their former Chief."

"I say you have an enemy."

"I say it is Mortimer."

"Why, then," said Godfrey, "do you continue to consult him about the case?"

"So that he shall not know I suspect him. He may then fall into a trap. Meantime, as I have told you, he is out of my will. He doesn't know *that*."

"Oh, you are always changing your will. No wonder you have enemies." Godfrey felt guilty at having gossiped to Olive about Lettie's changes in her will. "No wonder," he said, "you don't know the culprit."

"I haven't heard from Eric lately," Dame Lettie remarked, so that he felt more guilty, thinking of all he had told Olive.

Godfrey said, "He has been in London the past six weeks. He returned to Cornwall last night."

"But he hasn't been to see me. Why didn't you let me know before, Godfrey?"

"I myself did not know he was in London," said Godfrey, "until I learned it from a mutual friend yesterday."

"What mutual friend? What has Eric been up to? What friend?"

"I cannot recollect at the moment," said Godfrey. "I have long given up interest in Eric's affairs."

"You should keep your memory in training," she said. "Try going over in your mind each night before retiring everything you have done during the day. I must say I am astonished that Eric did not call upon me."

"He didn't come near us," said Godfrey, "so why should he come to see you?"

"At least," she said, "I should have thought he knew what side his bread's buttered."

"Ha, you don't know Eric. Fifty-six years of age and an utter failure. You ought to know, Lettie, that men of that age and type can't bear the sight of old people. It reminds them that they are getting on. Ha, and he's feeling his age, I hear. You, Lettie, may yet see him under. We may both see him under."

Lying in bed later that night, it seemed clear to Dame Lettie that Eric must really after all be the man behind the telephone calls. He would not ring himself lest she should recognise his voice. He must have an accomplice. She rose and switched on the light.

Dame Lettie sat in her dressing gown at dead of night and re-filled her fountain pen. While she did so she glanced at the page she had just written. She thought, How shaky my writing looks! Immediately, as if slamming a door on it, she put the thought out of sight. She wiped the nib of her pen, turned over the sheet and continued, on the back, her letter to Eric:

... and so, having heard of your having been in London these past six weeks, your not having informed me, far less called, does, I admit, strike me as being, to say the least, discourteous. I had wished to consult you on certain matters relating to your Mother. There is every indication that we shall have to arrange for her to be sent to the nursing home in Surrey of which I told you when last I saw you.

She laid down her pen, withdrew one of the fine hairpins from her thin hair, and replaced it. Perhaps, she thought, I should take an even more subtle line with Eric. Her face puckered in folds under the desk-lamp. Two thoughts intruded simultaneously. One was: I am really very tired; and the other: I am not a bit tired, I am charging ahead with great energy. She lifted the pen again and continued to put the wavering marks across the page.

I have recently been making some slight adjustments in my own affairs, about which I could have wished to consult you had you seen fit to inform me of your recent visit to London.

Was that subtle enough? No, it was too subtle, perhaps, for Eric.

These *minor* adjustments, of course, have some bearing upon my Will. It has always seemed to me a pity that your cousin Martin, though doing so well in South Africa, should not be remembered in some small way. I would wish for no recriminations among the family after my passing. Your position is of course substantially unchanged, but I could wish you had made yourself available for consultation. You will recall the adjustments I made to existing arrangements after your cousin Alan fell on the field of battle. . . .

That is good, she thought, that is subtle. Eric had got out of the war somehow. She continued,

I could have wished for discussions with you, but I am an old woman and quite realise that you, who are nearing

488

the end of your prime, must be full of affairs. Mr. Merrilees is now drawing up the amended Will and I would not wish to further interfere with existing arrangements. Nevertheless, I could have wished to discuss them with you had you seen fit to present yourself during the six weeks of your recent stay in London, of which I did not hear until after your return.

That ought to do it, she thought. He will come wheezing down from Cornwall as fast as the first train will carry him. If he is the guilty man he will know that I *know*. No one, she thought, is going to kill me through fear. And she fell to wondering again, who her enemy could be. She fell to doubting whether Eric had it in him ... whether he had the financial means to employ an accomplice. Easier, she thought, for Mortimer. Anyway, she thought, it must be someone who is in my Will. And so she sealed and stamped her letter to Eric, placed it on the tray in the hall, took a tot of whisky and went to bed. Her head moved slowly from side to side on the pillow, for she could not sleep. She had caught a chill down there in the study. A cramp seized her leg. She had a longing for a strong friend, some major Strength from which to draw. Who can help me? she thought. Godfrey is selfish, Charmian feeble, Jean Taylor is bedridden. I can talk to Taylor, but she has not got the strength I need. Alec Warner ... shall I go to see Alec Warner? I never got strength from him. Neither did Taylor. He has not got the strength one needs.

Suddenly she sprang up. Something had lightly touched her cheek. She switched on the light. A spider on her pillow, large as a penny, quite still, with its brown legs outspread! She looked at it feverishly then pulled herself together to try to pick it off the pillow. As she put forth her hand another, paler, spider-legged and fluffy creature on the pillow where the bed-lamp cast a shade, caught her sight. "Gwen!" she screams. "Gwen!"

But Gwen is sleeping soundly. In a panic Dame Lettie

plucks at the large spider. It proves to be a feather. So does the other object.

She dropped her head on her pillow once more. She thought: My old pillows, I shall get some new pillows.

She put out the light and the troubled movements of the head began again. Whom, she thought, can I draw Strength from? She considered her acquaintances one by one—who among them was tougher, stronger than she?

Tempest, she thought at last. I shall get Tempest Sidebottome to help me. Tempest, her opponent in forty years' committee-sitting, had frequently been a painful idea to Dame Lettie. Particularly had she resented Tempest's bossy activeness and physical agility at Lisa's funeral. Strangely, now, she drew strength from the thought of the woman. Tempest Sidebottome would settle the matter if anyone could. Tempest would hunt down the persecutor. Dame Lettie's head settled still on the pillow. She would go over to Richmond tomorrow and talk to Tempest. After all, Tempest was only seventy. She hoped her idiotic husband Ronald would be out. But in any case, he was deaf. Dame Lettie turned at last to her sleep, deriving a half-dreamt success from the strength of Tempest Sidebottome as from some tremendous mother.

"Good morning, Eric," said Charmian as she worked her way round the breakfast table to her place.

"*Not* Eric," said Mrs. Pettigrew. "We are a bit confused again this morning."

"Are you, my dear. What has happened to confuse you?" said Charmian.

Godfrey sensed the start of bickering, so he looked up from his paper and said to his wife, "Lettie was telling me last night that it is a great aid to memory to go through in one's mind each night the things which have happened in the course of the day."

"Why," said Charmian, "that is a Catholic practice.

490

We are always recommended to consider each night our actions of the past day. It is an admirable—"

"Not the same thing," said Godfrey, "at all. You are speaking exclusively of one's moral actions. What I'm talking about are things which have happened. It is a great aid to memory, as Lettie was saying last night, to memorise everything which has occurred in one's experience during the day. Your practice, which you call Catholic, is, moreover, common to most religions. To my mind, that type of examination of conscience is designed to enslave the individual and inhibit his freedom of action. Take yourself, for example. You only have to appeal to psychology—"

"To whom?" said Charmian cattily, as she took the cup which Mrs. Pettigrew passed to her.

Godfrey turned back to his paper. Whereupon Charmian continued the argument with Mrs. Pettigrew.

"I don't see that one can examine one's moral conduct without memorising everything that's happened during the day. It is the same thing. What Lettie advises is a form of—"

Godfrey put down his paper. "I say it is not the same thing." He dipped an oblong of toast in his tea and put it in his mouth.

Mrs. Pettigrew rose to the opportunity of playing the peacemaker. "Now hush," she said to Charmian. "Eat your nice scrambled egg which Taylor has prepared for you."

"Taylor is not here," stated Charmian.

"Taylor—what do you mean?" said Godfrey.

Mrs. Pettigrew winked at him.

Godfrey opened his mouth to retort, then shut it again.

"Taylor is in hospital," said Charmian, pleased with her clarity.

Godfrey read from the newspaper, " 'Motling—' are you listening, Charmian?—'on 10th December at Zomba, Nyasaland; Major Cosmos Petwick Motling, G.C.V.O., husband of the late Eugenie, beloved father of Patricia and Eugen, in his 91st year.' Are you listening, Charmian?"

"Was he killed at the front, dear?"

"Ah, me!" said Mrs. Pettigrew.

Godfrey opened his mouth to say something to Mrs. Pettigrew, then stopped. He held up the paper again and from behind it mumbled, "No, Zomba. Motling's the name. He went out there to retire. You won't remember him."

"*I* recall him well," said Mrs. Pettigrew; "when his wife was alive, Lisa used to—"

"Was he killed at the front?" said Charmian.

"The front," said Mrs. Pettigrew.

" 'Sidebottome,' " said Godfrey, "are you listening, Charmian?— 'On 18th December at the Mandeville Nursing Home, Richmond; Tempest Ethel, beloved wife of Ronald Charles Sidebottome. Funeral private.' Doesn't give her age."

"Tempest Sidebottome!" said Mrs. Pettigrew, reaching to take the paper from his hand. "Let me see."

Godfrey withdrew the paper and opened his mouth as if to protest, then closed it again. However, he said, "I am not finished with the paper."

"Well, fancy Tempest Sidebottome," said Mrs. Pettigrew. "Of course, cancer is cancer."

"She always *was* a bitch," said Godfrey, as if her death were the ultimate proof of it.

"I wonder," said Mrs. Pettigrew, "who will look after poor old Ronald now. He's so deaf."

Godfrey looked at her to see more closely what she meant, but her short broad nose was hidden by her cup and her eyes stared appraisingly at the marmalade.

She was, in fact, quite shocked by Tempest's death. She had only a month ago agreed to join forces with the Sidebottomes in contesting Lisa Brooke's will. Tempest,

when she had learnt of Guy Leet's hitherto secret marriage
to Lisa, had been driven to approach Mrs. Pettigrew and attempt to make up their recent differences. Mrs. Pettigrew
had rather have worked alone, but the heavy costs deterred
her. She had agreed to go in with Tempest against Guy
Leet on the grounds that his marriage with Lisa Brooke
had not been consummated. They had been warned that
their case was a slender one, but Tempest had the money
and the drive to go ahead, and Mrs. Pettigrew had in her
possession the relevant correspondence. Ronald Sidebottome had been timid about the affair—didn't like raking
up the scandal, but Tempest had seemed to have the
drive. Tempest's death was a shock to Mrs. Pettigrew. She
would have to work hard on Ronald. One got no rest.
She stared at the marmalade pot as if to fathom its possibilities.

Godfrey had returned to his paper. "Funeral private.
That saves us a wreath."

"You had better write to poor Ronald," said Charmian,
"and I will say a rosary for Tempest. Oh, I do remember
her as a girl. She was newly out from Australia and her
uncle was a rector in Dorset—as was also my uncle, Mrs.
Pettigrew—"

"Your uncle was not in Dorset. He was up in York-
shire," said Godfrey.

"But he was a country rector, like Tempest's uncle.
Leave me alone, Godfrey. I am just telling Mrs. Pettigrew."

"Oh, do call me Mabel," said Mrs. Pettigrew, winking
at Godfrey.

"Her uncle, Mabel," said Charmian, "was a rector and
so was mine. It was the thing we had in common. We had
not a great deal in common, Mrs. Pettigrew, and of course
as a girl she was considerably younger than me."

"She is still younger than you," said Godfrey.

"No, Godfrey, not now. Well, Mrs. Pettigrew, I do so

remember our two uncles together and we were all staying down in Dorset. There was a bishop and a dean, and our two uncles. Oh, poor Tempest was bored. They were discussing the Scriptures and this manuscript called 'Q.' How Tempest was in a rage when she heard that 'Q' was only a manuscript, because she had imagined them to be talking of a bishop and she said out loud *'Who* is Bishop Kew?' And of course everyone laughed heartily, and then they were sorry for Tempest. And they tried to console her by telling her that 'Q' was nothing really, not even a manuscript, which indeed it wasn't, and I must confess I never understood how they could sit up so late at night fitting their ideas into this 'Q' which is nothing really. As I say poor Tempest was in a rage, she could never bear to be made game of."

Mrs. Pettigrew winked at Godfrey.

"Charmian," said Godfrey, "you are over-exciting yourself." And true enough, she was tremulously crying.

Chapter Nine

Partly because of a reorganisation of the Maud Long Ward and partly because of Tempest Sidebottome's death, Sister Burstead was transferred to another ward.

She had been a protégée of Tempest's, and this had mostly accounted for the management committee's resistance to any previous suggestion that the sister could not cope with the old people's ward. The committee, though largely composed of recently empowered professional men and women, had been in many ways afraid of Tempest. Or rather, afraid to lose her lest they should get someone worse.

It was necessary for them to tolerate at least one or two remnants of the old-type committee people until they should die out. And they chiefly feared, in fact, that if Tempest should take offence and resign, she would be replaced by some more formidable, more subtle private welfare-worker and busybody. And whereas Tempest had many dramatic things to say in committee, whereas she was imperious with the matron, an opponent on principle of all occasions of expenditure, scornful in the extreme of physiotherapists and psychiatrists (everything beginning "psycho-" or "physio-" Tempest lumped together, believed to be the same thing, and dismissed)—although she was in reaction against the committee's ideals, she was so to the point of parody, and it was for precisely this reason, because she so much demonstrated the errors of her system, that she was retained, was propitiated from time to time, and allowed to have her way in such minor matters as that of Sister Burstead. Not that the committee were not afraid of Tempest for other, less evident reasons; but these were matters of instinct and not openly admitted. Her voice in committee had been strangely terrifying to many an eminent though small-boned specialist, even the bossy young heavily-qualified women had sometimes failed to outstare the little pale pebble-eyes of the great unself-questioning matriarch, Mrs. Sidebottome. "Terrible woman," everyone always agreed when she had left.

"After the fifties are over," said the chairman who was himself a man of seventy-three, "everything will be easier. This transition period . . . the old brigade don't like change. They don't like loss of authority. By the middle-sixties everything will be easier. We will have things in working order." Whereupon the committee surrendered themselves to putting up with Tempest, a rock of unchanging, until the middle-sixties of the century should arrive, leaving behind her on the committee a Tempest-shaped vacuum which they immediately attempted, but had not yet been able to fill.

In the meantime, as if tempting Providence to send them another Tempest, they transferred Sister Burstead, on the first of January, to another ward. That the old people's ward was being reorganised provided a reasonable excuse, and Sister Burstead made no further protest.

News of the transfer reached the grannies before the news of the reorganisation.

"I'll believe it when I see it," said Granny Barnacle.

She saw it before that week-end. A new ward sister, fat and forceful with a huge untroubled faceful of flesh and brisk legs, was installed. "That's how I like them," said Granny Barnacle. "Sister Bastard was too skinny."

The new sister, when she caught Granny Green absent-mindedly scooping the scrambled egg off her plate into her locker, put her hands on her slab-like hips and said, "What the hell do you think you're doing?"

"That's how I like them," said Granny Barnacle. She closed her eyes on her pillow with contentment. She declared herself to feel safe for the first time for months. She declared herself ready to die now that she had seen the removal of Sister Bastard. She sprang up again from her pillow and with outstretched arm and pointing finger prophesied that the whole ward would now see the winter through.

Miss Valvona, who was always much affected by Miss Barnacle's feelings, consulted the stars: "Granny Barnacle—*Sagittarius*. 'Noon period best for commencing long-distance travel. You can show your originality to-day.' "

"Ho!" said Granny Barnacle. "Originality to-day, I'll wear me britches back to front."

The nurses came on their daily round of washing, changing, combing and prettifying the patients before the matron's inspection. They observed Granny Barnacle's excitement and decided to leave her to the last. She was usually excitable throughout this performance in any case. During Sister Burstead's term of office, especially, Granny Barnacle would screech when turned over for her back to be dusted with powder, or helped out of bed to sit on her chair.

"Nurse, I'll be covered with bruises," she would shout.

"If you don't move, Gran, you'll be covered with bed-sores."

She would scream to God that the nurses were pulling her arms from their sockets, she would swear by the Almighty that she wasn't fit to be sat up. She moaned, whenever the physiotherapist made her move her fingers and toes, and declared that her joints would crack.

"Kill me off," she would command, "and be done with it."

"Come on, Gran, you've got to get exercise."

497

"Crack! Can't you hear the bones crack? Kill me off and—"

"Let's rub your legs, Gran. My, you've got beautiful legs."

"Help, she's killing me."

But at the best of times Granny Barnacle really liked an excuse for a bit of noise, it livened her up. In a sense, she gave vent to the whole ward's will to shout, so that the others did not make nearly so much noise as they might otherwise have done. It was true some of the other grannies were loud in complaints, but this was mostly for a few seconds when their hair was being combed. Granny Green would never fail to tell the nurses after her hair was done:

"I had a lovely head of hair till you cut it off," although in reality there had been very little to cut off.

"It's hygiene, Granny. It would hurt far more when we combed it if your hair was long."

"I had a lovely head. . . ."

"Me, too," Granny Barnacle would declare, especially if Sister Burstead had been within hearing. "You should have seen my head before they cut it off."

"Oh, short hair is cooler when one is in bed," Granny Taylor, whose hair had really been long and thick, and who actually preferred it short, would murmur to herself.

"Let's give you a nice wave to-day, Granny Barnacle."

"Oh, you're killing me."

On the day of the new sister's arrival, Granny Barnacle and her obvious excitement having been left to the last, it was found, when her turn came, that she was running a temperature.

"Get me out of bed, love," she implored the nurse. "Let's sit up to-day, seeing Bastard's gone."

"No, you've got a temperature."

"Nurse, I want to get up to-day. Get me a will-form,

there's a bob in my locker, I want to make a new will and put in the new sister. What's her name?"

"Lucy."

"Lucy Locket," shrieked Granny Barnacle, "lost her—"

"Lie still, Granny Barnacle, till we make you better."

She submitted after a fuss. Next day, when they told her she must keep her bed she protested louder, even struggled a little, but Miss Taylor in the opposite bed noticed that Granny Barnacle's voice was unusually thin and high.

"Nurse, I'm going to get up to-day. Get me a will-form. I want to make a new will and put in the new sister. What's her name?"

"Lucy," said the nurse. "Your blood pressure's high, Gran."

"Her last name, girl."

"Lucy. Sister Lucy."

"Sister Lousy," screamed Granny Barnacle. "Well, she's going in my will. Give me a hand. . . ."

When the doctor had gone she was given an injection and dozed off for a while.

At one o'clock, while everyone else was eating, she woke. Sister Lucy brought some milk custard to her bed and fed her with a spoon. The ward was quiet and the sound of grannies' spoons tinkling on their plates became more pronounced in the absence of voices.

About three o'clock Granny Barnacle woke again and started to rave in a piping voice, at first faintly, then growing higher and piercing. "Noos, E'ning Noos," fluted the old newsvendor. "E'ning pap-*ar*, Noos, E'ning Stan-*ar*, E'ning Stah Noos *an* Stan-*ar*."

She was given an injection and a sip of water. Her bed was wheeled to the end of the ward and a screen was put round it. In the course of the afternoon the doctor came, stayed behind the screen for a short while, and went.

The new ward sister came and looked behind the screen

from time to time. Towards five o'clock, when the few visitors were going home, Sister Lucy went behind the screen once more. She spoke to Granny Barnacle, who replied in a weak voice.

"She's conscious," said Miss Valvona.

"Yes, she spoke."

"Is she bad?" said Miss Valvona as the sister passed her bed.

"She's not too well," said the sister.

Some of the patients kept looking expectantly and fearfully at the entrance to the ward, whenever anyone was heard approaching, as if watching for the Angel of Death. Towards six o'clock came the sound of a man's footsteps. The patients, propped up with their supper trays, stopped eating and turned to see who had arrived.

Sure enough, it was the priest, carrying a small box. Miss Valvona and Miss Taylor crossed themselves as he passed. He went behind the screen accompanied by a nurse. Though the ward was silent, none of the patients had sharp enough ears, even with their hearing-aids, to catch more than an occasional humming sound from his recitations.

Miss Valvona's tears dropped into her supper. She was thinking of her father's Last Sacrament, after which he had recovered to live a further six months. The priest behind the screen would be committing Granny Barnacle to the sweet Lord, he would be anointing Granny Barnacle's eyes, nose, mouth, hands and feet, asking pardon for the sins she had committed by sight, by hearing, smell, taste and speech, by the touch of her hands, and by her very footsteps.

The priest left. A few of the patients finished their supper. Those who did not were coaxed with Ovaltine. At seven the sister took a last look behind the screen before going off to the dining-room.

"How is she now?" said a granny.

"Sleeping nicely."

About twenty minutes later a nurse looked behind the screen, went inside for a moment, then came out again. The patients watched her leave the ward. There she gave her message to the runner who went to the dining-room and, opening the door, caught the attention of the ward sister. The runner lifted up one finger to signify that one of the sister's patients had died.

It was the third death in the ward since Miss Taylor's admittance. She knew the routine. "We leave the patient for an hour in respect for the dead," a nurse had once explained to her, "but no longer than an hour, because the body begins to set. Then we perform the last offices— that's washing them and making them right for burial."

At five past nine, by the dim night-lamps of the ward, Granny Barnacle was wheeled away.

"I shan't sleep a wink," said Mrs. Reewes-Duncan. Many said they would not sleep a wink, but in fact they slept more soundly and exhaustedly that night than on most nights. The ward lay till morning still and sound-less, breathing like one body instead of eleven.

The reorganisation of the Maud Long Ward began next day, and all patients declared it a mercy for Granny Barnacle that she had been spared it.

Hitherto, the twelve beds in the Maud Long Ward had occupied only half of the space in the room; they had been a surplus from another, larger, medical ward, com-prised mainly of elderly women. The new arrangement was designed to fill up the remaining half of the Maud Long Ward with a further nine elderly patients. These were to be put at the far end. Already, while the prep-arations were still in progress, this end of the ward was referred to among the nurses as the "geriatric corner."

"What's that word mean they keep saying?" Granny Roberts demanded of Miss Taylor.

"It's to do with old age. There must be some very old patients coming in."

"We supposed to be teen-agers, then?"

Granny Valvona said, "Our new friends will probably be centenarians."

"I didn't catch—just a minute till I get the trumpet right," said Granny Roberts, who always referred to her small hearing fixture as the trumpet.

"See," said Granny Green, "what they're bringing in to the ward."

A line of cots was being wheeled up the ward and arranged in the new geriatric corner. These cots were much the same as the other hospital beds, but with the startling difference that they had high railed sides like children's cots.

Granny Valvona crossed herself.

Next, the patients were wheeled in. Perhaps this was not the best introduction of the newcomers to the old established set. Being in varying advanced states of senility, and also being specially upset by the move, the new arrivals were making more noise and dribbling more from the mouth than usual.

Sister Lucy came round the grannies' beds, explaining that they would have to be patient with these advanced cases. Knitting needles must not be left lying about near the geriatric corner, in case any of the newcomers should hurt themselves. The patients were not to be alarmed if anything *funny* should occur. At this point the sister had to call a nurse's attention to one of the new patients, a frail, wizened, but rather pretty little woman, who was trying to climb over the side of her cot. The nurse rushed to settle the old woman back in bed. The patient set up an infant-like wail, yet not entirely that of a child—it was more like that of an old woman copying the cry of an infant.

The sister continued addressing the grannies in confidential tones. "You must try to remember," she said, "that these cases are very advanced, poor dears. And don't get upset, like good girls. Try and help the nurses by keeping quiet and tidy."

"We'll soon be senile ourselves at this rate," said Granny Green.

"Sh-sh," said the sister. "We don't use that word. They are geriatric cases."

When she had gone Granny Duncan said, "To think that I spent my middle years looking forward to my old age and a rest!"

Another geriatric case was trying to climb over the cot. A nurse bustled to the rescue.

"A mercy," said Granny Duncan, "poor Granny Barnacle didn't live to see it. Poor souls— Don't you be rough with her, Nurse!"

The patient had, in fact, pulled the nurse's cap off and was now clamouring for a drink of water. The nurse replaced her cap, and while another nurse held a plastic beaker of water to the old woman's lips, assured the ward, "They'll settle down. The moving's upset them."

After a stormy night, the newcomers did seem quieter next morning, though one or two made a clamour in the ordinary course of conversation, and most, when they were helped out of bed to stand shakily upheld for a moment by the nurse, wet the floor. In the afternoon a specialist lady and an assistant came with draught-boards which she laid on the floor beside four of the new patients who were sitting up in chairs, but whose hands were crippled. They did not protest when their socks and slippers were removed and their feet manipulated and rubbed by the younger woman. Their socks and slippers were replaced and they seemed to know what to do when the draught-boards were set in front of their feet.

"Look, did you ever," said Granny Valvona. "They're playing draughts with their feet."

"I ask you," said Granny Roberts, "is it a bloody circus we are here?"

"That's nothing to what you'll see in Geriatrics," said the nurse proudly.

"A blessing poor Granny Barnacle wasn't spared to see it."

Miss Taylor absorbed as much of the new experience as she could, for the sake of Alec Warner. But the death of Granny Barnacle, her own arthritic pains, and the noisy intrusion of the senile cases, had confused her. She was crying towards the end of the day, and worried lest the nurse should catch her at it, and perhaps report her too sick to be wheeled down next morning to the Mass which she and Miss Valvona had requested for the soul of Granny Barnacle who had no relatives to mourn her.

Miss Taylor dropped asleep, and waking in the middle of the night because of her painful limbs, still pretended to sleep on, and went without her injection. At eleven o'clock next morning Miss Valvona and Miss Taylor were wheeled into the hospital chapel. They were accompanied by three other grannies, not Catholics, from the Maud Long Ward who had been attached to Granny Barnacle in various ways, including those of love, scorn, resentment and pity.

During the course of the Mass an irrational idea streaked through Miss Taylor's mind. She dismissed it and concentrated on her prayers. But this irrational idea, which related to the identity of Dame Lettie's tormentor, was to return to her later again and again.

Chapter Ten

"Is that Mr. Godfrey Colston?" said the man on the telephone.

"Yes, speaking."

"Remember you must die," said the man.

"Dame Lettie is not here," he said, being flustered. "Who is that speaking?"

"The message is for you, Mr. Colston."

"Who is speaking?"

The man had hung up.

Though Godfrey was still tall, he had seemed to shrink during the winter, to an extent that an actual tape-measure would perhaps not confirm. His bones were larger than ever; that is to say, they remained the same size as they had been throughout his adult life, but the ligaments between them had gradually shrunk, as they do with advancing age, so that the bones appeared huge-grown. This process had, in Godfrey, increased rapidly in the months between the autumn of Mrs. Pettigrew's joining his household and the March morning when he received the telephone call.

He put down the receiver and walked with short steps into the library. Mrs. Pettigrew followed him. She herself was looking healthier and not much older.

"Who was that on the phone, Godfrey?" she said.

"A man . . . I can't understand. It should have been

for Lettie but he definitely said it was for me. I thought
the message—"

"What did he say?"

"That thing he says to Lettie. But he said 'Mr. Colston,
it's for you, Mr. Colston.' I don't understand. . . ."

"Look here," said Mrs. Pettigrew, "let's pull ourselves
together, shall we?"

"Have you got the key of the sideboard on you?"

"I have," said Mabel Pettigrew. "Want a drink?"

"I feel I need a little—"

"I'll bring one in to you. Sit down."

"A stiff one."

"Sit down. There's a boy."

She came back, spritely in her black dress and the new
white-streaked lock of hair among the very black, sweeping
from her brow. Her hair had been cut shorter. She had
painted her nails pink and wore two large rings
which gave an appearance of opulent ancient majesty to
the long wrinkled hand which held Godfrey's glass of
brandy and soda.

"Thanks," said Godfrey, taking the glass. "Many
thanks." He sat back and drank his brandy, looking at her
from time to time as if to see what she was going to do and
say.

She sat opposite him. She said nothing till he had
finished. Then she said, "Now, look."

She said, "Now, look. This is all imagination."

He muttered something about being in charge of his
faculties.

"In that case," she said—"in *that* case, have you seen
your lawyer yet?"

He muttered something about next week.

"You have an appointment with him," she said, "this
afternoon."

"This afternoon? Who—how . . . ?"

"I've made an appointment for you to see him at three this afternoon."

"Not this afternoon," said Godfrey. "Don't feel up to it. Draughty office. Next week."

"You can take a taxi if you don't feel up to driving. It's no distance."

"Next week," he shouted, for the brandy had restored him.

However, the effects wore off. At lunch Charmian said, "Is there anything the matter, Godfrey?"

The telephone rang. Godfrey looked up, startled. He said to Mrs. Pettigrew, "Don't answer."

Mrs. Pettigrew merely said, "I wonder if Mrs. Anthony has heard it? I bet she hasn't."

Mrs. Anthony's hearing was beginning to fail, and she had obviously not heard the telephone.

Mrs. Pettigrew strode out into the hall and lifted the receiver. She came back presently and addressed Charmian.

"For you," she said. "The photographer wants to come to-morrow at four."

"Very well," said Charmian.

"I shan't be here, you know, to-morrow afternoon."

"That's all right," said Charmian. "He does not wish to photograph *you*. Say that four o'clock will be splendid."

While Mrs. Pettigrew went to give the message, Godfrey said, "Another reporter?"

"No, a photographer."

"I don't like the idea of all these strangers coming to the house. I had a nasty experience this morning. Put him off." He rose from his seat and shouted through the door, "I say, Mrs. Pettigrew, we don't want him coming here. Put him off, will you?"

"Too late," said Mrs. Pettigrew, resuming her place.

Mrs. Anthony looked round the door.

"Was you wanting something?"

507

"We did hope," said Mrs. Pettigrew very loudly, "to have our meal without interruptions. However, I have answered the telephone."

"Very good of you, I'm sure," said Mrs. Anthony, and disappeared.

Godfrey was still protesting about the photographer. "We'll have to put him off. Too many strangers."

Charmian said, "I shall not be here long, Godfrey."

"Come, come," said Mrs. Pettigrew. "You may well last another ten years."

"Quite," said Charmian, "and so I have decided to go away to the nursing home in Surrey, after all. I understand the arrangements there are almost perfect. One has every privacy. Oh, how one comes to appreciate privacy."

Mrs. Pettigrew lit a cigarette and slowly blew the smoke in Charmian's face.

"No one's interfering with your privacy," Godfrey muttered.

"And freedom," said Charmian. "I shall have freedom at the nursing home to entertain whom I please. Photographers, strangers—"

"There is no need," said Godfrey desperately, "for you to go away to a home now that you are so much improved."

Mrs. Pettigrew blew more smoke in Charmian's direction.

"Besides," he said, glancing at Mrs. Pettigrew, "we can't afford it."

Charmian was silent, as one who need not reply. Indeed, her books were bringing in money, and her small capital at least was safe from Mrs. Pettigrew. The revival of her novels during the past winter had sharpened her brain. Her memory had improved, and her physical health was better than it had been for years in spite of that attack of bronchitis in January, when a day and a night nurse had been in attendance for a week. However, she still had to move slowly and was prone to kidney trouble.

She looked at Godfrey who was wolfing his rice pudding without, she was sure, noticing what he was eating, and she wondered what was on his mind. She wondered what new torment Mrs. Pettigrew was practising upon him. She wondered how much of his past life Mrs. Pettigrew had discovered, and why he felt is necessary to hush it up at all such costs. She wondered where her own duty to Godfrey lay—where does one's duty as a wife reach its limits? She longed to be away in the nursing home in Surrey, and was surprised at this longing of hers, since all her life she had suffered from apprehensions of being in the power of strangers, and Godfrey had always seemed better than the devil she did not know.

"To move from your home at the age of eighty-seven," Godfrey was saying in an almost pleading voice, "might kill you. There is no need."

Mrs. Pettigrew, having pressed the bell in vain, said, "Oh, Mrs. Anthony is quite deaf. She must get an aid," and went to tell Mrs. Anthony to fetch her tea and Charmian's milk.

When she had gone, Godfrey said,

"I had an unpleasant experience this morning."

Charmian took refuge in a vague expression. She was terrified lest Godfrey was about to make some embarrassing confession concerning Mrs. Pettigrew.

"Are you listening, Charmian?" said Godfrey.

"Yes, oh yes. Anything you like."

"There was a telephone call from Lettie's man."

"Poor Lettie, I wonder he isn't tired of tormenting her."

"The call was for me. He said, 'The message is for you, Mr. Colston.' I am not imagining anything, mind you. I heard it with my ears."

"Really? What message?"

"You *know* what message," he said.

"Well, I should treat it as it deserves to be treated."

"What do you mean?"

"Neither more nor less," said Charmian.

"I'd like to know who the fellow is. I'd like to know why the police haven't got him. It's preposterous when we pay our rates and taxes to be threatened like that by a stranger."

"What did he threaten to do?" said Charmian. "I thought he merely always said—"

"It's upsetting," said Godfrey. "One might easily take a stroke in consequence. If it occurs again I shall write to *The Times*."

"Why not consult Mrs. Pettigrew," said Charmian. "She is a tower of strength."

Then she felt suddenly sorry for him, huddled among his bones. She left him and climbed the stairs slowly, clinging to the banister, to take her afternoon rest. She considered whether she could bring herself to leave Godfrey in his plight with Mrs. Pettigrew. After all, she herself might have been in an awkward situation, if she had not taken care, long before her old age, to destroy all possibly embarrassing documents. She smiled as she looked at her little bureau with its secretive appearance, in which Mrs. Pettigrew had found no secret, although Charmian knew she had penetrated behind those locks. But Godfrey, after all, was not a clever man.

In the end Godfrey submitted, and agreed to keep the appointment with his lawyer. Mrs. Pettigrew would not absolutely have refused to let him put it off for another day, had she not been frightened by his report of the telephone call. Obviously, his mind was going funny. She had not looked for this. He had better see the lawyer before anyone could say he had been talked into anything.

He got out the car and drove off. About ten minutes later Mrs. Pettigrew got a taxi at the end of the street and followed him. She wanted just to make sure he was at the lawyer's, and she merely intended to drive past the offices to satisfy herself that Godfrey's car was outside.

His car was not outside. She made the driver take her round Sloane Square. There was still no sign of Godfrey's car. She got out and went into a café opposite the offices and sat where she could see him arrive. But by quarter to four there was still no sign of his car. It occurred to her that his memory had escaped him while on his way to the lawyer. He had sometimes remarked that his oculist and his chiropodist were in Chelsea. Perhaps he had gone, by mistake, to have his eyes tested or his feet done. She had trusted his faculties; he had always seemed all right until this morning; but after his silly talk this morning about that phone call anything could happen. It was to be remembered he was nearly eighty-eight.

Or was he cunning? Could the phone call have come from the lawyer, perhaps to confirm the appointment, and Godfrey have cancelled it? After all, how could he have suddenly gone crazy like his sister without showing preliminary signs? Possibly he had decided to feign feebleness of mind merely to evade his obligations.

Mrs. Pettigrew paid for her coffee, resumed her brown squirrel coat, and set off along the King's Road. She saw no sign of his car outside the chiropodist. Anyway, he had probably gone home. She glanced up a side turning and thought she saw Godfrey's car in the blue half-light parked outside a bombed building. Yes indeed, on investigation, it proved to be Godfrey's Vauxhall.

Mrs. Pettigrew looked expertly around her. The houses opposite the bombed building were all occupied and afforded no concealment. The bombed building itself seemed to demand investigation. She walked up the dusty steps on which strangely there stood a collection of grimy milk bottles. The broken door was partly open. She creaked it further open and looked inside. She could see right through, over the decayed brick and plaster, to the windows at the back of the house. She heard a noise as of rustling paper—or could it be rats? She stepped back and stood once more outside the door considering whether and how long she could bear to stand in that desolate doorway and see, without being seen, from which direction Godfrey should return to his car.

Charmian woke at four and sensed the emptiness of the house. Mrs. Anthony now went home at two in the afternoons. Both Godfrey and Mrs. Pettigrew must be out. Charmian lay listening, to confirm her feeling of being alone in the house. She heard no sound. She rose slowly, tidied herself and, groping for one after another banister rail, descended the stairs. She had reached the first half-landing when the telephone rang. She did not hurry, but it was still ringing when she reached it.

"Is that Mrs. Colston?"

"Yes, speaking."

"Charmian Piper—that's right, isn't it?"

"Yes. Are you a reporter?"

"Remember," he said, "you must die."

"Oh, as to that," she said, "for the past thirty years and more I have thought of it from time to time. My memory is failing in certain respects. I am gone eighty-six. But somehow I do not forget my death, whenever that will be."

"Delighted to hear it," he said. "Goodbye for now."

"Goodbye," she said. "What paper do you represent?" But he had rung off.

Charmian made her way to the library and cautiously built up the fire which had burnt low. The effort of stooping tired her and she sat for a moment in the big chair. After a while it was tea-time. She thought, for a space, about tea. Then she made her way to the kitchen where the tray had been set by Mrs. Anthony in readiness for

Mrs. Pettigrew to make the tea. But Mrs. Pettigrew had gone out. Charmian felt overwhelmed suddenly with trepidation and pleasure. Could she make tea herself? Yes, she would try. The kettle was heavy as she held it under the tap. It was heavier still when it was half-filled with water. It rocked in her hand and her skinny, large-freckled wrist ached and wobbled with the strain. At last she had lifted the kettle safely on to the gas ring. She had seen Mrs. Anthony use the automatic lighter. She tried it but could not make it work. Matches. She looked everywhere for matches but could not find any. She went back to the library and took from a jar one of Godfrey's home-made tapers. She stooped dangerously and lit the taper at the fire. Then, cautiously, she bore the little quivering flame to the kitchen, holding it in one shaking hand, and holding that hand with her other hand to keep it as steady as possible. At last the gas was lit under the kettle. Charmian put the teapot on the stove to warm. She then sat down in Mrs. Anthony's chair to wait for the kettle to boil. She felt strong and fearless.

When the kettle had boiled she spooned tea into the pot and knew that the difficult part had come. She lifted the kettle a little and tilted its spout over the tea-pot. She stood as far back as she could. In went the hot water, and though it splashed quite a bit on the stove, she did not get any over her dress or her feet. She bore the tea-pot to the tray. It wafted to and fro, but she managed to place it down gently after all.

She looked at the hot-water jug. Should she bother with hot water? She had done so well up to now, it would be a pity to make any mistake and have an accident. But she felt strong and fearless. A pot of tea without the hot-water jug beside it was nonsense. She filled the jug, this time splashing her foot a little, but not enough to burn.

When all was set on the tray she was tempted to have her tea in the kitchen there in Mrs. Anthony's chair.

But she thought of her bright fire in the library. She looked at the tray. Plainly she could never carry it. She would take in the tea-things one by one, even if it took half-an-hour.

She did this, resting only once between her journeys. First the tea-pot, which she placed on the library hearth. Then the hot-water jug. These were the dangerous objects. Cup and saucer; another cup and saucer in case Godfrey or Mrs. Pettigrew should return and want tea; the buttered scones; jam; two plates, two knives, and two spoons. Another journey for the plate of Garibaldi biscuits which Charmian loved to dip in her tea. She could well remember, as she looked at them, the fuss about Garibaldi in her childhood, and her father's eloquent letters to *The Times* which were read aloud after morning prayers. Three of the Garibaldi biscuits slid off the plate and broke on the floor in the hall. She proceeded with the plate, laid it on a table, and then returned to pick up the broken biscuits, even the crumbs. It would be a pity if anyone said she had been careless. Still, she felt fearless that afternoon. Last of all she went to fetch the tray itself, with its pretty cloth. She stopped to mop up the water she had spilt by the stove. When she had brought everything into the room she closed the door, placed the tray on a low table by her chair and arranged her tea-things neatly upon it. The performance had taken twenty minutes. She dozed with gratitude in her chair for five more minutes, then carefully poured out her tea, splashing very little into the saucer. Even that little she eventually poured back into the cup. All was as usual, save that she was blissfully alone, and the tea was not altogether hot. She started to enjoy her tea.

Mrs. Pettigrew stood under the chipped stucco of the porch and looked at her watch. She could not see the dial in the gloom. She walked down the steps and consulted her watch under a lamp-post. It was twenty to five. She turned to resume her station in the bombed porch. She had mounted two steps when, from nowhere, a policeman appeared.

"Anything you wanted, madam?"

"Oh, I'm waiting for a friend."

He went up the steps and pushing open the creaking door flashed his torch all over the interior, as if expecting her friend to be there. He gave her a curious look and walked away.

Mrs. Pettigrew thought, It's too bad, it really is, me being put in a predicament like this, standing in the cold, questioned by policemen; and I'm nearly seventy-four. Something rustled on the ground behind the door. She looked; she could see nothing. But then she felt something, like the stroke of a hand over her instep. She shuffled backwards, and catching the last glimpse of a rat slithering through the railings down the area, screamed.

The policeman crossed over the street towards her, having apparently been watching her from some doorway on the other side.

"Anything wrong?" he said.

"A rat," she said, "ran across my feet."

"I shouldn't stand here, madam, please."

"I'm waiting for my friend. Go away."

"What's your name, madam?"

She thought he said, "What's your game?" and it occurred to her, too, that she probably looked years younger than she thought. "You can have three guesses," she replied pertly.

"I must ask you to move along, madam. Where do you live?"

"Suppose you mind your own business?"

"Got anyone to look after you?" he said; and she realised he had not much underestimated her years, but probably suspected she was dotty.

"I'm waiting for my friend," she said.

The policeman stood uncertainly before her, considering her face, and possibly what to do about her. There was a slight stir behind the door. Mrs. Pettigrew jumped nervously. "Oh, is that a rat?"

Just then a car door slammed behind the policeman's bulk.

"That's my friend," she said, trying to slip past him. "Let me pass, please."

The policeman turned to scrutinise the car. Godfrey was already driving off.

"Godfrey! Godfrey!" she called. But he was away.

"Your friend didn't stop long," he observed.

"I've missed him through you talking to me."

She started off down the steps.

"Think you'll get home all right?" The policeman seemed relieved to see her moving off.

She did not reply but got a taxi at King's Road, thinking how hard used she was.

Godfrey, on her arrival, was expostulating with Charmian. "I say you *couldn't* have made the tea and brought it in here. How could you? Mrs. Pettigrew brought in your tea. Now think. You've been dreaming."

Charmian turned to Mrs. Pettigrew. "You have been out all afternoon, haven't you, Mrs. Pettigrew?"

"Mabel," said Mrs. Pettigrew.

"Haven't you, Mabel? I made my tea myself and brought it in. Godfrey won't believe me, he's absurd."

"I brought in your tea," said Mrs. Pettigrew, "before I went out for an airing. I must say I feel the need of it these days since Mrs. Anthony started leaving early."

"You see what I mean?" said Godfrey to Charmian.

Charmian was silent.

"A whole long story," said Godfrey, "about getting up and making your own tea. I knew it was impossible."

Charmian said, "I am getting feeble in mind as well

516

as body, Godfrey. I shall go to the nursing home in Surrey. I am quite decided."

"Perhaps," said Mrs. Pettigrew, "that would be the best."

"There's no need, my dear, for you to go into a home," said Godfrey. "No one is suggesting it. All I was saying—"

"I'm going to bed, Godfrey."

"Oh, dear, a supper tray," said Mrs. Pettigrew.

"I don't want supper, thank you," said Charmian. "I enjoyed my tea."

Mrs. Pettigrew moved towards Charmian as if to take her arm.

"I can manage quite well, thank you."

"Come now, don't get into a tantrum. You must get your beauty sleep for the photographer to-morrow," said Mrs. Pettigrew.

Charmian made her slow way out of the room and upstairs.

"See the lawyer?" said Mrs. Pettigrew.

"It's damn cold," said Godfrey.

"You saw the solicitor?"

"No, in fact, he'd been called away on an urgent case. Have to see him some other time. I say I'll see him to-morrow, Mabel."

"Urgent case," she said. "It was the lawyer you had an appointment with, not the doctor. You're worse than Charmian."

"Yes, yes, Mabel, the lawyer. Don't let Mrs. Anthony hear you."

"Mrs. Anthony has gone. And, anyway, she's deaf. Where have you been all afternoon?"

"Well, I called in," he said, "at the police."

"What?"

"The police station. Kept me waiting a long time."

"Look here, Godfrey, you have no evidence against me,

517

you understand? You need proof. Just you try. What did you tell them? Come on, what did you say?"

"Can't remember exact words. Time they did something about it. I said, 'My sister has been suffering from this man for over six months.' I said, 'Now he has started on me,' I said, 'and it's high time you did something about it,' I said. I said—"

"Oh, your phone call. Is that all you have to think about? I ask you, Godfrey, is *that all* . . . ?"

He huddled in his chair. "Damn cold," he said. "Have we got any whisky there?"

"No," she said, "we haven't."

He silently opened Charmian's door on his way to bed.

"Still awake?" he said in a whisper.

"Yes," she said, waking up.

"Feeling all right? Want anything?"

"Nothing, thank you, Godfrey."

"Don't go to the nursing home," he said in a whisper.

"Godfrey, I made my own tea this afternoon."

"All right," he said, "you did. But don't go—"

"Godfrey," she said. "If you will take my advice you will write to Eric. You will make it up with Eric."

"Why? What makes you say that?"

But she would not say what made her say this, and he was puzzled by it, for he himself had been thinking of writing to Eric; he was uncertain whether Charmian knew more about him and his plight than he thought, or whether her words represented merely a stray idea.

"You must promise," said Olive Mannering, "that this is to be treated as a strictly professional matter."

"I promise," said Alec Warner.

"Because," said Olive, "it's dangerous stuff, and I got it in strictest confidence. And I wouldn't tell a soul."

"Nor I," said Alec.

"It's only for purposes of research," said Olive.

"Quite."

"How do you make your notes?" Olive enquired. "Because there mustn't be names mentioned anywhere."

"All documents referring to real names are to be destroyed at my death. No one could possibly identify my case-histories."

"O.K.," said Olive. "Well, goodness, he was in a terrible state this afternoon. I was really sorry for him. It's Mrs. Pettigrew, you see."

"Garters and all that lark?"

"No, oh no. He's finished with that."

"Blackmail."

"That's right. She has apparently discovered a lot about his past life."

"The affair with Lisa Brooke."

"That and a lot more. Then there was some money scandal at the Colston Breweries which was hushed up at the time. Mrs. Pettigrew knows it all. She got at his private papers."

"Has he been to the police?"

"No, he's afraid."

"They would protect him. What is he afraid of? Did you ask?"

"His wife, mostly. He doesn't want his wife to know. It's his pride, I think. Of course, I haven't met her but it sounds to me that she's always been the religious one, and being famous as an author off and on, she gets all the sympathy for being more sensitive than him."

Alec Warner wrote in his book.

"Charmian," he remarked, "would not be put out by anything she learnt about Godfrey. Now, you say he's *afraid* of her knowing?"

"Yes, he is, really."

"Most people," he said, "would say she was **afraid** of him. He bullies her."

"Well, I've only heard his side. He looks pretty bad just now."

"Did you notice the complexion?"

"High coloured. Goodness he's lost weight."

"Stooping more?"

"Oh, much more. The stuffing's knocked out of him. Mrs. Pettigrew keeps the whisky locked up."

Alec made a note. "Do him good in the long run," he commented. "He drank too much for his age. What is he going to do about Mrs. Pettigrew?"

"Well, he pays up. But she keeps demanding more. He hates paying up. And the latest thing, she wants him to make a new will in her favour. He was supposed to be at the lawyer to-day, but he called in on me instead. He thought I might persuade Eric to come and frighten her. He says Eric wouldn't lose by it. But as you know, Eric feels very bitter about his family, and he's jealous of his mother, especially since her novels are in print again, and the fact is, Eric is entitled to a certain amount, it's only a question of time. . . ."

"Eric," said Alec, "is not one of us. Go on about Godfrey."

"He says he'd like to make it up with Eric. I promised to write to Eric for him, and so I shall, but as I say—"

"Has Mrs. Pettigrew any money of her own?"

"Oh, I don't know. You never know with a woman like that, do you? I don't think she has much, because of something I heard yesterday."

"What was that?"

"Well," said Olive, "I got the story from Ronald Sidebottome, he called yesterday. I didn't get it from Godfrey."

"What was the story?" said Alec. "You know, Olive, I always pay extra if it entails an extra interview on your part."

"O.K.," said Olive, "keep your hair on. I just wanted you to know this makes another item."

Alec smiled at her like an uncle.

"Ronald Sidebottome," she said, "has finally decided not to contest Lisa Brooke's will now that Tempest is dead. The case was really Tempest's idea. He said the whole thing would have been very distasteful. All about Lisa's marriage with Guy Leet not being consummated. Mrs. Pettigrew is awfully angry about the case being withdrawn, because she was working in with the Sidebottomes when Tempest died. And she hasn't managed to get her hold on Ronald, though she's been trying hard all winter. Ronald is a very independent type at heart. You don't know old Ronald. He's deaf, I admit, but—"

"I have known Ronald over forty years. How interesting he should strike you as an independent type."

"He has a nice way with him on the quiet," she said. She had met Ronald Sidebottome while strolling round a picture gallery with her grandfather shortly after Tempest's death, and had brought the two old men back to supper. "But if you've known Ronald for forty years, then you don't want to hear any more from me."

"My dear, I have known Ronald over forty years but I can't know him as you do."

"He hates Mrs. Pettigrew," Olive observed with an inward-musing smile. "She won't get much of Lisa's bequest. All she has so far is Lisa's squirrel coat, that's all."

"Does she think of contesting the will on her own account?"

"No, she's been advised her case is too weak. Mrs. Brooke paid her adequately all the time; there's no case. Anyway, I don't think she has the capital to finance it. She was depending on the Sidebottomes. Of course, under the will, the money goes to her when Guy Leet dies. But he's telling everyone how fit he feels. So you can be sure

Mrs. P. is going to get all she can out of poor old Godfrey."

Alec Warner finished his notes and closed the book. Olive passed him a drink.

"Poor old Godfrey," said Olive. "And he was upset by something else, too. He had an anonymous phone call from that man who worries his sister—or at least he thinks he had. It amounts to the same thing, doesn't it?"

Alec Warner opened his notebook again and got his pen from the pocket of his waistcoat. "What did the man say?"

"The same thing. 'You are going to die' or something."

"Always be exact. Dame Lettie's man says, 'Remember you must die'—Was that what Godfrey heard?"

"I think so," she said. "This sort of work is very tiring."

"I know, my dear. It must be. What time of day did he receive this call?"

"The morning. That I do know. He told me it was just after the doctor had left Charmian."

Alec completed his notes and closed his book once more. He said to Olive, "Has Guy Leet been informed of the withdrawal of the law-suit?"

"I don't know. The decision was only made yesterday afternoon."

"Perhaps he does not know yet," said Alec. "Lisa's money will make a great difference to a man of Guy's tastes. He has been feeling the pinch lately."

"He can't have long to live," said Olive.

"Lisa's money will make his short time pleasanter. I take it this information is not particularly confidential?"

"No," said Olive, "only what I told you of Mrs. Pettigrew's hold on Godfrey—that's confidential."

Alec Warner went home and wrote a letter to Guy Leet:

DEAR GUY—I do not know if I am the first to inform you that neither Ronald Sidebottome nor Mrs. Pettigrew are now proceeding with their suit in contest of Lisa's will.

I offer you my congratulations, and trust you will long enjoy your good fortune.

Forgive me for thus attempting to anticipate an official notification. If I have been successful in being the first to convey this news to you, will you kindly oblige me by taking your pulse and your temperature immediately upon reading this letter, and again one hour afterwards, and again the following morning, and inform me of the same, together with your normal pulse-rate and temperature if you know it?

This will be invaluable for my records. I shall be so much obliged.

Yours,
Alec Warner

P.S. Any additional observations as to your reaction to the good news will of course be much appreciated.

Alec Warner went to post the letter and returned to write up his records. Twice, the telephone rang. The first call was from Godfrey Colston, whose record-card, as it happened, Alec held in his hand.

"Oh," said Godfrey, "you're in."

"Yes. Have you been trying to get me?"

"No," said Godfrey. "Look here, I want to speak to you. Do you know anyone in the police?"

"Not well," said Alec, "since Mortimer retired."

"Mortimer's no good," said Godfrey. "It's about these anonymous calls. Mortimer has been looking into them for months. Now the chap has started on me."

"I have an hour to spare between nine and ten. Can you come round to the club?"

Alec returned to his notes. The second telephone call came a quarter of an hour later. It was from a man who said, "Remember you must die."

"Would you mind repeating that?" said Alec.

The speaker repeated it.

"Thank you," said Alec, and replaced the receiver a fraction before the other had done so.

He got out his own card and made an entry. Then he made a cross-reference to another card which he duly annotated. Finally he wrote a passage in his diary, ending it with the words, "Query: mass-hysteria."

Chapter Eleven

In the fine new sunshine of April which fell upon her through the window, Emmeline Mortimer adjusted her glasses and smoothed her blouse. She was grateful to be free of her winter jumpers and to wear a blouse and cardigan again.

She decided to sow parsley that morning and perhaps set out the young carnations and the sweet peas. Perhaps Henry would prune the roses. Henry was over the worst, but she must not let him hoe or weed or in any way strain or stoop. She must keep an eye on him without appearing to do so. This evening, when the people had gone he could spray the gooseberries with lime-sulphur in case of mildew and the pears with Bordeaux mixture in case of scab. And the black-currants in case of big bud again. There was so much to be done, and Henry must not overdo it. No, he must not spray the pears for he might over-reach and strain himself. The people would certainly exhaust him.

Her hearing was sharp that morning. Henry was moving about briskly upstairs. He was humming. The scent of her hyacinths on the window ledge came in brief irregular waves which she received with a sharp and pleasant pang. She sipped her warm and splendid tea and adjusted the cosy round the pot, keeping it hot for Henry. She touched her glasses into focus and turned to the morning paper.

Henry Mortimer came down in a few moments. His wife turned her head very slightly when he came in and returned to her paper.

He opened the french windows and stood there for a while satisfying his body with the new sun and air and his eyes with his garden. Then he closed the windows and took his place at the table. "A bit of hoeing to-day," he said.

She made no immediate objection, for she must bide her time. Not that Henry was touchy or difficult about his angina. It was more a matter of principle and habit; she had always waited her time before opposing any statement of Henry's.

He gestured with the back of his hand towards the sunny weather. "What d'you think of it?" he said.

She looked up, smiled, and nodded once. Her face was a network of fine wrinkles except where the skin was stretched across her small sharp bones. Her back was straight, her figure neat, and her movements easy. One half of her mind was busy calculating the number of places she would have to set for the people this afternoon. She was four years older than Henry, who had turned seventy at the beginning of February. His first heart attack had followed soon after, and Henry, half-inclined to envisage his doctor as a personification of his illness, had declared himself much improved since the doctor had ceased to pay regular daily visits. He had been allowed up for afternoons, then for whole days. The doctor had bade him not to worry, always to carry his box of tablets, to stick to his diet, and to avoid any exertion. The doctor had told Emmeline to ring him any time if necessary. And then, to Henry's relief, the doctor had disappeared from the house.

Henry Mortimer, the former Chief Inspector, was long, lean, bald and spritely. At the sides and back of his head his hair grew thick and grey. His eyebrows were thick and black. It would be accurate to say that his nose and lips were thick, his eyes small and his chin receding into his neck. And yet it would be inaccurate to say he was not a handsome man, such being the power of unity when it exists in a face.

He scraped butter sparingly on his toast in deference to the departed doctor, and remarked to his wife, "I've got these people coming this afternoon."

She said, "There's another bit about them in the paper to-day." And she held her peace for the meantime about his having to take care not to wear himself out with them; for what was the point of his being retired from the Force if he continued to lay himself out on criminal cases?

He stretched out his hand and she put the paper into it. "Hoax Caller Strikes Again," he read aloud. Then he read on to himself:

Police are still mystified by continued complaints of a number of elderly people who have been receiving anonymous telephone calls from a male hoax-caller since August last year.

There may be more than one man behind the hoax. Reports on the type of voice vary from "very young," "middle-aged" to "elderly" etc.

The voice invariably warns the victim, "You will die to-night."

The aged victims' telephones are being tapped by the authorities, and police have requested them to keep the caller in conversation if possible. But this, and all other methods of detecting hoax-callers have so far failed, the police admitted yesterday.

It was thought at first that the gang's activities were confined to the Central London area. But a recent report from former critic Mr. Guy Leet, 75, of Stedrost, Surrey, indicates that the net is spreading wider.

Among numerous others previously reported to be recipients of "the Call" are Dame Lettie Colston, O.B.E., 79, pioneer penal reformer, and her sister-in-law Charmian Piper (Mrs. Godfrey Colston) the novelist, 85, author of *The Seventh Child*, etc.

Dame Lettie told reporters yesterday, "I am not satisfied that the C.I.D. have taken these incidents seriously enough. I am employing a private agency. I consider it a great pity that flogging has been abolished. These vile creatures ought to be taught a lesson."

Charmian Piper, whose husband, Mr. Godfrey Colston, 86, former Chairman of Colston Breweries, is also among the victims of the hoax, said yesterday, "We are not in the least perturbed by the caller. He is a very civil young man."

A C.I.D. spokesman said everything possible is being done to discover the offender.

Henry Mortimer put down the paper and took the cup his wife was passing him.

"An extraordinary sort of case," she said.

"Embarrassing for the police," he said, "poor fellows."

"Oh, they'll get the culprit, won't they?"

"I don't see," he said, "how they ever can, all evidence considered."

"Well, you know the evidence, of course."

"And considering the evidence," he said, "in my opinion the offender is Death himself."

She was not really surprised to hear him say this. She had followed his mind all through its conforming life and late independence, so that nothing he said could surprise her very much. He had lived to see his children cease to take him seriously—his word carried more force in the outside world. Even his older grand-children, though they loved him, would never now understand his value to others. He knew this; he did not care. Emmeline could never, however, regard Henry as a dear old thing who had taken to developing a philosophy, as other men, on their retirement, might cultivate a hobby. She did not entirely let her children see how she felt, for she liked to please them and seem solid and practical in their eyes. But she trusted Henry, and she could not help doing so.

She let him busy himself in the garden before she sent him indoors to rest. A few more weeks and he would be watching the post for that particular letter from his old friend in the country inviting him to come for a fortnight's fishing. It seemed miraculous that another spring had begun and that soon Henry would announce, "I've heard from Harry. The *mayfly's* on the river. I'd better be off day after tomorrow." Then she would be alone for a while, or perhaps one of the girls would come to stay after Easter and the younger children would roll over and over on the lawn if it was dry enough.

She sowed her parsley, and wondered excitedly what the deputation who were calling to see Henry this afternoon would look like.

The Mortimers' house at Kingston-on-Thames was not difficult to reach, if one followed Henry's directions. However the deputation had found it a difficult place to find. They arrived shaken in nerve and body, half an hour late in Godfrey's car and two taxis. In Godfrey's car, besides Godfrey himself, were Charmian, Dame Lettie and Mrs. Pettigrew. The first taxi bore Alec Warner and Dame Lettie's maid, Gwen. In the second taxi came Janet Sidebottome, that missionary sister of Lisa Brooke; accompanying her were an elderly couple and an aged spinster who were strangers to the rest.

Mrs. Pettigrew, spruce and tailor-made, stepped out first. Henry Mortimer came beaming down the path and shook her hand. Godfrey emerged next, and meantime there was a general exit from the two taxis, and a fussy finding and counting of money for the fares.

Charmian, from the back of Godfrey's car, said, "Oh, I have so enjoyed the drive. My first this year. The river is splendid to-day."

"Wait a minute, wait a minute, Godfrey," said Dame Lettie who was being helped out. "Don't pull me." She had grown stouter and yet more fragile during the past winter. Her sight was failing, and it was obviously difficult for her to find the kerb with her foot. "Wait, Godfrey."

"We're late," said Godfrey. "Charmian, sit still, don't move till we've got Lettie out."

Mrs. Pettigrew took Dame Lettie's other arm while Henry Mortimer stood holding the door. Lettie yanked her arm away from Mrs. Pettigrew, so that her handbag dropped to the pavement and the contents spilled out. The occupants of the taxis rushed to rescue Lettie's belongings, while Lettie herself drew back into the car and sank with a plump sound into her seat.

Young Gwen, whom Dame Lettie had brought as a witness, stood in the gateway and laughed aloud.

Mrs. Mortimer came briskly down the path and addressed Gwen. "Look lively, young person," she said, "and help your elders instead of standing there laughing."

Gwen looked surprised and did not move.

"Go and pick up your aunt's belongings," said Mrs. Mortimer.

Dame Lettie, fearful of losing her maid, called out from the car,

"I'm not her aunt, Mrs. Mortimer. It's all right, Gwen."

Mrs. Mortimer, who was not normally an irate woman, took Gwen by the shoulders and propelled her over to the little group who were stiffly bending to retrieve the contents of the bag. "Let the girl pick them up," she said.

Most of the things were, however by now collected, and while Alec Warner, directed by Henry Mortimer, stooped to fish with his umbrella under the car for Dame Lettie's spectacle-case, Gwen so far overcame her surprise as to say to Mrs. Mortimer, "I got nothing to do with *you*."

"All right, Gwen. It's all right," said Dame Lettie from the car.

Mrs. Mortimer now kept her peace although it was clear she would have liked to say more to Gwen. She had been troubled, in the first place, by the sight of these infirm and agitated people arriving with such difficulty at her door. Where are their children? she had thought, or their nieces and nephews? Why are they left to their own resources like this?

She edged Gwen aside and reached into the car for Dame Lettie's arm. At the opposite door Henry Mortimer was reaching for Charmian's. Mrs. Mortimer, as she assisted Dame Lettie, hoped he would not strain himself, and said to Dame Lettie, "I see you have brought the spring weather." As Lettie finally came to rest on the pavement Mrs. Mortimer looked up to see Alec Warner's eyes upon her. She thought, That man is studying me for some reason.

Charmian tottered gaily up the path on Henry Mortimer's arm. He was telling her he had just read, once more, her novel *The Gates of Grandella* in its fine new edition.

"It is over fifty years," said Charmian, "since *I* read it."

"It captures the period," said Mortimer. "Oh, it brings everything back. I do recommend you to read it again."

Charmian slid her eyes flirtatiously towards him—that gesture which the young reporters who came to see her found so enchanting—and said, "You are too young, Henry, to remember when the book first came out."

"No indeed," he said, "I was already a police constable. And a constable never forgets."

"What a charming house," said Charmian, and she

caught sight of Godfrey waiting inside the hall, and felt she was, as always when people made a fuss over her, making him sick.

The conference did not start for some time. Emmeline Mortimer consulted in low tones with the ladies of the deputation in the hall, whether they would first like to go "upstairs," or, if the stairs were too much for them, there was a place downstairs, straight through the kitchen, turn right. "Charmian," said Mrs. Pettigrew out loud, "come and make yourself comfortable. I'll take you. Come along."

Henry Mortimer piled the men's coats and hats neatly on a chest, and, having shown the way upstairs to the male candidates, ushered the rest of the men into the dining-room where, at the long table, bare except for a vase of shining daffodils, and at the top, a thick file of papers, Gwen was already seated, fuming sulkily to herself.

When Godfrey came in he glanced round at the furnishings with an enquiring air.

"Is this the right room?" he said.

Alec Warner thought: He is probably looking for signs of a tea-tray. He probably thinks we are not going to get any tea.

"Yes, I think this is most suitable," said Henry, as one taking him into consultation. "Don't you? We can sit round the table and talk things over before tea."

"Oh!" said Godfrey. Alec Warner congratulated himself.

At last they were settled round the table, the three strangers having been introduced as a Miss Lottinville and a Mr. and Mrs. Jack Rose. Mrs. Mortimer withdrew and the door clicked behind her like a signal for the start of business. The sunlight fell mildly upon the table and the people round it, showing up motes of dust in the air, specks of dust on the clothes of those who wore black, the wrinkled cheeks and hands of the aged, and the thick make-up of Gwen.

Charmian, who was enthroned in the most comfortable chair, spoke first, "What a charming room."

"It gets the afternoon sun," Henry said. "Is it too much for anyone? Charmian—another cushion."

The three strangers looked uneasily at each other, simply because they were strangers and not, like the others, known to each other for forty, fifty years it might be.

Godfrey moved his arm to shoot back his sleeve, and said, "This telephone man, Mortimer, I must say, it's a bit thick—"

"I have a copy of your statement here, Colston," said Henry Mortimer, opening his file. "I propose to read each one aloud by turn, and you may add any further comments after I have read it. Does that course meet with approval?"

No one seriously disagreed with that course.

Gwen looked out of the window. Janet Sidebottome fiddled with the electric battery of her elaborate hearing-aid. Mrs. Pettigrew laid her arm on the table and her chin on her hand and looked intense. Charmian sat with her heart-shaped face composed beneath her new blue hat. Alec Warner looked carefully at the strangers, first at Mrs. Rose then at Mr. Rose and then at Miss Lottinville. Mrs. Rose had her eyebrows perpetually raised in resignation, furrowing deep lines into her forehead. Mr. Rose held his head sideways; he had enormous shoulders; his large mouth drooped downwards at the same degree of curvature as his chin, cheeks and nose. The Roses must be nearly eighty, perhaps more. Miss Lottinville looked small and slight and angry. The left side of her mouth and her right eye kept twitching simultaneously.

Henry Mortimer's voice was not too official, but it was firm:

". . . just after eleven in the morning . . . on three separate occasions . . . It sounded like that of a common man. The tone was menacing. The words on each occasion were . . ."

". . . at various times throughout the day . . . the first occasion was on 12th March. The words were . . . The tone was strictly factual. . . . He sounded young, like a Teddy-boy. . . ."

". . . first thing on the morning . . . every week since the end of August last. It was the voice of a cultured, middle-aged man . . . the tone is sinister in the extreme. . . ."

"It was the voice of a very civil young man. . . ." This was Charmian's account. Godfrey broke in. "How could he be a civil young man saying a thing like that? Use your head, Charmian."

"He was," said Charmian, "most civil on all three occasions."

"Perhaps," said Henry, "if I could continue . . . ? Then Charmian can add her comments."

He finished Charmian's statement. "That is correct," said Charmian.

"How could he be *civil?*" said Godfrey.

"Mr. Guy Leet," Henry announced, taking up the next paper. "Oh, Guy isn't here, of course—"

"Guy asked me to say," said Alec, "we could discuss his case as much as we like so long as we don't discuss his private life up to 1940."

"Has to get about on two sticks," commented Godfrey.

"Guy's account," said Henry, "is substantially the same as the others, with the most interesting exception that he gets Tol calls from London at between six and seven in the evening when the cheap rate is on. In his opinion the offender is a schoolboy."

"Nonsense," said Dame Lettie. "A middle-aged man."

"It is simple," said Henry, "to trace a Tol call from London to the country. And yet the police have not yet traced any caller to Guy Leet at Stedrost."

"Quite," said Dame Lettie. "The police—"

"However, we will discuss these factors later," said Henry. "Next Mr. Ronald Sidebottome— Oh, Ronald's not here either. What's happened to Ronald, Janet?"

"He was a youth—a Teddy-boy, as I've said," Janet Sidebottome replied.

"Ronald" roared Godfrey into her ear. "Why hasn't Ronald turned up? He said he was coming."

"Oh, Ronald. Well, he was to call for me. I suppose he forgot. It was most annoying. I waited and then I rang him up but he wasn't at home. I really can't answer for Ronald these days. He is never at home."

Alec Warner took out a small diary and scribbled something in pencil.

"Ronald's statement," said Mortimer, "describes the caller as a man well advanced in years with a cracked and rather shaky voice and a suppliant tone."

"There must be something wrong with his phone," said Dame Lettie. "The man's voice is strong and sinister. A man of middle years. You must remember, Henry, that I have had far more experience of the creature than anyone else."

"Yes, Lettie, my dear, I admit you have been greatly tried. Now Miss Lottinville, your statement . . . 'At three o'clock in the morning . . . A foreigner . . .' "

Mrs. Mortimer put her head round the door. "Tea is ready, Henry, when you are. I have laid it in the breakfast room so that—'

"In five minutes, Emmeline."

She disappeared and Godfrey looked yearningly after her.

"Finally, Mr. Rose," said Henry. " 'I received the call at my business premises at twelve noon on two days running . . . the man sounded like an official person . . . late middle age. . . .' "

"That sounds accurate," said Dame Lettie. "Only I would describe the voice as *sinister*."

"Did he have a lisp?" said Godfrey.

"Mr. Rose has not mentioned a lisp in his statement—Had he a lisp, Mr. Rose?" said Henry.

"No, no. Like an official. My wife says an army man, but I would say a government chap."

Everyone spoke at once.

"Oh no," said Janet Sidebottome, "he was—"

"A gang," said Dame Lettie, "there must be a gang."

Miss Lottinville said: "I assure you, Chief Inspector, he—"

Henry waited for a while till the noise subsided. He said to Mr. Rose,

"Are you satisfied with your account as I have read it?"

"A hundred per cent," said Mr. Rose.

"Then let's continue the discussion after tea," said Henry.

Miss Lottinville said: "You have not read the statement of this lady on my left." The lady on her left was Mrs. Pettigrew. "*I* haven't had any of your phone calls," she said. "I've made no statement."

Alec Warner wondered, from the vehemence of her tone, if she were lying.

Mrs. Mortimer sat with her silver tea-pot poised at a well-spread table.

"Come and sit by me," she said kindly to Gwen, "and you can help to pass the cups."

Gwen lit a cigarette and sat down sideways at the place indicated.

"Have you been afflicted with these phone calls?" Emmeline Mortimer asked her.

"Me? No, I get wrong numbers."

Mrs. Pettigrew said confidentially to Mrs. Mortimer: "I've had no trouble myself from any phone calls. Between ourselves, I think it's all made up. I don't believe a word of what they say. They're trying to draw attention to themselves. Like kids."

"What a delightful garden," said Charmian.

They were assembled once more in the dining-room where a fire sparkled weakly in the sunlight.

Henry Mortimer said: "If I had my life over again I should form the habit of nightly composing myself to thoughts of death. I would practise, as it were, the remembrance of death. There is no other practise which so intensifies life. Death, when it approaches, ought not to take one by surprise. It should be part of the full expectancy of life. Without an ever-present sense of death life is insipid. You might as well live on the whites of eggs."

Dame Lettie said suddenly and sharply, "Who is the man, Henry?"

"My dear Lettie. I can't help you, there."

She looked so closely at him, he felt almost that she suspected himself.

"Lettie thinks you are the man," said Alec wickedly.

"I hardly think," said Henry, "Lettie would attribute to me such energy and application as the culprit evidently possesses."

"All we want," said Godfrey, "is to stop him. And to do that we've got to find the man."

"I consider," said Janet Sidebottome, "that what Mr. Mortimer was saying just now about resigning ourselves to death is most uplifting and consoling. The religious point of view is too easily forgotten these days, and I thank you, Mr. Mortimer."

"Why, thank you, Janet. Perhaps 'resigning ourselves to death' doesn't quite convey what I mean. But of course, I don't attempt to express a specifically religious point of view. My observations were merely confined—"

"You sound most religious to me," said Janet.

"Thank you, Janet."

"Poor young man," mused Charmian. "He may be lonely, and simply wanting to talk to people and so he rings them up."

"The police, of course, are hopeless. Really, Henry, it is time there was a question in the House," said Lettie warningly.

"Considering the fairly wide discrepancies in your various reports," said Henry, "the police at one stage in their investigations assumed that not one man but a gang was at work. The police have, however, employed every method of detection known to criminology and science, so far without success. Now, one factor is constant in all your reports. The words, 'Remember you must die.' It is, you know, an excellent thing to remember this, for it is nothing more than the truth. To remember one's death is, in short, a way of life."

"To come to the point—" said Godfrey.

"Godfrey," said Charmian, "I am sure everyone is fascinated by what Henry is saying."

"Most consoling," said Janet Sidebottome. "Do continue, Mr. Mortimer, with your words."

"Ah yes," said Miss Lottinville who was also enjoying Henry's philosophising.

And Mrs. Rose, with her longanimous eyes and resignation, nodded her head in sad, wise and ancient assent.

"Have you considered," said Alec Warner, "the possibility of mass hysteria?"

"Making telephones ring?" said Mr. Rose, spreading wide his palms.

"Absurd!" said Dame Lettie. "We can eliminate mass hysteria."

"Oh no," said Mortimer. "In a case like this we can't eliminate any possibility. That is just our difficulty."

"Tell me," Alec asked the Chief Inspector with his piercing look, "would you describe yourself as a mystic?"

538

"Never having previously been called upon to describe myself, I really couldn't say."

"The question is," said Mr. Rose, "who's the fellow that's trying to put the fear of God in us?"

"And what's the motive?" said Godfrey. "That's what I ask."

"The question of motive may prove to be different in each case, to judge by the evidence before us," said Mortimer. "I think we must all realise that the offender is, in each case, whoever we think he is ourselves."

"Did you tell them," said Emmeline Mortimer when they had gone, "what your theory is?"

"No—oh no, my dear. I treated them to brief philosophical sermons instead. It helped to pass the time."

"Did they like your little sermons?"

"Some of the women did. The young girl seemed less bored than at other times. Lettie objected."

"Oh, Lettie."

"She said the whole afternoon had been pointless."

"How rude. After my lovely tea."

"It was a lovely tea. It was my part that was pointless. I'm afraid it had to be."

"How I wish," said Emmeline, "you could have told them outright, 'Death is the culprit.' And I should like to have seen their faces."

"It's a personal opinion. One can't make up one's mind for others."

"Can they make up their own minds, then?"

"No. I think I'll go and spray the pears."

"Now, darling," said Mrs. Mortimer. "You know you've done enough for one day. I'm sure it's been quite enough for me."

"The trouble with these people," he said, "they think that the C.I.D. are God, understanding all mysteries and all knowledge. Whereas we are only policemen."

He went to read by the fire in the dining-room. Before he sat down he straightened the chairs round the table and put back some of them in their places round the wall. He emptied the ash-trays into the fire. He looked out of the window at the half-light and hoped for a fine summer. He had not mentioned it to Emmeline yet, but this summer he hoped to sail that yacht of his for which, in his retirement, he had sacrificed a car. Already he could feel the bright wet wind about his ears.

The telephone rang. He went out to the hall, answered it. Within a few seconds he put down the receiver. How strange, he thought, that mine is always a woman. Everyone else gets a man on the line to them, but mine is always this woman, gentle-spoken and respectful.

Chapter Twelve

"I told him straight what I feel," said Mrs. Pettigrew to Mrs. Anthony. "I said, 'It's all a lot of rot, Inspector. It started with Dame Lettie Colston, then Godfrey feels he's got to be in the picture and one sets off the other. To my dying day I'll swear it's all make up.' But he didn't side with me. Why? I'll tell you why. He'd be put out of Dame Lettie's will if he agreed it was all her imagination."

Mrs. Pettigrew, though she had in fact, one quiet afternoon, received the anonymous telephone call, had chosen to forget it. She possessed a strong faculty for simply refusing to admit an unpleasant situation, and to go quite blank where it was concerned. If, for instance, you had asked her whether, eighteen years before she had undergone a face-lifting operation, she would have denied it, and believed the denial, and moreover would have supplied gratuitously, as a special joke, a list of people who had, "really" had their faces lifted or undergone other rejuvenating operations.

And so Mrs. Pettigrew continued to persuade herself she had not heard the anonymous voice on the telephone; it was not a plain ignoring of the incident; she omitted even to keep a mental record of it, but put down the receiver and blacked it out from her life.

"A lot of imagination all round," said Mrs. Pettigrew.

"Ah well," said Mrs. Anthony, "we all got to go some

day. But I shouldn't like to have that chap on the phone to me. I'd give him something to get along with."

"There isn't any chap," said Mrs. Pettigrew. "You hear what I say?"

"I got my deaf-aid in, and I hear what you say. No need to raise your voice."

Mrs. Pettigrew was overcome by that guilt she felt whenever she had lowered herself to the intimacy of shouting at Mrs. Anthony, forgetting to play her cards. By way of recompense she left the kitchen aloofly, and went to find Godfrey.

He was sitting by the fire, maddeningly, opposite Charmian.

"Please, Godfrey, let us not have all this over again. Ah, it's you, Mrs. Pettigrew," said Charmian.

"She is not Taylor," said Godfrey, with automatic irritability.

"I know it," said Charmian.

He looked unhappily at Mrs. Pettigrew. There was really no consolation left in the house for a man. He was all the more disturbed by Charmian's increasing composure. It was not that he wished his wife any harm, but his spirits always seemed to wither in proportion as hers bloomed. He thought, looking at his wife, It is only for a time, this can't last, she will have a relapse. He felt he was an old man in difficulties. Mrs. Pettigrew had made another appointment for his lawyer that afternoon. He did not feel up to keeping it. He supposed he would have to see the lawyer some time, but that long fruitless going to and from Kingston yesterday had left him exhausted. And that madman Mortimer, making a fuss over Charmian—everyone making a fuss over Charmian, as if she were still somebody and not a helpless old invalid—roused within him all those resentments of the long past; so that, having made the mistake of regarding Charmian's every

542

success as his failure, now, by force of habit, he could never feel really well unless she were ill.

Charmian was saying to him, "We did talk over the whole matter quite a lot last night. Let us leave the subject alone. I for one like Henry Mortimer, and I thoroughly enjoyed the drive."

Mrs. Pettigrew, too, was alarmed by this mental recovery of Charmian's, induced apparently, by the revival of those old books. In reality it was also, in part, due to an effortful will to resist Mrs. Pettigrew's bullying. Mrs. Pettigrew felt that there might now even be some chance of Charmian's outliving Godfrey. Charmian should be in a home, and would be, if Godfrey were not weak-minded about it, trying to play on his wife's sympathy and keep her with him.

Godfrey looked across the fireplace at his ally and enemy, Charmian, and at Mabel Pettigrew, whom he so tremendously feared, sitting between them, and decided to give Mrs. Pettigrew the slip again this afternoon and go to see Olive.

Mabel Pettigrew thought: I can read him like a book. She had not read a book for over forty years, could never concentrate on reading, but this nevertheless was her thought; and she decided to accompany him to the solicitor.

After Charmian had gone to lie down after lunch Mrs. Pettigrew came in to her.

Charmian opened her eyes. "I didn't hear you knock, Mabel," she said.

"No," said Mrs. Pettigrew. "You didn't."

"Always knock," said Charmian.

"Mrs. Anthony," said Mrs. Pettigrew, "is getting too forgetful to manage the cooking. She has left out the salt three days running, as you know. There was a caterpillar cooked in yesterday's greens. She put all that garlic in the sweetbread casserole, said she thought it was celery—well

I mean to say. She boiled Godfrey's egg hard this morning, he couldn't touch it."

"Keep an eye on her, Mabel. You have little else to do."

Mrs. Pettigrew's feelings—those which prompted every action—rose to her throat at this independent attitude which Charmian had been gradually accumulating all winter. Mrs. Pettigrew's breath, as she stood over Charmian's bed became short and agitated.

"Sit down, Mabel. You are out of breath," said Charmian.

Mrs. Pettigrew sat down. Charmian watched her, trying to sort out in her mind this new complaint about Mrs. Anthony, and what it could signify, apart from its plain meaning. Her thoughts drifted once more, for reassurance, to the nursing home in Surrey, in the same way that, as she knew, Jean Taylor's thoughts would, in the past, rest on her savings in the bank when from time to time her life with the Colstons had become too oppressive.

Mrs. Pettigrew's breathing was worse. She had been suddenly caught in a gust of resentment which had been stirring within her since Charmian's partial recovery. She felt a sense of great injustice at the evident power Charmian exerted over Godfrey—so strong that she did not seem conscious of it. It was a spell of her personality so mighty that, for fear of his miserable infidelities in Spain and Belgium with Lisa Brooke coming to Charmian's knowledge, he had been, so far, docile before all the threats and deprivations of the past winter. Mabel Pettigrew had only needed to indicate that she was in possession of the full correspondence between Lisa Brooke and Godfrey, dated 1902, 1903 and 1904, and his one immediate idea had been: Charmian must not know. Tell Eric, tell everyone. But keep it from Charmian.

Mrs. Pettigrew was aware that in this he was not displaying any special consideration for Charmian's feelings. That might have been endurable. The real reason was

beyond her grasp, yet undeniably present. It was real enough to render Godfrey limp in her hands. What he seemed to fear was some superiority in Charmian and the loss of his pride before her. And, though Mabel Pettigrew indeed was doing better out of Godfrey than she had hoped, she sat in Charmian's bedroom and overwhelmingly resented the inexplicableness of Charmian's power.

"You seem to have a mild touch of asthma," Charmian remarked. "Better keep as still and quiet as possible and presently I will get Godfrey to ring the doctor."

Mrs. Pettigrew was thinking of that business scandal at Colston Breweries which had been hushed up at the time, the documents of which she now had in her keeping. Now, if Godfrey had been really frightened about her possible disclosure of these documents she would have understood him. But all he worried about were those letters between himself and Lisa Brooke. Charmian must not know. His pride before Charmian, Charmian, an old wreck like Charmian.

Charmian stretched her hand towards the bell-push by her bed. "Godfrey will ring for the doctor," she said.

"No, no, I'm better now," said Mrs. Pettigrew, gradually controlling her breath, for she had the self-discipline of a nun where business was concerned. "It was just a little turn. Mrs. Anthony is such a worry."

Charmian leaned back on her pillow and moved her hand wearily over her heart-shaped face. "Have you had asthma before, Mabel?"

"It is not asthma. It's just a little chest trouble." Mrs. Pettigrew's face was less alarmingly red. She breathed slowly and deeply after her ordeal, and lit a cigarette.

"You have great courage, Mabel," Charmian observed, "if only you would employ it to the proper ends. I envy your courage. I sometimes feel helpless without my friends around me. Very few of my friends come to see me now. It isn't their fault. Godfrey did not seem to want them after my stroke. When my friends were around me every day, what courage I had!"

"You would be better off in the home," said Mabel Pettigrew. "You know you would. Lots of company, your friends might even come and visit you sometimes."

"It's true I would prefer to be in the nursing home. However," said Charmian, "Godfrey needs me here."

"That's where you're wrong," said Mrs. Pettigrew.

Charmian wondered, once more, which of Godfrey's secrets the woman could have got hold of. The Colston Brewery affair? Or merely one or more of his numerous infidelities? Of course, one was always obliged to appear to know nothing where a man like Godfrey was concerned. His pride. It had been the only way to live reasonably with him. For a moment, she was tempted to go to Godfrey and say, "There is nothing you can tell me about your past life which would move me in the slightest. I know most of your supposed secrets, and what I do not know would still not surprise me."

But she did not possess the courage to do this. He might—he would certainly—turn on her. He would never forgive her for having played this game, for over fifty years, of knowing nothing while at the same time knowing everything, as one might be "not at home" while actually in the house. What new tyranny might he not exert to punish her knowledge?

And the simple idea of *facing* each other with such a statement between them was terrible. This should have been done years ago. And yet, it should not have been done. There was altogether too much candour in married life; it was an indelicate modern idea, and frequently led to upsets in a household, if not divorce. . . .

And she, too, had her pride to consider. Her mind munched over the humiliations she had received from Godfrey. Never had she won a little praise or recognition but she had paid for it by some bitter, petty, disruptive action of Godfrey's.

But I could sacrifice my pride, she thought, in order to release him. It is a matter of courage. The most I can do is to stay on here at home with him. She envied Mrs. Pettigrew her courage.

Mrs. Pettigrew rose and came to stand by her bed.

"You're more of a hindrance to Godfrey here than you would be in a nursing home. It's ridiculous to say he needs you."

"I shall not go," said Charmian. "Now I think I must have my nap. What is the time?"

"I came," said Mrs. Pettigrew, "to tell you about Mrs. Anthony. She can't do the cooking any more, we shall all have stomach trouble. I will have to take over the meals. And besides, this cold supper she leaves for us at night is not satisfactory. It doesn't agree with me, going to bed on a cold supper. I will have to take over the cooking."

"That is very good of you," murmured Charmian, calculating meanwhile what was behind all this, since, with Mrs. Pettigrew, something always seemed to be behind her statements.

"Otherwise," said Mrs. Pettigrew, "one of us might be poisoned."

"Well, really!" said Charmian.

"*Poisoned*," said Mrs. Pettigrew. "Poison is so easy. Think it over."

She left the room.

Charmian was frightened, and at the same time a long-latent faculty stirred in her mind to assess the cheap melodrama of Mrs. Pettigrew's words. But Charmian's fear predominated in the end, and, as she lay fearfully in her bed, she knew she would not put it past Mrs. Pettigrew to poison her once she took control of the food. A poisoning was not easy to accomplish, but still Mrs. Pettigrew might know of undetectable methods. Charmian thought on and on, and frightened herself more and more. Another woman, she thought, would be able to go to her husband and say, "Our housekeeper is threatening to poison me" —or to insist on an investigation by her friends, her son, the doctor. But Godfrey was craven, Eric was hostile, the doctor would attempt to soothe her down, assuming she had started to entertain those wild suspicions of the aged.

Then it is settled, Charmian thought. This is the point where my long, long duty to Godfrey comes to an end. I shall go to the nursing home.

The decision gave her a sense of latitude and relief. In the nursing home she could be a real person again, as she had been yesterday with Henry Mortimer, instead of a frightened invalid. She needed respect and attention. Perhaps she would have visitors. There, she could invite those whom she was prevented from seeing here at home through Godfrey's rudeness. The nursing home was not far from Stedrost. Perhaps Guy Leet would be driven over to see her. Guy Leet was amusing.

She heard the front door slam and then the slam of the car door. Mrs. Pettigrew's footsteps followed immediately, clicking towards the front door. Charmian heard her open the door and call, "Godfrey, I'm coming with you. Wait." But the car had already started and Godfrey was gone. Mrs. Pettigrew slammed the door shut once more and went to her room. A few seconds later she had descended the stairs and left the house.

Mrs. Pettigrew had informed Godfrey of her intention of accompanying him to his solicitor. When she found he had once given her the slip she felt pretty sure he had no intention of keeping his appointment with the lawyer. Within a few moments she had put on her hat and coat and marched up the road to find a taxi.

First of all she went to the bombed building off the King's Road. There, sure enough, was Godfrey's car.

There was, however, no sign of Godfrey. She ordered the taxi to drive round the block in a hope that she would catch Godfrey before he reached his destination, wherever that might be.

Godfrey, meanwhile, was on his way to Olive's flat, about seven minutes' walk for him at his fastest pace. He turned into Tite Street, stooping his head still more than his natural stoop, against a sudden shower of rain. He hoped Olive would have tea ready. He hoped Olive would not have any other visitors to-day, obliging him to enquire, in that foolish way, for the address of her grandfather. Olive would be in a listening mood, she was a good consoling listener. She would probably have heard from Eric. Godfrey wondered what she had heard from Eric. Olive had promised to write and tell Eric, in strictest confidence, about his difficulties with Mrs. Pettigrew. She had promised to appeal to Eric. Eric would no doubt be only too glad to be on good terms with his parents again. Eric had been a disappointment, but now was his chance to prove himself. Eric would put everything right, and no doubt Olive had heard from Eric.

He reached the area gate and pushed it open. There was an unusual amount of litter down in the area. The dust-bin was crammed full; old shoes, handbags and belts were sticking out beneath the lid. On the area pavement were scattered newspapers, tins, rusty kitchen utensils, empty bottles of numerous shapes, and a battered lampshade. Godfrey thought: Olive must be having a spring-clean, turning out all her things. Very wasteful and untidy. Always complaining of being hard up; no wonder.

No one answered his ring. He walked over to the barred window of Olive's front room and it was then he noticed the curtains had gone. He peered in. The room was quite bare. Must he not have come to the wrong house? He walked up the steps and looked carefully at the number. He walked down the steps again and peered once more into the empty room. Olive had definitely departed. And on realising this his first thought was to leave the vicinity of the house as quickly as possible. There was something mysterious about this. Godfrey could not stand anything mysterious. Olive might be involved in some scandal. She had said nothing, when he had seen her last week, about moving from her flat. As he walked away down Tite Street he feared more and more some swift, sudden scandal, and his one desire was to forget all knowledge of Olive.

He cut along the King's Road, bought an afternoon paper, and turned up the side street where his car was waiting. Before he reached it a taxi drew up beside him. Mrs. Pettigrew got out.

"Oh, there you are," she said.

He stood with the newspaper hanging from his hand while she paid the taxi, bewildered by guilt. This guilt was the main sensation Mrs. Pettigrew touched off in him. No thought, word or deed of his life had roused in him any feeling resembling the guilt he experienced as he stood waiting for Mrs. Pettigrew to pay the taxi and turn to ask him, "Where have you been?"

"Buying the paper," said Godfrey.

"Did you have to park your car here in order to walk down the road to buy the paper?"

"Wanted a walk," said Godfrey. "Bit stiff."

"You'll be late for your appointment. Hurry up. I told you to wait for me. Why did you go off without me?"

"I forgot," said Godfrey as he climbed into the car, "that you wanted to come. I was in a hurry to get to the lawyer's." She went round to the other side of the car and got in.

"You might have opened the door for me," she said.

Godfrey did not at first understand what she meant, for he had long since started to use his advanced years as an excuse to omit the mannerly conformities of his younger days, and he was now automatically rude in his gestures as if by long-earned right. He sensed some new frightful upheaval of his habits behind her words, as he drove off fitfully towards Sloane Square.

She lifted the paper and glanced at the front page.

"Ronald," she said. "Here's Ronald Sidebottome in the paper. His photo; he's got married. No, don't look. Watch where you're going, we'll have an accident. Mind out—there's the red light."

They were jerked forward roughly as Godfrey braked for the red light.

"Oh, do be careful," she said, "and a little more considerate."

He looked down at her lap where the paper was lying. Ronald's flabby face beamed up at him. He stood with Olive simpering on his arm, under the headline, "Widower, 79, weds girl, 24."

"Olive Mannering!" Godfrey let out.

"Oh, you know her?"

"Grand-daughter of my friend the poet," Godfrey said.

"The lights, Godfrey," said Mrs. Pettigrew in a tired tone.

He shot the car forward.

" 'Wealthy ex-stockbroker . . .' " Mrs. Pettigrew read out. "She knows what she's doing, all right. 'Miss Mannering . . . film extra and B.B.C. actress . . . now given up her flat in Tite Street, Chelsea . . .' " The jig-saw began to piece itself together in Mrs. Pettigrew's mind. As heart is said to speak unto heart, Mrs. Pettigrew looked at Olive's photograph and understood where Godfrey had been wont to go on those afternoons when he had parked his car outside the bombed building.

"Of course, Godfrey, this will be a blow to you," she said.

He thought: God, she knows everything. He went up to his solicitor's offices like a lamb, while Mrs. Pettigrew waited in the car below. He did not even attempt to circumvent her wishes, as he had half-hoped to do when finally forced to the alteration of his will. He did not now even think of the idea he had previously dabbled with, of confiding the facts to his lawyer. Mabel Pettigrew knew everything. She could tell Charmian everything. He instructed a new will to be drawn up leaving the minimum required by law to his son, and the bulk to Mrs. Pettigrew, and even most of Charmian's share, should she outlive him, in trust for Mrs. Pettigrew.

"Now," said the solicitor. "This might take some time to prepare, of course."

"It must be done right away," said Godfrey.

"Would you not like some time, Mr. Colston, to think it over? Mrs. Pettigrew is your housekeeper?"

"It must be done right away," said Godfrey. "No delay, if you please."

"Disgusting," said Godfrey later that evening to Charmian. "A man going on eighty marrying a girl of twenty-four. Absolutely disgusting. And he's deaf as a post."

"Godfrey," she said, "I am going to the nursing home on Sunday morning. I have made arrangements with the doctor and the bank. Universal Aunts are coming to-morrow to pack my things. Janet Sidebottome will accompany me. I do not wish to put you out, Godfrey. It might distress you to take me yourself. I am afraid I simply can't stand these anonymous telephone calls any longer. They will bring me speedily to my grave. I must be protected from the sight of the telephone. I have spoken to Lettie, and she approves my decision. Mrs. Pettigrew thinks, too, it will be the best course—don't you, Mabel? Everyone is agreed. I must say, I feel most sad. However, it had to be eventually. You yourself have often said—"

"But you don't mind the telephone calls!" he shouted. "You don't care about them at all."

"Oh yes, I do, I do. I can't put up with them any longer."

"She does mind them," said Mrs. Pettigrew.

"But you don't need to answer the phone," he shouted.

"Oh but every time the telephone rings I feel it must be *him*." Charmian gave a little shudder.

"She feels so bad about the telephone," said Mrs. Pettigrew.

He knew he could not refute their words.

Chapter Thirteen

"What surprised me, I must confess," Alec Warner said to Miss Taylor, "was that, for a moment or two, I felt positively jealous. Olive, of course, was a friendly type of girl, and most conscientious in giving me all the information she could gather. I shall miss her. But the curious thing was this pang, this envy of Ronald, my first reaction to the news. Not that Olive, at any time, would have been my type."

"Did you make a note of your reaction?"

"Oh, I made a note."

I bet he did, thought Miss Taylor.

"Oh, I made a note. I always record these surprise deviations from my High-Churchmanship."

His "High-Churchmanship" was a figure of speech he had adopted from Jean Taylor when, at some buoyant time past, she had applied it to him, merely on account of the two occasions when he had darkened the doors of a church, to observe, with awe and curiosity, a vicar of his acquaintance conducting the service of evensong all by himself in the empty building; Alec's awe and curiosity being directed exclusively towards the human specimen with his prayer book and splendid persistence in vital habits.

"Granny Green has gone," said Miss Taylor.

"Ah yes, I noticed a stranger occupying her bed. Now what was Granny Green?"

"Arterio-sclerosis. It affected her heart in the end."

"Yes, well, it is said we are all as old as our arteries. Did she make a good death?"

"I don't know."

"You were asleep at the time," he said.

"No, I was awake. There was a certain amount of fuss."

"She didn't have a peaceful end?"

"No, not peaceful for us."

"I always like to know," he said, "whether a death is a good or bad one. Do keep a look out."

For a moment she utterly hated him. "A good death," she said, "doesn't reside in the dignity of bearing but in the disposition of the soul."

Suddenly he hated her. "Prove it," he said.

"Disprove it," she said wearily.

"I'm afraid," he said, "I've forgotten to ask how you are keeping. How are you keeping, Jean?"

"A little stronger, but the cataract is a trouble."

"Charmian is gone to the nursing home in Surrey at last. Would you not like to join her there?"

"Godfrey is left alone with Mrs. Pettigrew, then."

"You would like to be with Charmian, surely."

"No," she said.

He looked round the ward and up to the noisy end. There the senile cases were grouped round the television and so were less noisy than usual, but still emitting, from time to time, a variety of dental and guttural sounds and sometimes a whole, well-intentioned speech. Those who were mobile would occasionally leave their chairs and wander up the ward, waving or talking to the bedridden. One tall patient poured herself a beaker of water and began to raise it to her lips, but forgetting the purpose before the act was accomplished, poured the water into another jug; then she turned the beaker upside down on her head so that a little water, left in the beaker, splashed over her forehead. She seemed pleased with this feat. On the whole, the geriatrics were keen on putting objects on their heads.

"Interesting," said Alec. "The interesting thing is, senility is somewhat different from insanity. The actions of these people, for instance, differ in many particulars from those of the aged people whom I visit at St. Aubrey's Home in Folkestone. There, some of the patients have been mad most of their lives. In some ways they are more coherent, much more methodical than those who merely turn strange in their old age. The really mad old people have had more practice in irrational behavior, of course. But all this," said Alec, "cannot be of much interest to you. Unless one is interested in gerontology, I cannot see that their company, day and night, can be pleasant to you."

"Perhaps I'm a gerontologist at heart. They are harmless. I don't mind them, now. Alec, I am thinking of poor Godfrey Colston. What can have possessed Charmian to go away just when her health was improving?"

"The anonymous telephone calls were worrying her, she said."

"Oh no. Mrs. Pettigrew must have forced her to go. And Mrs. Pettigrew," said Miss Taylor, "will most certainly make Godfrey's remaining years a misery."

He reached for his hat. "Think over," he said, "the idea of joining Charmian in the nursing home. It would so please me if you would."

"Now Alec, I can't leave my old friends. Miss Valvona, Miss Duncan—"

"And this?" He nodded towards the senile group.

"That is our memento mori. Like your telephone calls."

"Goodbye then, Jean."

"Oh Alec, I wish you wouldn't leave just yet. I have something important to say, if you will just sit still for a moment and let me get my thoughts in order."

He sat still. She leaned back on her pillow, removed

her glasses, and dabbed lightly with her handkerchief at one eye which was inflamed. She replaced her glasses.

"I shall have to think," she said. "It involves a question of dates. I have them in my memory but I shall have to think for a few minutes. While you are waiting you may care to speak to the new patient in Granny Green's bed. Her name is Mrs. Bean. She is ninety-nine and will be a hundred in September."

He went to speak to Mrs. Bean, tiny among the pillows, her small toothless mouth open like an "O," her skin stretched thin and white over her bones, her huge eye-sockets and eyes in a fixed infant-like stare, and her sparse white hair short and straggling over her brow. Her head nodded faintly and continuously. If she had not been in a female ward, Alec thought, one might not have been sure whether she was a very old man or a woman. She reminded him of one of his mental patients at Folkestone, an old man who, since 1918, had believed he was God. Alec spoke to Mrs. Bean and received a civil and coherent answer which came, as it seemed, from a primitive reed instrument in her breast-bone, so thin and high did she breathe, in and out, when answering him.

He stepped over to Miss Valvona, paid his respects, and heard from her his horoscope for the day. He nodded to Mrs. Reewes-Duncan, and waved to various other occupants of the ward familiar to him. One of the geriatric set came and shook hands with him and said she was going to the bank, and, having departed from the ward, was escorted back by a nurse who said to her, "Now you've been to the bank."

Alec carefully watched the patient's happy progress back to the geriatric end, reflected on the frequency with which the senile babble about the bank, and returned to Jean Taylor who said:

"You must inform Godfrey Colston that Charmian was unfaithful to him repeatedly from the year after her marriage. That is starting in the summer of 1902 when Charmian had a villa on Lake Geneva, and throughout that year, when Charmian used often to visit the man in his flat in Hyde Park Gate. And this went on throughout 1903 and 1904 and also, I recall, when Charmian was up in Perthshire in the autumn—Godfrey could not leave London at the time. There were also occasions at Biarritz and Torquay. Have you got that, Alec? Her lover was Guy Leet. She continued to see him at his flat in Hyde Park Gate through most of 1905—up to September. Listen carefully, Alec, you are to give Godfrey Colston all the facts. Guy Leet. So she gave him up in the September of 1907, I well remember, I was with them in the Dolomites, and Charmian became ill then. You must remember Guy is ten years younger than Charmian. Then in 1926 the affair began again, and it went on for about eighteen months. That was about the time I met you, Alec. Guy wanted her to leave Godfrey, and I know she thought of doing so quite often. But then she knew Guy had so many other women—Lisa Brooke, of course, and so on. Charmian couldn't really trust Guy. Charmian missed him, he did so amuse her. After that she entered the Church. Now I want you to give these facts to Godfrey. He has never suspected Charmian, she managed everything so well. Have you got a pencil on you, Alec? Better write it down. First occasion, 1902—"

"You know, Jean," he said, "this might be serious for poor Godfrey and Charmian. I mean, I can't think you really want to betray Charmian after all those years."

"I don't want to," she said, "but I will, Alec."

"Godfrey probably knows already," he said.

"The only people who know about this are Charmian, Guy, and myself. Lisa Brooke knew, and in fact she blackmailed Charmian quite cruelly. That was when Charmian had her nervous breakdown. And in fact the main reason Guy married Lisa was to keep her quiet, and save Charmian from the threat of scandal. It was never a proper marriage, but, however, as I say, Guy did marry Lisa for Charmian's sake. I will say that for him. Of course, Guy Leet did have charm."

"He still has charm," said Alec.

"Has he? Well, I don't doubt it. Now, Alec, write this down, will you?"

"Jean, you would regret it."

"Alec, if you won't give Godfrey this information I shall have to ask Dame Lettie to do so. She would make the matter far more unpleasant for Charmian. I see it is necessary that Godfrey Colston should stop being morally afraid of Charmian—at least it is worth trying. I think, if he knows of Charmian's infidelity he won't fear any disclosures about his. Let him go and gloat over Charmian. Let him—"

"Charmian will be shocked. She trusts you." He put the case for the opposition, but she knew he was stirred and excited by her suggestion. He had never, in the past, hesitated to make mischief if it served his curiosity: now he could serve her ends.

"There is a time for loyalty and a time when loyalty comes to an end. Charmian should know that by now," she said.

He looked at her curiously as if to find in her face something that he had previously overlooked, some latent jealousy.

"The more religious people are, the more perplexing I find them. And I think Charmian would be hurt by your action."

"Charmian herself is a religious woman."

"No, only a woman with a religion." He had always found it odd that Miss Taylor, having entered the Church only to please Charmian, should have become the more addicted of the two.

He made notes of the information Miss Taylor gave to

him. "Make it clear," she said, "that this is a message from me. If my hands were in use I would write to him myself. Tell him from me he has nothing to fear from Mrs. Pettigrew. Poor old man."

"Were you ever jealous of Charmian?" he said.

"Of course I was," she said, "from time to time."

Alec was wondering as he wrote down the details of Charmian's love affair, if Godfrey Colston would be agreeable to taking his pulse and temperature before and after the telling. On the whole, he thought not. Guy Leet had been obliging in this respect, but then Guy was a sport. Still, one might try.

"You know, Taylor," said Dame Lettie, "I do not feel I can continue to visit you. These creatures are too disturbing, and now that I am not getting my proper sleep my nerves are not up to these decrepit women here. One wonders, really, what is the purpose of keeping them alive at the country's expense."

"For my part," said Miss Taylor, "I would be glad to be let die in peace. But the doctors would be horrified to hear me say it. They are so proud of their new drugs and new methods of treatment—there is always something new. I sometimes fear, at the present rate of discovery, I shall never die."

Dame Lettie considered this statement, uncertain whether it was frivolous or not. She shifted bulkily in her chair and considered the statement with a frown and a downward droop of her facial folds.

Miss Taylor supplied obligingly: "Of course the principle of keeping people alive is always a good one."

Dame Lettie glanced along the ward at the geriatrics who were, at that moment, fairly docile. One old lady sat up in her cot singing a song or something; a few were being visited by relatives who spoke little but for the most part simply sat out the visiting time with their feeble forebears, occasionally breaking the silence with some piece of family news, spoken loudly into the half-comprehending faces, and accepting with blank calm the response, whether this were a cluck or a crow, or something more substantial. The rest of the geriatric patients were grouped at the television corner, watching and commenting. Really, there was nothing one could complain of in them.

But Lettie had been, in any case, jittery beyond the usual when she arrived. She had not answered Miss Taylor's greeting, but had scraped the bedside chair closer to Miss Taylor and started talking immediately.

"Taylor, we all went to see Mortimer. It was utterly futile—"

"Oh, yes, Mr. Warner told me yesterday—"

"Quite useless. Mortimer is not to be trusted. The police are, of course, shielding him. He must have accomplices—one of them is apparently a young man, another a middle-aged man with a lisp, and then there is a foreigner, and also—"

"Chief Inspector Mortimer," said Miss Taylor, "always used to seem to me rather sane."

"Sane, of course he's sane. I am not saying he isn't sane. I made the great mistake, Taylor, of letting him know I had remembered him in my will. He always appeared to be so helpful on the committees, so considerate. But I see now, he has been a schemer. He did not expect me to live so long, and he is using these methods to frighten me to death. Of course I have now taken him out of my will, and I took steps to make this fact known to him, hoping his persecution would then cease. But now, in his rage, he has intensified his efforts. The others who receive the anonymous calls are merely being used as a blind, a cover, you see, Taylor, a blind. And Eric, I believe, is working in with him. I have written to Eric, but have received no reply, which alone is suspicious. I am their main objective and victim. Now, a further development. A few weeks ago, you remember I arranged to have my telephone disconnected."

"Oh yes," said Miss Taylor, closing her eyes to rest them.

"Well, shortly after that, as I was going to bed, I could swear I heard a noise at my bedroom window. As you know, my window looks out on the . . ."

Dame Lettie had, in the past few weeks, got into the habit of searching the house every night before going to bed. One could not be too careful. She searched the house from top to bottom, behind sofas, in cupboards, under beds. And even then there were creaks and unaccountable noises springing up all over the place. This nightly search of the house and the garden took three-quarters of an hour, by the end of which Dame Lettie was in no condition to deal with her maid's hysterics. After a week of this routine Gwen had declared the house to be haunted and Dame Lettie to be a maniac, and had left.

Thus, Dame Lettie was not in the mood for the geriatrics when she visited Miss Taylor in the Maud Long Ward.

"I suppose," ventured Miss Taylor, "you have informed the police of your suspicions. If someone is trying to get into the house, surely the police—"

"The police," Dame Lettie explained with long-tried emphasis, "are shielding Mortimer and his accomplices. The police always stick together. Eric is in with them. They are all in it together."

"Perhaps a little rest in a country nursing home would do you good. All this must be very exhausting."

"Not me," said Dame Lettie. "Oh no, Taylor, no nursing home for me while I have my faculties and am able to get about on my feet. I am looking for another maid. An older woman. They are so difficult to come by, they all want their television." She looked over to the senile patients gathered round their television receiver.

"Such an expense to the country. An abominable invention."

"Really, in cases like theirs, it is an entirely suitable invention. It does hold their attention."

"Taylor, I cannot come here again. It is too distressing."

"Go away for a holiday, Dame Lettie. Forget about the house and the phone calls."

"Even the private detective whom I employed is in league with Mortimer. Mortimer is behind it all. Eric is . . ."

Miss Taylor dabbed her sore eye under her glasses. She wanted to close her eyes, and longed for the bell to ring which marked the end of the visiting hour.

"Mortimer . . . Mortimer . . . Eric," Dame Lettie was going on. Miss Taylor felt reckless.

"In my belief," she said, "the author of the anonymous telephone calls is Death himself, as you might say. I don't see, Dame Lettie, what you can do about it. If you don't remember Death, Death reminds you to do so. And if you can't cope with the facts the next best thing is to go away for a holiday."

"You have taken leave of your senses, Taylor," said Dame Lettie, "and I can do no more for you." She stopped at the outer office and, demanding to speak to the ward sister, registered her opinion that Miss Taylor was off her head and should be watched.

When Gwen had left Dame Lettie's employment she quite understandably told her boy friend all about the nightly goings-on, how the mad Dame would go round the house, poking into all the cupboards and corners, and the garden, poking into the shrubberies with an electric torch, no wonder her eyesight was failing.

"And she wouldn't let me tell the police," said Gwen. "She doesn't trust the police. No wonder, they'd have laughed at her. Oh, but it gave me the creeps because when you're looking for noises, you keep hearing them all over the house and you think you see shapes in the darkness, and half the time it was herself I bumped into in the garden. Oh, but that house is just about haunted. I couldn't stand it a minute longer."

Gwen's boy friend thought it a good story and recounted it at his work which was in a builder's yard.

"My girl was in with an old girl, some dame or countess or other up Hampstead way . . . went round the place every night . . . kept hearing burglars . . . wouldn't get the police . . . My girl walked out on her a week past, too much of it. . . ."

"There's some cranky ones going about," commented one of his friends, "I'll tell you. I remember during the war when I was batman to a colonel, he . . ."

So it was that a labourer, new to the yard, picked up Gwen's story—a youth who would not have considered himself a criminal type, but who knew a window cleaner who would give two or perhaps three pounds an item for likely information. But you had to have an address.

"Where'd you say this countess was living?" he said to Gwen's boy. "I know all up Hampstead and round the Heath."

Gwen's boy said, "Oh, this is a posh part, Hackleton Rise. My girl says the old woman'll be carted off looney in the end. She's one of them. Did you see in the papers about the phone-call hoax? She's cut off her phone now . . ."

The young labourer took his information to the window cleaner, who did not pay him immediately. "I got to check the address with my contact."

The window cleaner himself never actually touched a job like this, but there was money in information. In a few days' time his contact expressed himself satisfied, and paid over ten pounds, remarking that the old girl in question wasn't a countess after all. The window cleaner duly paid a small share to the young labourer remarking that the information was a bit faulty, and that he'd better not be leaky with his mouth the next few days.

So it came about that Dame Lettie's house and nocturnal searching fell under scrutiny.

On the day of her last visit to Miss Taylor she returned to Hampstead by taxi shortly after five. She called in at the employment agency to see if they had found her a woman yet, a middle-aged woman, clean with good references, to live in. No, they had found no one yet, Dame Lettie, but they were keeping their eyes open. She walked the rest of the way home.

Gloomily she made a pot of tea and drank a cup standing in the kitchen. She then puffed her way into her study and started writing a letter to Eric. Her fountain-pen ran out of ink. She refilled it and continued,

... I am thinking only of your poor mother put away in a home, and your poor old father who has done so much for you, and who is rapidly failing in health, when I demand that at least you should write and explain your silence. There has been bitterness between your parents and yourself, I know. But the time is come, surely, in their declining years, for you to make what amends you can. Your father was telling me only the other day, that, for his part, he is willing to let bygones be bygones. In fact, he asked me to write to you in this vein.

She stopped and looked out the window. An unfamiliar car had pulled up at the house opposite. Someone visiting the Dillingers, apparently, not knowing the Dillingers were away. She began to feel chilly and got up to draw the curtain. A man was sitting waiting in the car. As she drew the curtains, he drove off. She returned to her desk and continued,

> Do not suppose I am not aware of your activities in
> London and your attempts to frighten me. Do not sup-
> pose I am in the least alarmed.

She scored these last sentences through with her pen.
That was not what she had meant to write. She had, at
first, thought of writing in this manner, but her second
thoughts, she now recalled, had decided her to write something more in the nature of an appeal. One had to employ
cunning with a man like Eric. She took a fresh sheet and
began again, stopping once to look over her shoulder at
a potential noise.

> I am thinking only of your poor mother put away in a
> home, and your poor old father, enfeebled and rapidly
> failing in health, when I . . .

She finished the letter, addressed and sealed it, and called
Gwen to catch the six o'clock post. Then she remembered
Gwen had left.

Dame Lettie laid the letter helplessly on the hall table
and pulled herself together so far as to think of supper
and to switch on the news.

She prepared her supper of steamed fish, ate it and
washed up. She listened to the wireless till half-past nine.
Then she turned it off and went into the hall where she
stood for about five minutes, listening. Eventually, various
sounds took place, coming successively from the kitchen
quarters, the dining-room on her right, and upstairs.

She spent the next forty-five minutes in a thorough
search of the house and the garden, front and back. Then
she locked and bolted the front door and the back door.
She locked every room and took away the keys. Finally
she climbed slowly up to bed, stopping every few steps to
regain her breath and to listen. Certainly, there was somebody on the roof.

She locked her bedroom door behind her and tilted a chair under the door knob. Certainly, there was someone down there in the garden. She must get in touch with the Member tomorrow. He had not replied to her previous letter which she had posted on Monday, or was it Tuesday? Well, there had been time for a reply. Corruption in the police force was a serious matter. There would have to be a question in the House. One was entitled to one's protection. She put her hand out to feel the heavy walking-stick securely propped by her bed. She fell asleep at last. She woke suddenly with the noise in her ears, and after all, was amazed by the reality of this.

She switched on the light. It was five past two. A man was standing over by her dressing-table, the drawers of which were open and disarranged. He had turned round to face her. Her bedroom door was open. There was a light in the passage and she heard someone else padding along it. She screamed, grabbed her stick, and was attempting to rise from her bed when a man's voice from the passage outside said, "That's enough, let's go." The man by the dressing-table hesitated nervily for a moment, then swiftly he was by Lettie's side. She opened wide her mouth and her yellow and brown eyes. He wrenched the stick from the old woman's hand and, with the blunt end of it, battered her to death. It was her eighty-first year.

Chapter Fourteen

Four days passed before the milkman reported an accumulation of four pints of milk on Dame Lettie's doorstep, and the police entered her house to find the body, half in, half out of her bed.

Meanwhile Godfrey did not wonder, even vaguely, why he had not heard from Lettie. Now that her telephone was disconnected he seldom heard from her. In any case, he had other things to think about that morning. Alec Warner had been to see him with that extraordinary disturbing, impudent, yet life-giving message from Taylor. He had, of course, ordered Warner out of the house: Alec had seemed to expect this and had departed with easy promptitude to Godfrey's "Get out," like an actor who had rehearsed the part. He had, however, left a slip of paper behind him, bearing a series of dates and place-names. Godfrey examined the document and felt unaccountably healthier than he had been for some months. He went out and bought himself a whisky and soda while he decided what to do. And, over his drink, he despised Guy Leet yet liked the thought of him, since he was associated with his new sense of well-being. He had another whisky, and chuckled to himself to think of Guy bent double over his two sticks. An ugly fellow; always had been, the little rotter.

Guy Leet sat in his room at the Old Stable, Stedrost, Surrey, laboriously writing his memoirs which were being

568

published by instalments in a magazine. The laboriousness of the task resided in the physical, not the mental effort. His fingers worked slowly, clutched round the large barrel of his fountain-pen. His fingers were good for perhaps another year—if you could call these twisted, knobble-knuckled members good. He glanced reproachfully at them from time to time—perhaps good for another year, depending on the severity of the intervening winter. How primitive, Guy thought, life becomes in old age, when one may be surrounded by familiar comforts and yet more vulnerable to the action of nature than any young explorer at the Pole. And how simply the physical laws assert themselves, frustrating all one's purposes. Guy suffered from an internal disorder of the knee-joints which caused one leg to collapse across the other whenever he put his weight on it. But although he frequently remarked, "The law of gravity, the beast," he was actually quite cheerful most of the time. He also suffered from a muscular rheumatism of the neck which caused his head to be perpetually thrust forward and askew. However, he adapted his eyesight and body as best he could to these defects, looking at everything sideways and getting about with the aid of his servant and his car, or on two sticks. He had in his service a pious, soft-spoken, tip-toeing unmarried middle-aged Irishman for whom Guy felt much affection, and whom he called Tony to his face and Creeping Jesus behind his back.

Tony came in with his morning coffee and the mail, which always arrived late. Tony placed two letters beside the paper-knife. He placed the coffee before Guy. He stroked the fronts of his trousers, wriggled and beamed. He was doing a Perpetual Novena for Guy's conversion, even though Guy had told him, "The more you pray for me, Tony, the more I'm a hardened sinner. Or would be, if I had half a chance."

He opened the larger envelope. Proofs of the latest instalment of his memoirs. "Here, Tony," he said, "check these proofs."

"Ah, ye know I can't read without me glasses."

"That's a euphemism, Tony." For Tony's reading capacity was not too good, though he managed when necessary by following each word with his finger.

"Indeed, sir, 'tis a pity." Tony disappeared.

Guy opened the other letter and gave a smile which might have appeared sinister to one who did not realise that this was only another consequence of his neck being twisted. The letter was from Alec Warner.

Dear Guy,

I'm afraid I sent Percy Mannering the last instalment of your *memoirs*. He would have seen it, in any case. I'm afraid he is a trifle upset about your further reference to Dowson.

Mannering in replying to thank me for sending him the article, tells me he is coming down to see you, no doubt to talk things over. I hope he will not prove too difficult and that you will make all allowances.

Now, dear fellow, you will, I know, assist me by taking the old fellow's pulse and temperature as soon as it can conveniently be done after he has discussed the article with you. Preferably, of course, *during* the discussion, but this may prove difficult. Any further observations as to his colour, speech (clarity of, etc.) and general bearing *during* the little discussion will be most welcome, as you know.

Mannering will be with you tomorrow, i.e. the day on which you will, I expect, receive this letter—at about 3.40 p.m. I have supplied him with train times and all necessary directions.

My dear Fellow,
I am, most gratefully,
Alec Warner

Guy put the letter back into its envelope. He telephoned to the nursing home where Charmian was now resident and asked if he might call and see her that afternoon, and was informed, after the nurse had been to make enquiries, that he might. He then told Tony to have the car ready at three-fifteen.

He had intended to see Charmian, in any case. And to-day was warm and bright, though clouds came over at intervals. He held no resentment against Alec Warner. The chap was a born mischief-maker; but he didn't know it, that was the saving grace. He was sorry poor Percy would have to undergo the journey for nothing that afternoon.

When he left at a quarter past three he left a message on the door of his Old Stable, "Away for a few days." Quite improbable, it sounded, but Percy would have to take it or leave it.

" 'Tis a lie," commented Tony, sliding into the car to drive his master off.

Charmian liked her new room. It was large and furnished with bright old-fashioned chintzes. It reminded her of her headmistress's room at school in those times when the days were always, somehow, sunny, and everyone seemed to love each other. She had been quite eighteen years of age before she had realised that everyone did not love each other; this was a fact which she had always found it difficult to convey to others. "But surely, Charmian, you must have come across spitefulness and hatred before you were eighteen?"

"Only in retrospect," she would reply, "did I discern discord in people's actions. At the time, all seemed harmony. Everyone loved each other."

Some said she was colouring the past with the rosy glow of nostalgia. But she plainly remembered her shock when, at the age of eighteen, she became conscious of evil—a trifling occasion; her sister had said something detrimental about her—but it was only then that Charmian discovered the reality of words like "sin" and "calumny" which she had known, as words, for as long as she could remember.

The window of her room looked out on a lawn in the centre of which stood a great elm. She could sit at her window and watch the other patients walking in the grounds, and they might have been the girls at her old school sauntering at their recreation period, and she with her headmistress taking tea by the window.

"Everything," she said to Guy some time after he had made his difficult way across the room, "has an innocent air in this place. I feel almost free from Original Sin."

"How dull for you, dear," said Guy.

"It's an illusion, of course."

A young nurse brought in tea and placed it between them. Guy winked at her. The nurse winked back, and left them.

"Behave yourself, Guy."

"And how," he said, "did you leave Godfrey?"

"Oh, he was most depressed. These anonymous telephone calls worry him." She gestured towards her white telephone receiver. The civil young man had vaguely assumed in her mind the shape of a telephone receiver. At home he had been black; here he was white. "Does he worry you, Guy?"

"Me? No. I don't mind a bit of fun."

"They worry Godfrey. It is surprising how variously people react to the same thing."

"Personally," said Guy, "I tell the young fellow to go to hell."

"Well, he vexed Godfrey. And then we have an unsuitable housekeeper. She also worries him. Godfrey has a lot of worries. You would see a change in him, Guy. He is failing."

"Doesn't like this revival of your books?"

"Guy, I don't like talking against Godfrey, you know. But, between ourselves, he *is* rather jealous. At his age, one would have thought he had no more room for these feelings, somehow. But there it is. He was so rude, Guy, to a young critic who came to see me."

"Fellow has never understood you," said Guy. "But still I perceive you have a slight sense of guilt concerning him."

"Guilt? Oh no, Guy. As I was saying, I feel unusually innocent in this place."

"Sometimes," he said, "a sense of guilt takes a self-righteous turn. I see no cause for you to feel either in the right or in the wrong where Godfrey's concerned."

"I have regular visits from a priest," she said, "and if I want moral advice, Guy, I shall consult him."

"Oh quite, quite." Guy placed his gnarled hand on her lap; he was afraid he was forgetting how to handle women.

"And then," said Charmian, "you know he has estranged Eric. It is really Godfrey's fault, Guy. I do not like to say these things, and of course Eric was a disappointment, but I can't help feeling Godfrey's attitude—"

"Eric," said Guy, "is a man of fifty-five."

"Fifty-seven," said Charmian, "next month."

"Fifty-seven," said Guy. "And he has had time to acquire a sense of responsibility."

"That," sighed Charmian, "Eric has never possessed. But I did think at one time he might have been a painter. I never had much hope for his writing, but his paintings— he did seem to have talent. At least, to me. But Godfrey was so mean about money, and Godfrey—"

"If I remember," said Guy, "it was not until Eric was past forty-five that Godfrey refused to give him any more money."

"And then Lettie," said Charmian, "has been so cruel about her wills. Always promising Eric the earth, and then

573

retracting her promises. I don't know why she doesn't do something for Eric while she is still alive."

"Do you think," said Guy, "that money would make Eric any less spiteful?"

"Well, no," said Charmian, "I don't. I have been sending Eric sums of money for some years, secretly, through Mrs. Anthony who is our daily woman. But he is still spiteful. Of course he disapproves of my books."

"They are beautiful books," said Guy.

"Eric doesn't approve the style. I'm afraid Godfrey has never handled Eric tactfully, that is the trouble."

"Beautiful," said Guy. "I have just been re-reading *The Seventh Child*. I love particularly that scene at the end with Edna in her mackintosh standing at the cliff's edge on that Hebridean coast being drenched by the spray, and her hair blown about her face. And then turning to find Karl by her side. One thing about your lovers, Charmian, they never required any preliminary discussions. They simply looked at each other and *knew*."

"That," said Charmian, "is one of the things Eric cannot stand."

"Eric is a realist. He has no period-sense, no charity."

"Oh, my dear Guy, do you think these new young men read my books from charity?"

"Not from indulgence and kindness. But charity elevates the mind and governs the inward eye. If a valuable work of art is rediscovered after it has gone out of fashion, that is due to some charity in the discoverer, I believe. But I say, without a period-sense as well, no one can appreciate your books."

"Eric has no charity," she said.

"Well, perhaps it is just that he is middle-aged. The really young are so much pleasanter," said Guy.

She was not listening. "He is like Godfrey in so many ways," she said, "I can't help remembering how much I

had to shut my eyes to in Godfrey. Lipstick on his handkerchiefs—"

"Stop feeling guilty about Godfrey," Guy said. He had expected a livelier meeting with Charmian. He had never known Charmian to complain so much. He wished he had not enquired after Godfrey in the first place. Her words depressed him. They were like spilt sugar; however much you swept it up some grains would keep grinding under your feet.

"About your novels," he said. "The plots are so well-laid. For instance in *The Seventh Child,* although of course one feels that Edna will never marry Gridsworthy, you have this tension between Anthony Garland and Colonel Yeoville, and until of course their relationships to Gabrielle are revealed, there is every likelihood that Edna will marry one or the other. And yet, of course, all along one is aware of a kind of *secret life* within Edna, especially at that moment when she is alone in the garden at Neuflette, and then comes unexpectedly upon Karl and Gabrielle. And then one feels sure she will marry Gridsworthy after all, merely for his kindness. And really, right up to the last page one does not know Karl's true feelings. Or rather, one knows them—but does *he* know them? I must admit, although I remembered the story well, I felt the same enormous sense of relief, when I read it again the other day, that Edna did not throw herself over the cliff. The suspense, the plot alone, quite apart from the prose, are superb."

"And yet," said Charmian, smiling up at the sky through the window, "when I was halfway through writing a novel I always got into a muddle and didn't know where it was leading me."

Guy thought: She is going to say—dear Charmian—she is going to say, "The characters seemed to take on a life of their own."

"The characters," said Charmian, "seemed to take control of my pen after a while. But at first I always got into a tangle. I used to say to myself,

> 'Oh what a tangled web we weave
> When first we practise to deceive!'

Because," she said, "the art of fiction is very like the practise of deception."

"And in life," he said, "is the practise of deception in life an art too?"

"In life," she said, "everything is different. Everything is in the Providence of God. When I think of my own life . . . Godfrey . . ."

Guy wished he had not introduced the question of life, but had continued discussing her novels. Charmian was upset about Godfrey, that was plain.

"Godfrey has not been to visit me yet. He is to come next week. If he is able. But he is failing. You see, Guy, he is his own worst enemy. He . . ."

How banal and boring, Guy thought, do the most interesting people become when they are touched by a little bit of guilt.

He left at five. Charmian watched him from the window being helped into his car. She was vexed with herself for going on so much about Godfrey. Guy had never been interested in her domestic affairs. He was such an amusing companion. The room, with its chintzes, felt empty.

Guy waved out of his car window, a stiff, difficult wave. It was only then that Charmian noticed the other car which had drawn up while Guy had been helped into his seat. Charmian peered down; it looked like Godfrey's car. It was, and Godfrey was climbing out, in his jerky way. She supposed he had come on an impulse to escape Mrs. Pettigrew. If only he could go to live in a quiet private hotel. But as he walked across the path, she noticed

576

he looked astonishingly bright and healthy. She felt rather tired.

Guy Leet considered, as he was driven home, whether in fact he was enjoying that sense of calm and freedom that is supposed to accompany old age or whether he was not. Yesterday he had been an old, serene man. To-day he felt younger and less peaceful. How could one know at any particular moment what one's old age finally amounted to? On the whole, he thought, he must be undergoing the experience of calm and freedom, although it was not like anything he would have anticipated. He was, perhaps, comparatively untroubled and detached, mainly because he became so easily exhausted. He was amazed at Charmian's apparent energy—and she ten years his senior. He supposed he must be a dear old thing. He was fortunate in possessing all his material needs, and now that Lisa's will was being proved, he might possibly spend the winter in a really warm climate. And he had earned Lisa's money. And he bore no grudge against Charmian for her ingratitude. Not many men would have married Lisa simply to keep her quiet for Charmian's sake. Not many would have endured the secrecy of such a marriage, a mere legal bond necessary to Lisa's full sensual enjoyment of her many perversions. "I've got to be married," she would say in that hoarse voice, "my dear, I don't want the man near me, but I've got to know I'm married or I can't enjoy myself."

Foolishly, they had exchanged letters on the subject, which might have upset his claim on Lisa's money. He did not think Tempest's suit would have succeeded, but it would have been unpleasant. But that eventuality had come to nothing. He would get Lisa's money; he had earned it. He had given satisfaction to Lisa and safety to Charmian.

He doubted if Charmian ever thought with gratitude of his action. Still, he adored Charmian. She had been wonderful, even when he had met her a year ago at a time when her mind was failing. Now that she was so greatly improved, what a pity she had this Godfrey trouble on her mind. However, he adored Charmian for what she had been and what she still really was. And he had earned Lisa's money. Trinidad might be delightful next winter. Or Barbados. He must write for some information.

When they drew up at the Old Stable Percy Mannering appeared out of the back garden and approached the car waving a magazine in the direction of the front door where Guy's message was pinned up.

"Away for a few days," shouted Percy.

"I have just returned," said Guy. "Tony will give me a hand, and then we will go indoors for a drink. Meanwhile let us not alarm the lilies of the field."

"Away for a few days," shouted Percy, "my foot."

Tony trotted round the car and took Guy by the arms.

"I've been waiting," shouted Percy, "for you."

Guy, as he was helped to his feet, was trying to recall what exactly he had written about Ernest Dowson in the latest published instalment of his memoirs which so enraged Percy. Guy was not a moment inside the door before he found out, for Percy then started to inform him.

"You quote from the poem about Cynara,

" 'I have been faithful to thee, Cynara! in my fashion.'

"You then comment, 'Yes, that was always Dowson's way, even to the point of dying in the arm of another man's wife—his best friend's!'—That's what you wrote, is it not?"

"It must be," said Guy, sinking into his chair, "if you say so."

"And yet you know as well as I do," shouted Percy, "that Sherrard rescued Dowson from a pub and took him home to be nursed and fed. And Dowson did indeed die in Mrs. Sherrard's arms, you utter snake; she was sustaining and comforting him in a sudden last spasm of his consumption. You know that as well as I do. And yet you write as if Dowson and she—"

"I am but a hardened old critic," said Guy.

Percy banged his fist on the table. "Critic— You're an unutterable rat."

"A hardened old journalist," said Guy.

"A steaming scorpion. Where is your charity?"

"I know nothing of charity," said Guy. "I have never heard of the steaming properties of the scorpion. I never cared for Dowson's verse."

"You're a blackguard—you've slandered his person. This has nothing to do with verse."

"What I wrote is the sort of thing, in my opinion, that *might* have happened," said Guy. "It is as near enough my meaning."

"A cheap jibe," yelled Percy. "Anything for a cheap joke, you'd say anything—"

"It was quite cheap, I admit," said Guy. "I am under-paid for these essays of mine."

Percy grabbed one of Guy's sticks which were propped beside his chair. Guy grabbed the other stick and, calling out for Tony, looked up with his schoolboy face obliquely at Percy.

"You will write a retraction," said Percy Mannering, with his wolf-like look, "or I'll knock your mean little brains out."

Guy aimed weakly with his stick at Percy's stick, and almost succeeded in knocking it out of the old man's quivering hand. Percy adjusted his stick, got it in both hands and with it knocked Guy's stick to the floor, just as Tony came in with a tray and a rattle of glasses.

"Jesus, Mary," said Tony and put down the tray.

"Tony, will you kindly recover my walking stick from Mr. Mannering."

Percy Mannering stood fiercely displaying his two greenish teeth and gripping the stick ready to strike, it seemed, anyone.

Tony slithered cautiously round the room until Guy's desk was between him and Percy. He lowered his head, rolled up his eyes, and glared at them from beneath his sandy eyebrows like a bull about to charge, except that he did not really look like a bull. "Take care what ye do," he said to them both.

Percy removed one of his hands from the shaking stick and took up the offensive journal. He fluttered this at Tony.

"Your master," he declared, "has uttered a damnable lie about a dead friend of mine."

" 'Tis within the realm of possibility," said Tony, clutching the edge of the desk.

"If you will lay a piece of writing paper on the desk, Tony," said Guy, "Mr. Mannering wishes to write a letter of protest to the editor of the magazine which he holds in his hand."

The poet grinned wildly. The telephone, which was on a side table beside Guy's chair, mercifully rang out.

"Come and answer the phone," said Guy to Tony.

But Tony was looking at Percy Mannering who still clung to the stick.

The telephone rang on.

"If ye will lift the instrument I'll lay out the paper as requested," said Tony, "for a man can do but one thing at a time." He opened a drawer and extracted a sheet of paper.

"Oh, it's you," Guy was saying, "well now, sonny, I'm busy at the moment. I have a poet friend here with me and we are just about to have a drink."

Guy heard the clear boyish voice continue: "Is it Mr. Percy Mannering who's with you?"

"That's right," said Guy.

"I'd like to talk to him."

"For you," said Guy, offering the receiver to Percy.

"Me? Who wants me, what?"

"For you," said Guy, "a youngster of school age I should think."

Percy bawled suspiciously into the telephone, "Hallo, who's there?"

"Remember you must die," said a man's voice, not at all that of a young person.

"This is Mannering here. Percy Mannering."

"That's correct," said the voice, and rang off.

Percy looked round the room with a bewildered air. "That's the chap they're talking about," he said.

"Drinks, Tony," said Guy.

"That's the man," roared Percy, his eyes gleaming as with some inner greed.

"Nice youngster, really. I suppose he's been overworking at his exams. The cops will get him, of course."

"That wasn't a youngster," said Percy, lifting his drink and draining it off, "it was a strong mature voice, very noble, like W. B. Yeats."

"Fill Mr. Mannering's glass, Tony," said Guy. "Mr. Mannering will be staying for dinner."

Percy took his drink, laid down the stick, and sank into a chair.

"What an experience!" he said.

"Intimations of immortality," commented Guy.

Percy looked at Guy and pointed to the telephone. "Are you behind this?"

"No," said Guy.

"No." The old man drained his glass, looked at the clock and rose from his chair. "I'll miss my train," he said.

"Stop the night," said Guy. "Do stay."

Percy walked uncertainly about the room. He picked up the magazine, and said,

"Look here—"

"There is a sheet of paper laid out for you to write your protest to the editor," Guy said.

"Yes," said the old man. "I'll do that tomorrow."

"There is a passage in *Childe Harold*," said Guy, "I would like to discuss with you. It—"

"No one," stated Percy, "in the past fifty years has understood *Childe Harold*. You have to *begin* with the last two cantos, man. That is the SECRET of the poem. The episodes—"

Tony put his head round the door. "Did ye call me?"

"No, but while you're here, Mr. Mannering will be stopping the night."

Percy stayed the night and wrote his letter of protest to the editor next morning. He stayed for three weeks during which time he wrote a Shakespearian sonnet entitled "Memento Mori," the final couplet of the first version being,

> Out of the deep resounds the hollow cry,
> *Remember—oh, remember you must die!*

The second version being,

> But slowly the reverberating sigh
> Sounds in my ear: *Remember you must die!*

The third being,

> And from afar the Voices mingle and cry
> O mortal Man, *remember you must die!*

and there were many other revisions and versions.

Eric Colston and Mrs. Pettigrew were waiting for Godfrey's return.

"There's something funny going on in the old man's mind to-day," Mrs. Pettigrew said. "I should judge it was

582

something to do with a visit from old Warner this morning. He couldn't have stayed long. I had just gone across the road for cigarettes and when I got back there was Warner on the doorstep. I asked him if he wanted to see Godfrey. He said, 'I've seen Godfrey, thanks.' But I'll find out what it's all about—you just wait, I'll find out. Then, when I got indoors Godfrey gave me a really wild grin and then *he* went out. I was too late to catch him. He didn't come back to lunch, there's his fish fingers lying on the table. Oh, I'll find out."

"Has he signed the will yet?" said Eric.

"No, the lawyers are taking their time."

Eric thought: I'll bet they are taking their time. He had taken the first train to London on receiving that letter from Olive. His first action had been to call on the solicitor. His next was to get in touch with Mrs. Pettigrew.

Mrs. Pettigrew filled Eric's glass. She noticed, as she had done earlier in the day, his little hands, and she felt quite frightened.

Eric was a stocky man, rather resembling his mother in appearance except that the feminine features and build looked odd in him. His hips were broad, his head was large. He had Charmian's wide-spaced eyes, pointed chin and small neat nose. His mouth was large like that of Dame Lettie whose battered body was later that evening to be discovered.

But, Mrs. Pettigrew told herself, she was experienced with men like Eric. Not that she had ever encountered quite the same details of behaviour in any other man. But she was familiar with the general pattern; she knew he was not normal, for though he greatly desired money he yet seemed willing to sacrifice quantities of it to gain some more intense and sinuous satisfaction. She had in her life before met men prepared to sacrifice the prospect of money in order to gain, for instance, a social ambition.

To that extent she felt she knew her man. She felt it

was not surprising that such a man would sacrifice anything for revenge. And yet, could she trust him?

"I am doing this," he had told her, "for moral reasons.
I believe—I firmly believe, it will do the old man good.
Teach him a lesson."

Oh, but Eric was a mess! She looked at his little hands
and the feminine setting of the eyes like Charmian's and
felt perhaps she was foolish to trust him.

Eric was a mess. Olive's letter had told him his father
was being blackmailed by "a certain Mrs. Pettigrew" into
bequeathing a large portion of his fortune to her. Eric had
acted promptly and without a moment's thought. Even in
the train up from Cornwall he had not taken thought but
had flirted all the way with delicious ideas—the discomfi-
ture of Godfrey; the undermining of Charmian; the possible sympathetic-bosomed qualities of this Mrs. Pettigrew
under her possibly tough exterior; the thrill of being able
to expose everyone to everyone if it proved expedient to
do so; and the thrill of obtaining sufficient immediate
cash to enable him to go and tell his Aunt Lettie what
he really thought of her.

Not that he knew what he thought of her. He retained
in his mind an axiom from his youth: the family had let
him down badly. Everyone, even the family, had agreed
upon that in the years when Eric was between twenty-two
and twenty-eight, and the century was between twenty-
three and twenty-nine years old. He had rejected every
idea his family had ever held except this one idea, "Somehow or other we have let Eric down. How did it happen?
Poor Eric, Charmian has mothered him too much. Charmian has not been a mother enough to him. Godfrey has
been too occupied, has never taken any notice of the boy.
Godfrey has been too lenient, too strict, too mean, has
given him too much money." The elders had grown out
of these sayings when the fashion changed, but by then

Eric had taken them for his creed. Lettie bore him off on consoling holidays. He robbed her, and the hotel staff got the blame. She tried to get him interested in prison-visiting. He started smuggling letters and tobacco into Wormwood Scrubs. "Poor Eric, he hasn't had a chance. He should never have been sent to that crank school. How could he ever be expected to pass an exam? I blame Charmian . . . I blame Lettie . . . Godfrey has never cared . . ." He went to an art school and was caught stealing six tubes of paint. They sent him to a Freudian analyst whom he did not like. They sent him to an Adlerian, and subsequently to an individualist. Meanwhile, there was an incident with a junior porter of a club, in the light of which he was sent to another psychiatrist of sympathetic persuasion. He was so far cured that he got one of the maids into trouble. Charmian was received into the Church.

"Eric will grow out of this phase," said Charmian. "My grandfather was wild as a youth."

But Eric was amazed when his elders eventually stopped blaming themselves for his condition. He thought them hypocritical and callous to go back on their words. He longed for them to start discussing him again in the old vein; but by the time he was thirty-seven they had said quite bitter things to him. He had bought a cottage in Cornwall, where he drank their money. He was in a home for inebriates when the war broke out. He emerged to be called up by the military, but was turned down on account of his psychological history. He loathed Charmian, Godfrey and Lettie. He loathed his cousin Alan who was doing so well as an engineer and who, as a child, had always been considered dull in comparison with Eric. He married a negress and got divorced six months later; a settlement being made on her by Godfrey. From time to time he wrote to Charmian, Godfrey and Lettie, to tell them that he loathed them. When, in 1947, Godfrey refused him any more money, he made it up with Lettie and obtained small revenues and larger promises from her. But Lettie, when she saw so little return for her cash by way of his company, reduced her bounty to mere talk about her will. Eric wrote a novel, and got it published on the strength of Charmian's name. It bore a similarity to Charmian's writing. "Poor Eric," said Charmian, "has not much originality. But I do think, Godfrey, now that he is really doing some work, we ought to assist him." She sent him, over a period of two years, all she possessed. Eric thought her mean, he thought her envious of his novel, and said so. Godfrey refused to write him. Charmian had confided to Guy Leet, "I suspect that Godfrey has a secret horror of another novelist in the family." And she added, what was not strictly true, but was a neat conclusion, "Of course, Godfrey always wanted Eric to join that dreary firm."

By the time he was fifty Eric began to display what looked like a mind of his own. That is, instead of sending wild vituperative accusations to his family, he now sent cold reasoned denunciations. He proved, point by point, that they had let him down badly from the time of his first opening his eyes.

"In his middle-age Eric is becoming so like Godfrey," said Charmian, "though of course, Godfrey does not see it."

Eric no longer called Charmian's novels lousy muck. He analysed them piece by piece, he ridiculed the spare parts, he demolished the lot. He had some friends who applauded his efforts.

"But he takes my work so seriously," said Charmian. "Nobody ever wrote of it like that."

Charmian's health had failed by the mid-fifties. The revival of her novels astonished Eric, for he had by some fractional oversight misjudged an element in the temper of his age. He canvassed his friends and was angered and bewildered to find so many had fallen for the Charmian Piper period-cult.

Charmian's remittances, smuggled through Mrs. Anthony, were received with silence. His second book had secretly appealed to Dame Lettie. It had been described as "realistic and brutally frank," but the energy which he might have put into developing his realistic and brutally frank talents was now dispersed in resentment against Charmian. The revival of her novels finished him off and he found he could no longer write.

Even the reports in the papers that Godfrey, Charmian and Lettie had been recipients of threatening telephone calls failed to stimulate him.

Throughout the war, and since, he had been mainly living on women of means, the chief of whom had been Lisa Brooke. He had found it hard, after Lisa's death, to replace her. Everyone was hard up, and Eric put on weight with the worry of it all, which did not help. His difficulties were approaching a climax at the moment he had received Olive's letter. "Your father is being cruelly blackmailed by a certain Mrs. Pettigrew, the housekeeper. I think he would be willing to make up the past differences, if there was anything you could do without letting your mother know. . . ."

He took the first train up to London, in a state of excitement, and spent the journey visualising the possibilities before him.

When he arrived at Paddington at a quarter to six he had no idea what he was going to do. He went into the bar and had a drink. At seven he emerged and saw a telephone box. He telephoned to the home of his father's solicitor, and on the strength of his communication, obtained an interview that evening. He got from the solicitor an assurance that preparations for the new will would be delayed as long as possible. He received some additional advice to which he did not listen.

He went to call on Olive, but found her flat deserted. He stayed the night with some reluctant acquaintances in Notting Hill Gate. At eleven next morning he telephoned to Mrs. Pettigrew and met her for lunch in a café in Kensington.

"I wish you to know, Mrs. Pettigrew," he said, "that I'm with you. The old man deserves a lesson. I take the moral point of view, and I'm quite willing to forgo the money."

"I'm sure," said Mrs. Pettigrew at first, "I don't know what you mean, Mr. Eric." She wiped the corners of her mouth with her handkerchief, pulling her lower lip askew in the process.

"He would die," said Eric, "rather than my poor mother got to know about his gross infidelities. And so would I. In fact, Mrs. Pettigrew," he said with his smile which had long ceased to be winning, "you have us both in your hands, my father and I."

Mrs. Pettigrew said, "I've done a lot for your parents. Your poor mother, before she was taken away, I had to do *everything* for her. There aren't many that would have put up with so much. Your mother was inclined to be—well, you know what old people are. I suppose I'm old myself, but—"

"Not a bit," said Eric. "You don't look a day older than sixty."

"Well, I felt my years while I had your mother to attend to."

"I'm sure you did. She's impossibly conceited," said Eric; "impossible."

"Quite impossible. And, now, your father—"

"He's impossible," said Eric, "an old brute."

"What exactly," said Mrs. Pettigrew, "had you in mind, Mr. Eric?"

"Well, I felt it my duty to stand behind you. And here I am. Money," he said, "means hardly anything to me."

"Ah, you can't go far without money, Mr. Eric—"

"Do call me Eric," he said.

"Eric," she said, "your best friend's your—"

"Well, of course, a little cash at the right time is always useful. At the right time. It's surprising, really, my father has lived so long after the life he's led."

"Eric, I would never let you go short. I mean, until the time comes . . ."

"You can always get ready cash out of him?"

"Oh yes."

Eric thought: I bet you can.

"I think we should see him together," said Eric.

She looked at his little hands. Can I trust him? she wondered. The will was not yet signed and sealed.

"Trust me," said Eric. "Two heads are better than one."

"I would like to think it over," she said.

"You would prefer to work alone?"

"Oh, don't say that. I mean, this plan of yours is rather sudden, and I feel, after all I've done for Godfrey and Charmian, I'm entitled to—"

"Perhaps, after all," said Eric, "it is my duty to go down to Surrey to see Mother and inform her of her husband's little indiscretions. Distasteful as that course might be, in fact, it might save a lot of trouble. It would take a load off my father's mind, and there would then be no need for you to take any further interest in him. It must be a strain on you."

She came back on him sharply: "You don't know the details of your father's affairs. I do. You have no evidence. I have. Written proof."

"Oh yes," he said, "I have evidence."

Is it bluff? she wondered.

"When do you want to come and see him?" she said.

"Now," he said.

But when they got back, Godfrey was still out. Mrs.

589

Anthony had left. Mrs. Pettigrew felt quite frightened. And when Eric started roaming about the house, picking up the china ornaments and turning them upside down to look at them, she felt quite vexed. But she held her peace. She felt she knew her man. At least she ought to, with all her experience.

When he sat down, eventually, in Charmian's old chair, she ruffled his hair, and said, "Poor Eric. You've had a raw deal from them, haven't you?" He leaned his large head against her bosom and felt quite nice.

After tea Mrs. Pettigrew had a slight attack of asthma and withdrew to the garden, where she got it under control. On her return she thought she saw Godfrey in the chair where she had left Eric. But it was Eric all right. He was asleep, his head lolling sideways; although in features he most resembled Charmian, he looked remarkably like Godfrey in this pose.

Charmian's impression of Godfrey's brightness and health, when she saw him from her window, became more pronounced when he was shown into her room.

"Cheerful place," he said, looking round.

"Come and sit down, Godfrey. Guy Leet had just gone. I'm afraid I'm rather tired."

"Yes, I saw him leaving."

"Yes, poor soul. It was kind of him to visit me. He has such difficulty getting about."

"So different," said Godfrey, leaning back in his chair like a satisfied man, and stretching his legs apart, "from the way he got about in the summer of 1902 in the villa on Lake Geneva, up to 1907 at his flat in Hyde Park Gate, in Scotland and Biarritz and Torquay and then in the Dolomites when you were taken ill. Then nineteen years later when he was living in Ebury Street, up to the time of—"

"I should like a cigarette," said Charmian.

"What?" said Godfrey.

"Give me a cigarette, Godfrey, or I shall ring and ask the nurse to fetch one."

"Look here, Charmian, you'd better stay off cigarettes. I mean—"

"I would like to smoke a cigarette before I die. As to Guy Leet—you yourself, Godfrey, have hardly any room to talk. You yourself. Lisa Brooke. Wendy Loos. Eleanor—"

"The little rotter," said Godfrey. "Well, just look what he's come to and only seventy-five. Bent double over two sticks."

"Jean Taylor must have talked," she said. She stretched out her hand and said, "A cigarette, Godfrey." He gave her one and lit it.

"I'm getting rid of Mrs. Pettigrew," he said. "A most domineering bitch. Always upsetting Mrs. Anthony."

Charmian inhaled her cigarette. "Any other news?" she said.

"Alec Warner," he said, "is losing control of his faculties. He came to see me this morning and wanted me to take my pulse and temperature. I ordered him out of the house."

Charmian began to laugh, and could not stop, and eventually had to be put to bed, while Godfrey was taken away and given a soft-boiled egg with thin bread and butter, and sent off home.

At eight o'clock they had finished supper. Mrs. Pettigrew said, "If he isn't home by nine I'd better ring the police. He might have had an accident. That car, it isn't safe. He's a menace on the road."

"I shouldn't worry," said Eric, reflecting that, after all, the new will was not signed.

"Oh, I always worry about him," she said. "That's what I mean when I say that I'm entitled to . . ."

Godfrey drove more carefully than usual. Having satisfied himself that Warner's information was accurate he
felt that life was worth taking care of. Not that one had
doubted Warner's information. Poor Charmian. At any
rate, she had no call, now, to be uppish and righteous.
Not that she really had been priggish; but she had always
assumed that air of purity which made one feel such a
swine. Poor Charmian; it was very catty of Taylor to
gossip about her after all these years. Still, Taylor had
done one a good turn without knowing it. . . .

Here he was at home. A long drive for an old man.

Godfrey came in with his glasses in his hand, rubbing
his eyes.

"Where on earth have you been?" said Mrs. Pettigrew.
"Eric is here to see you."

"Oh, good evening, Eric," said Godfrey. "Have a
drink."

"I've got one," said Eric.

"I'm keeping quite well, thank you," said Godfrey,
raising his voice.

"Oh, really?" said Eric.

"Eric wishes to speak to you Godfrey."

"Mrs. Pettigrew and I are in this together, Father."

"In what?"

"The question of the new will. And in the meantime,
I expect to be remunerated according to the situation."

"You're growing a paunch," said Godfrey. "I haven't
got a paunch."

"Otherwise we shall really have to present Mother with
the facts."

"Be reasonable, Godfrey," said Mrs. Pettigrew.

"Get to hell out of my house, Eric," said Godfrey. "I
give you ten minutes or I call the police."

"I think we're a little tired," said Mrs. Pettigrew, "aren't
we?"

"And you leave tomorrow morning," he said to her.

The door bell rang.

"Who can that be?" said Mrs. Pettigrew. "Did you forget to leave the car lights on, Godfrey?"

Godfrey ignored the bell. "You can't tell Charmian anything," he said, "that she doesn't know already."

"What did you say?" said Mrs. Pettigrew.

The door bell rang again.

Godfrey left them and went to open it. Two men stood on the doorstep.

"Mr. Colston?"

"That's right."

"Could we have word with you? It's the C.I.D."

"The car lights are on," said Godfrey.

"It's about your sister," said the senior-looking of the men, "Dame Lettie Colston, I'm afraid."

Next day was Sunday. "Hoax Caller Strikes at Last" declared the headlines. *"Aged Welfare Worker, 81, killed in bed. Jewellery and valuables missing."*

Chapter Fifteen

"If you look for one thing," said Henry Mortimer to his wife, "you frequently find another."

Mrs. Mortimer was opening and closing her mouth like a bird. This was because she was attempting to feed a two-year-old boy with a spoon, and as he opened his mouth to take each spoonful of soft egg, she involuntarily opened hers. This child was her grandson whom she was minding while her daughter was confined with a second child.

Mrs. Mortimer wiped the infant's mouth and pushed a jug of milk out of his reach.

"Look for one thing and you find another," said Henry Mortimer. "They found twenty-two different wills amongst Lettie Colston's papers, dated over the past forty years."

"Silly woman," said Emmeline Mortimer, "to change her mind so often." She tickled the cheek of her grandson and clucked into his face, and while his mouth was open in laughter she popped in the last spoonful of egg, most of which he spluttered out. "I was sorry for poor old Godfrey breaking down at the inquest. He must have been fond of his sister," she said.

She gave the child his mug of milk which he clutched in both hands and drank noisily, his eyes bright above the rim, darting here and there.

When the child was settled in a play-pen in the garden Mrs. Mortimer said to her husband,

594

"What's that you were saying about poor Lettie Colston's wills?"

"The chaps were checking up on her papers in the course of routine, in case they should provide any clue to the murder, and of course they checked up on all her beneficiaries. Quite a list out of twenty-two consecutive wills."

"The murderer wasn't known to her, was he?"

"No—oh no, this was before they got him. They were checking up, and . . ."

Dame Lettie's murderer had been caught within three weeks of her death and was now awaiting trial. In those three weeks, however, her papers had been thoroughly examined, and those of the beneficiaries of her twenty-two wills who were still alive had been quietly traced, checked, and dismissed from suspicion. Only one name had proved a very slight puzzle; Liza O'Brien of Nottingham, whose name appeared in a bequest dated 1918. The records, however, showed that Lisa Brooke, nee Sidebottome, aged 33, had married a man named Matthew O'Brien aged 40 at Nottingham in that year. The C.I.D. did not look much further. Lisa O'Brien in the will must be a woman of advanced years by now and, in fact, it emerged that she was dead; O'Brien himself, if still alive, would be beyond the age of the suspect. The police were no longer interested, and ticked the name O'Brien off their list.

Henry Mortimer, however, as one acquainted with the murdered woman and her circle, had been approached, and had undertaken to investigate any possible connection between the murder and the anonymous telephone calls. Not that the police believed these calls had taken place; every possible means of detection had failed, and they had concluded, with the support of their psychologists, that the old people were suffering from hallucinations.

The public, however, had to be satisfied. Henry Mortimer was placed in charge of this side of the case. The police were able to announce:

> The possibility of a connection between the murder and the anonymous telephone calls which the murdered woman was reported to receive from time to time before her death, is being investigated.

Mortimer fulfilled his duties carefully. Like his colleagues, he suspected the murderer to be a chance criminal. Like his colleagues, he knew the anonymous voice would never be traced in flesh and blood. Nevertheless, he examined the police documents, and finally sent in a report which enabled the police to issue a further statement:

> The authorities are satisfied that there is no connection between the murder of Dame Lettie Colston and the anonymous telephone calls of which she had been complaining some months before her death.

Meantime, however, Henry had noticed the details of Lisa O'Brien, and was interested.

"You look for one thing and you find another," he had said to himself. For he had never before heard of this marriage of Lisa's. Her first marriage with rich old Brooke had been dissolved in 1912. Her secret marriage with Guy Leet had recently come to light, when Guy had claimed her fortune. But Matthew O'Brien—Henry did not recall any Matthew O'Brien. He must be quite old now, probably dead.

He had requested the C.I.D. to check further on Matthew O'Brien. And they had found him quite quickly, in a mental home in Folkestone where he had been resident for more than forty years.

"And so," said Mortimer to his wife, "you look for one thing and you find another."

"Do Janet and Ronald Sidebottome know anything of this husband?" said Mrs. Mortimer.

"Yes, they remember him quite well. Lisa went touring Canada with him. They didn't hear from her for a year. When she turned up again she told them he had been killed in an accident."

"How long has he been in this mental home?"

"Since 1919—a few months after their marriage. Janet is going down to identify him tomorrow."

"That will be difficult after all these years."

"It is only a formality. The man is undoubtedly Matthew O'Brien whom Lisa Brooke married in 1918."

"And she said he was dead?"

"Yes, she did."

"Well, what about Guy Leet? Didn't she marry him? That make them bigamists, doesn't it?"

"I shouldn't think for a moment Guy knew the man was still alive. Everyone, apparently believed he was dead."

"The police won't trouble poor Guy about it?"

"Oh, the police won't bother him now. Especially at his age."

"What a woman," said Mrs. Mortimer, "that Lisa Brooke was. Well, I expect her money—Oh, what will happen to her money, now? Guy Leet is surely—"

"That's a question, indeed. Lisa's fortune belongs to Matthew O'Brien by rights, sane or insane."

Henry went out into the garden and said to his squealing grandson,

"What's all this racket going on?" He rolled him over and over on the warm stubbly grass. He picked up the child and threw him into the blue sky and caught him again.

"He'll throw up his breakfast," remarked Emmeline, who stood with her head on one side, and smiled proudly at the child.

"Up-up-ee," demanded the child.

Henry rolled him over and over, left him yelling for more, and went indoors to catch Alec Warner on the telephone before he should go out.

"You're interested in the St. Aubrey's Home at Folkestone?" Henry said.

"Yes. But only in the older patients. I've been visiting them on private research for ten years."

"Do you know a man there called Matthew O'Brien?"

"Matt O'Brien, oh yes, a private patient. A dear old chap, nearly eighty. He's bedridden now. Quite batty, of course, but he always knows me."

"Were you thinking," said Henry, "of going down there any time this week?"

"Well, I only go once a month, as a rule, and I went last week. Is there anything special?"

"Only," said Henry, "that Janet Sidebottome has agreed to go down to Folkestone tomorrow to identify Matthew O'Brien. I won't go into details, but if you would care to accompany her, since you are acquainted with the home, it would be a kindness to Janet who will probably be distressed. Ronald can't go with her, he's in bed with a chill."

"What has Janet Sidebottome to do with Matt O'Brien?"

"Can you go?" said Henry.

"Yes," said Alec.

"Then Janet will explain everything. Do you know her number?"

"Yes," said Alec.

"And one of our men will be there to meet you."

"A copper?" said Alec.

"A detective," said Mortimer. "The affair might be of some incidental interest to you."

"That's just what I was thinking," said Alec.

Janet said, "It is all most distressing. Ronald should have been here to assist me. He met Matthew several times. It can't think why Ronald should have a chill in this fine weather."

Alec shouted above the rattle of the taxi.

"No need to be distressed. I shall do my best to replace Ronald."

"Oh, no, don't distress Ronald," she said. "I only meant—"

He gave her a smile. She sadly adjusted her hearing equipment, and said, "My hearing is rather poor."

"You may not be able to recognise Matt O'Brien," he articulated. "He's an old man, and the years of insanity may have changed him beyond recognition. They get drugs, you know, and then the drugs have an affect on the appearance. But don't worry if his features are not familiar to you. I think the authorities already have evidence that he's Lisa's husband. They have Lisa's signature, for instance, from the time of his admission."

"I will do my best," said Janet. "But it is a distressing experience."

"He is gentle," shouted Alec. "He thinks he is God. He has never been violent."

"I am distressed about my late sister," Janet said. "I don't like to admit it, but I must; Lisa was never straight in her dealings. It is a blessing she was never found out in this business."

"It would have been bigamy," said Alec.

"It was bigamy," she said. "There was no excuse for Lisa, she had every opportunity in life. But it was the same when she was a girl. She caused our dear father a great deal of sorrow. And when Simon Brooke divorced her, there was all that scandal. Scandal was serious in those days."

"What did you think of Matt O'Brien at the time?"

"Well, he was an Irishman, a lawyer. He talked a great deal, but then he was an Irishman, and he was quite charming. And do you know, when Lisa told me he was

599

dead, I could hardly believe it. He had seemed to me so lively. Of course, we did not suspect the truth. It is very distressing."

"It will soon be over," said Alec. "We shall not be with him for long."

The interview with Matt O'Brien was soon over. The detective met them in the hall and a nurse took them up to Matt's room where he lay on his pillow among his loose white hair.

"Hallo, Matt," said Alec, "I've brought two friends of mine to see you."

The detective nodded to the old man and stood back discreetly and formally beside the nurse.

Janet approached his bedside and lifted his limp hand in greeting. He raised his other hand in benediction.

The old man moved his pale eyes towards Alec.

"It's you, Alec," he said in a blurred voice, as if his tongue were in the way.

"I was wondering," said Alec, "if you remember a lady called Lisa, at all? Lisa Brooke. Lisa Sidebottome."

"Lisa," said the old man.

"You don't remember Lisa—a red-haired lady?" said Alec.

"Lisa," said the old man, looking at Janet.

"No, this isn't Lisa. This is her sister, Janet. She's come to see you."

The old man was still looking at Janet.

"Don't you remember Lisa?—Well, never mind," said Alec.

The old man shook his head. "I recollect all creatures," he said.

"Lisa died last year," Alec said. "I just thought you might know of her."

"Lisa," said the old man and looked out at the sky through the window. It was a bright afternoon, but he must have seen a night sky full of stars. "My stars are shining in the sky," he said. "Have I taken her to Myself?"

Janet was served with tea downstairs and invited to put her feet up for a while.

She put away her handkerchief. "I did not," she said, "at first find any resemblance. I thought there must be a mistake. But as he turned his head aside to the window, I saw the profile, I recognised his features quite plainly. Yes, I am sure he is the same Matthew O'Brien. And his manner, too, when he spoke of the stars. . . ."

Alec declined tea. He took a notebook from his pocket and tore a page from it.

"Will you excuse me if I scribble a note to a friend? I have to catch the post." He was already scribbling away when Miss Sidebottome gave him leave to do so.

DEAR GUY—I believe I shall be the first to give you the following information.

A man named Matthew O'Brien has been discovered, who was already married to Lisa when you married her.

Mortimer will give you the details, which have now been fully established.

As it happened, I have been visiting this man, in the course of research, at St. Aubrey's Home for mental cases, for the past ten years, without suspecting any such association.

I imagine there will be no blame imputed to you. But of course, as your marriage with Lisa was invalid, you will not now benefit from her estate. Lisa's money, or at least the great bulk of it, will of course go to her legal husband—I fancy it will be kept in trust for him as he is mentally incapacitated.

Be a good fellow, and, immediately on reading this letter, take your pulse and temperature, and let me know . . .

Alec begged an envelope from the receptionist. He slipped in his note, and addressed and stamped it. He slid the letter into the post-box in the hall, and returned to comfort Janet.

Alec felt, when he left Janet Sidebottome's hotel after escorting her painfully home, that he had had a fruitful though exhausting day.

Reflecting on Matt O'Brien's frail and sexless flesh and hair on his pillow, and how the old man had looked back and forth between Janet and himself, he was reminded of that near-centenarian, Mrs. Bean, who had replaced Granny Green in the Maud Long Ward. So different from each other in features, they yet shared this quality, that one would not know what was their sex from first impressions. He resolved to make a note of this in Matt O'Brien's case-history.

He felt suddenly tired and stopped a taxi. As it drove him home he ruminated on the question, why scientific observation differed from humane observation, and how the same people observed in these respective senses, actually seemed to be different people. He had to admit that Mrs. Bean, for instance, to whom he had not paid close attention, had none the less rewarded him with one of those small points of observation that frequently escaped him when he was deliberately watching his object. However, the method he had evolved was, on the whole, satisfactory.

A fire-engine clanged past. Alec leaned in his corner and closed his eyes. The taxi turned a corner. Alec shifted his position and looked out into the evening. The taxi was purring along the Mall towards St. James's Street.

The driver leaned back and opened the communicating window.

"A fire somewhere round here," he said.

Alec found himself on the pavement outside his block of chambers, in a crowd. There were policemen everywhere, smoke, people, firemen, water, then suddenly, a cry from the crowd and everyone looking up as a burst of flame shot from the top of the building.

Alec pushed through to the inner edge of the crowd. A policeman barred his way with a strong casual arm. "I live here," Alec explained. "Let me pass, please."

"Can't go in there," said the policeman. "Stand back, please."

"Get back," shouted the crowd.

Alec said, "But I live there. My things. Where's the porter?"

"The building is on fire, sir," said the policeman.

Alec made a rush advance and got past the policeman into the smoke and water at the entrance to the building. Someone hit him on the face. The crowd fell back as a wave of smoke and flame issued from a lower window. Alec stood and looked into the interior while another policeman from the opposite side of the crowd walked over to him.

"Come back," said the policeman, "you're obstructing the firemen."

"My papers are up there," Alec said.

The policeman took him by the arm and pulled him away. "There is a cat," Alec said desperately, "in my rooms. I can't let pussy burn. Let me dash up and let her out. I'll take the risk."

The policeman did not reply, but continued to propel Alec away from the fire.

"There's a dog up there. A beautiful husky from a polar expedition," Alec haggled. "Top floor, first door."

"Sorry, too late guvnor," said one of the firemen. "Your dog must have had it by now. The top storey's burnt out."

One of the residents among the crowd said, "There are no pets in those flats. Pets are not allowed."

Alec walked away, he went to his club and booked a room for the night.

Chapter Sixteen

The summer had passed and it was Granny Bean's birthday, for which the ward had been preparing for some days.

There was a huge cake with a hundred candles. Some men from the newspapers came in with their cameras. Others talked a while to Granny Bean, who was propped up in a new blue bed-jacket.

"Yes," Granny Bean answered them in her far-away flute, "I've lived a long time."

"Yes," said Granny Bean, "I'm very happy."

"That's right," she agreed, "I seen Queen Victoria once as a girl."

"What does it feel like to be a hundred, Mrs. Bean?"

"All right," she said weakly, nodding her head.

"You mustn't tire her," Sister Lucy who had put on her service medal for the occasion, told the newsmen.

The men took down notes from the sister. "Seven children, only one now alive, in Canada. Started life as a seamstress hand at the age of eleven. . . ."

The matron came in at three o'clock and read out the telegram from the Queen. Everyone applauded. Granny Valvona commented, " '. . . on your hundredth birthday,' doesn't sound quite right. Queen Mary always used to say, 'on the occasion of your centenary.' " But everyone said it came to the same thing.

The matron stood proxy for Granny Bean in blowing

out the candles. She was out of breath by the twenty-third. The nurses took turns to blow out the rest.

They were cutting the cake. One of the newsmen called, "Three cheers for Granny Bean."

The hilarity was dying down and the men had gone by the time the normal visitors started to arrive. Some of the geriatrics were still eating or doing various things with their slice of cake.

Miss Valvona adjusted her glasses and reached for the newspaper. She read out for the third time that day: " 'September 21st—to-day's birthday. Your year ahead: You can expect an eventful year. Controversial matters may predominate from December to March. People associated with music, transport, and the fashion industry will find the coming year will bring a marked progress.' Now, were you not connected with the fashion industry, Granny Bean? It says here in black and white . . ."

But Mrs. Bean had dropped asleep on her pillow after the nurse had given her a warm drink. Her mouth was formed once more into a small "O" through which her breath whistled faintly.

"Festivities going on?" said Alec Warner, looking around at the party decorations.

"Yes, Mrs. Bean is a hundred to-day."

The deep lines on Alec's face and brow showed deeper. It was four months since he had lost his entire notes and records in the fire.

Jean Taylor had said, "Try to start all over again, Alec. You will find a lot of it will come back to your mind while you work."

"I could never trust my memory," he had said, "as I trusted those notes."

"Well, you must start all over again."

"I haven't got it in me," he said, "to do that at my age. It was an accumulation of years of labour. It was invaluable."

He had seldom, since then, referred to his loss. He felt, sometimes, he said once, that he was really dead, since his records had ceased to exist.

"That's rather a metaphysical idea for you, Alec," she said. "For in fact you are not dead, but still alive."

He told her, it was true he frequently went over his vast notebooks in his mind, as through a card index. "But never," he said, "shall I make another note. I read instead. It is in some ways a better thing."

She caught him looking almost desirously at Granny Bean on her hundredth birthday. He sighed and looked away.

"We all appear to ourselves frustrated in our old age, Alec, because we cling to everything so much. But in reality we are still fulfilling our lives."

"A friend of mine fulfilled his yesterday."

"Oh, who was that?"

"Matt O'Brien in Folkestone. He thought he was God. He died in his sleep. He has left a fortune, but never knew about it. Lisa's money of course. No relatives."

"Will Guy Leet—?"

"No, Guy has no claim. I think Lisa's estate will now go according to her will to Mrs. Pettigrew."

"In that case," said Miss Taylor, "she will, after all, have her reward."

Mrs. Pettigrew had her reward. Lisa's will was proved in her favour and she inherited all her fortune. After her first stroke Mrs. Pettigrew went to live in a hotel at South Kensington. She is still to be seen at eleven in the morning at Harrod's Bank where she regularly meets some of the other elderly residents to discuss the shortcomings of the hotel management, and to plan various campaigns against the staff. She can still be seen in the evening jostling for a place by the door of the hotel lounge before the dinner gong sounds.

Charmian died one morning in the following spring, at the age of eighty-seven.

Godfrey died the same year as the result of a motor accident, his car having collided with another at a bend in Kensington Church Street. He was not killed outright, but died a few days later of pneumonia which had set in from the shock. It was the couple in the other car who were killed outright.

Guy Leet died at the age of seventy-eight.

Percy Mannering is in an old men's home, where he is known as "The Professor" and is treated with special respect, having his bed put in an alcove at the far corner of the dormitory—a position reserved for patients who have known better days. His grand-daughter, Olive, sometimes visits him. She takes away his poems and letters to editors; she types them out, and despatches them according to Percy's directions.

Ronald Sidebottome is allowed up in the afternoons but is not expected to last another winter.

Janet Sidebottome died of a stroke following an increase in blood pressure, at the age of seventy-seven.

Mrs. Anthony, now widowed, had a legacy from Charmian, and has gone to live at a seaside town, near her married son. Sometimes, when she hears of old people receiving anonymous telephone calls, she declares it is a good thing, judging by what she has seen, that she herself is hard of hearing.

Chief Inspector Mortimer died suddenly of heart-failure at the age of seventy-three, while boarding his yacht, *The Dragonfly*. Mrs. Mortimer spends most of her time looking after her numerous grandchildren.

Eric is getting through the Colston money which came to him on the death of his father.

Alec Warner had a paralytic stroke following a cerebral haemorrhage. For a time he was paralysed on one side and his speech was incoherent. In time he regained the use of his limbs, his speech improved. He went to live permanently in a nursing home and frequently searched through his mind, as through a card index, for the case-histories of his friends, both dead and dying.

What were they sick, what did they die of?

Lettie Colston, he recited to himself, comminuted fractures of the skull; Godfrey Colston, hypostatic pneumonia; Charmian Colston, uraemia; Jean Taylor, myocardial degeneration; Tempest Sidebottome, carcinoma of the cervix; Ronald Sidebottome, carcinoma of the bronchus; Guy Leet, arterio-sclerosis; Henry Mortimer, coronary thrombosis. . . .

Miss Valvona went to her rest. Many of the grannies followed her. Jean Taylor lingered for a time, employing her pain to magnify the Lord, and meditating sometimes confidingly upon Death, the first of the Four Last Things to be ever remembered.